Praise for *The Joshua Files*

"A gripping survival story . . . a fantasy of
pyramids, caves and tunnels"
Daily Telegraph

"Fast-paced and exciting, this is one for fans of
Alex Rider and Young Bond"
Bookseller

"A splendid adventure story of UFOs, ancient Mayan
documents and a lost city"
Mail on Sunday

"It's the Mexican and Mayan flavourings that give
Harris's adventure yarn that bit of extra bite as she weaves
a satisfyingly twisty plot around the science fiction
staples of UFOs and time travel"
Financial Times

Also by M.G. Harris

The Joshua Files
Invisible City
Ice Shock

ZeRO MoMeNT

M. G. HARRIS

■ SCHOLASTIC

First published in the UK in 2010 by Scholastic Children's Books
An imprint of Scholastic Ltd
Euston House, 24 Eversholt Street
London, NW1 1DB, UK
Registered office: Westfield Road, Southam, Warwickshire, CV47 0RA
SCHOLASTIC and associated logos are trademarks and/or registered
trademarks of Scholastic Inc.

ISBN 978 1407 12062 1

A CIP catalogue record for this book is available
from the British Library.

Printed in the UK by CPI Bookmarque, Croydon, Surrey
Papers used by Scholastic Children's Books are made from
wood grown in sustainable forests.

3 5 7 9 10 8 6 4 2

www.scholastic.co.uk/zone

For Ana-Elena, Kizzie, Deborah and Alison,
in memory of wonderful days in Brazil.

I would like to swim against the stream of time.

Italo Calvino

The Oxford Repor

DNA scientist found dead in Middle East yacht mystery

DOHA, QATAR The body of Cambridge professor and biotech entrepreneur Melissa DiCanio was discovered earlier today by fishermen in a yacht off the coast of Doha, Qatar. The boat was abandoned and had floated into the Persian Gulf.

DiCanio had been missing since the middle of January. The cause of death has not been released.

CCTV footage from Doha Harbour has helped police to make an arrest. Three men were photographed at the site, and one has been arrested – Simon Madison, who is also wanted by the FBI and CIA as a suspected terrorist.

Authorities intend to bring Madison to the United States of America. It is believed he will be charged with a number of offences.

Doha police were unable to comment as to the possible motive for the murder.

A spokesman for the FBI said, "We've been after Madison for a long time. This is an important and rather satisfying arrest."

DiCanio was born in Houston, Texas. She began her career at Baylor College of Medicine before moving to Oxford University in 1997 as a visiting professor at Aquinas College.

In 1999 she co-founded the pharmaceutical company Chaldexx BioPharmaceuticals, a privately held company which developed and markets the drug Tripoxan, with annual sales of US$50 m.

In 2005 DiCanio was awarded the Chaldexx Chair of Molecular Genetic Neuroscience at Cambridge University. DiCanio divided her time between her university research group and her post as Chief Scientific Officer at Chaldexx BioPharmaceuticals, based in Interlaken, Switzerland.

Dr Marcus Anthony, Master of Aquinas College, Oxford, said, "Melissa was a brilliant scientist, a true innovator. It was an honour to know her during her time at Aquinas College. She will be sorely missed."

From: Ixchel<ixchel1996@aol.com>
To: MariposaJosh<mariposajosh@gmail.com>
Subject: Hey there, Mister Promise-I'll-Write...

Josh!

You said you'd write but you haven't. What's going on with you? Benicio tells me a few things about his life there in Oxford with you.

But it's not the same as hearing it from YOU.

How is Oxford? Your friend Tyler? Your mother?

I visit your father's grave every week, just the way I promised. The sun shines on him for many hours here. I enjoy my visits. I don't forget anything that happened. I'm there with him, for you.

Come on, write me a little message. And what happened about your blog?

You've gone pretty quiet, Josh. Should I be worried?

I have some important news for you. It's about the strange inscription on the Adaptor, in case you're still interested. . .

Your friend always,

Ixchel

Hey Ixchel,

Yeah . . . it's been a while. I've just not been on the computer much. Benicio keeps me busy . . . I'm not sure how, but we seem to hang out quite a bit. Which is cool, you know? All the girls at school want to know about this college-student cousin of mine. Tyler and me, we've been training hard for a capoeira thing in Brazil. We're leaving in a couple of weeks.

It's like . . . finally I'm starting to have a life again. A normal life, I mean. I try not to think about what happened, but when things go quiet, when I'm alone, I can't stop thinking about. . . Well, you know. I try to be out all the time doing stuff. I try not to think. Kind of hard to talk about it, really. I'd rather not, if it's all the same to you.

So I'm not sure I want to know about any "strange inscription".

It was nice to hear from you, I mean that.

Josh

Subject: Something I really think you'll want to know about
Importance: High

Josh,

But you're talking to someone about this, yes? It's no good to keep such strong, hard feelings inside. You have Benicio and Tyler and your mother. Do you talk to them?

About the inscription on the Adaptor – we found something that I think you WILL want to know. I don't want to write details in an email; you never can be sure where it will finish up.

I think YOU should know because . . . well, because of the You Know What. (I'm guessing we have to call it something like this?)

We need a more secure way to communicate than email. Do you know anything about that?

A hug,

Ixchel

De: Ixchel<ixchel1996@aol.com>
Para: MariposaJosh<mariposajosh@gmail.com>
Asunto: Re: Something I really think you'll want to know about
Importancia: Alta

Hey Ixchel,

Wow . . . I wasn't expecting this. I don't know what to

say. Of course I'm interested in anything new about the You Know What. But on the other hand, maybe I should let sleeping dogs lie, right?

Things have settled down for me since then. I'm in a proper routine here: I get up at six-thirty and go to the gym with Ty. We mark each other – he's bigger and stronger than me, so he does more reps and heavier weights than me but I'm gaining on him. This is every day. It wasn't my idea to be like a maniac but Ty is obsessed, OBSESSED with winning a medal at the World Capoeira Championships next month and he wants to be WELL buff. But after about a month I started to notice that I was starting to get pretty ripped too. I've got these biceps and shoulder muscles now and even a six-pack! Not like Ty, obviously, but he had one to start with. So I'm not going to stop now – I'll turn back into a flabby shrimp.

Then we train for a bit. Not fighting, just the moves. Handstands, backflips, cartwheels without hands. So we can start our capoeira routine with something really awesome. I can hold a handstand for ninety seconds. That's freestanding. Then we go to school, then home and after a snack and some Xbox, we're back to the training.

We meet every single day. We only call each other by our *apelidos* – capoeira nicknames. We're getting so good now; we're faster and faster. People stand around and watch us. Benicio usually turns up too – doing his job, keeping an eye on me.

I'll tell you straight – I don't like remembering what happened on that mountain. Don't even want to think about it. Because every time I do I feel sick, sick in my guts. I can feel that rope tightening around me again, all my internal organs being squeezed like it's going to slice me in two. I think about the moment when my dad cut the rope. Over and over again. The rope going slack. Him falling without making a sound. His last words – "This isn't over."

And why did it happen; why did I go up that mountain? Who is – or was – Arcadio? How did he know so much about me? Why did I listen to him – why did I let him lead me to Mount Orizaba?

I used to have this dream, last year, about my dad. Maybe I told you? I can't remember if I did or not. In the dream, Dad wasn't really dead. Him and Mum, they'd been pretending, keeping things from me. Pretty crazy, right? It made me sad, but at least it was like seeing Dad, like being with him again. Then I *did* see Dad – for real.

That's when it all went to pieces.

I mean, was it all meant to happen? I don't know anything any more.

I don't like these questions. It's enough to drive you crazy.

So . . . let me think about it some more, before I decide

7

whether I want to start with this stuff again. OK?

Hugs,

Josh

To: Josh Garcia<mariposajosh@gmail.com>
From: Ixchel<ixchel1996@aol.com>
Subject: reps? ripped? buff??

Josh,

It's good that you've found something to take your mind off the painful memories. You seem very focused on the capoeira, but I don't really know what you are talking about when you write "reps" and "buff" and "six-pack" and "ripped". Something to do with getting muscles, yes? That's good too – you told me that you were going to get stronger so you could protect yourself and your mother.

But the world keeps turning, doesn't it? We're still here in Ek Naab and everything is going to happen in 2012 exactly the way it is written. The galactic superwave – all the computers in the world are going to be wiped, the end of civilization. Unless we can stop it, using all the information in the codex you found, the Book of Ix. No wonder no one in Ek Naab really thinks about anything but our job now – solving the 2012 problem.

What I've learned about the inscription – it isn't just about the You Know What. There is also a link with the

2012 problem.

This is a big deal in Ek Naab. I can sense it in the air. It's the usual thing, Josh. People talking in hushed voices. *Don't-tell-that-I-said-this-but* . . . is how every sentence starts. The only person who has all the information is . . . we both know who I'm talking about.

Please let me tell you what I've discovered. You are the only person I can tell.

A hug,

Ixchel

De: Ixchel<ixchel1996@aol.com>
Para: MariposaJosh<mariposajosh@gmail.com>
Asunto: Re: reps? ripped? buff??

Ixchel,

OK, you got me. Now I'm really curious. . .

There is a way we can communicate secretly.

I've set up a room for us at this online 3D place. We can talk with avatars and put up pictures and videos and stuff. The room is locked – I'll send you the password and all the details. Delete the email after reading, then meet me in the chat room. I'll be online all evening, waiting.

Josh

<J-MARIPOSA has joined>
<MENINHA has joined>

MENINHA: Hello . . . J-MARIPOSA! Josh – you're named
    after a butterfly?

J-MARIPOSA: It's my *apelido* – my capoeira nickname.
    After my favourite move.

MENINHA: And I'm just "girl" . . . *meninha* is Portuguese for
    "girl", am I right?

J-MARIPOSA: *grin* Sorry. Couldn't think what you'd like.
    Ooh, how do you make your avatar scowl like that. . .?

MENINHA: I've never seen you dressed in white pyjama
    bottoms and no shirt. . .

J-MARIPOSA: They're *abada* trousers. For capoeira.

MENINHA: Oh. Please give your avatar a shirt next time.

J-MARIPOSA: *sigh* There's so much I have to teach
    you. . .

MENINHA: So – you have a favourite move?

J-MARIPOSA: Yep. *Mariposa* – the butterfly twist. It's
    awesome.

MENINHA: We can talk freely here?

J-MARIPOSA: Talk away. What's this big news?

MENINHA: OK. You remember the Adaptor? That weird
    object that Simon Madison stole, then we found it in the
    hands of the Sect of Huracan, in that strange chamber
    under the pyramid in Becan?

10

J-MARIPOSA: Course I remember. I was carrying the
    Adaptor around in my back pocket trying not to let it
    blow poison gas in your face most of the time . . . how
    could I forget it???
MENINHA: Sorry, Josh, it's just that you said you've been
    trying not to think about what happened last time you
    were here.
J-MARIPOSA: Trying not to think about it . . . don't see how
    I could ever forget. . .
MENINHA: Well, then you'll remember that the Adaptor has
    an inscription. . .
J-MARIPOSA: The same inscription that appears at the
    beginning of the Ix Codex, the fifteen symbols. I
    remember. And. . .?
MENINHA: Well, they deciphered the Adaptor inscription.
J-MARIPOSA: Whoa!
MENINHA: The entire project has locked down. All of a
    sudden – top secret! One of the decipherment team is
    my teacher at the Tec. You know I'm learning ancient
    Sumerian, yes?
J-MARIPOSA: You said you might.
MENINHA: My teacher stopped being able to say
    ANYTHING about the project. No one is allowed to
    know what's written in that inscription. Apart from the
    members of the ruling Executive.
J-MARIPOSA: I might have guessed Carlos Montoyo

wouldn't want to be left out.

MENINHA: You're right. But this time – he isn't in charge.

J-MARIPOSA: Then who is?

MENINHA: Lorena. The *atanzahab*, the matchmaker, you remember her? Our chief scientist.

J-MARIPOSA: They put a scientist in charge of this project? Why?

MENINHA: I have no clue.

J-MARIPOSA: Why are you so keen to tell me about this?

MENINHA: Because you want to fix the You Know What, don't you?

J-MARIPOSA: You can call it the Bracelet of Itzamna here. No one here but us chickens.

MENINHA: What. . .?

J-MARIPOSA: It's just a saying.

MENINHA: Here's the thing. The Bracelet needs a replacement Crystal Key. . .

J-MARIPOSA: We don't know that for sure.

MENINHA: Yes, but we know that some ancient technology uses the Key.

J-MARIPOSA: Yeah, yeah, how could I forget? The bit of the Ix Codex I gave away . . . with all those secret instructions about how to activate the Revival Chamber using the Adaptor and the Key. The Key can be a liquid . . . but works best in crystal form.

MENINHA: Nice of you to finally talk about the Ix Codex. All that secrecy about what you were allowed to say was getting kind of annoying.

J-MARIPOSA: Hmm. It's only because I reckon you know more about what's in the Ix Codex than me by now.

MENINHA: You may be right.

J-MARIPOSA: If only I'd always been as careful about the Ix Codex as I was with you. Thanks to me, the Sect of Huracan know how to make the Key. . .

MENINHA: You couldn't have known that your friend Ollie was spying on you. Her and Simon Madison working together . . . she used your friendship against you. That's why it's called a betrayal. Not your fault, Josh.

J-MARIPOSA: Believe me, I still feel like an idiot. At least the Key they made didn't work.

MENINHA: True. That was pretty funny, actually, when they tried to activate the Revival Chamber and it failed. Remember how those people from the Sect of Huracan, the Professor woman and Marius Martineau, started screaming at each other? And at Simon Madison too?

J-MARIPOSA: Didn't seem all that funny to me. I remember we were pretty scared they'd find us hiding in the tunnels.

MENINHA: I guess we were.

J-MARIPOSA: So . . . any news of what the Revival Chamber actually does?

MENINHA: No clue, it's all secret. Lorena had her team take over the chamber right away. They sealed the

Sect's secret entrance and created another, direct from
Ek Naab.

J-MARIPOSA: When we were climbing Mount Orizaba, you
told me you reckoned it might be a time-travel device.

MENINHA: Yeah. But now I'm not so sure. Your father –
he seemed to use the Bracelet of Itzamna to
transport from wherever he was to the volcano,
didn't he? So maybe the Revival Chamber does
something completely different. Like, maybe it
revives the dead?

J-MARIPOSA: Jeez. That would be cool! Do you think
Lorena's team has managed to activate it?

MENINHA: I don't know! Like I say, TOP SECRET! They
don't tell someone like me.

J-MARIPOSA: OK, what about this inscription on the
Adaptor? You need the Adaptor to activate the Revival
Chamber, yeah? The Key goes into the Adaptor and
makes it work in the Container . . . and that makes the
Revival Chamber work . . . isn't that how it goes?

MENINHA: I haven't been able to find out what the
inscription on the Adaptor says . . . but what I do know
is that Lorena's scientists – they're talking about the
Key. That's the whisper, the rumour. The inscription tells
them how to make the Key.

J-MARIPOSA: Those fifteen symbols on the Adaptor – they
tell you how to make the Key?

MENINHA: Correct. They're trying to make the crystal version – the Crystal Key. The ancient instructions in the Ix Codex say that the Crystal Key is the most stable form.

J-MARIPOSA: Make a crystal . . . like with a chemistry set?

MENINHA: I guess. . . Lorena is a scientist.

J-MARIPOSA: So those fifteen symbols are like . . . a chemical formula for the crystal?

MENINHA: That's what I think. But I haven't been able to see the deciphered text.

J-MARIPOSA: If it's chemistry, we're out of luck. I wouldn't know where to start with making a crystal.

MENINHA: Yes, the same with me. But here in Ek Naab, they are confident. They're going to have the Crystal Key here in a few weeks. A month at the most.

J-MARIPOSA: Are you sure?

MENINHA: I read some emails of Lorena's. Over her shoulder, actually – she didn't realize. It was just a short message to Montoyo. He asked *When will it be ready for a test?* And her reply was *Maybe a month.*

J-MARIPOSA: But when we were in the caves, I heard that Professor woman from the Sect say that you had to make the Crystal Key at zero gravity.

MENINHA: Yes, I remember that. But maybe zero gravity is not a problem for Ek Naab. They could take a Muwan up into space.

J-MARIPOSA: Hmmmmm. If I could get my hands on that crystal . . . even for a bit. Just to try it in the Bracelet.

MENINHA: YES! Just what I was thinking.

J-MARIPOSA: I need to find an excuse to go back to Ek Naab.

MENINHA: EXACTLY.

J-MARIPOSA: But what?

MENINHA: It could be me.

J-MARIPOSA: You?

MENINHA: Yes, your excuse for coming back to Ek Naab. Say you want to see me again.

J-MARIPOSA: *blush*

MENINHA: Say that you miss me. Montoyo and Lorena – they're so keen for us to like each other, since they tried so hard to arrange our marriage. They'll fall for it.

J-MARIPOSA: Okayyyy. . .

MENINHA: You and me, we'll know the truth.

J-MARIPOSA: Well, if you're sure. I'll tell Benicio. And he'll tell Montoyo.

MENINHA: Mmmm . . . maybe you should ask Montoyo directly. Don't involve Benicio.

J-MARIPOSA: Why not? He seems to like talking about you.

MENINHA: I'd prefer you and Benicio don't have that conversation. Later he might find out we weren't telling the truth. Then he won't trust us.

J-MARIPOSA: I guess.

MENINHA: Good. OK. Well, I'll drop by this room again in a few days.

J-MARIPOSA: We can leave messages for each other on the wall. THIS wall!

MENINHA: Goodbye, then.

J-MARIPOSA: Later.

MENINHA: What later?

J-MARIPOSA: I mean SEE YOU later.

MENINHA: Oh! OK . . . later!

Long minutes after Ixchel's avatar disappears in a puff of animated smoke, I still can't tear my eyes away from the screen. I can't seem to move from my chair.

Why did I choose the screen names "J-MARIPOSA" and "MENINHA"? Why do I try to be funny around Ixchel? I could kick myself – I don't seem to make her laugh. It's a good thing that the 3D chat room doesn't keep a log of our conversation because if I could, I'd read it over and over. Just to check how much of an idiot I made of myself.

I'm so distracted, it doesn't even occur to me – for well over an hour – to think seriously about what Ixchel is suggesting.

It's everything I've tried so hard to avoid. The mysteries of Ek Naab and 2012. The Bracelet of Itzamna.

Three months of struggling with the urge to bury that bracelet in the rubbish bin. Or to chuck it into the River Cherwell on a rainy day.

Three months of trying to forget about travelling back in time, to forget about fixing what happened to my dad.

Persuading myself to let things fall – wherever.

Then Ixchel sends me some messages about an inscription, and something creeps back, something I thought I'd banished.

Hope.

Since I got back from Mexico, Mum's treating me completely differently. It's as though she's heaved a big sigh of relief that her kid has finally grown up and she doesn't need to take care of him any more. He can take care of her.

You'd think a guy would be happy about it, and at first I was. Not any more. I don't mind putting up shelves and making furniture from IKEA, but I don't want to listen to Mum talk about how lonely she feels, how she misses my dad.

I feel pretty rubbish about it too. After all, I was there when he died. He died saving me – not something I'll ever, ever be able to put out of my mind.

Mum asks me to buy her cigarettes at the shop. I can't believe it – she's actually forgotten my age.

"You're almost sixteen," she says.

"I'm not even fifteen until summer!"

She frowns, exactly as if she'd forgotten where she put her keys. "Really?"

"Anyway you have to be eighteen," I tell her, annoyed.

I go to the shop all the same and buy her a paper, a bottle of Perrier and a cream cake. When I return Mum takes one look at the headline and remarks, "Melissa DiCanio – your father knew her."

It takes me a few seconds to focus on what Mum is saying. There's a story in the Oxford newspaper about a scientist who's been found dead in Qatar, a country in the Middle East. While Mum talks, trying to remember how Dad had known the woman, whether Mum had met DiCanio at this college dinner or that one, I read the story.

Right away, something leaps out at me: *one has been arrested – Simon Madison, who is also wanted by the FBI and CIA as a suspected terrorist.*

Simon Madison. Somehow he survived the avalanche that he started on Mount Orizaba, the avalanche that led to my father's death. Just as I'm feeling a surge of disappointment that Madison didn't get what was coming to him, I read the next bit.

Authorities intend to bring Madison to the United States of America. It is believed he will be charged with a number of offences.

So that's it, then. Madison has been caught. Too bad for DiCanio, that scientist he seems to have murdered. For her, it's too late.

Madison is not often out of my thoughts. How can I

forget him? He's bound up in my single most painful memory – the memory of my dad's death.

That day, the *whole* day, is the last thing I think about at night and the first thing I think about in the morning. It's in the back of my mind most of the time too, but night and morning are when it comes right to the surface. As soon as the thoughts start, I work at pushing them away. I visualize capoeira moves. I plug in some headphones and listen to music or a funny podcast. I get to sleep and everything goes blank. No more dreams.

Ground zero – blank.

For the first time in many weeks, I open the drawer with the Bracelet of Itzamna and gaze at it. Then I touch it, lightly. That ancient Erinsi technology. There's a really distinctive feel to those surfaces. I remember the same from the Adaptor and the cover on the Ix Codex. Like stroking a sheet of magnetized iron filings.

I put the Bracelet on my wrist, feel the familiar buzz of energy, so tiny that you could miss it if you weren't prepared. The hairs on my arms prickle and a shiver runs up my spine. But it's not me reacting to the Bracelet – it's the Bracelet reacting to me.

Those first few weeks after the avalanche that killed my dad . . . if I could have fixed the Bracelet, I would have. No question. I'd have gone back in time and done whatever it took to make sure he didn't end up on that volcano.

But then . . . then I had a bit of a think.

Everything I've done so far has been rushed. I get an idea into my head and I just go and do it. Find out what happened to my dad, go to Mexico, find the Ix Codex, break into J Eric Thompson's house, take on Simon Madison, follow some mysterious message in a bunch of coded postcards . . . climb a volcano and risk my life. . .

All in the name of some bizarre, prophetic letter from Arcadio Garcia – a weirdo who claims to know my future.

No planning. Just reacting.

Where has it got me?

My dad is dead. That's all I can see.

Any way you look at it, I've messed up. The only good thing I did was to find the Ix Codex. Everything else. . .?

You can talk about "destiny", the way Arcadio did in that letter. Yep, you can do that, and accept things, the way Montoyo said.

I don't buy it.

There has to have been a better way.

I have the Bracelet of Itzamna. A chance to travel in time. To put the clock back, to change the past: a way to fix everything. There's no way I can afford to screw this up.

The Bracelet is broken. It can't travel in time, because the crystal burned out. The Crystal Key might fix the Bracelet. It isn't just another lost relic waiting to be found.

The Crystal Key can be made.

I've been waiting for some news like this, some ray of hope. Didn't even dare to think it would happen so soon.

Problem is, it's too soon. This is make-or-break.

And I'm not ready.

Message Posted on the Wall of J-MARIPOSA's Place: GET READY . . .

. . . for a BIG surprise, Josh. Montoyo has a plan. I'm sworn to secrecy. Just to annoy you, I'm gonna join in with his little game.

So, do nothing till you hear from me.

"Meninha"

J-Mariposa says. . .

Woo, mysterious. . .

"Do Nothin' Till You Hear From Me" . . . that's a song, did you know? By Duke Ellington. Another of my dad's favourites. I guess I'm never forgetting stuff like that.

Meninha says. . .

Why would you want to forget things your father showed you? Like it or not, he's part of who you are.

I don't hear from Ixchel over the next few days . . . which stretch to a week, then eat into the following week. Maybe I'm taking it too literally – *do nothing till you hear from me.*

Well, whatever. Can't have the girl thinking I've got a thing for her, which she might if I emailed for no reason. . .

The time arrives to pack for Brazil. Me, Tyler, my mum, Benicio; we're all flying to the beach resort of Natal for the World Capoeira Championships. Sun, sand, sea and the land where capoeira was invented. Mum's been getting right into it; she's been showing me YouTube videos and everything.

"Children practise capoeira right there on the beach!" Mum tells me in a tone of discovery.

I just sigh. *Mum, I know.* . . Haven't I been going on about capoeira for two years now? Nice that she finally takes an interest.

The afternoon before we leave, Mum drives us all up to Shotover Country Park. For some reason we haven't taken

Benicio there yet. I'm pretty sure Benicio must be fed up with my mum insisting he spend every weekend learning something new about life in Oxford. I told her he'd be happier hanging out with some Oxford Uni students. But does she listen. . .?

The car park is almost full when we arrive – it's a typical family weekend type of outing. Most people disappear straight into the woods, following one of the walking trails. Tyler and I walk along in silence a little ahead of Benicio, who, as usual, is talking to my mum. The bluebells are out, dotted around the woodland undergrowth. That means a trip to the bluebell woods at the arboretum is next on Mum's list. Dad or no Dad, every year is just like the last.

Now I think about it, that's OK by me.

Every trail leads to the sandpit clearing, and that's where we end up. We stop for a while and sit on the log, looking out over the woods.

"Strange to think that there was sea here once . . . so far inland," Benicio says to no one in particular.

"And dinosaurs," I add. "The first one was found not far from here."

"Nothing lasts. . ." my mum says softly. "Not even the 'terrible lizards'."

"Overgrown chickens," Tyler says, sniffing. "Nothing to miss. . ."

26

"No one to miss them, Tyler," she murmurs. "It's different with people."

I look away, instinctively hiding my eyes from the others. It must show, what I'm thinking. How could it not? I feel it so strongly, it's as though it were seeping from my pores.

If I could fix the Bracelet of Itzamna, I wouldn't have to miss anything or anybody.

The past, the present, the future; they'd all open up before me.

When is Ixchel going to get back to me? I don't like having my hopes built up and then . . . silence.

"So . . . how is it you like to be called," Benicio says with a wicked grin, "*Mariposa* and *Eddy G*?"

"It's serious, man," Tyler says with a straight face. "The *apelidos* help us get into the zone. When I'm fighting, I'm not Tyler . . . I'm Eddy Gordo, capoeira titan."

Benicio smirks. "And what's Josh? A butterfly?"

Tyler winks. "He's a guy who *still* can't do the *mariposa* move."

For that, I shove Tyler hard enough that he lands on the ground, cracking up with laughter.

As evening draws in, we end with a final practice of our capoeira routine, up there on the sandy hill. Walkers and their children stop to watch as Tyler and I fling ourselves around, flying through the air, spinning kicks that miss each other by closely timed fractions of a second. Until my leg

27

links with Tyler's, wraps around his knee and he stops in mid-crouch, flashes me a quick grin, then pulls away.

My problem is, *I don't really want to miss*. Next time someone goes for me, I have to be ready.

Night falls. Before locking my laptop away in the cupboard, I log into the 3D chat room. Still no word from Ixchel.

I'm quiet all the way to Brazil. I think about Benicio getting into his Muwan, throwing a rucksack into the belly of the craft, putting his headset on over his scruffy student hair, starting up the anti-gravity engines, docking his iPod to listen to his favourite new rock tunes from England. Heading out alone, all the way to Brazil.

Yet it occurs to me how different everything would have been for us both if Benicio's grandmother had been a bloke.

He'd have been the son of a Bakab's son. Then *Benicio* would be the Bakab Ix. They'd never have needed me. My grandfather wouldn't have been the one to search for the Ix Codex. My dad would still be alive, and I would be living a quiet, ordinary life in Oxford. Never even dreaming that a place like Ek Naab could exist.

Whichever way you look at it, Fate dealt us all a pretty random hand.

I've always been kind of envious of Benicio. It's hard not to be – he's obviously a genius, gets to fly a futuristic spacecraft; he's the hand-picked secret lieutenant of Carlos Montoyo. And for some reason girls really like him.

But *I'm the Bakab*. One of the four sons of the god Itzamna, according to Mayan mythology. Only it turns out that Itzamna was real – he was the founder of Ek Naab. I don't know if the original Bakabs really were his sons, but they were definitely special. All male descendants of Bakabs inherit a genetic immunity against a poison – the ancient bio-defence toxin that protects each of the four Books of Itzamna. Those four books contain the inscriptions that Itzamna found in a super-ancient ruin near the Mayan city of Izapa. The inscriptions aren't Mayan – they're much older. The Books of Itzamna are the writings of the Erinsi – a civilization that's been lost from the record. Something destroyed the Erinsi civilization – the galactic superwave, a massive burst of energy from the centre of the galaxy. And it's coming our way again . . . at the end of 2012.

For hundreds of years, one of the Books of Itzamna had been missing – the Ix Codex. Only a Bakab Ix could find it. It should have been my grandfather, but he died in the search. Then my own dad disappeared after using the Bracelet of Itzamna to zap himself to another time and place. So it came down to me, the only Bakab Ix left. At least, as far as the people in Ek Naab knew.

The Bakabs are pretty important to Ek Naab – in fact, four of them sit on a ruling Executive of just six people.

As the Bakab Ix, I'll join the ruling Executive of Ek Naab, once I turn sixteen.

From the window of our aeroplane, my eyes search the endless horizon of clouds, hunting for even the tiniest sign of Benicio's Muwan. I wonder; could it be that Benicio envies *me*?

It's evening when we land at Natal's airport. The sun is just going down. As we step out of the airport, a blast of warm air hits us. Within minutes the thick weave of my T-shirt sticks to my back. Tyler grins in delight. "Proper heat! Hey, *Mariposa* – this is the life."

The guest house – Pousada Florianopolis – is right next to the promenade of Natal's wide beach. After dumping the luggage and changing into flashy board shorts, Tyler and I hit the beach.

It's flooded with yellow light from tall lamps all along the promenade. The sea disappears into dark shadows. White caps of surf lines glisten in the artificial light. We race into the sea, frothy warm water spreading around our legs. Wading along in the line of the first wave, we follow my mother. She's showered, changed into her evening beachwear, and strolls along the pavement above the sand, peering out towards us.

Mum was right about the capoeira on the beach. About fifty metres up the beach, two tanned, lean boys around twelve years old practise slow handstands followed by measured sweeping and turning kicks – *queixada* and *armada*. Tyler and I pause briefly to watch them. From the moves they're doing, I'd guess they're beginners, but still . . . their technique has a fluidity that mine has only just begun to capture.

We slosh along in the surf, keeping one eye out for Mum, who's taking her pick of the beachside bars. Finally she stops and waves us over. We cross the beach as white sand-crabs shimmy around our feet across the powder. In this light the sand looks like snow.

Tyler bounces along, gives me an experimental shove. With a low chuckle, he tries harder to unbalance me. In a second we're both cartwheeling across the beach, going into the final part of our routine. Our feet are a blur in the air.

Warm currents brush my skin as I whip through the air. The sand is cool to the touch under my hands and feet. I push back all memories of Tyler and me in the pool at Hotel Delfin, showing off in front of Ollie, seconds before Camila arrived. . .

Ollie, the gorgeous girl who betrayed me. I thought she was a little out of my league, OK, beautiful and a couple of years older than me. Never suspected that she was actually a spy, and even worse, agent of the Sect of Huracan and Simon Madison's girlfriend!

My sister, Camila – another painful memory. She was a fantastic girl – well, a woman, really. A husband who was crazy about her, and most of her life ahead. The memory of Camila drowning in that swamp is one of the most horrible things I have in my head. . . I try pretty hard to keep from remembering that.

At the beach bar, Mum orders drinks. Goblet-shaped glasses appear filled with foam-topped fresh juices, bright purple and orange; grape for me, passion fruit for Tyler.

We sip our drinks in contented silence. Mum drinks from a frosty glass of cold beer. Her eyes are still on the beach, continually sweeping back and forth. She seems distracted, but I'm too wrapped up in my own thoughts to notice right away.

Two tables down from us a couple of slender girls are sitting eating ice cream from sundae glasses. They both wear green-and-yellow-trimmed white *abada* trousers and short, sleeveless green tops. Capoeiristas. Here, they're everywhere.

So I don't notice my mum staring in the opposite direction until Tyler prods me, hard.

"Look."

When I do, I see something that, for just an instant, makes my heart bounce straight into my mouth.

Carlos Montoyo. But not just him . . . Ixchel, strolling towards us along the promenade, grins all over both their faces. Yep, Carlos's too. For once, even he looks happy.

I shuffle to my feet. Tyler follows.

"So this is your girlfriend," he murmurs under his breath. I hiss back, "She is not!"

I told Tyler everything when I got back from Mexico. I was fed up with keeping Ek Naab a secret from my mum and friends, with them thinking I was a crazy who invented stories about alien abduction. Looking back on it, obviously *Ollie* never thought I was making anything up. No; she knew everything, right from the beginning, right from when she set out to spy on me.

I didn't know that, though, and that's what counts. I'm the one who felt like a secretive freak.

So I wasn't having that with Tyler, not any longer. Now, he knows it all: Ek Naab, who Benicio is, Ixchel, the codex, almost everything. Of course he can hardly believe it – and he's not happy about the fact that Benicio refuses to let him see his Muwan. Then again, Tyler has to believe it, doesn't

33

he? By now my life doesn't make much sense unless you know the madder bits.

Except – Tyler doesn't know about the Bracelet of Itzamna. No one but Ixchel and me knows about that.

That's how it has to stay.

I might have guessed Ty would tease me about Ixchel.

"She's just a friend," I mutter as I step forward, pushing one hand through my hair before it hits me that I'm nervous.

I don't know which of them is making me feel this way – Montoyo or Ixchel. But that's what's going on as I wait for them to reach our table.

Ixchel looks nice – better than nice, actually; really cute. She's got a new haircut, she's using a little bit of make-up, and she's dressed in white beach shorts and a cropped, sleeveless top. She's not dressed up and elegant the way she was at my dad's funeral. The sassy-girl-waitress look has vanished too. But it's her smile that gets me.

Jeez. I don't remember her being this pretty.

I have to drag my eyes away from Ixchel to Montoyo. Probably already too late; I make a mental note to keep my eyes off Ixchel as much as possible for the rest of the evening.

Tyler whispers in my ear, "Mate, be cool. . ."

I manage a nod. Montoyo hugs me first, claps my back twice and looks deeply into my eyes, like he's searching for a sign of how upset I might still be about my dad. "Josh, look at you! You're really turning into a man now!"

I redden – can't help it. I guess he's talking about the bodybuilding. But of course I'm glad he noticed. This took work – and it didn't half hurt!

Then it's Ixchel's turn. Cool as silk, she gives me the once-over with her eyes. "Good work!" she says, like she's congratulating someone who just carried heavy suitcases to the door. We kiss hello, a bit awkwardly. Then she moves on to Tyler.

"This is Tyler," I say with a shrug. "He likes to be called Eddy G. . ."

"All right, Ixchel, mate," he says calmly, as though they've known each other for years. He pecks her cheek, even squeezes in a little shoulder hug. "Heard a lot about you. . ."

So of course, everyone looks straight at me. I blush so hard that I have to stare at the ground. I just about force a laugh. "Right! Yeah. . ."

Montoyo hugs my mum for what seems like a tiny bit too long. He says something to her quietly, staring for just a second right into her eyes. I don't catch what he says, but I sense it right away.

Things have changed.

In the past three months, while I've had my mind on other things, something has changed with my mother.

Sitting at the table with her and Montoyo, I can't escape the sensation; they know something that I don't.

As we sit down, I try to hide the fact that I'm concentrating hard, trying to work out what the heck is going on. Ixchel and Montoyo order snacks and drinks. It's obvious right away that Montoyo knows exactly what he's doing. Is there any place this guy doesn't look and act completely in his element? I watch for a few seconds as he stretches an arm around Ixchel whilst also patting my shoulder, eyes roving contentedly around our little group.

He walks in, he takes charge.

Montoyo looks almost exactly the same as the first time I saw him. Right down to the silk black shirt and grey-flecked, short ponytail. He carries a small leather briefcase across his left shoulder.

Montoyo orders something called *pastel* for both him and Ixchel, and a drink called *guarana*. He starts chatting easily about this part of Brazil; what there is to see, places we should take in after the capoeira championship, excursions we should book. It's the same sort of thing I've heard my mum talk about, but instead of saying "Yes, I know all about that," like you might expect, she just listens, like she's fascinated to be hearing this for the first time.

What the heck is going on with those two?

Ixchel starts asking Tyler and me about our capoeira routine, our workout regime, everything I told her about the gym and everything. She shows no sign whatsoever that she and I have been discussing this by email and in the chat room. I sit there saying almost nothing, letting Tyler do the talking.

So Ixchel and I, we're pretending that we haven't been talking about anything; I get it. I'm not sure why, but Ixchel seems to have it worked out. So I play along. I catch her eye every so often. No sign at all that this isn't the first time she's said this, either.

Ixchel and my mum are good at this play-acting thing.

Tyler enjoys talking. He gestures with his hands, demonstrating the theory of capoeira, explaining the rules of the competition.

"Josh and I are competing in the student tournament. I'm a higher belt than him, so we'll never be against each other in a match. We do have this routine, though, just for show, for our capoeira school in Oxford."

Meanwhile, Montoyo and my mum talk quietly between themselves. I try to look as though I'm involved in the Tyler–Ixchel conversation, which is louder and punctuated by short laughs. When actually I'm trying to hear what Montoyo is saying to my mum.

What could they have to talk about?

Listening to them, it slowly dawns on me that this isn't a conversation that began here and now, this evening on a Brazilian beach.

This is a conversation they've been having for some time.

Montoyo and my mum – they've been in touch with each other. By phone or who-knows-what. Since they met in Ek Naab around Christmas, they've got to know each other. They've become friends.

As I realize this, a wave of fury rises in my throat, tightening my chest.

He's got some nerve. . .

Montoyo glances at me. In that moment I see that he knows. He can tell I'm angry – I don't know how because I'm using all my energy to control my face. He purses his lips, narrows his eyes for a brief second.

"Tyler, Ixchel, I need to borrow your friend. We need to speak alone, Josh, if that's OK with you. There's Bakab business that you should know about."

With that Montoyo whisks me off on to the sand, where the rhythmic slapping of waves on the shore will drown our words.

I'm guessing he expects me to lose my cool.

He's right.

Montoyo and I head for the beach a few metres from the ocean. We walk in stony silence for a minute, put fifty metres between us and the beachside café where Ixchel, Tyler and my mum sit. Something about the way Montoyo gets me out of there – the very second he realizes I'm angry – makes me feel even angrier.

Almost as though it's OK for me to react that way. Like Montoyo thinks I'm justified.

"You don't seem happy to see me, Josh," he begins. He speaks slowly, every word considered. "Or Ixchel. Not a very warm welcome for a girl who's been . . . ."

"I'm not marrying her," I break in, speaking so mildly that it surprises even me.

Montoyo stops walking. His eyes widen. ". . . for a girl who's been through some very tough experiences with you . . . is what I was going to say. Josh! What's wrong with you? We've already explained – the arranged marriage only happens if you *both* agree."

You always get me to do what you want, is what I'm about to say. But I bite my lip. At least I'm still keeping the Bracelet a secret from Montoyo.

He looks at me in silence. I stare back, pushing out my chest.

"You're angry," he says. He sounds disappointed. "About my friendship with your mother."

In fact I'm so angry that I can't speak. I want to yell at him but I'm suddenly scared that it might come out as a sob. So instead I gulp hard and keep it in.

"We're just friends, Josh," Montoyo says, very simply. "I like her. Eleanor . . . she's a very interesting woman . . . very intelligent and cultured. We have had some nice conversations – principally about you. She's been telling me about her life with you, about how Benicio is getting on in Oxford."

There's another long silence.

"You're a credit to her and you should know – if you don't already – that your mother is tremendously proud of you."

As calmly, quietly as I can make myself speak, I say, "My dad's been dead for three months. That's all."

"Maybe so, but Eleanor has already been mourning him for almost a year," Montoyo says.

That does it. I let fly; I yell, right in his face, "So she can forget him, is that it? So she can move on . . . to you?"

Montoyo doesn't flinch, I'll give him that; he takes it on the chin.

"Maybe one day, if she decides. I would be the lucky one. But that's not your decision."

It's all I can do not to punch him.

"She's your mother, Josh, and I understand that you feel protective – even possessive – towards her. But women aren't possessions. I should know," he says, suddenly regretful. "I've made that mistake myself."

"Why couldn't you let her be?" I shout. I've barely heard a word he's said. "She's my mother! It's my life! It's like you have to be *everywhere* . . . Ek Naab . . . Oxford . . . here."

"Let this go, Josh," Montoyo says, very serious. "Or it's going to become a problem between you and Eleanor. Between you and me. Your mother's already worried enough about you."

"You could have fooled me," I say bitterly. "She's not even that interested."

Now that Montoyo's here in Brazil, it's suddenly obvious to me why Mum was so keen to come. Not to watch me do capoeira, after all.

He continues, "You're wrong. Just because she doesn't crowd you and coddle you as though you were a little boy. She respects you! She thinks of you as a young man . . . one who's ready to take his role in the world. But that doesn't mean that she doesn't worry about you."

I start to walk away from Montoyo, along the shore. Tears of fury are prickling in my eyes. I can't afford to let him see.

Montoyo walks along beside me. He pulls something out of his shoulder bag, puts a hand on my arm.

"Before we get back to the others, I brought something for you." He places a book into my hands. I recognize it immediately. What I see takes my mind right away from any worries about Montoyo and my mum.

Incidents of Travel in Central America, Chiapas and Yucatan Volume I, by John Lloyd Stephens.

It's part of the same book that was stolen from my house . . . same book, different volume. A copy of my dad's first-ever gift to my mum. The same edition that I tried to replace, the book I found in a bookshop in Oxford and had nicked right out from under me. All thanks to Simon Madison and the mysterious global network he works for – the Sect of Huracan.

"The book. . ." I say in wonder, turning it over. I look up at Montoyo and notice that now, he's hardly more than a couple of centimetres taller than me. "Is this supposed to be for my mum? Cos the one we had nicked was Volume II. . ."

He taps his shoulder bag with a hint of impatience. "Yes, yes, I have the second volume also. It's the first volume that interests me. I remembered what you told me about the dedication in that book you found in the shop. From John Lloyd Stephens to Arcadio."

I stare at him in disbelief. As if in a dream, I open the book to the flyleaf. In the top left-hand corner there's a scribbled name.

J Arcadio Garcia, 1843.

"No way! This book belonged to Arcadio Garcia too . . . you think it's the same Arcadio?" I mutter, amazed.

Montoyo nods. "Maybe."

"Where did you get it?"

"Ever since you told me about the letter that Arcadio Garcia left for you with Susannah St John . . . I've thought it an interesting coincidence," he replies. "It never occurred to you? A book dedicated to 'Arcadio' and then this strange letter from 'Arcadio Garcia'?"

"A coincidence? It's just the same first name."

Montoyo taps the flyleaf. "But this book was owned by Arcadio Garcia. The same name as your mysterious correspondent, Susannah St John's friend."

Well, OK . . . except that . . . it couldn't be the same guy. Could it?

"But the date. . ." I stammer. "1843? He couldn't still be alive in the 1960s, when he met Susannah."

Montoyo grins, showing his teeth. I get a little shiver, watching him smile like that. This must be how a mouse feels, being toyed with by a cat.

"Not unless he has a time machine."

OK, Montoyo . . . you got me.

I don't want him to see my excitement, so I pretend to stare closely at the book. But I can feel his eyes on me, watching me like a hawk.

Montoyo continues, "It struck me as an interesting coincidence, so I began looking out for that book in rare bookshops. Do you know what I found? There's a collector in the USA who's been collecting that same book. . ." He pauses for a minute, staring directly into my eyes. "All copies inscribed by J Arcadio Garcia."

"Weird," I agree, slowly. I don't really follow . . . yet.

"But the *dates*, Josh. That's the strange thing. The dates are all over the place. Nineteenth century, twentieth century. Always the same book. The collector has eight. He *had* nine; I persuaded him to sell one set of volumes to me."

"I bet that cost you," I say, flipping through the pages.

Drily Montoyo agrees. "He very nearly refused to sell. Now why do you suppose, Josh, that Arcadio Garcia had a collection of these books, all inscribed with different dates?"

I stare blankly. "No idea."

Montoyo gives me a long, searching look. Eventually he nods at the book. "Look at the back."

I turn to the back flap. There's more of the same handwriting – is it Arcadio's?

Curtly Montoyo says, "Read it."

I read aloud: "*I would like to swim against the stream of time: I would like to erase the consequences of certain*

events and restore an initial condition. But every moment of
my life brings with it an accumulation of new facts and each
of these new facts brings with it its consequences; so the
more I seek to return to the zero moment from which I set
out, the further I move away from it. . ."

I stop reading, face Montoyo with what I hope is a vague expression.

He asks me, "You understand . . . what this is saying?"

Maybe I do. I can't help but think these words have some kind of meaning for me.

But I don't want to let Montoyo know that. Then he might guess that these days, all I think about is how I can do exactly that: *to swim against the stream of time.*

To go back in time and change the past.

So I shake my head. "Not really, no."

"I looked this up. He's quoting from a writer named Calvino. The character in the story makes a terrible mistake and longs for a way to turn back the clock, to alter what went wrong in the past."

I force myself to shrug, act as uninterested as possible.

Montoyo taps the book. "Why do you suppose Arcadio is writing this?"

Mumbling, I reply, "I dunno."

"The inscription of Arcadio's name in the book says 1843. . ."

"So. . .?"

Montoyo gives me a quizzical smile. "And yet the quotation comes from a Calvino story . . . a story published in 1979. Over a hundred years later."

"Arcadio's a practical joker?" I suggest.

The smile doesn't leave Montoyo's lips. "You think so? What if I told you that I saw all the books in this collector's possession? *And every one of them has the same quotation at the back.* What do you say to that?"

I scowl. "Why ask me? I don't even know who this Arcadio is!"

"Who is Arcadio. . .?" Montoyo wonders. "Now *that* . . . that is really the question. Isn't it?"

We climb the stairs to the paved promenade and stroll back
to the café. Montoyo stops to buy some T-shirts from a stall.
They look a little tight for his beefy shoulders. I don't
comment. Then he surprises me by handing me one – it's
yellow and green, shows the flag of Brazil.

"We're going to a restaurant, Josh," he says, tight-lipped.
"So put on a shirt."

We pick up Mum, Tyler and Ixchel from the beachside
café and Montoyo leads us down to the main street on the
seafront of Natal. The narrow palm-lined boulevard is packed
with artists flogging their canvases, boys pushing wooden
carts on wheels loaded with pirated CDs. Their loud sound
systems blast out samba rhythms. The pavement crawls with
fortune tellers, mystics, crippled beggars, guys touting buggy
rides on the sand dunes. Opposite the sea there's a solid line
of restaurants and bars, half-filled with lazy-eyed tourists.

The whole place pulses with a warm, steady rhythm, a

rhythm that lies somewhere between *relaxing* and *energizing*.

As I pass one mystic's tent, he breaks off his conversation and stares at me from under a silky purple turban, a white fringe and thick black eyebrows. His expression is so piercing that I glance around to see if he's looking at something behind me. When I turn back he gives me a knowing smile.

Tyler notices him looking at me. "Check out the weirdo in the turban and cloak."

My eyes lock with the guy in the turban for one second before I look away. Something about the mystic makes me feel uneasy. He reminds me vaguely of the bus driver I met in Catemaco, the one who offered to interpret my dream for cash.

The dream, I remember with a shudder, which led me right to the Ix Codex.

Tonight, though, I don't want to think about the past. It's a warm, sultry night and Ixchel's here. So I ignore the weird vibe I get from the mystic and walk faster, catching up to Tyler and Ixchel.

Montoyo seems to know what he's doing. He picks a café, shakes hands with the owner and guides us upstairs. We take a table next to the concrete dance floor, by the stage. Talking directly to the owner, Montoyo orders plates of seafood, rice, beefsteak, chips, all without asking any of us what we want.

I glance slyly at my mum. Montoyo has decided that she's sharing a mixed seafood platter with him and drinking a *caipirinha* – the local lime-based, sugar cane spirit cocktail. Mum doesn't seem to mind having her food and drink chosen for her.

I sit quietly and seethe, then lean across to the waiter just as he's leaving and change my drink order from *guarana* to grape-flavoured Fanta.

Tyler and Ixchel have stopped talking. In fact, I notice they keep giving me these little glances – who knows what they mean. If they're bored with chatting to each other already, that's fine by me.

I'm wondering whether or not to tell Ixchel about the book I'm holding. I can see she's curious about why I'm carrying a famous old travel book about the Mayan ruins. She's smart enough to work out that Montoyo gave it to me on our walk just now. Aside from that, it won't mean much to her.

Then Tyler speaks up. "Oi, isn't that the same book we were after in Jericho that time?"

I glance at him, taken aback. "Actually. . ."

The stage comes to life then – musicians start up on the conga drums. Two capoeiristas emerge from the edges and burst across the smooth concrete floor, flying head over heels in a series of spectacular criss-crossing somersaults.

The words freeze in my mouth as I watch. Tyler's just the same – eyes riveted to the stage.

More capoeiristas follow, bouncing on to the stage in pairs. They fly at each other with cartwheels and backflips and then perform a couple of swift, basic moves before moving aside to let others join them on stage.

When the entire group has assembled, they pair off and begin to spar, whirling in a blur of yellow and green *abada* trousers. The musicians on stage sing the same capoeira songs that Tyler and I have learned. I notice that like me, Tyler sings along quietly, under his breath.

The players perform within metres of us. Their moves become faster and more violent with every turn they take. Within moments all the men gleam with a shiny film of sweat, whilst the two girls still look daisy-fresh. By the end of the show I know for a fact that I'm watching the best capoeira players I've seen in my life. The students at the championship aren't going to be a patch on these guys. When they're really going for it, their kicks have the power and speed to kill . . . and yet every move is intricately timed. They miss each other by the breadth of a hair, laughing with delight, clapping as they land from another daredevil handstand and backflip.

Tyler and I are speechless. We're clapping along with everyone else in the audience. I notice Montoyo watching me.

You like this, don't you, Josh? he seems to be saying. *I finally found a way to put a smile on your face.*

Well, OK, Montoyo. Maybe this time. . .

On stage, the *berimbau* player hands the instrument to another guy and then he bounces lightly, lands barefoot on the dance floor. They start playing "Happy Birthday" to a capoeira rhythm. Everyone grins happily as the capoeiristas take turns sparring with Birthday Guy.

At the table next to us, two women in their twenties remove their flip flops and line up to dance with the birthday guy. The capoeira moves are now the slow, light-hearted, easy moves that two beginners might play. If anybody accidentally lands a kick it's dodged, blocked and laughed away like an old joke between friends.

Tyler stands up.

"I'm gonna have a go," he says.

Ixchel smiles. "Go on – Eddy G! That would be so great!"

Just like that – he does. Tyler steps in, touches hands with Birthday Guy, and without a word, they begin. Birthday Guy can handle more than the easy moves he's been playing so far. When Tyler moves the pace up a notch, so does he. Their movements speed up rapidly. I can see that Tyler is being pushed right to the edge of his abilities.

Tyler looks incredible. I've never seen him do capoeira with anyone this good. Now I realize just how talented Tyler is. Soon everyone in the restaurant is cheering him along.

They give him a round of applause and a cheer when he finishes.

When Tyler returns to our table, breathing hard, he wipes a sheen of sweat from his forehead and neck.

"Wow, Ty, that was amazing." I'm filled with pride in my pal.

"Yeah. . ." Tyler says with a quick grin at everyone at the table. "Thanks. It was all right, wasn't it?"

It's only then that I notice another presence at our table. Benicio. Without any fuss he's joined us. He's already sipping a drink and clapping Tyler, who's the first one to greet him.

"Hey, man, you made it!"

There's something like a squeal of joy from Ixchel. She turns around, delight in her eyes, and throws herself against Benicio. I sit by, uncomfortable once again. I watch as Benicio and Ixchel hug tightly. Her hand lingers on his shoulder. For some reason I can't tear my eyes away from that hand. When I finally glance away, I catch Montoyo gazing at me again, with a sort of knowing look.

Montoyo is really starting to get on my nerves.

On the dance floor the capoeira players have given way to three couples dressed in casual black. They dance together to tropical music with an accordion backbeat. It looks a bit like ballroom dancing, only funkier, less formal. The lead singer calls it *forro*. After the demonstration, the dancers invite people to join them on the dance floor.

Benicio winks at Ixchel. He offers his hand. "Do you dare?" She grins back, putting her hand in his.

So then I have to watch them dance. It gets worse. Montoyo leads my mum on to the stage, where it's obvious immediately that he knows what he's doing on the dance floor too. My eyes flicker from them to Benicio and Ixchel, who aren't anything like as proficient. But at least they can dance in time. When they make a mistake they just giggle helplessly, pressing their foreheads together.

I feel something then that is completely new. Nausea throbbing somewhere underneath my diaphragm. The feeling gets more intense when I finally put a name to it.

I'm actually *jealous*; more than I can remember being in my entire life.

It's so overpowering that for a few seconds the sheer novelty is almost funny. It's like unlocking a whole new part of my brain.

Who knew it could feel this bad?!

Looking from Benicio with Ixchel and Montoyo with my mum, it's hard to tell which of them is causing the feeling. In fact, they both are. But it's worse with Ixchel. After a while I literally can't bear to watch her dance with Benicio – I have to look away, suddenly act very interested in the lobster tank in the middle of the restaurant.

I'm conscious of my heart pounding like a metronome. I concentrate on the lobsters crawling around in their tank. It

suddenly strikes me as pitiful, watching them experience
their last few minutes of life. I sense the tropical rhythms of
the dance band; they enter through the soles of my feet,
through my fingers, deep into my bones, which feel like
they're trembling inside my skin. Try as I might, I can't stop
exhaling sharply – more like a tiny gasp of pain.

I like Ixchel; I like her *a lot*. When did this happen? Why
didn't I see it coming?

Later, Tyler lies snoring in the bed next to mine. I'm hypnotized by the ceiling fan, watching it slowly rotate among the shadows. In my head, I can still hear the music from the beach restaurant, pulsing away in the background.

I've been awake for almost twenty-four hours since waking up in Oxford. Although I'm shattered, I can't sleep.

My mind can't stop motoring along, not for a second. My thoughts flit from the last minutes of my dad's life, replaying the whole incident on the volcano in detail. Then I think about Ixchel. She's falling asleep against me on the bus to Tlacotalpan. She's holding my hand as we whisper to each other, the night before we climbed the volcano. She's standing beside me at the funeral. I remember how aware I was of her, our shoulders almost touching all the way through that ordeal. The way she took my hand and murmured, *You'll get through this, Josh. . .*

Then I'm on to thoughts of the Bracelet. That quotation

in the John Lloyd Stephens book that Montoyo brought me: *I would like to swim against the stream of time.*

A perfect way of putting it. That poet Arcadio quoted from, Borges, in the letter he left me all those years ago . . . Borges wrote that *time is a river.*

Well, if that's the way things are, then yes, I want to swim upstream.

Why is Arcadio writing something like that in so many copies of the John Lloyd Stephens book? Is that the reason why Madison stole a copy of the book from our house? As Montoyo says – who is Arcadio Garcia?

From there I think about Montoyo. The way he looked at my mum. The way she smiled at him. Jeez . . . she's *my* mother! I'm not thinking of her as a possession – what a jerk that Montoyo can be. I've never thought of a girl as a possession, either. But what my mum is to me, she can't be to anyone else. I'm her first-born and only child, her son. I have rights, whatever Montoyo thinks. I don't have to just stand by and watch him try to steal her away from my dad.

Dad is not just a memory. For us, things can be different.

I have the Bracelet of Itzamna. *I can change everything.*

I roll out of bed, fed up with hearing Tyler snoozing so happily. I step out on to the balcony, listen to the breeze whispering over the sound of the waves. In the garden below, the palms are lit up with blue and red lights. Suddenly I notice a movement in the shadows, beyond the pool. I stare hard into the depths of that darkness. The more I stare, the more I grow certain that someone is sitting there quietly, concealed by the dark, on a deckchair.

As I lean on the rail of the balcony, I have a keen sensation of being watched. My gaze falls into the blackness, with nowhere to focus. Whoever sits down there can probably see me clearly, outlined by the dim orange glow of a citronella candle.

I suddenly hear my mother's voice. She's speaking very quietly, but there's no doubt about it – it's her.

Is she down there in the darkened garden with Montoyo? Immediately, I lose interest in the mysterious presence in the garden below.

I've gone rigid with tension when I realize that I hear *both* their voices – Montoyo's and my mother's. The sounds are coming not from the garden but from the path which leads to the beach.

Montoyo and my mother have been together at the beach. They've only just returned to the hotel.

I pull back from the rail and against the hammock that's stretched across the balcony. I fall into the hammock, carefully wrap it around me so they can't see that anyone is on this balcony. I lie rigid inside the hammock, one arm against the balcony door, holding the hammock perfectly still. I listen out for their footsteps on the stairs. There's the sound of one door shutting and then another.

They've each gone to their own rooms, which is a relief. Yet clearly Montoyo and Mum wanted to keep their conversation going. They fancied a midnight walk together, along a tropical beach. Well, that's enough to put me off my sleep for the rest of the night.

It's a disaster. Tomorrow is the first day of the capoeira contest. I'm going to be wrecked.

Outside, it begins to rain. Within minutes the downpour has built to a torrent, drumming loudly on the roof and balcony.

Back in the room, I turn on my bedside lamp. I pick up the two volumes of the John Lloyd Stephens book and flick through them. I'm looking for the story my dad always told me about – where Stephens relates hearing rumours of a living city of the Maya – in 1840, hundreds of years after the Maya collapse, and after the Spanish invasion too.

There shouldn't have been Mayans still living in the ancient cities – not by 1840. Only in Ek Naab – the secret city beneath the ruins.

Ever since I discovered their invisible city, I've always wondered whether that story could have been a clue. Was it John Lloyd Stephens' way of hinting about Ek Naab?

Montoyo once told me that Stephens had secretly been to Ek Naab. That Stephens taught the people of Ek Naab English. And that's how they finally worked out that the Ix

Codex is written in Mayan hieroglyphs which spell out words in English.

On page 195 of Volume II, I find what I'm looking for. *A Living City.*

I read the page once, quickly, then more carefully. That's when I notice that two of the letters on the page are very faintly ringed with pencil. I glance through the rest of the book to see if there are any similar marks anywhere else.

There aren't.

I pick up Volume I and make the same check. Nothing in the pages. But now that I'm examining the second volume closely, I find something bizarre in the back flap, tucked right under an old Stanford University library sticker.

A series of numbers, beginning with 195.

195: 1, 1, 6; 2, 7, 4; 5, 3, 2; 6, 1, 4; 6, 4, 4; 6, 6, 1; 8, 5, 3; 8, 5, 5; 9, 1, 2; 9, 2, 2; 10, 4, 3; 10, 5, 4; 15, 2, 3; 16, 2, 1; 16, 2, 5

I'm so still, I can almost hear my own pulse. I stare at the numbers; tiny, meticulous handwriting. Like something a librarian might write, or a bookshop owner, to help them catalogue the book. But I'm fairly certain this is no coincidence. A set of numbers starting with 195 in Volume I of a book I . . . and then traces of pencilled rings on *page* 195 of Volume II . . . ?

The whole situation seems to remind me of something. It feels like there's a telephone ringing in the distance, muffled, and I'm hunting down the phone in room after room.

This should make sense to me. This should be easy.

I'm just so tired, though. I can't force my brain to calm down and think it through in a nice, calm, logical way. It's like a TV image when the satellite signal breaks down. Doesn't make sense.

Yet it should. Volume I and Volume II. Numbers in one volume of a book, ringed letters in the other.

Like a jolt of electricity, it hits me. An idea so incredible and yet simple that I can't believe it could be true. . .

The numbers in Volume I refer to the page in Volume II.

My hands shake slightly as I open the two books again, locate the first ringed letter on page 195. It's a Y. I mumble slightly, counting how many lines down, how many words across and how many letters along the word the Y appears.

Five lines down, three words across, two letters along. Y.

Now, my breath catching with excitement, I scan the long list of numbers in Volume I for that same triplet: 5, 3, 2.

The triplet is there. Amazing. . .

I struggle to calm myself as I test the theory a second time, now with the second ringed letter: a K.

Fifteen lines down, two words across, three letters along. K.

Now I'm looking for the triplet 15, 2, 3. And there it is.

I gasp, stuff a fist into my mouth to stop myself from yelling with triumph.

Each triplet of numbers corresponds to one letter. Two of them have been ringed – a Y and a K.

The string of numbers written in Volume I is a cipher – a coded message.

Someone started to decode this message. Who?

I work my way through the entire cipher text, translating the triplet code into the single letters. But after the first three letters, my spirits begin to plummet.

This doesn't spell any word in English . . . in fact, it doesn't look like any kind of word.

I plough on right until the end. But by then I'm totally disillusioned.

AGYLIHRPPREIKGR

It's meaningless to me. Might as well be another code.

I still can't sleep, and I don't see why Ixchel should. So I slink into the corridor of the guest house and knock softly on her door, then a little louder. She comes to the door instantly. Although she's in her pyjamas – shorts and a T-shirt – it doesn't seem like she was asleep either.

"Hey," she says with a surprisingly shy grin. "Couldn't sleep?"

"I found something."

"Your mum's in the shower. She just got back from the beach with Montoyo."

Impatiently I reply, "I know. Let's go to my room. We can sit on the balcony."

The instant I say the words, I realize that's a bad idea. It takes me a few seconds to work out why. Thinking about the balcony gives me a creepy feeling – a sense of being silently observed by whoever was just sitting out in the darkened garden.

It's OK, though, because Ixchel kicks the idea out. "Too dark. Let's go downstairs, to the lobby."

Behind the high reception counter of the lobby, a tall rangy-looking guy with a shaven head and trendy black glasses sits reading a paperback folded almost double. He glances up for just a moment when we approach. We help ourselves to a fistful of sweets from a goldfish bowl crammed with fruit drops. It's late and everyone else in the guest house is in bed, but after we sit on the sofas he doesn't give us a second look.

I unwrap a grape-flavoured drop and pop it into my mouth. Ixchel chooses lime.

"OK, Josh . . . what have you found?"

I show her the volume of the John Lloyd Stephens book I've been carrying as well as the separate piece of paper on which I've scrawled the deciphered code. I explain how I worked it out, and then my voice trails away as I watch for her reaction.

Ixchel is quiet for a couple of minutes.

"You worked this out, just now?" She looks at me keenly and I find myself stammering slightly.

"Well, yeah. . ."

"You really have a talent for codes, Josh. This is brilliant, you know."

She really seems to mean it.

"Thanks," I mumble, feeling myself redden. "But it doesn't get us any further."

"Yes," Ixchel says. "It does. It tells us a lot. I just don't understand how or why. . ."

"Huh?" I say. "Explain."

"Well," Ixchel says, pointing at the string of letters. "Have you noticed that there are fifteen of these letters?"

I actually hadn't bothered to count them. If I'd noticed that there were fifteen, I probably wouldn't have thought too much about it. But now that Ixchel mentions it. . .

"You're right," I mutter. "That is fully weird." And a crackle of excitement zips along my spine.

"Fifteen symbols on the Adaptor," Ixchel whispers. "Fifteen glyphs in the front of the Ix Codex fragment. And now *fifteen letters* in Arcadio's book."

"You think it's the same thing?"

Ixchel chuckles. "I know it is! Look – see this combination near the end. RPPR-something-something-something-something-R. I've seen it before."

"You've seen this sequence of letters before?"

"No . . . not as R and P. It could have been ABBA something-something-something-something-A. Or BCCB – and the rest. I never knew what it was – I just saw the glyphs. I saw them plenty of times. This pattern is pretty memorable. The same pattern of two different glyphs: glyph A, glyph B, glyph B, glyph A, then four other glyphs, then glyph A again."

A slow grin spreads across my lips. "You think this is the Adaptor sequence?"

"What are the chances of a sequence like that happening by accident – in a fifteen-letter sequence?"

"Hmm . . . I'm not great at maths."

"This could be the formula for the Key, Josh. Don't you think?"

"I think you're right, *Meninha*," I say. I can't help smiling at her. "You're a bit of a genius yourself."

"Yes," she says, no hint of joking, ignoring that I just called her "girl" in Portuguese – or at a stretch, "babe". "I know."

"Doesn't look like any chemical formula I've seen."

"Well, me neither, but I don't know chemistry. We could find one – a chemistry expert."

"You want to find a chemist here in Brazil?"

"Well, sure," Ixchel replies with a smile. "We'll use the Internet."

She's been strangely calm all the way through this. Me,

I'm sizzling with wonder at our discovery. But then Ixchel puts her finger on the one thing that makes me a little uneasy.

"The thing is, Josh – why? Why is Arcadio writing the Key sequence in code? And why in these books?"

I don't know the answer to that yet. But for some reason, the question sets off a tiny little alarm bell. It feels like the source of something dangerous.

Maybe even life and death.

7

Next morning, Tyler has to shake me awake. I can hardly
move. He's shouting at me to get dressed, but it's all I can do
to prise my eyelids apart.

"Hnuhhh?"

"Breakfast in an hour!" Tyler says. "Just time for a swim
first. . ." He chucks a pair of shorts at my head.

Maybe the ocean will wake me.

When we get down there it's barely 8 a.m. yet I can
already feel my shoulders roasting under the sun's rays. The
beach is nicely empty; just a few guys are selling sunglasses,
bags of fresh-roasted cashew nuts, ice lollies. I'm a little
surprised to see that Montoyo and Mum are already
lounging under a beach parasol. The ocean is blue-metal
grey, speckled with foam. Waves are dotted with surfboards,
their riders bobbing around the breakers. Once in a while
someone catches a long wave and rides it all the way to
shore.

Ixchel is in the water, riding a boogie board amongst the surfer dudes. She's not very good at it. I guess she's hardly ever been to the beach. I watch her for a minute. She looks happy, laughing every time a wave knocks her off the board.

Mental note – teach Ixchel how to bodysurf.

Tyler and I have a quick dip in the ocean and then hit the beach for another capoeira warm-up session. We go through the routine twice and then do some freestyle. A handful of local people watch us, smiling in appreciation.

With capoeira, when everything is going well, there's an energy which flows through my entire body. The air, my hands, the ground; it all merges into one. I am a free particle, energized, bursting with *axé* – an Afro-Brazilian word we use in capoeira. It means something like "life force" but also "cool".

But today there's no *axé*. Today I'm slow, clumsy, rough.

When we finish, Tyler eyes me curiously for a few seconds.

"Something wrong, Josh?"

"Yeah," I tell him tightly. I want to talk but I don't. I hate this feeling. Can't take a step forward for fear of going back. I glance out towards the surf again. Tyler follows my eyes to Ixchel and then back again to me. He raises an eyebrow.

"You *like* her."

I snort. It's probably not very convincing.

"But she likes *him*, don't she?" Tyler continues thoughtfully. "She likes Benicio."

So simple and everyday when Tyler says it. Ice cream is cold; the girl you like wants *someone else*.

"Hmmm. Change the subject."

Tyler stares at me curiously. He throws me a towel. "All right, Josh. Try to keep your mind on the capoeira. What was up with those *queixadas*? Even your *ginga* looks off."

Annoyed, I say, "Think I don't know?"

He's right, though; I can't even pull off the basics today. I'm doing the moves but my mind is somewhere else completely.

Even worse – I hardly care. I just want to be alone with Ixchel so that we can sort out this mystery. Instead, I have to go and compete in the capoeira tournament.

Tyler is going to kill me, because he's right; my heart isn't in it. Not today.

The championships are being held in a fancy hotel further along the beach to the north. After the morning swim and a quick breakfast of ripe yellow mangoes, pineapple juice and fried eggs, we head out as a group, walking along the sand. Montoyo is even more brazen than last night – he offers my mother his arm as they walk. Benicio strolls along with one arm dangling around Ixchel's shoulders.

I couldn't feel more gutted if she actually kicked me in the stomach.

It's almost like they're doing it to irritate me. I'm itching to hit someone. That or find some isolated place and vent my rage. Tyler and I walk on ahead. He keeps flashing me these anxious looks.

"Chill, Josh."

"Shut up."

"I know what it's like, man."

"No," I scowl. "You don't."

"Yeah," he says calmly. "My mum and her new boyfriend. That's rubbish, that is. And how do you think I felt about you and Ollie?"

I turn to Tyler in amazement. "Me and Ollie? There is no 'me and Ollie', never was."

"Yeah, I know that now, but she played me too. All part of her plan to spy on you. She used me. Winding me up, going on and on about you."

I stop walking, staring. "You're joking. You liked Ollie? You never said."

Tyler presses his lips together. "I liked her. And course I didn't say nothin', muppet."

My eyes focus lazily on the sand, the horizon, anywhere but Tyler's flat, bitter gaze.

"So I know what it's like, man."

With a throat so dry it almost chokes me to speak, I say, "With Ixchel, I think I might be. . . You know."

"Blatantly," he agrees. "She's *nice*."

I sigh with relief that I don't have to spell it out for Tyler.

"But Ty . . . I mean, how? I thought . . . me and her . . . we're just mates, right? Then I see her again and it's . . . like . . . *bam*. Just hits me."

Tyler just nods. "It was probably there all along. That stuff is weird."

I stare at him. "You were supposed to tell me I'm imagining things. . ."

He grins, shaking his head. "Nope. I reckon you've got it bad."

"What am I going to do?"

Tyler laughs, shrugging. "No idea."

The others have almost caught up with us, so I start walking again. Tyler follows.

"Let it out in the capoeira, Josh."

That sounds like a great idea. If only I knew how.

The hotel is one of those big fancy ones with lots of marble and a bunch of ritzy swimming pools surrounded by palm trees. As we approach the conference room we hear the pulse of the *pandeiro* drum and a raw, stringy twang, the buzz notes of the *berimbau*, the chorus chanting in response to the singer: the music of capoeira.

Tyler perks up the moment he hears the sounds, turns to me with a huge grin. "Mate, we're here, we're really here!"

The conference room has been laid out with tiered seating around a wooden roll-out dance floor. By the time we arrive, the early stages of the tournament are almost

70

over. Just five more matches for students with the same belt as me.

I've drawn a fifteen-year-old boy from Austria. One look at him stretching is enough to make me worry. He's about the same height as me, looks skinnier actually, less muscular. But he's got that long, raggedy, sun-bleached, ski-bum hair. I just know he's one of those mountain kids who spend six months of the year on a snowboard.

I don't like snowboarders. Ever since Madison got my dad and a bunch of other climbers killed by starting an avalanche whilst riding a snowboard.

Snowboarders are reckless.

I shake my head in silence, going into my breathing exercises. I can see Tyler having words with the British team coach, Mestre Joandy. I'm expecting a massive pep talk before I get into the *roda* with the snowboarder.

But all Mestre Joandy says is, "Have fun, Josh. Relax. Enjoy – that's capoeira."

I look up, mystified. I guess they've really given up on me.

From the second we touch hands, Snowboarder really is wild, totally fearless, throws himself into the match with a quick series of flips ending with a *mortal* – a somersault. From then, he keeps upping the ante – I do an overhead kick and he'll do *aú sem mão* – an aerial cartwheel with no hands. If I miss him by ten centimetres, he'll skirt my face by five. I go for the *mariposa*. It's not the best one I've ever done but as I fly past Snowboarder, I catch his delighted grin. This guy is not just good – he lives capoeira. Winning doesn't matter to him. He just wants to play. His own *mariposa* follows – faster and sleeker than mine. Then a barrage of rapid variations on *meia lua* – circular kicks.

The judges don't even need to discuss it. They pick Snowboarder to go through to the next round. Snowboarder can't stop beaming. I should be happy for him. A guy like that *should* win. But none of that helps. I wasn't as good as I can be and I know it. I never once got into the zone. With all these people watching, too. . .

"There's still plenty more team display stuff to look forward to," Tyler says. He pulls on his UK team shirt, getting ready for the next round – the yellow/blue belts.

I glance up into the audience, where Mum is giving me a "never mind" sort of look.

"I guess," I mutter.

Ixchel joins me at the side of the dance floor, watching as Tyler and the other yellow/blue belts warm up. I can hardly look at her, so I just give a quick nod.

"You're not in the mood, are you?" she says, in what for Ixchel is a very kind voice.

Slowly, I say, "Nope . . . seems not."

She seems to consider her next words. "This whole Bracelet thing . . . it's taken over you. Hasn't it?"

I can hardly believe what I'm hearing. Has she only just worked that out?

Ixchel continues, "Because maybe . . . maybe you should be thinking more carefully about what you'll do . . . if you fix it."

I've never really talked about that in detail, not with anyone.

"You're going to use it to go back and save your father . . . right?"

"Yes."

"What if that changes things?"

I gaze at Ixchel in disbelief. "I want it to change things!"

"If your father isn't there on the volcano when we climb it – how do you know that you won't die? Or me?"

Exasperated, I say, "No one will die! I'll bring Dad back *in the past*. None of that mountain stuff will have happened. Dad can find the Ix Codex. Then everything will go on like before. Except that *Dad* will be the Bakab and I'll be back to my normal life."

Looking right into my eyes with what I'm sure is a hint of a blush, Ixchel says, "So if this works . . . you and me . . . we might never meet?"

I mumble, "I'm sure Dad will introduce us one day . . . he's the one who agreed to us being fixed up, after all."

Softly she says, "And you're so sure that your father will find the Ix Codex?"

"Yeah . . . course . . . he had the same dream as me, the one with the *brujo* who says *Summon the Bakab Ix. . ."*

Ixchel shakes her head. "You're taking a big risk. Your father had that same dream since he was a child. But even so, it never occurred to him to search for a Mayan codex in Catemaco."

"Me neither."

"No, Josh – *you* were led there."

I laugh. "It was a coincidence. I took a bus. Never planned it. I just wound up in Catemaco."

Incredulous, Ixchel says, "After everything that's happened to you – after the ghosts of Chan and Albita saved us in the caves – you still believe that it's all been a coincidence?"

"Yes," I say firmly. "A coincidence! They happen all the time. My dad could have found the Ix Codex in Catemaco, just the same as me!"

I stop talking. Why is she trying to talk me out of this? It's not so complicated. This isn't a Chosen One-type situation. Anyone with the Bakab Ix gene could do what I did.

Even Madison – and all those other guys in the Sect of Huracan who happen to have the Bakab genes.

I move away from Ixchel, let her see the anger that's rising within me. "I just want things back the way they're supposed to be."

Then I turn and walk away. From behind I hear Ixchel's firm, quiet voice following me.

"But Josh . . . how can you know *what that is*?"

I ignore her. To my surprise, the ache I feel when I look at Ixchel is replaced by something colder, something easier to take: *resentment*.

This is good. This will cure me. Get mad at her! I should have thought of it before.

As I leave the dance floor, a spectator who's been sitting in the front row stands up. I catch his eye for a second and he gives me a quick nod. Now I think about it, he was watching my game very closely. He's fair-haired, too. Maybe another one from the Austrian team?

I don't give him another thought. But I should.

We're outside and there's drinks and general festivity beside the moonlit waves. The capoeira tournament is over and Tyler has won not one but two medals – best in his belt class and best all-round under-sixteen. I'm happy for him – really happy. It's everything Tyler has wanted for months and months. Watching his incredible performance in the finals this afternoon, it struck me that I couldn't be prouder of my best mate. Which, I realized today, Tyler has become.

The tournament closed with celebratory team displays. Followed by another beach party.

Boy, do the Brazilians know how to party!

With music pumping through my senses, feeling dizzy from drinking lime juice laced with sugar cane brandy, it's hard to have a care in the world. Of course Mum doesn't let me have enough *cachaça* to really forget my troubles. So it's not long before I'm back to brooding, watching Benicio and Ixchel laughing, chatting and dancing together on the sand.

OK, she asked me to dance first. It was only because she knows I'm going to say no. I can't dance, Ixchel knows it, and I'm not going to look like an idiot in front of everyone.

Get mad at her.

It's working. Anger is something I can deal with. If Ixchel's not going to support me, if she's going to be all weird about me using the Bracelet, then she's going to find herself off my friend list. I stare out at the bluish-black beyond the horizon, where a half-moon is on the ascent.

In a beach paradise like this, surrounded by friends and family, I should be happy. I'm not.

Montoyo notices that I've broken away from the group. He joins me, our feet submerged in warm surf every time the waves break.

"So Josh," he begins. "Having a good time?"

"Yeah." I attempt a smile. "Tyler was amazing. He made up for me being so useless."

"You weren't useless. You were . . . distracted."

I nod, resigned. "True."

Montoyo eyes me watchfully. "The question is . . . by what?"

The real answer to that would bring me scarily close to mentioning the Bracelet. So I try to be vague. "By wondering why . . . why everything has to be so complicated."

Montoyo seems perplexed. "What is complicated? Your life?"

"Yeah. Being a Bakab and that. When all I want is. . ."

"What, Josh?" Montoyo's eyes take on a stern glint. "What do you want?"

I shrug. "I just want to be happy."

I don't know if I'm expecting sympathy or what, but I don't expect Montoyo to actually laugh.

"Happy?! But what *is* that?"

It seems pretty obvious to me, so obvious that I start to think he's making fun of me. "Happiness. . ." I blurt. "Like, having fun and mates and things to look forward to and not be dreading stuff all the time."

Not feeling jealous, either. Or sick when certain memories flash into your mind. . .

"Is that actually happiness? The pursuit of pleasure, the avoidance of pain? That's not what Aristotle believed. You know Aristotle, the philosopher? He thought that happiness was about seeking personal excellence."

I shake my head slightly. "Personal excellence" sounds like a recipe for hard work.

Montoyo continues, "For men like us, Josh; for men of will, men of action, happiness is something else. It's about always having someone needing you, depending on you. Always having someone to protect. Always having difficult problems to solve. Always having so much work to do that . . . sometimes you don't have time even to drink a glass of water."

78

I stare at Montoyo in silence. He's actually smiling. He *does* look happy.

"Maybe it's time you were really honest with yourself, Josh. What's really important to you in life?"

Before I've even realized, my gaze has wandered over to Benicio and Ixchel. Like Tyler earlier today, Montoyo's eyes follow mine: he watches me watch Ixchel. Then he breathes a light sigh of discovery.

"Ah. . .!"

I force my stare to become glazed; move my eyes in a controlled fashion so that they appear to sweep the dancing couples, the bar, the restaurant; all with the same feigned lack of interest. A last-ditch attempt to make Montoyo doubt what he thinks he saw.

Montoyo shifts his position in the water-furrowed sand. This time, he sighs deeply. "Well, you'll be happy tomorrow, I guarantee it."

"Why?"

"We're gonna take a nice long ride on the dune buggies. Ride down giant sand dunes. Eat barbecued shrimp by a river in the cashew-nut forest. Zip-wire into a freshwater lagoon. And drive right along the sand until we find a beautiful beach that's just for us."

"Really. . .?" I can hardly believe my ears.

Montoyo nods. He claps a heavy hand on my shoulder, squeezes once. "That sound OK for you, Josh?"

"Yeah," I manage. "That sounds *amazing*."

The party winds down. We walk back along the beach to the hotel. Ixchel catches up to Tyler and me.

"Josh, is there something wrong?"

Tyler throws me a knowing look and then hangs back, leaving me to walk alone with Ixchel.

I make myself look at her, as vaguely as possible. "Nothing wrong," I answer shortly.

We walk along in silence for a few seconds. Beside me, I can sense Ixchel tensing.

"You're mad because of what I said," she begins. "About not changing the past."

Yes, Ixchel, and so much more. . .

But all I say is, "You're entitled to your opinion."

Ixchel reaches out, takes my arm. "Stop it, Josh."

"Stop what?"

"This. I've never seen you like this before. Cold. Angry. Just because I warned you not to do something that could be incredibly dangerous?"

I stop moving, facing her. "What did you think I was going to use the Bracelet for?"

A confused expression comes over Ixchel's face. "I don't know . . . maybe I didn't think it through properly either."

Challenging her, I say, "You didn't think I'd ever fix it."

"Well, sure! It's still a long shot."

"I know the formula of the Key. And I know they

80

probably have the Crystal in Ek Naab. One way or another, I'm going to fix the Bracelet, Ixchel." I pause, enjoying the look of unease on her face. "With or without you."

She looks hurt, withdraws her hand from my arm.

Get mad at her.

"So this is how you get when people don't agree with you, is it?"

"That's right." I nod, staring directly at her. "This is how I get."

In the artificial glow of the beach lights, I notice tears glistening in her eyes. I don't allow the shock of what I've done to register on my face. A cool wave of relief seems to pass through me. When it's gone, I feel numb.

Controlling her voice with difficulty, Ixchel says, "Well, I'm glad I found out."

I can only nod. "Uh huh."

She turns and slowly walks back to where Benicio, Montoyo and my mother are ambling along in a leisurely fashion. Tyler picks up speed, jogging slightly until he's alongside me again. I'm already walking even faster than before.

He asks, "What happened?"

"Oh, she's just having a strop."

"What about?!"

"That's between me and Ixchel."

Tyler pauses. "At least Benicio's got the guts to own up to liking her."

Now Tyler's annoying me, too. "This has nothing to do with any of that."

"No?"

"No, this is about. . ."

"What?"

But my voice trails off. Suddenly it hits me that by pushing Ixchel away, I've lost the one person I trusted to help me work out how to use the Bracelet.

I've left myself totally alone in my quest – again.

Well . . . OK. Good.

Trust no one.

9

I sleep fitfully that night. At least twice I'm stirred awake,
certain that I've heard my mobile phone buzzing underneath
my pillow. I don't answer it, of course. It costs a fortune to
take a call from someone in the UK. And there's really no
one there I want to talk to right now. The second time it
happens I turn the phone off. And then I think I even dream
that the phone is buzzing.

I don't let myself think too much about Ixchel, or Benicio,
or Montoyo.

Instead I focus on the next steps in fixing the Bracelet.
First I need to understand that fifteen-letter chemical
formula. Then I need to work out who Arcadio is – and if
there's any way of contacting him.

Unless I decide to patch things up with Ixchel, I'll be
doing it alone. Which suits me fine.

What worries me slightly is this: what if Ixchel decides to
tell Montoyo about my plans for the Bracelet? Montoyo has

been after the Bracelet of Itzamna since the day I met him. If he finds out that I've got it, he'll take it from me. It's as simple as that.

Next morning we all meet for a quick breakfast in the reception area. Tyler, Ixchel and I are all wearing the matching yellow and green Brazil-flag T-shirts that Montoyo bought at the beachside stall. Tyler and I think it's funny but Ixchel seems a bit miffed to be dressed in matching outfits. She's about to go and change, but Montoyo tells her it's too late: the dune buggies are here.

Stepping on to the beach outside we meet our buggy drivers – the *bugeiros* – tanned guys in their twenties who wear uniform white T-shirts made of football-shirt fabric. They stand beside two stocky, squat-looking buggies with chunky wheels. A scent of sweet, alcohol-blended petrol hangs over the vehicles. They look something like beefed-up Mini cars with the roofs sawn off. An overhead bar sits across the middle of each car, from which a plastic tarpaulin sheet hangs, protecting the front seat passenger and driver from the sun. For passengers in the back, though, there are no seat belts and zero shade, just the cool of a racing breeze to keep them from frying.

Mum chooses to sit in the shade at the front of the red buggy. She straps herself into a front seat with the only safety belt. Tyler and I sit up on the back of the roofless, brightly painted car. We grip the overhead bar in front, our

84

sandalled feet on the plastic-covered, cushioned bench at the back.

Benicio and Ixchel do the same in the back of a second, silver-coloured car, whilst Montoyo takes the front seat.

We take off, racing over the cobbled streets of Natal behind the hotels, up to the highway and then along the main beach road. It's only nine a.m. but once again the sun pelts down from a deep blue sky. A wind whips through the buggy, refreshing, exhilarating.

After about twenty minutes of careering through the city, our drivers leave the main road. We head for narrow chaos in the backstreets of hillside fishing villages. We cross a red-tinged river on wooden rafts punted by muscular villagers. They laugh and joke with each other, talking in laid-back, slangy-sounding Portuguese.

The buggies storm through another couple of villages, splashing through mud and cloudy puddles of last night's rain. Then the *bugeiros* veer off-road. We cut across damp, brick-red sand and shallow mangrove swamps, towards a golden mountain – the beginning of the giant sand dunes.

Up there, it's like being in a ski resort – except instead of the gleam of white powdery snow it's just pinkish-yellow sand as far as the eye can see. Behind the dunes in the distance, a line of deep blue – the sea.

We climb out of the vehicles, stretch our legs and take some photos. A young girl approaches, holding a plump green lizard along her arm. Ixchel, Tyler and Benicio are immediately drawn to the lizard girl, cooing over her exotic pet.

A third buggy pulls up beside ours. The driver is short and squat, his mouth a straight line under wrap-around sunglasses and a baseball cap. His green uniform shirt looks too tight for him, stretched thin across thick shoulder muscles. Four male passengers climb out, snap a couple of photos, swig from water bottles. Three of them are probably Brazilian; strong-looking guys accompanying one fair-haired European – or maybe Canadian? He looks kind of familiar, although behind his dark glasses I can't be sure. Seconds later the passengers climb back in. Their buggy pulls away sharply, disappears down the nearest slope.

I stroll away some distance, gazing out over the sands. I notice then that Mum has followed me.

"Josh . . . you've got to stop sulking. It isn't fair on your friends, or me."

I'm stunned. *Sulking?*

She continues. "Ixchel was crying last night. She was very quiet, but I heard. What did you say to her? It's really not on to be horrid to your friends, just because you're upset about your performance."

I draw myself up to my full height. Something feels ready to explode inside me. I wish Mum would just shut up.

"And Carlos mentioned that you were a bit stroppy with him too. . ."

"What, suddenly I'm surrounded by all these telltales?" I say coldly. "But you, Mum; you don't understand anything. You don't know anything about me at all!"

"If I don't, it's because you don't tell me anything! Josh, be careful. Or you're going to grow into one of those cold, distant men. It won't make your life easy, I promise you."

The explosion feels very close now. In disbelief I say, "Easy. . .?"

"Yes. You should be more open. None of us can read your mind, you know."

"Easy. . ." I repeat, even more amazed. "You think my life is easy now? Well, it's not!"

"You're still upset about your father, aren't you?"

I stagger. "Upset. . .? Mum . . . are you kidding . . . upset?"

"I should have insisted you see a bereavement counsellor. I'm sorry, that was my oversight."

That does it.

"A counsellor? You think you can just fob me off on some counsellor and it all goes away? Like back when I was the only one who refused to believe that Dad's death was an accident? You *never* listen to me!"

Mum tries to touch me but I push her hand away. "You don't listen to me," I repeat, "and you know what, Mum?

What I've learned is this: I can't count on anyone but myself. When I needed you, you couldn't help me. You couldn't think about anyone but yourself. Maybe if you'd listened to me, things would have been different. Maybe I would never have ended up on that mountain."

There's a long, agonizing silence.

In a voice that trembles slightly, Mum says, "I don't pretend to understand everything in your life, no, but I do try my best to be supportive. As for everything that's happened, Josh . . . you must learn to accept things. To let things go."

Now I'm trembling too. Maybe a part of me – a tiny part – can see the sense in what Mum says. But that part is swamped by raw anger.

I hate that Mum is so wrong about me. I hate that she is so right about me. I hate that I can't control anything – outside of me or inside. That I just want Mum to hug me and make it better but she can't, ever, and I can't rely on anyone but myself.

"I can't . . . *let things go*. I won't. Because everything in our life is wrong – can't you see that?"

But I can fix it. . .

Mum's tone becomes disappointed. "I'm sorry that you feel I'm such a failure as a mother. . ."

I give a bitter laugh. "That's right; try to guilt trip me."

With that I storm off, right past the red buggy and into the silver one, where I sit fuming in the back.

Ixchel approaches. "I think you've really upset your mother, Josh."

I squint up at her in dazzling sunlight. "What's it to you?"

Ixchel shakes her head. "Wow. You have a real mean streak, don't you?"

To that, I don't reply, just glare back at Ixchel. After a second or two she picks her bag out of the silver-coloured buggy. "I'm gonna ride with Eleanor. This isn't a nice way to treat her. You're lucky to still have a mother."

With that, Ixchel walks over to the red buggy, where Mum is standing, dabbing at her eyes.

I almost give it up right there and then, go over and apologize. But what would I say? I wouldn't know where to begin. This has all somehow spiralled out of control. All because of this . . . *thing* . . . I have for Ixchel. What kind of an idiot does that make me?

This is too complicated. I'm not going to have everyone feeling sorry for me just because I've gone soft – over a girl who likes someone else.

Better that they think I'm moody, angry, whatever.

So I stay put, blinking in the intense light because, stupidly, I've left my baseball cap in the other buggy. The way things are now, it would just be too undignified to fetch it. Then I notice that Ixchel has put my cap on. She turns around and glares back at me, shadowed under the peak of the cap. Daring me to come and get it. But I won't.

Eventually Montoyo, Tyler and Benicio gather around the silver buggy.

Tyler gives me a steady look. "You want me to ride with you, mate?"

I shake my head. "Stay with them, Ty."

He looks thoughtful. "OK."

Montoyo's expression doesn't alter. He doesn't even glance at me, just sits in the front seat and straps himself in. Benicio resumes his seat in the back, next to me. We both avoid each other's eyes, saying nothing.

I can almost hear Benicio's mind whirring away. If Tyler guessed, then so will Benicio. I exhale very slowly, fix a blank gaze on the nearby slope of the dune.

If this is what love feels like, then . . . you can keep it.

Ahead, a valley of shimmering sand stretches across our entire field of view – a view which might easily belong to the Sahara. The dunes are dotted with a few other buggies. Their riders screech with pleasure as the buggies tumble down the slopes like giant sledges. But even that thrill is going to leave me untouched. The weather may be sizzling hot, but inside there's a cold front sweeping through me.

Oblivious doesn't even come close.

The *bugeiros* are probably wondering why their fun party of dune-surfers has suddenly turned so cold. As they rev up the buggies to tackle the first slippery slope, we're all a bit po-faced. But once we start hurtling down the monstrous sand hills, even I perk up.

It does feel amazing.

The drivers seem to have the curves of the dunes etched into their minds. From the top, the craters at the bottom of the dunes seem terrifyingly distant. The expanse of sand is so bright that staring at it, I lose all sense of perspective. The next patch might be wildly steep or loose, require a hard bank to the left . . . or to the right: who knows? As a passenger you can hardly predict where you'll be going next, which gives a mad exhilaration to the ride.

Soon enough, we're all whooping as we zigzag across the landscape. It's as much as Benicio and I can do to hang on to the overhead bar. A couple of times we're actually lifted off our seats. It only adds to the thrill.

Holding on takes concentration. We're aware of the other buggies on the dunes, but don't pay much attention to their positions.

So what happens next really takes us by surprise.

Apparently from nowhere, a metallic-blue car leaps through the air in front of us. It lands between our silver buggy and the red one that carries Mum, Ixchel and Tyler. Our driver curses loudly to himself but doesn't alter his course. For some reason the blue car's driver was desperate to overtake us in the craziest way, scrambling across a patch of trees and scrub to cut in.

Now we're one of three buggies in a row. The red one carrying Mum, Tyler and Ixchel; then the weirdo-blue buggy; then us in the silver.

Between catching my breath as we swoop down and up those sandy hills, I begin to catch glimpses of something odd happening ahead. I don't speak Portuguese, but from his tone, I can tell that our driver is getting irritated with the driver of the blue vehicle in front. He keeps muttering under his breath until Montoyo asks him something – I'm guessing it's "What's going on?"

Our *bugeiro* gestures wildly towards the blue car.

Benicio shouts into the wind, "What's up?"

Montoyo turns unsteadily in the front seat. The buggy

jumps slightly. Montoyo's head bounces against the soft tarpaulin sun shade.

Still wincing, Montoyo tells us, "That driver . . . he's being very aggressive . . . trying to force them off the hills."

I look around, puzzled. There's sand for at least three hundred metres in either direction.

"Force them off . . . into where?"

Montoyo shrugs blankly. He turns away and faces forward again, rubbing his head. I glance at Benicio. Both he and Montoyo go very quiet. I sense there's something they're not saying. I stare at the red buggy. The blue one is right behind it.

No doubt about it – red is in trouble.

The crest of the last slope looms ahead, fleshy pink against the white-flecked, navy blue of the sea. A three-hundred-metre sheer drop, straight into the Atlantic Ocean.

For safety, our *bugeiro* pulls back as we near the edge. There's no hiding his astonishment when the blue buggy driver does the opposite, sticking dangerously close to the red buggy as it tumbles down the slope.

Benicio gasps. "That guy is nuts! Someone's going to get hurt."

Finally, the driver of the red buggy seems to have got it into his head that he has a crazy guy on his tail. He uses the drop to speed up, pulling away at the bottom of the hill. The red buggy is already a hundred metres ahead, almost at the shoreline as we go into the final drop. The blue buggy speeds up too.

Benicio speaks again, this time ominously. "I don't think that buggy is trying to overtake Ixchel's." I turn to him. He pauses. I definitely don't want to hear Benicio complete this thought. "I think they're chasing them."

The driver of the red buggy seems to have reached the same conclusion. He's really turned the speed on now, trying to get away from the nutjob behind him. Ixchel and Tyler are yellow and green blurs in the distance as their buggy zips across the flat wet sands. The blue buggy speeds up too, its four burly passengers sitting impassively in their seats.

"Josh, Benicio, time to sit properly. Hold tight!" Montoyo yells. Then he tells our *bugeiro* to speed up.

As I drop from the back on to the rear car seat, a sense of foreboding flashes across my mind. Something bad is happening – in probably the last place I expected. In the very next second our buggy takes its turn at the sickening, almost-vertical drop. We zip down the sand, sometimes sliding, sometimes bumping. Tangy sea air and sand sting our faces. We practically fly down the dune. I hardly breathe.

Then we're on to the beach, rushing to catch the blue car in front. The low tide whips at the wheels of our vehicle; a spray of salty water lashes our skin. Blue buggy chases red buggy. Silver chases blue. Could it all be a stupid game? If this was happening to anyone but me, I'd be tempted to say it was just some local *bugeiros*, rivals possibly, playing a joke.

But this *is* me. In my life, incidents like this have a habit of turning nasty.

A few minutes into the situation, I'm more than nervous. I'm downright scared.

In the red buggy, Ixchel, Mum and Tyler are still around a hundred metres ahead when their buggy actually jumps across a stream of water slicing into the sand. They make a hard left, disappear into a tangle of cashew trees behind the low dunes.

A second or so later, the blue buggy follows suit. Another second after that, so do we.

The path cut through the cashew trees is just wide enough for one buggy. All three *bugeiros* are driving like crazies – I'm not surprised to spot tourists spreadeagled against the side of the path, desperately trying to stay out of our way.

The forest path twists and turns – I can only just spot the blue buggy ahead. The obstacles have slowed it down. Now I can see the passengers more clearly. It's the three muscular blokes with their fair-haired guy. They don't even glance behind them. They're obsessed with chasing the buggy in front.

Why?

In a few minutes, we clear the cashew forest. We crash

through broken fencing and on to the red, sandy dirt track of a village. The makeshift road is lined with single-storey shacks; simple houses from where locals stare at us as we zoom by.

I'm starting to wonder where this will end. Are we just going to hurtle madly through all the fishing villages until we get to Natal? What then?

The road is riddled with deep puddles of milky, reddish-brown rainwater. The *bugeiros* swerve to avoid the deepest puddles, but it's not always possible. The blue and red buggies ahead keep being lost from view, hidden behind a cloud of brick-coloured spray.

As the town gets more built-up, the road narrows. We hit a tarmac-covered section. Even though we're in the thick of the village now, the drivers hardly slow down at all. Why doesn't the red buggy driver just stop, call off the chase? I crane my neck to get a better look at the passengers in the blue buggy. But every time I move, my head or knees get a wallop from some part of the buggy.

"Why don't they just stop?" I yell at Montoyo.

He replies curtly, not bothering to turn around, "Because they have a gun. In the front seat. He's pointing a gun at them."

"What?!"

Montoyo doesn't answer. I steal a glance at Benicio.

"What the heck. . .?"

Benicio frowns. "It looks bad, Josh."

Ignoring the fact that my head crashes against the overhead bar, I raise myself up to a place where I can see over the three guys in the back of the blue buggy.

Montoyo's right. Calm as you like, the guy in the front has a large pistol trained on the red buggy.

Yet he's not firing. Why?

Villagers are literally leaping out of our way now. Some of them hurl rubbish at us, furious at the ruckus. But nothing seems to stop us.

The road slopes along a steep hill. Buildings here are a mixture of ramshackle concrete huts that might be half-built or half-destroyed – it's hard to tell which. Wheels slip and slide as the driver forces the buggy to climb way too fast. At the top of the hill, the red buggy halts.

It's not just the hill. There's something in the way – two more buggies packed with passengers. They've come up against something. I peer up the hill. There seems to be a white van across the road, blocking it.

The blue buggy stops a few metres behind the red one carrying Mum, Ixchel and Tyler. The guy in front, the fair-haired white guy, steps out. The gun is raised now, held sideways at eye level.

He shouts towards the red buggy in heavily accented English, "Get out, all of you!"

Montoyo grabs our driver's arm. "Stop!"

The three dark guys in the back of the blue buggy are climbing out. Two of them turn towards us.

Urgently Montoyo hisses, "Reverse!"

Our *bugeiro* slams the buggy into reverse. We screech down the hill backwards.

The two guys from the blue buggy are reaching into their shirts. One pulls out a gun. Our *bugeiro* forces a handbrake turn. We spiral for a second, then jolt forward. The buggy leaps across someone's front yard, bursting through a line of hanging laundry. We head for the workshop at the side. We keep going, breaking down the makeshift straw wall at the rear and heading into a construction site. Labourers in hard hats leap out of our way, yelling out in fury. The buggy skids unsteadily over patches of wet concrete, clambers over a pile of scree that blocks the only exit.

That takes us into another alleyway, for the moment deserted. The buggy driver mutters again. But like us, he can see there's no choice but to keep moving.

Those guys have guns.

"That was a roadblock!" Benicio shouts, breathless as we navigate the narrow, dusty lane. "Those guys were organized!"

I'm stunned. "You saying it was a trap?"

Before anyone can answer, there's an engine roar from behind us. It's the blue buggy, revving loudly, screaming down the tight street to catch up with us.

Our driver turns into an even narrower alley. The sides of the vehicle scrape against crumbling concrete walls. Instinctively, I suck in my breath. We squeeze through the narrow gap and on to a dusty clearing – overlooking the edge of a ravine. The *bugeiro* curses loudly. He spins the buggy round and round, throwing up clouds of sandy red powder.

He's looking for options. There's only one.

The blue buggy has followed us again. This time it's carrying only one passenger – and he's armed. It blocks the narrow lane as, carefully, its driver forces through. In two seconds they'll be on the patio with us.

We're pointing straight at the edge of the flat clearing. The ravine is beyond, about four metres wide. On the other bank, a line of banana trees. Behind them, more scrub-covered sand dunes.

Our driver drops into first gear and slams the pedal; the buggy leaps forward until we reach the edge of the ravine. We're airborne. It only lasts a fraction of a second. I can hardly believe we're going to make it. We drop dangerously low; almost slam into a wall of banana palms. But amazingly, the driver manages to land between two of them. We're through, on to the sand dunes. I turn around just in time to see the blue buggy stalled at the edge of the patio.

They've stopped.

Benicio gasps with relief. "I guess we weren't worth the extra risk. . ."

Montoyo replies grimly, "Or they need to leave someone to pay the ransom."

Ransom?

"They've been kidnapped, Josh," he says gravely. "Benicio is right. This was a trap."

For several long minutes I struggle to grasp what Montoyo has just said.

Kidnapped?

Ominous tales of South American kidnapping gangs spring to mind. I didn't know this kind of thing happened in Brazil – at least not in a nice place like Natal. Mexico, Colombia, Peru, sure; everyone's heard of kidnapping in those countries. It's a big business in Mexico City these days, so I've heard my parents say. A bloody one at that.

People get kidnapped, yanked right out of their cars on the street. Young people, old people; it doesn't matter. What matters is that they matter to someone – someone who will pay.

Simple economics. Give us cash or your son, daughter, cousin gets it.

On the way, victims can lose a finger or two, maybe an ear. Sliced off by ruthless kidnappers, delivered to the terrified relatives. When the kidnappers get impatient, people die.

My mind reels. Mum. Tyler. Ixchel.

The things they're going to go through. I'm sick with fear.

Benicio and Montoyo are silent with their own thoughts. A sense of deep shock settles over us. The *bugeiro* drives along, no more muttering or cursing, chewing nervously on his shirtsleeve.

I summon up the courage to speak, my voice cracking. "What happens now?"

"Let's get back to the hotel first, Josh," Montoyo says. "Try to relax if you can." He twists backwards in the seat, faces me. "And breathe. The next few days are going to be difficult. You need to be strong."

He's right, I realize. I'm so tense that it's hard to breathe.

This can't be happening. Not now, not after everything we've been through.

The buggy driver takes us on to the main highway. Soon we're crossing a huge bridge into Natal. I stare up at the parallel lines of the bridge's suspension, slicing the sky into deep-blue segments.

I'd forgotten about the real world, the outside world. So wrapped up in my own problems: Ek Naab and its massive destiny, the mystery of Arcadio, the Bracelet of Itzamna and a fate I believed I could alter. . .

I forgot about the everyday brutality of the real world.

Why should I be immune to ordinary crime? Obviously, I'm not. But it doesn't seem fair.

This is just too much.

The second we arrive at the hotel, Benicio leaps out of the buggy. Without a word or a glance, he storms into the room he's sharing with Montoyo. I watch him climb the stairs two at a time.

Benicio is angry with me.

I don't understand why, but there's no mistaking the rage pouring off him. It must have brewed up over the buggy ride. I look at Montoyo, puzzled.

"Why's he angry with me?"

"Don't worry about Benicio now," Montoyo advises. He sits me down in the lobby. It's deserted apart from one maid laying the dining table for lunch.

The receptionist strolls over and murmurs quietly to Montoyo, in Portuguese. When she's gone, Montoyo stares at me, his eyes deadly serious, his mouth set.

"The kidnappers have been in touch."

Hesitantly, I nod.

His voice becomes soft, deliberately calm. "Let me explain what has happened. It looks as though your mother and friends have been abducted by a new gang that's operating in the area. They also took seven other tourists, the ones in the two buggies in front of your mother's. They blocked the road with that white van, rounded them up and took everyone into their van at gunpoint. Minutes later, they were gone."

"A new gang?"

"Kidnapping is rather unusual in this part of Brazil. But the gang members seem to be from a place where kidnapping is big business – Rio de Janeiro. Definitely professionals. "

"I get it. . ." I mutter.

But I don't.

Montoyo says carefully, "This is all about money. The kidnappers judge how much they can ask for each hostage. They will come back to us with what's known as 'proof of life' – photo evidence that the hostages are alive and well. Then will follow a named sum of money. That's when we start to negotiate. Somewhere in the middle ground, we find a figure we can all agree on."

"So Mum, Tyler, Ixchel – they won't be hurt?" I'm starting to glimpse some hope.

Montoyo shakes his head. "Try not to worry. We have access to plenty of cash. Obviously we'll negotiate, just so that it looks like we're being pushed to our limit. The fact that we're staying in such a simple hotel should make the kidnappers believe we aren't rich."

I can't keep the admiration out of my voice. "You can fix this?"

With a little smile, Montoyo says, "Don't worry. I've dealt

with many, many difficult people in my life. I will handle this. Stay calm, stay in your room as much as possible. Don't be alone, even in the pool. In a few days hopefully this will be over. Like a bad dream."

"What about the police?"

"If we go to the police, we force them to act for us."

"So?"

A shadow seems to cross Montoyo's face. "It makes things harder to resolve quietly. Pride comes into it. The police want to win, catch the criminals. The safety of the hostages may not be their main objective. For now we deal directly with the gang."

With that he stands up, pulling me to my feet. I'm sent upstairs to my room while Montoyo waits for the phone call.

Somehow I'm not surprised that Montoyo has completely taken charge. He didn't ask me once about how I felt or what I thought we should do. Montoyo seems pretty confident about the situation. Me – I'm out of ideas.

I close the door behind me, feeling shivery and numb. I lie on the bed staring up at the motionless ceiling fan. Minutes tick by, time stretching in the growing afternoon heat. After a while I break out into a sweat. It trickles down my head and neck, into the pillowcase. I don't budge an inch. I can't stop remembering.

The things I said to Mum. The way I acted around Ixchel.

It seems hard to believe that was me, even a couple of hours later.

What I'd really wanted this morning was simply to sit next to Ixchel, maybe put my arm around her. To be all relaxed and smiling, sharing a joke. Why was that so hard? In my imagination it was easy – no problem. In my imagination I was just like Benicio with Ixchel. Relaxed, cool, confident – the kind of guy every girl likes.

But searching my memories, I don't think I've ever let her see that side of me. Not once. I know I'm not usually a jerk around girls. Why can't I just be normal with Ixchel?

Mum's another story. She's my mum – she'll forgive me. When we see each other again, I bet it will be like it never happened.

The events of the afternoon begin to take shape in my memory, like pieces of a jigsaw puzzle. The face of the fair-haired guy in the blue buggy. I recognized him from somewhere, but where? It'll come to me eventually, I know. I replay the entire morning in my head. Slowly. As though in a dream, I watch myself walk away from my mother at the sand dunes, and go to the silver buggy, watch Ixchel take her belongings and join Mum in the red buggy, watch Tyler offer to ride with me but return to the red buggy.

No wonder Benicio's angry.

If not for my outburst against my mother, I'd have been

the third passenger in the red buggy. Ixchel would have been with Benicio.

Ixchel would have been safe.

I want to believe Montoyo that it's all going to be OK. But a deep current of fear runs through me. How all this happened . . . how it's all going to turn out . . . it's like some complex mathematical equation.

I can't balance it.

It all looks so simple on the surface – a simple case of bad luck: wrong place, wrong time. With such a simple solution – cash.

I'd love to believe it. Can it really be true?

When I'm finally starting to relax, nicely cooled by the dampness of my pillow – it comes to me. Things that weren't in order. In a place where there should have been nothing odd, things that stuck in my mind.

The fair-haired guy in the blue buggy was at the capoeira contest.

He was watching as I walked away from my bout – the one I lost to Snowboarder. At the time I thought he might be with the Austrian team – that's why I was confused. I didn't expect to see him in a dune buggy with three Brazilians.

That first night in Natal, when I sensed that someone was watching me from the shade of the darkened garden. . . Is there some connection? I sit up rapidly, grab my shoes. Montoyo needs to know about this. The blue buggy being on the dunes at the same time as us – what if it's no coincidence? What if something started the day we arrived in Brazil?

What if this is no ordinary kidnap?

I lock the room behind me, then leap down the short flight of marble stairs to the lobby. Montoyo's there, holding a phone to his ear. He looks up at me, his expression wide, hopeful. He gestures at me to be silent as he nods twice. He speaks briefly in Portuguese before ending the call.

"There's news, Josh. We have a proof of life."

MESSAGE FROM IXCHEL

Hi Carlos, Benicio, Josh. First thing: try not to worry. We haven't been harmed. We're staying with some guys called Tiago, Nando, Mario and Gaspar. Gaspar and Nando were in the buggy behind us at the dunes. Tiago and Mario were in the white van.

Gaspar was at the capoeira match too, maybe you noticed? He'd been watching us for a while, Josh.

There are some other tourists with us too. I'm allowed to tell you that there are seven others and that they are all fine, in case you've been in touch with their families.

So far no one has gone to the police. Gaspar told me to tell you that everyone is cooperating. If everyone keeps doing that, everything will be fine and no one will get hurt. They have people watching all our families. If they get any idea that you are going to the police, then it's going to make things bad for us.

As you can see from the photos, we're all fine, no injuries. Eleanor was very shocked and needed some medicine, but they let her take one of her own diazepam pills. She's feeling better now.

We have to spend most of the time tied up. I'm dictating this via Gaspar. I guess there's no way I can make you believe that these are my actual words. You'll just have to accept it. I can't tell you anything else about where we are.

Gaspar says that he'll let us communicate via the comments on this blog. He said not to bother to trace the IP address, that he's smart enough to know how to shield that information. If they detect any IP tracing activity they'll assume the police are involved. So please don't!

Josh – your mother asked me to tell you that she's concerned about the bad mood you were in this morning. She says that she understands you sometimes feel things are hard and that's OK, of course she loves you anyway, so don't feel bad.

Gaspar says that if you do exactly what they want, we'll be home in a few days.

We send you lots of hugs and kisses; we are trying to be strong. Please don't do anything dangerous. Let's all stay calm and this will soon be just a bad memory.

Montoyo pores over the photos on the computer screen. I've never seen him this anxious. I'm the same; I can hardly believe my eyes. Ixchel and Tyler, sitting on two shabby-looking plastic chairs, hands behind their backs – presumably tied. Mum sitting on another chair, her face drawn, looking ten years older than she actually is. She's holding a copy of today's newspaper. The strain shows on their faces. These aren't cheerful shots of hopeful hostages just waiting for their inevitable freedom.

These are photos of terrified people trying hard to appear relaxed.

Montoyo reads Ixchel's message over and over, muttering to himself as if it were some kind of code.

"Is this what you were expecting?" I say, breaking the tension.

"It's more high-tech than I expected," he admits slowly, "using the Internet and blogs to make a proof of life. But it makes sense. If they really do know what they are doing, it would take some serious intervention to track them down. They're probably using a mobile satellite to get their signal. Which means they can just keep moving from place to place. Using technology to track them down would be unreliable. Risky, too."

"Track them down? I thought you were just going to pay up."

Montoyo gives me a guarded look. "Did you notice that nobody has mentioned money yet?"

I'm thrown. "What else would they want?"

"I don't know what else, Josh. But Ixchel didn't write most of that message – however it looks. And these four names are just normal Brazilian names – they tell us nothing."

"Maybe they're still wondering how much money to ask for?"

"Money is top of the agenda for kidnappers."

I hesitate. "What if this is no ordinary kidnap?"

Montoyo goes silent, clicking a fingernail against the keyboard. Then I tell him all my worries, the dark suspicions that have rumbled away since the first night.

"You should have told me," he says eventually.

I say nothing. It's hard to explain how unimportant those tiny little details had seemed, with everything else to think about. All that anger and frustration, all those plans I made with Ixchel about fixing the Bracelet of Itzamna. Plans that are fading with every passing second. I sense the weight of the Bracelet in my pocket. Right now, it might as well be a worthless chunk of metal.

Montoyo continues, "For whatever reason, these kidnappers have identified us as a target. It's not unusual for kidnappers to stalk their prey, but. . ." His voice trails off, as though he's lost in thought.

"What?" I ask, anxiously.

Montoyo eyes me cautiously. "I don't want you to worry, Josh. Let's take this one step at a time, OK?"

I can't stop myself, though. "'Stalk their prey'? Why? Tell me!"

After a pause, Montoyo speaks again, reluctantly. "There's something called a 'tiger kidnap'. When they take someone in order to coerce someone to do something. . ."

"Coerce someone? Like who?"

I can see from Montoyo's expression that I've pushed him as far as he'll go on this. "Leave this now, Josh. There is something strange about this kidnap, it's true. Most likely we've wandered into some kind of territorial struggle between two gangs. The kidnappers appear to be new to Natal. That will make them many enemies here."

Benicio arrives in the lobby. His hair is all messy, his eyes blazing with unspoken anger. Montoyo calmly explains the situation to date. Benicio stays silent. Only a single, resentful glance flashed in my direction gives a hint that he blames me.

I can't return his look. Deep down I agree with him. I'm the reason that Ixchel's in danger.

We're still staring at the computer screen in the lobby when the receptionist comes over with the phone. Yet another call for Montoyo. She rolls her eyes, grins in mock sympathy. Bet she's got no idea what's going on. She probably imagines it's a travel agent playing phone tennis with him.

Montoyo takes the phone confidently. He says "yes" a couple of times and then goes silent. His expression doesn't change one bit as he listens. Then, very slowly, almost incredulously, he hands the phone back to the receptionist.

"What?" Benicio asks. We wait impatiently. Montoyo doesn't seem to know where to start.

"We've found them!"

Benicio and I gasp. It's the last thing we expected to hear. But Montoyo's expression makes me suspicious.

"Something's dodgy, isn't it?"

Montoyo shrugs. "It just seems too incredible. But one of the *bugeiros* has a contact who has a contact who *saw* them. We're all forgetting that one of the buggy drivers was kidnapped too. I assumed that he was in on the plan. But maybe not." He frowns. "That was the head of the buggy tourism company. He's organizing a rescue mission. The hostages are being held about twenty minutes away, in an abandoned construction site."

I say, "But they said no police."

Benicio adds, "And why do you trust that guy who spoke to you? What if it's a trap – a way to lure the rest of us?"

Nodding, Montoyo says, "You have a point. But we cannot risk that this may be genuine information. It's typical – plans go wrong. You think you have a secure plan, all the *t*'s crossed and *i*'s dotted. But you forget about the friend of a friend who works for another friend. . . Information finds a way to leak. We're just very lucky that it's leaked this early. We cannot delay. However," he adds thoughtfully, "the time may have arrived to call for reinforcements."

Benicio grins. "You're gonna call the Chief?"

"I think it's time some more of our guys from Ek Naab joined us at the beach," Montoyo says with a thin smile. "Don't you?"

We all go up to Montoyo and Benicio's room. Montoyo makes some lengthy calls, including one to Chief Sky Mountain, the head of Ek Naab's tiny armed force. The whole time he speaks Yucatec – the language they mostly speak in Ek Naab. I can't understand a word. Benicio paces up and down, mumbling to himself.

I feel totally left out. I get the distinct impression that I'm not going to be asked to help.

When the call is over, Montoyo sits us all down. Carefully

he closes the balcony door, turns up the air conditioning so that there's a loud background hum to our conversation.

"The Chief is sending six people in two Muwans. With weapons. I'm afraid we have to use ordinary guns, because anything else will leave a very suspicious trace."

I chime in, "What else would you use?" Do they have some kind of laser gun? It's the first time I've heard anyone from Ek Naab talking about weapons.

Montoyo ignores the question.

"We're going in tonight, as soon as it gets dark. We'll land all three Muwans – yours and the other two – on the roof of the building. It's one of those unfinished hotels. The developers ran out of money – it's the same story all over Natal. This place has been deserted for over a year. The intelligence says that the staircase is only partly completed. So we'll lower ourselves down more than ten storeys, and then go in to the staircase. They'll never be expecting an attack from above." Montoyo pauses. "We could use some independent intelligence on that hotel building. But it's a risk. Chances are that any request for information may be detected. Asking the wrong person . . . could be fatal." ·

Benicio says, "I could take the Muwan – fly some reconnaissance."

"And if you're spotted? What then?"

Benicio bristles. "You prefer we take our information from the buggy company guy? It could be a trap."

"He's taking his group in on foot, from the ground. Naturally, he doesn't know that we're planning anything."

"So why is he telling you anything about his plan?"

I agree with Benicio. Why tell us anything?

"Because he wants my help."

Benicio and I, we sneer in disbelief. "Then it's definitely a trap!"

Now, Montoyo seems annoyed. "Of course I didn't offer him any men. I offered money – if the rescue is successful. He's agreed."

"How much?"

Montoyo pauses. "It's quite a sum."

Benicio can't hide his scorn. "In that case, it's one kidnapper buying the debt from another! He's gonna kidnap the hostages and then he's gonna pass them on to his guaranteed buyer!"

"I agree, it could be." Montoyo's answer is spoken mildly. But his eyes have narrowed.

Montoyo doesn't like Benicio talking to him like this, but I can tell that he doesn't want Benicio to notice. Benicio hasn't, though – he's on a roll now. In fact, he's getting more confident by the second.

"The guy who runs the buggies might even be in on the original kidnap. . ."

My mind reels as I try to understand the implications of what Benicio is suggesting.

"Hang on," I say. "Are you saying this is a kidnap within a kidnap?"

Benicio looks triumphant. "Exactly!"

Still Montoyo doesn't seem fazed. "There are many possibilities. Who to trust, who not to trust. Maybe it's genuine. The guy is taking a big risk to deal with me openly. If he really is another kidnapper."

Benicio snorts. "No, he's legitimized the whole business! You won't be able to call him a kidnapper – he'll just claim to the police that he rescued the hostages and you paid towards the rescue."

Patiently, Montoyo says, "That is precisely why I'm not telling him about our own plan."

Sitting there with Montoyo and Benicio, listening to them plan the rescue, a feeling of exhilaration grows inside me. Turns out that they are going to let me get involved – I'm going to fly in with them, help guard the Muwans in case anyone from the kidnap gang manages to get on to the roof.

A kidnap within a kidnap.

Well, OK, maybe that's how these things are done.

Either way, the rescue is going to be one terrific adventure. What a way to improve my image with Ixchel, to earn Tyler's admiration, to make it up to my mum. Just as much as Benicio, I'll be one of the heroes.

Now that we know we're being watched, we take care to lie low in the hotel all afternoon and evening. The question is, who's watching us now? The original kidnappers or the buggy company guy?

It's hard not to marvel at the convoluted game that's being played here. Gang A watches a bunch of buggy-riding tourists, rounds them up on a day out, and then calls all the relatives. *No police, do as you're told* . . . the whole thing. But they make a mistake and kidnap a guy from Gang B. So Gang B puts together another deal with the relatives who all hired buggies. Gang B swoops the hostages away from Gang A.

It could even be like Benicio says – maybe Gang A and Gang B were working together from the start.

Montoyo's right, though – none of that really matters. Either way, we're going to get our guys back. With or without assistance.

As the sun sets, Benicio and I change into our darkest clothes. In my case, that's an old black rock concert T-shirt and some black jeans. In Benicio's case, it's his Muwan pilot's jacket over his jeans. Benicio mutters something about getting me a bulletproof jacket later on, when we get to the Muwan. It's obvious from his tone that every word he has to speak to me is one more than he'd like.

Does that mean I'll be getting a gun too?

I'm not sure I'd be much good if it comes to shooting someone. I remember when I had a gun on Simon Madison that time we fought in the nunnery ruins. He was knocked out cold, but I couldn't even shoot him in the leg. Real-life violence is nothing like computer games.

I don't want to see anyone else die. I'll never forget how I watched those two US agents dying from the poison gas released by the Ix Codex. Their screams bubbled with the sound of blood. And Camila and Dad. . . They both died near me, but thank God I didn't actually see Camila drown, or watch Dad break his neck. Although what I've imagined might be worse.

I decide that if I have to shoot, I'm aiming for their knees.

When it's properly dark outside, Montoyo receives the signal. It's go time. We leave the hotel by taxi. The taxi driver is probably in the pay of Gang A or Gang B – but who cares? By later tonight, no one will believe a word they say about us.

Montoyo tells the taxi driver to take us to the Serhs Grand Hotel, where the capoeira championship was hosted. We talk about capoeira all the way, pretending to our taxi driver that we have teammates staying there. When we arrive Benicio and I step out, saying that we're going to pick up a friend who's waiting in the lobby.

Instead we go straight to the motorbike parking, where Benicio's left his Harley Davidson. He used it the first night to drive from where he hid the Muwan, then down to the beach. Benicio starts the machine in a hurry, looking around nervously as the engine revs. I grip the pillion as we take off. No time for helmets. We fire off into the brightly lit beach highway. Within minutes we've pulled off into a side road and we're climbing into the hillside neighbourhoods – the poorer backwaters of Natal.

I don't know how Montoyo's going to find his way to the construction site where they're holding Mum, Tyler and Ixchel. When I asked him, he just looked grim and told me, "You let me worry about that."

Benicio and I make such a quick getaway, it seems at first that we're not followed. But I guess we make a distinctive pair – two teenage boys without helmets on a Harley. It's not long before someone's on our tail.

Unfortunately, it's the police.

A traffic cop is the first to spot us. He flashes us from behind to pull over. Naturally, Benicio ignores him and speeds up. He makes a few rapid turns and we're in another network of higgledy-piggledy streets. Eateries, pedestrians, cars and bikes clog the road. It's so busy, it could be the middle of the day. The police car switches on its siren. A few people look around curiously. Benicio curses. We're stalled behind a delivery van. On its open load, stacks of plastic crates packed with bottles of Antarctica-brand *guarana* clink against each other, precariously balanced. Then we hear another siren – a second cop. This one's on a motorbike.

"I guess they don't like these Mexican number plates. . ." Benicio says ruefully.

We probably look like a couple of thieving kids on some rich foreigner's bike.

Benicio jumps the bike on to the pavement. I hold on even tighter. We zoom along, watching people dive out of our way. We outrun the traffic jam, but then so does the bike cop.

We try to shake him with another series of crazy turns into alleyways, down a flight of stairs, then out on to some scrubland behind a narrow street. We lose him just as we reach the edge of the city. Our headlamp beams straight ahead, lighting up scrub and occasional heaps of rubbish. There's just enough ambient light from the glowing cityscape – we can make out trees in the distance.

Benicio activates the Muwan via remote. Shadowed behind some trees, the aircraft's lights turn on. Not too far behind, I hear the familiar roar of the police bike, still looking for us.

Why doesn't the cop just give up?

Close to the Muwan now, we slow to a halt. Benicio scrambles into the cockpit to start the engines. I take care to stow the Harley in the hold. When I close the door there's a brilliant light beaming straight at me. It's the other bike approaching through the trees.

"Hurry!" Benicio calls, jangling the rope ladder. I follow him into the aircraft, begin strapping myself in.

We take off right in front of the biker cop. Later tonight he'll be the person that everyone will think is UFO-crazy. I mention this to Benicio as he engages the in-flight stealth mode, turning off all the outside lights.

Benicio is not so convinced that it's going to be laughed away. "It's bad when police see us. Police have to make a report, however dumb it sounds. The National Reconnaissance Office – they're pretty high-tech guys, Josh. A joint organization of the United States Department of Defense and the Central Intelligence Agency? Not short of a few dollars, the NRO. They have computer programs that can trawl all the data of all the police forces in the world. They've known about us for a long time now, believe me. They know what to look for. They're gonna know we were in Natal."

There's no time to worry about the consequences of the NRO pinning down a Muwan sighting to Natal. We're in the air for only five minutes. Benicio has set the navigation systems to lock on to a signal broadcast by the other two Muwans – both are the smaller Mark Is. They've already landed on the roof of the unfinished hotel. Benicio takes our Muwan down, lands in the remaining space with barely a whisper.

In the planning meetings, Montoyo was given information that the building is about twenty storeys high, but past the twelfth floor, only the outer walls have been built. There aren't too many other buildings around, and nothing above five floors. It's a commercial district, and it seems that most people have gone home.

The strike team from Ek Naab has already assembled on the roof. The two pilots stay in their Muwans. Four guys wearing balaclavas are dressed in black from head to toe. I don't recognize any of them – but then I was never exactly given the keys to the city. One of them hands me a large bundle without a word.

It's a bulletproof jacket and a gun. I pull on the jacket and stare at the gun.

"Ever used one?" he asks. I shake my head.

"OK. I wondered. We've been told you can handle yourself. Didn't know if that was with a gun or without."

I stare up at him, flushed with pride. I wonder – who told him that I could handle myself?

"You point, you shoot. Keep both eyes open to aim. Keep

your arm really firm, and watch out for the kickback. Got that?"

I nod, biting my lip.

I'm the lookout guy. I patrol the roof and warn the pilots if anyone's coming. The gun is only for emergencies.

The strike team lower themselves down the side of the building on fast-moving quick-release nylon rope winches. They enter around the empty windows of the sixth floor. The kidnappers are holed up in a space that was planned as a conference suite, on the third floor. The plan is that they'll burst in on the kidnappers, shoot them and grab the hostages.

They'll arrive silently, from above and not below, as the kidnappers would expect. They'll strike with deadly speed and accuracy. "These are our best marksmen," Montoyo promised me earlier today. "The kidnappers won't stand a chance."

Standing on the roof I listen out, tense with anticipation. I keep expecting to hear gunshots. But there's nothing. Just the noises of a seaside city, calming down for the night.

I wander over to Benicio's Muwan, calling up to him.

"What's going on?"

Benicio is listening to a communication via his headset. There's a tense silence. He finally breaks off. Staring at me, his eyes fill with astonishment and confusion.

"They've all gone!"

14

Benicio and I drop down to the third floor using the rope
winch. It's an adrenaline rush, but I'm too frazzled at what's
happened to enjoy the moment.

Montoyo and the four members of the strike team make
a painstaking search of the space, hunting for clues. I just
stand there feeling useless. I stare into the dark corners of
the four bare walls that imprisoned my mother, best friend
and Ixchel until less than an hour ago. It's chilling to think of
them here in this grey, empty place, tied up, not knowing
how much longer they'd be held.

"My contact has double-crossed me," Montoyo
concludes. He stands still, his tone deadly calm. "He made
the raid an hour sooner than we agreed. They must have
disturbed the kidnappers. Now they've moved on and taken
the hostages."

"How do you know it was an hour ago?"

Montoyo indicates the floor near to him. "There's blood

here. It's congealed but still wet. And over there, the floor and the wall. The concrete is still slightly warm. My guess is that's where they had their portable power generator."

I don't take much in after "blood".

"How much blood?"

"Someone's been shot, but perhaps not fatally. They probably managed to stop the bleeding before they got out. The drops fall in a trail that reaches here. . ." Montoyo takes a few steps towards the door. "And then they stop. There's a small pool. This is probably where the person stopped to be patched up."

But who?

I remember the searing pain of the bullet that I took in the leg when Madison shot me last year in Tlacotalpan. It was like being stabbed with a red-hot poker. Thinking that the same may have happened to Mum or Ixchel makes me feel a powerful surge of rage. If the kidnappers have hurt either of them, I swear I'll get revenge.

There's a rustling sound from behind us, by the doorway to the elevator shafts. The four black-clad marksmen from Ek Naab turn in one fluid motion, assault rifles at the ready. One of them shines a powerful beam into the gloom.

A figure steps forward.

Standing in the doorway, his hands up, shaking, is Tyler. One side of his Brazil T-shirt is stained almost black.

I rush straight at my pal. Montoyo tells the strike team to

126

lower their rifles. I grab Ty by the shoulders, but when he winces I pull away.

"I'm a bit shot, man."

"No kidding."

I look at Tyler. That's when I notice his eyes – they're glassy, staring. His teeth are chattering. He's on the verge of passing out. He falters slightly, falls against me.

Montoyo and Benicio surge forward. They help me to catch Tyler and lower him to the ground.

"He's going into shock."

"I've got morphine," Benicio says. He reaches for his backpack and starts fumbling around.

I pull my hand away from Tyler's side. It's sticky with his blood.

"He's been shot in the side."

There's a makeshift bandage over the wound. Montoyo's right – someone tried to patch him up. And then, what? Was it the kidnappers? Or someone from Gang B? Did they actually manage to rescue anyone? Did they just abandon Tyler?

Benicio injects Tyler with something. Then he drags a piece of dark cloth from his backpack – a fleece blanket, which he places over Tyler's shivering body. We squat in silence for a few minutes whilst Tyler starts to regain awareness.

"They've gone," Tyler begins, speaking quietly, short

bursts of laboured breath. "They got a tip-off . . . someone was coming. One of the lookouts got suspicious. So they packed everything up. Gaspar put his gun down to untie me from the chair. I saw a chance. I got in a few good kicks . . . then cleared off. Doing handflips so that they couldn't easily shoot me. One of them caught me in the side. I didn't get much further . . . staggered on a bit . . . fell down. They were so mad . . . they were really in a hurry. Gaspar slapped something on me to stop the bleeding. From that minute I could see – they weren't that bothered with me. Wasn't really me they wanted, was it?" He shoots me a tiny glance, eyes hooded with fear.

"They hustled everyone else downstairs. Didn't even give me a chance to say goodbye. The lookout called again. Gaspar got really mad then. He told me this. *Tell Montoyo – you can have this one for free. And he can have the other two when he gives us the boy – Joshua Garcia.*"

I'm frozen solid. Montoyo leans in closer. "Tyler . . . how did they know Josh's name?"

Tyler shivers from head to toe, staring from me to Montoyo. "They know about all of us."

Montoyo asks, "What did they do with the other hostages?"

"I didn't see what happened after they went downstairs. A bit after that, some other blokes turned up, about ten of them. I hid in the elevator shaft. They didn't stay long. They scarpered the minute they could see everyone had gone."

Tyler's eyes cloud over again. "This is about you, Josh. It's not money. They want *you*. They were following our buggy cos they thought it was you, me and your mum. We was all wearing this same Brazil T-shirt, remember? You, me, Ixchel."

In a hollow voice, Benicio says, "But Josh wanted to switch seats."

I return Benicio's cold, accusing stare. No. I'm not going to let him lay this all on me.

Tyler closes his eyes again. "I'm so tired. . ."

With effort, Montoyo stands up. "I'm finished playing games with these people. We're taking you both back to Ek Naab."

I stare at him open-mouthed. "What about Mum and Ixchel?"

Montoyo looks suddenly old, like something's sucked all the life out of him. "These aren't any ordinary kidnappers, Josh. I'm afraid your fears were justified. Unless I'm very much mistaken . . . what we're dealing with here . . . is the Sect of Huracan."

15

Montoyo wants to put me in a Muwan right away with Tyler and Benicio, send us all to Ek Naab. I don't see that I have any choice. I won't leave Tyler alone in this state.

I'm not happy to think of Montoyo back at the hotel, going through my mum's things, packing them up. The whole idea makes my blood boil. Then there's my John Lloyd Stephens books. At least I stashed the paper with the decoded message. I doubt that Montoyo will be looking too carefully at my books, not at a time like this.

I glance at Benicio. He's concentrating hard, sitting in the pilot's seat. After the way he looked at me, blaming me for the fact that Ixchel's in danger, I don't particularly want to be around him.

It's the same old story – things have been taken out of my hands. All the time we're flying to Ek Naab I keep thinking, how did I let this happen?

One minute I was making plans to travel back in time, to

change the past so that my dad doesn't die. I cracked a code that's been sitting in a book for decades – some kind of chemical formula for making the Crystal Key. A massive step on the way to repairing the Bracelet.

And now . . . this. My mother and Ixchel snatched right in front of me. I don't know where they are. I don't know where they're going. Something tells me that I may never see them again.

This is no ordinary kidnap. This is personal – as personal as it gets. There's something about my genes – my DNA – that makes the Sect desperate to get their hands on me. This is about genetic experiments – experiments the Professor woman from the Sect muttered about in the tunnels under Becan. Marius Martineau – Madison's father – had suggested that they kill me, but the Professor told him that I was more useful alive – as a test subject. They're experiments that require someone with the Bakab gene. Most of the blokes in the Sect have one of the four Bakab genes, but these experiments, they didn't dare to try on their own people.

I remind Montoyo of all this and he just nods. "We can't risk you falling into their hands, Josh. I hope you'll remember that and understand some of the choices I may be forced to make."

Montoyo can talk all he likes about negotiating with the Sect, or even about mounting another rescue attempt. Deep down I know it's pointless. The Sect wants me. They might even kill a hostage to get me. I imagine my mother tied up in some dark, dank cellar with a sack over her head, terrified that she's going to be dragged away and shot. Even the mental image leaves me gasping for breath.

Ixchel, too . . . I still can't stand to think about what I said to her. It was worse than what I said to my mum: I actually *meant* to hurt Ixchel.

How can I let that be the last thing Ixchel remembers about me?

I lose myself staring into the midnight purple of the sky. The last time I remember feeling this powerless was when, thanks to Madison, I almost drowned in the Caribbean Sea. At least I kept fighting until the end. Which probably saved me – a few minutes later and I'd have sunk too far under the waves for anyone to drag me out.

There's only one thing I can think of doing.

I could give the Sect what they want. I could hand myself over.

Benicio doesn't say more than five words to me on the way over. We're all reeling from how deeply serious this has become. It's as though the air is heavy with fear.

Tyler sleeps through most of the flight, woozy from a painkilling injection that Benicio gave him. I think about how much I'd be looking forward to showing Tyler Ek Naab, if only it was the three of us. The way it should be: me, Ixchel, Tyler.

Until I actually watch Brazil disappearing beneath us, I don't realize how strong the link is to my mother and to Ixchel. It's like I'm being torn away from an invisible anchor – a thread which connects me to them both. Deep inside my chest there's an actual physical pain.

I think about the first time I met Ixchel. It was in the middle of the jungle, and she was dressed in a football shirt and jeans. She seemed so distant. Not angry with me, exactly, but as if leading me through the jungle was a chore. I remember trying to hide that I was crying about Camila's death. I remember how Ixchel wouldn't pretend not to notice.

Now that I think about it, that's when it began: the instant that I felt Ixchel's sympathy – sympathy which I turned down. Something was planted then, a seed of curiosity. I wanted to know more about this strange girl who appeared from nowhere with all her jungle knowledge.

Right at this moment, I think I'd do anything to have Ixchel beside me again. Just to know she's safe, just to hear her say one more time, "Listen to who's talking."

Now there's no way that can happen. The kidnappers will kill Ixchel unless I hand myself in. It's literally her or me.

"You all right, man?"

Tyler's voice snaps me out of my trance. When I look at him, I'm amazed to see him giving me a weak smile. I check the level of the blood bag that's hooked up to Tyler's arm. It's almost half empty.

"That's some hard-core medicine Benicio gave me," Tyler mutters. "I feel exactly like I'm flying."

I manage a chuckle. "They've got great doctors in Ek Naab. You'll be fine in a bit."

"So I'm finally going to see Ek Naab."

"Yep."

"Always reckoned you'd made it up, if I'm honest."

"Ty, I couldn't. Not even if I tried. You just wait."

We fall silent then, both of us thinking hard. Still looking out of the window, I say, "So, these kidnappers. What are they like?" When my gaze falls back on Tyler, I see that he's staring at me with a mixture of dread and sympathy.

"I'm sorry, Josh," he says quietly. "They're . . . bad."

It's the only thing he can say. After that his voice cracks and dries up.

I pause. "You think they'd actually . . ."

". . . kill one of them?" He nods, then breathes, "Yeah."

Tyler's hand goes to his wound. His face creases up. I can tell that the pain is creeping back.

I touch the Bracelet in my pocket, feeling the familiar rustle of energy when my fingertips connect. Tyler's eyes follow my hand. "What've you got there?"

I look at him for a few seconds, wondering whether to tell.

"Can I trust you?"

He nods. "Course."

I lower my voice so that Benicio won't hear. "It's a relic – from the ancient civilization that founded Ek Naab. My dad had it with him when we met on Mount Orizaba. He gave it to me before he died."

"Huh? I thought Ek Naab was Mayan?"

"Not exactly. Itzamna was a time traveller. He copied the writings of an ancient civilization called the Erinsi. What he wrote became the four Books of Itzamna. One of them was the Ix Codex, the one we were searching for."

Tyler takes a moment to consider this. "You never told me that. About the time travelling."

"I don't tell you everything," I tell him. "Not sure if it's safe."

"You can't do everything by yourself, Josh."

I don't respond to that.

"What . . . does the bracelet do?"

I rub my eyes briefly. "It travels in time. At least it would. Only, it's broken."

"Whoa. Does Montoyo know you have it?"

"Not a clue." I hesitate. "Well, maybe just a bit of a clue."

"Yeah, well, he wants it, I bet."

"He's been after it from the beginning, since the day I met him. Ever since my dad took it from Ek Naab. Actually, a strange old guy gave it to him."

"Blanco Vigores? Ain't he the blind bloke?"

"That's him. I told you about him – the one who lives in some weird, creepy, deeper-underground bit of Ek Naab."

"The place with all the hibiscus flowers that grow in the dark? Yeah, you did. Reckon we'll see him in Ek Naab?"

For some reason, at the thought of meeting Vigores again, a tiny shiver of excitement runs through me.

"No idea."

The truth is, I'm dying to see Vigores again. There's something I've been wondering about, something I need to ask him. Vigores knows more than he's telling – that's how I see it. Dad used the Bracelet to get from wherever he was being imprisoned to the slopes of the volcano. Which means that before Dad lost his memory, the Bracelet was working and Dad knew how to use it.

Someone told my father how to use the Bracelet of Itzamna. That someone is Vigores.

16

Somewhere in the jungle of Campeche, a vault in the ground opens up and swallows the Muwan whole. I'm back in Ek Naab.

The medical team is waiting with a stretcher. They take Tyler straight to the military hospital that's attached to the aircraft hangar. While they operate, I'm told that he'll be kept lying down for at least a day. "But it doesn't look complicated," a white-coated medic tells me. "No major organ damage. He's young. He'll be OK in two, maybe three days."

They let me stay in a room in the compound so that I can be close to Tyler. Benicio shows me to Tyler's room and stands in the doorway for a second, preparing to leave.

He seems to struggle for words, which is rare for him. "I'm sorry," he begins, speaking stiffly. "For what I said about you . . . being the cause of the kidnappings."

I point out, "In a way, I was."

"It's not your fault. It's ours. We should have protected you better."

The look we exchange says it all. He's trying to apologize for blaming me about Ixchel. But the words just won't flow.

"The Sect is everywhere," I say eventually, "with members all over the world. I guess we finally get that now."

Benicio nods, stiffly. "Yeah. I think we do."

When he leaves, I sleep. Just like the other night in Natal, I'm woken by the vibration of my UK mobile phone. This time I'm really annoyed, because I made a point of turning it off. Or thought I had. I miss the call but when I try to see who phoned, no number comes up. It's weird: the phone doesn't register any missed calls.

In the morning, I check on Tyler. He's still out – they tell me he'll sleep for hours. As ever, Benicio has been appointed to escort me around Ek Naab. Today, he doesn't even pretend to be pleased about the assignment.

"Babysitting duty again?" I say as we stroll down the corridors towards the chair lift.

"You got it," he agrees.

"So. Montoyo still doesn't trust me to get around Ek Naab by myself. . ."

"It's not you," Benicio says with a touch of irritation. "Like I told you last time you were here, it's other people. You might be surprised at how many people in Ek Naab would like a quiet five words with you."

I stop walking and look at him. "All right," I say loudly. "Enough with the *mystery*. What would they say? What's Montoyo trying to hide?"

Benicio takes my arm. He steers me back down the corridor. "Keep walking. Don't make a scene. Keep your voice down." We carry on and he continues. "You said it yourself last night. The Sect is everywhere. Even here, Josh."

Now that he's said it aloud, I realize that deep down, I've suspected for ages. Ever since Ixchel and Benicio told me about the secret gatherings and people who are afraid of talking to Montoyo, I've wondered. I thought maybe I was being paranoid, seeing the Sect everywhere, but maybe not.

"And you know who they are?"

"Me?" Benicio sounds shocked. "Of course I don't. There are enough people in Ek Naab who don't like Montoyo. It wouldn't be impossible for the Sect to find someone willing to betray him."

"But what would be in it for them? Won't the Sect destroy everything that Ek Naab stands for?"

"Well. . ." He pauses. "We don't exactly know what the Sect want."

"Huh? We *do* know! They want to get hold of all that ancient Erinsi knowledge that's in the Books of Itzamna. They want our technology, they want to know how to use that chamber me and Ixchel found. The one that's written about in the Ix Codex – the Revival Chamber. And when they have all that – they'll be able to work out how to stop the galactic superwave in 2012. Except – they won't stop it. They'll make sure that it happens. And all over the world, civilization will collapse."

Benicio gives me a curious look. "That's what you believe?"

"That's what Ollie told me, when she was trying to persuade me that I'd be better off with the Sect."

Slowly considering, he says, "But . . . it doesn't make sense."

"I know! They're insane! You should hear how they talk about the human population harming the planet and needing to be wiped out and all . . . they're psychos!"

"I don't know what you heard, Josh, but people don't behave like that. Soldiers, maybe – obeying orders, getting indoctrinated to believe they're doing the right thing."

"That's what I said – they're crazy."

Benicio shrugs. "I don't know. . ."

I can't put my finger on it, but there's something funny about his voice. He actually seems pretty uncomfortable talking to me about this. "The people at the top of the Sect, they will have their reasons. You can be sure of this: their reasons are things that even you and I can understand. In the end it always comes down to wanting the same thing – power, money, influence."

We reach the chair-lift station from where suspended

seats whisk travellers through the underground tunnels to Ek Naab. We ride through more slowly than I remember doing in the past. I guess that like me, Benicio is in no mood for fun.

When we arrive in Ek Naab, sunlight floods the underground city through the wire-mesh ceiling. I follow Benicio as he strolls to the plaza, crosses it and reaches the outdoor café. But he doesn't take a table, or order anything. Instead he grabs the waiter, who whispers something into his ear. Then he's back with me, now leading me towards the building with a fancy marble lobby and an elevator. We ride to the top of the building, to the jewel of Ek Naab's camouflage – the surface-level eco-resort.

Then we're strolling through the tables of the restaurant under a giant palm-thatched roof. Citizens of Ek Naab are enjoying a typical Mexican buffet breakfast. My mouth waters at the sight of plates of sizzling-hot spicy dishes, stacks of pancakes and heaps of fresh tropical fruit. When Benicio actually stops at a table, my stomach starts to rumble. I sigh with relief.

"Let's take a quick breakfast," he says, turning over a coffee cup. A waiter approaches and fills up the cup. Benicio and I approach the buffet and pile our plates high with scrambled eggs, black beans, chorizo sausage with fried potatoes, shredded tortillas and chicken in green tomato sauce. I fill another plate with warm, crusty muffins topped with crushed pecans.

"I'm so starved," I murmur. We don't talk for several minutes as we pack away the food. It's delicious, but I can't let myself think too much about how great it is. I have to steer my thoughts away from any of the horrible things going on with my mother and Ixchel, or I start to lose my appetite.

Which would be a bad idea. You never know when you'll need energy.

"So, Benicio, where are we going?"

"To see the Bakab Kan, Blanco Vigores. Remember his instructions – every time you visit Ek Naab, he wants to be the first to see you."

"Yeah," I say. "You mentioned that last time I was here. But my dad's funeral – Vigores wasn't there, even though everyone else was – all the others from the Executive."

Benicio just looks at me, his irritation obvious. "Well, Josh, the members of the Executive don't tell me everything. I'm just trying to help out here."

The ruling Executive. One day not far from now, I'll replace Montoyo on the Executive. When I reach sixteen I'll have that right – as the Bakab Ix.

"Things will be different when I'm on the Executive," I tell Benicio. "It's not right, all this secrecy. It makes people uncomfortable."

But even as the words are coming out of my mouth, I'm aware of the Bracelet, covered up, high on my arm under a sleeve.

I'm as bad as any of them. With me it's secret after secret after secret.

Vigores doesn't know I'm here, Benicio tells me. That's why Benicio had to ask the waiter at the café – his brother works for Vigores in his apartments in the "Garden". Vigores doesn't often emerge from the hibiscus-lined labyrinth in which he lives. But when Benicio put in a call this morning, it turned out that Vigores was on a rare visit to the surface.

Not to sunbathe or swim in the shimmering blue pools of the eco-resort; he was actually at the church near the cemetery.

I freeze a little when I hear that. The cemetery is where my father is buried.

"So is he very religious?" I ask Benicio. We're striding down a shady avenue lined with tall palms, their thick trunks painted white.

Benicio shakes his head. "I don't really know much about Vigores, Josh. I keep telling you that. I've seen him just a few times in my life and hardly ever spoken to him."

"Why not? Does he spook you?"

"Not even a bit. If anything, he's the one who avoids me."

"Huh? Why?"

Benicio shrugs. "You're asking the wrong person."

We emerge from the palm-lined avenue and into the outlying orange groves near the cemetery. The path slopes gently upwards towards the hill, on which sits the small, perfectly white Spanish-style church. But before we even reach the gravestones, I notice a white-enamelled bench under a tree dripping with oranges. On it sits the figure of an old man hunched over in his cream-coloured linen suit and panama hat. The hat casts a light shadow across his features, but I'm struck by how pale he is: a sharp contrast with Benicio's tanned, olive-coloured skin. Vigores is all milky-white, the flesh on his face stretched thin over his cheekbones, like paper.

Benicio clicks his tongue. "There he is."

We approach from the front so that the blind Vigores will have plenty of chances to hear us.

"Señor Vigores – it's Benicio. I've a surprise for you . . . Josh Garcia is with me."

The old man looks up, reaches for his white stick and then rises unsteadily to his feet. Blue veins stand out on the hand that grips the stick.

Benicio shakes his hand and then I stand in front of

him, reach for his hand. His bony fingers grab one of my arms and then the other. I notice that his hand hesitates slightly as he touches the Bracelet of Itzamna under my sleeve. I freeze, waiting for him to say something, but he doesn't react in any other way. He moves his hands up my arms to my shoulders and then my neck. Through his fingers he constructs an image of me. It brings a smile to his face.

"You've grown so much! Hah – much stronger now! Are you a 'monitor' yet, Josh? Or still a 'student'?"

I gasp and glance at Benicio to see his reaction. He gives an appreciative wink. Like me, Benicio is impressed that Vigores knows about the capoeira grading system. Someone must have told him about my interest in capoeira – I don't remember telling him myself.

"I'm still a student, sir."

"Your *apelido*?"

"They call me *Mariposa*."

He grins broadly. "*Mariposa!* That's a wonderful move. You've mastered it?"

I nod silently, then, reminding myself that he's blind, I add, "Yes, sir."

"That's marvellous. I wish I could see you do it."

I just stand there, not knowing what to do or say. Vigores sits back down, carefully, pushing away a low-hanging branch heavy with oranges.

"Sit down, Josh. Benicio, please leave us."

Benicio backs away slowly. He shrugs at me as if to say *You see?* Vigores doesn't move or change his expression. We sit in silence for perhaps two whole minutes. Finally he says, "Is he gone?"

"Yeah . . . ages ago."

"I want you to feel that you can talk freely, Josh. This time above all."

"OK. . ." I hesitate. It's hard to know what I could have to say to this strange old guy, but anyway. . .

"Do you remember what we talked about last time we met?"

"Umm. . ." I cast my mind back. The answer actually surprises me. "I think we talked about . . . girls!"

Very gently, he corrects me. "We talked about love."

"Right." I'm already uncomfortable.

"I asked if you'd ever been in love."

"Uh huh."

"And. . .?"

"I dunno. . . I'm too young for all that."

He chuckles. "Now I know you're hiding something. No fourteen-year-old thinks he's 'too young' for anything."

A flush of heat rises inside me. Even hearing the word "love" disturbs me. It's like being poked with a stick in an old, deep, and still-tender wound.

"The girl . . . in question . . . is in danger, isn't she?"

147

I gape. How does he know?

"Montoyo told me," Vigores says, almost as if he'd read my mind. "He's noticed what's happening with you two. Now she's been abducted. And your mother too. This is very painful for you." He lifts his face as if to look at me, but of course his eyes look straight past mine. There's a sadness to his expression. Real sympathy.

My lips tremble slightly – and for a moment I'm grateful that he's blind and can't see. It's always hardest to stay calm when people show me sympathy.

"I'm going to give you some advice now, young Josh, which may surprise you."

"Uh . . . OK. . ."

"In the matter of this kidnap, you *must* trust your instincts."

"What?"

"You've begun to doubt them, no? Hardly surprising, given the way your father died. But instinct consists not of magic or 'the Force'. It's simple intuition based on lightning-fast data processing. With you, young Josh – the power of intuition is strong."

He faces me again with those watery blue eyes, and actually winks.

"Data comes in through all your senses. Much more than you're aware of. It is processed by your conscious as well as your subconscious mind. Intuition ignores nothing.

Everything is given the appropriate weight of importance. Some things are *just so*."

"So . . . you're saying that what I think is jumping to a conclusion . . . might be the right thing to do?"

"Data comes in through all your senses," he repeats, this time even more solemnly. "Some senses that you perhaps aren't aware of." Then he leans forward, whispering, "Ignore nothing!"

I peer at him closely, watching his expression change from secrecy to determination. He seems to stare out through the foliage of the orange trees, past the clean stone of the graves and even beyond the glistening, whitewashed walls of the church.

I follow his gaze but I can't see anything special. Yet it strikes me then – with a strange rush of what I guess I'd have to call *intuition* – that this is a moment I'm going to remember for a very long time. Elements of the memory become solid, each piece falling into place: chinks of blue sky behind dark green leaves, the faint scent of oranges, the sharp blades of grass beneath my feet.

Ignore nothing.

It's as though I can almost grasp what he's saying. Somehow it's still just out of reach.

Then I speak. "Can I ask you something?"

"You may."

I pick my words carefully. If he's talking about me to

Montoyo then there's a chance that anything I say might be reported.

"Montoyo once asked me to find out whatever I could about the Bracelet of Itzamna. He reckoned that my dad stole it when he visited Ek Naab."

Vigores wags a finger. "That's incorrect. I *gave* it to him."

I knew my dad was no thief, but it's a huge relief to hear it from Vigores's own lips.

"Why?"

Very simply he says, "Because he asked me for it."

"What – you gave the Bracelet to him, just like that? Did you know what it can do?"

Vigores nods. "Indeed I do know, and did then too. It's a highly dangerous object."

"You told him that, yeah?"

"Naturally. I warned him that operating the Bracelet can cause you to materialize inside a rock. A painful way to die, I'm certain."

I gasp. "It can do *what*?"

"The Bracelet of Itzamna is thought to be a time-travel device, Josh, as I'm sure you know. What travels in time, however, must also travel in space."

"Why?"

"Because the earth flies through space. And spins on its axis – constant motion. Wherever you are on the earth at a given point in time, if you are to travel to the same place

150

but at a different point in time, you must also shift in space."

I consider this. "So the Bracelet is also a teleport device?"

"Correct."

Dad jumped in space – but not time.

I ask, "Have . . . have you ever used it?"

Silently he nods. "But I've also seen what can happen when the Bracelet is used without . . . due care." It sounds like he was going to say something else but stopped himself.

"You've actually used it? What happened?"

There's a deep sigh. "Yes. I was lucky – I survived. I was a young man. It happened soon after I first came across the Bracelet of Itzamna."

I interrupt. "*You* found the Bracelet? That's news to me. . ."

Why didn't Montoyo tell me any of this?

He hesitates, like he doesn't want to admit something. "I did."

"Where?"

"In a place called Izapa."

Again I gasp. "Izapa, near Mount Tacana? Was it anywhere near the Temple of the Inscriptions – where Itzamna copied. . .?"

"The ancient Erinsi writings that became the four Books of Itzamna? Yes, Josh, I found the Bracelet not far from that temple."

I lean back. "Wow! I mean – sorry – I never thought of you as a *Tomb Raider* type."

Drily Vigores says, "It wasn't a tomb."

I guess he's never heard of the computer game. . .

"The Bracelet that I gave your father – it's broken," Vigores tells me. There's no doubt whatsoever in his voice. "Or more strictly, the Bracelet is incomplete. It lacks the crystal that – presumably – controls the time circuit. Without that, there's no way to know where the Bracelet will send you. The chances are you'd end up in outer space and die."

"And my dad knew this?"

Vigores nods. "He did. He wanted to find a way to repair it. I tried to tell him that the crystal has never been found. Still. . ." Vigores seems to be searching for the words. "Your father . . . he insisted."

I fall silent, wondering. If Dad knew that using the Bracelet might kill him, why did he use it anyway and end up on the slopes of a volcano?

Vigores breaks across my thoughts. "You're thinking about your father again, yes? The Bracelet of Itzamna and why he wanted it, whether the Bracelet sealed his fate."

"Yes," I tell him slowly, "*sealed his fate* . . . I think it did. My dad lost his memory after using it. He ended up on Mount Orizaba. And later. . ."

"Later he sacrificed himself to save you," Vigores says

firmly. His tone becomes sharp. "So don't you think you should visit your father's grave now? To pay your respects?"

With that, he stands up and makes to shake my hand goodbye.

There's one final question I'm itching to ask.

"You showed him how to use the Bracelet. Didn't you?"

Vigores looks sad. "Yes. As a precaution – so that he didn't activate it by accident."

I'd do anything to ask how to use the Bracelet of Itzamna. But I can't think of a single way to do *that* . . . without giving the game away that I actually have it.

The Bracelet can be activated by accident.

One wrong move and I could suffocate in the vacuum of space.

18

Benicio is waiting for me when I finally leave my father's grave. The old man is nowhere to be seen. I get the feeling that Benicio wants to ask me about my talk with Vigores. Maybe because I've just been visiting my dead father, he lets me be.

I'm lost in thought all the way back. About the Bracelet. About my dad. Could it be that Ixchel was right, telling me that maybe I shouldn't meddle with the way things turned out? Perhaps that cemetery is where he's meant to be.

Yet, that doesn't make any sense. Ever since it happened, I've had the feeling that there is a reason why Dad made the effort to leave me the Bracelet. It's like he was asking me to fix it, to come back in time to rescue him. What else could he have meant by those last words – *"This isn't over"*?

Then there's Vigores. I'm so disoriented after meeting him. Not for the first time – he has this way of getting to me, every time we meet. I've never hung on to someone's words the way I do with his. I can only understand half of what he says. The other half, though, seems to worm its way deep inside. Words that just tick over, quietly. One day maybe they'll make sense.

As we're approaching the elevator in the thatched-roof restaurant where we had breakfast, overlooking the pools and the gardens decorated with banana palms, pink oleander and purple bougainvillea flowers, Benicio gets a call on his mobile.

"Your friend is awake now," he tells me. "Feeling much better, too."

I want to be with Tyler all the way from the beginning of his first visit to Ek Naab. So I go back to the aircraft hangar to pick him up. Benicio leaves me there and gets back to his own work.

Montoyo is with Tyler in the medical room. He's trying to act like we're the focus of his attention. But after only a few seconds his phone goes and he stands quietly in the corner, talking. Tyler is dressed in some clean jeans and one of Benicio's T-shirts. Poor old Benicio – he's always having to hand over his clothes. Tyler looks about a thousand times better than he did the last time I saw him awake. He even manages a broad smile.

"Hey, man," he says.

"You all right then?"

"Right as rain," he grins. I know he's fibbing. When I was shot in the leg last December I was in pain for days, even after Susannah St John stitched me up.

Susannah. Where is she now, I wonder? Back in Tlacotalpan? Or did Montoyo let her stay in Ek Naab? I decide to ask him.

"How is Susannah St John?"

Montoyo's just put his phone away. "Susannah St John," he repeats, very slowly.

"*Who* is Susannah St John?" Tyler asks.

"She's the old lady I met in Mexico last time I was here," I tell Tyler. "Last December. The one who sent the postcards . . . remember?"

Tyler nodded. It had been a crazy few hours, I recall. Phoning Tyler at all hours of the day as Ixchel and I travelled through Mexico by bus. Getting him to read out the coded messages on the backs of a bunch of postcards that kept arriving at my house. With his help we'd deciphered a code that the mysterious letter-writer Arcadio told Susannah St John to send me. Susannah must have wondered what kind of strange message she was carrying – since Arcadio had her wait over forty years before she mailed those postcards.

Montoyo says, "Well, Josh, why don't you ever write her a letter? Then you'd know."

"I'm not much of a letter-writer."

"On the contrary, you're a tremendous correspondent. What else is a blog?"

"But letters . . . to, well, someone older like Susannah, you know, with all the 'I hope you are well' and 'I have been keeping very well myself' and all that. . ." I wrinkle my nose. "I can't be bothered, honestly."

"I'm sure she'd be grateful even for something written in that strange text language you youngsters use," Montoyo comments.

"Do you write to her?"

"No," he admits. "But I use the telephone. She's well. Back in Tlacotalpan, most of the time."

"Why did you let her come here? Why tell her about us?"

Montoyo smiles briefly. "It's nice to hear you say 'us' when you talk about Ek Naab."

I hadn't even noticed, but he's right . . . I think of myself as part of Ek Naab.

"I told her, Josh, because, well. . ." He pauses. "Because she already knew!"

I say nothing. Ixchel and I had tried hard not to talk about Ek Naab in Susannah's presence. I guess we hadn't been careful enough. Then my mother arrived in Mexico after the avalanche and my father's death. . . At that point, I have to admit, the beans had to spill. Yet Susannah had taken it all in her stride – and Montoyo let her.

Meanwhile, even though in a couple of years I'll be on

157

the ruling Executive, I still have to be escorted around. I don't understand Montoyo.

We begin the tour. It feels so odd – wrong, almost – to be having such an interesting time with Tyler when Ixchel and my mum are going through something so nightmarish. Neither of us mentions them, and neither does Montoyo. I really want Tyler to enjoy his first day here. Looking back, I hadn't really been able to enjoy my first sight of Ek Naab. The day before I'd arrived, I was in a car crash with my half-sister and saw her drown. So I understand how Tyler must feel as we get into the chair lift and swoop through the tunnels, zooming past pools of phosphorescent water, stalactites and stalagmites.

Just like me on my first day in Ek Naab, Tyler will be grateful for the distraction.

A short while later we stand on the steps of the chair-lift station as they lead into Ek Naab, looking out over the gleaming mixture of modern, Mayan and Spanish architecture.

Tyler gives a low, soft whistle. "Man, that is quality!"

Montoyo watches him with a wry smile. "We don't get many visitors, as you know." He pats Tyler on the back. "You have excellent taste, my boy."

Montoyo walks us through the city, from the stone staircase down to the path that leads to the *cenote*, through the main town square where the daily market is in full flow, traders selling hot tortillas, fresh tropical fruit, dried chillies, warm bread, ice cream, clothes, paintings, today even books. We wander around, being given the spiel by Montoyo. Then he leads us back to the *cenote* – the ancient sacrificial sinkhole – the "dark water" for which Ek Naab is named.

After his initial whistling, Tyler actually doesn't say very much. He looks around mostly in silence, asking a question now and again, and that's all. Noticing how thoughtful Tyler has become, I take him aside slightly for a quiet word out of Montoyo's earshot. Staring at the smooth surface of the water, I prod his arm.

"So . . . what do you reckon?"

Tyler turns to me. There's a light in his eyes, but his expression is sad. He shakes his head. "I dunno, man. This is . . . it is like . . . so random. There's this. There's the world, and that superwave *thing* coming in 2012. The end of the world and whatnot. All these people here trying to stop it." He raises a finger and slowly prods me back. "And then there's you."

I grin slightly, puzzled. "Yeah . . . I know . . . I told you all that."

Tyler shrugs. "Seeing it, though, that's different. It's like . . . some impossible secret. Yeah. Something impossible. This is too much, Josh."

"Too much, I know! It's am-a-zing."

Tyler looks down, shakes his head. He turns away from

Montoyo, and speaking in a low voice says, "No. That's not what I mean. This is too much for you to handle alone. This Montoyo guy is *connected*, man. This morning in the hospital, when you were out? Never off his mobile. People coming to see him. But you, you want to travel in time, change the past. You ever think about all the things you might affect?"

I take a step backwards. "What are you saying?"

Tyler can see he's crossed me. He steps closer, whispers, "I'm on your side, Josh, you know that. But just think about it, yeah? Maybe you should hand the Bracelet over. . ." He cocks his head towards Montoyo. "Maybe he knows what he's doing?"

Horrified, I whisper, "Did you tell him I have it?"

Emphatically, he shakes his head. "No way! I'm thinking about *you*. We've got real problems here and now – with the kidnap. Montoyo is busting a gut to save your mum and Ixchel. All I'm saying is. . ."

"Maybe I should trust him?" I glance over my shoulder at Montoyo. He's on another phone call. Slowly I breathe out, releasing some of the tension. "OK. I'll think about it."

At that minute my UK mobile phone goes off. It vibrates against my left thigh. I pull the phone out, turn off the keypad lock. All I can do is stare.

It's a text message.

Nothing so unusual there, perhaps. But the sender? On

the phone screen flashes a name I typed into my phone during a fateful car journey down Highway 186 to Becan. The drive that led to my sister Camila's death. Moments before the agent of the Sect turned up and started shooting at our car, Camila and I, we'd had a moment. A real connection, me with the sister I didn't even know I had. *Next time you feel like you're missing our father*, she'd told me, *call me. Put my number in your phone. "Camila, Call Me!" or "Call Me! Camila!" Either way, it's with a "C".*

The number of times I'd seen her name come up on my phone, when I'd been browsing through the Cs. I never had the heart to delete it. I even thought I'd seen it the night we went out with Camila's husband, Saul, after it was all over and I'd found the codex. It seemed impossible to me then, that so much could be left of Camila except Camila herself. But that's how it is when people die, as I've come to realize. The person is gone, yet you're surrounded by all their stuff.

It's so hard to accept that they're not just a phone call away. That the phone will never ring again because of them – the telephone that rings, but who's to answer? That's what I told Camila about our dad, that exact thing. Now it looks as if I'm being haunted by her phone number.

It wasn't easy to let go of Camila. Maybe it's because I'd only known her for a few hours. Just didn't seem fair that life could give you something amazing like her, only to snatch her away.

Yet staring my mobile phone, there's no doubt – I don't even need to pinch myself to see if I'm awake. Incredible, impossible, and yet there it is, plain as day. My dead sister's name.

Camila Call Me.

19

I'm still boggling at my phone when Montoyo finishes his call and interrupts us.

"We need to get on the Internet right away. Ixchel's made another post."

Hurriedly, he leads us beyond the church to a very narrow little lane. Decorative hanging baskets drip flowers from the apartment windows above. The lane is so narrow that it seems that petals might almost meet across the gap. Montoyo disappears into a doorway about ten metres down the alley. Tyler and I follow him to a second-floor apartment. It's almost empty – three small rooms, a kitchen and two with hammocks. In one room there's a shiny new laptop computer, the box and packaging strewn around the room.

"I put you in this building," Montoyo says, logging on to the computer. "It's small but the best we have right now. Your things – and your mother's – are in the bedrooms."

I take in my surroundings – the newly whitewashed smell and four bare walls. The floors are covered with hard, glossy sisal carpeting. The windows are empty, still covered with the builders' dusty handprints. They face into a balcony across the lane, bursting with orange and yellow pot flowers.

"This is . . . my place?"

He nods. "For you and your mother."

"We never said we were coming to live here. . ." I say with a flash of anger.

Montoyo looks up suddenly, genuinely astonished. "Josh – at this point, the debate is over."

I stare back at my phone. We rushed off so quickly that I still haven't had time to check the actual message. While Tyler's looking over Montoyo's shoulder at the computer screen, I sneak a peek at the screen.

So you visit the old man, but how about me?

There's nothing else. Every single sound in the room is drowned out – by the sound of my own heart thumping. I can almost feel it in my throat.

How on earth can I be getting a text message from Camila?

On the computer, the familiar sight of Ixchel's new blog pops up. We all lean in to read.

MESSAGE TWO FROM IXCHEL

Well, you've probably heard from Tyler by now that our new friends aren't your usual gold-digging kidnappers. In fact, they traded all the other hostages yesterday for a very reasonable sum.

But not us. They want us for something else – as a trade for you. The kidnappers have a simple offer – just like they told Tyler. I'm guessing he's still alive? I really hope so.

A trade – one of us in exchange for Josh. If you agree, they'll arrange a place to swap hostages. If you don't agree, they'll shoot one of us. Then maybe you'll see sense and save whoever is left. (That's what Gaspar told me to write.)

You choose who to swap. They'll choose who to kill.

You can't begin to imagine what it feels like to write something like that about what might be my own death. How weird. It just seems unreal. I can't quite get it into my thoughts.

So now you know. That's what they say.

There've been a lot of threats. We haven't been hurt so far. Unlike Tyler, we haven't tried to escape.

Josh's mum has been having panic attacks. They're getting more tranquillizers for her . . . it seems she has a very nervous disposition.

What I've been told to tell you is this. We've been moved. I don't have any idea what country we're in now. They took us out of that empty building in Natal and into a van. We drove for many hours. Then we stopped, they drugged us and we moved on.

165

We have to spend all our time handcuffed together and locked in a room. They've offered us some books to read. It's not easy to concentrate, though. It's slow going. I've been trying to read a book called *Fictions* by Jorge Luis Borges. You'd like it, Josh, I think.

That's all from me. Sorry, I'm just not in the mood to write.

XXXXXX

This is straight from Gaspar: you have until 1800 hours Eastern Standard Time to decide. Let me know your decision by posting a comment here. We'll take it from there.

Ixchel's flat, empty tone breaks my heart. All the worries I've been suppressing for the past few hours suddenly tumble free. Ixchel is facing her own death again, like in the underground river where we almost drowned, like on the slopes of Mount Orizaba. Because of me – or because of how close she is to me. And my mother – she must be in some sorry kind of state if she can't even put down some words for her only son.

I check my watch. We've got just less than six hours. By this evening, my mother or Ixchel could be dragged out of a darkened room to be murdered.

I can scarcely comprehend the full scale of the horror. It's like looking at a vast painting – your eyes can only take in small chunks at a time.

I realize that I'm breathing faster. Montoyo's hand rests upon my shoulder.

"It won't happen," he tells me. "I won't let anything happen to them, Josh. Do you believe me?"

I blink as tears fill my eyes. I want to believe Montoyo, but there's a catch in his voice . . . this time even he sounds unconvinced. I glimpse Tyler, rigid, helpless, his face ashen.

They're both as scared as me.

I stand up straight, wipe away the tears. "They've really got us this time."

"No. . ."

I insist. "They're not going to kill me. Are they? Those genetic experiments they want me for – I won't die from them."

Montoyo shakes his head, appalled at what I'm suggesting. "We don't know that. And Josh . . . if this is the Sect . . . you can't expect me to deliver you into their hands."

"Yes . . . I can. You've got to!"

The tears begin to flow again. I know that deep down . . . *I'm lying.*

"Yes, yes," I say, trying to sound like I'm begging. "Let me go. Please! You can't let one of them die. We don't have a choice!"

Montoyo grabs my arms firmly. "Josh, calm down. This isn't the way, trust me."

But I get more agitated, pushing him away.

Even though the last thing I want is for him to stop.

"You have to let me go!"

Montoyo pulls me to him hard, buries my head against his shoulder. "I'm going to protect you, you hear me? That's my first duty. We're going to rescue them. Don't worry, don't be scared!"

Then I really let the tears go.

He's saying everything I want him to say. I know then that Montoyo will never put me in real danger. Which is how I want it to be.

All this time I've let myself believe I could be brave, heroic. But when it comes down to it, I'm nothing but a lousy, stinking coward. More worried about my own life than about my mother's or Ixchel's.

Worst of all, I'm a liar, making out to Montoyo and Tyler that I'm some wannabe hero.

I don't deserve to live.

The sightseeing tour of Ek Naab ends abruptly. Montoyo
dashes off to plan the rescue mission, leaving Tyler and me in
the apartment. There doesn't seem to be much to do there,
so we wander out into the lane.

I realize suddenly that Montoyo's left us alone.
Unsupervised, in Ek Naab.

"What do you wanna do?" Tyler asks. "And who was
that text from? You went white when you saw it – like you'd
seen a ghost."

Slowly and without a word, I take out my phone and
show him. Tyler stares, baffled, from me to the phone.
"What . . . you don't think . . . mate, don't be daft."

"What's your explanation?"

Tyler's eyes widen, astonished. "Josh, someone's pulling
your leg. Someone's got hold of your sister's phone, yeah?
And they're having a laugh. Did you try calling her back?"

"Great idea, man. Only, oh yeah, I already tried that."

"And. . .?"

"Number unknown."

Tyler shrugs. "Huh!" For a moment he seems properly stumped. "But . . . your sister. . .?"

"Read the text, Ty! I was visiting my dad's grave just before I got this. The 'old man' – she means our dad. How could anyone know that except. . .?"

"A ghost?"

"That's right." I take a gulp of breath, think back to the past two nights when I've been woken by my phone buzzing – calls from a mysterious, unrecorded number. There's some part of me that is somehow not surprised. "Yes," I say, more firmly. "A spirit – a ghost. I don't understand how it works or why me and not everyone else. But Ty, stuff like this happens to me. The world isn't as simple as you imagine. With me, this is normal."

"I mean this as a friend, Josh, but you – are not normal."

I lick my lips, thinking. The kidnap scenario has escalated into something so scary that it's too painful to think about right now. Montoyo's taken total command . . . I'm in the clear.

There's only one thing I can think of that will help now – apart from handing myself over, which Montoyo will never allow.

I can fix the Bracelet. I can go back in time, save my dad

and make sure that none of this nightmare that I'm living ever comes true.

"Come on, Ty," I tell him, turning around in front of the church, trying to get my bearings. "We're gonna go and find a Crystal Key. . ."

With that I head off towards the Tec – where I'm guessing Lorena the Chief Scientist must have her labs. Tyler follows, asking, "Find a what-now?"

"It's not a key made of crystal, exactly. . ." I begin. "But a crystal that *acts* as a key . . . to unlock some special activity in objects with Erinsi technology."

"A crystal," Tyler repeats, a touch sceptical.

"A crystal made of chemicals . . . and I know the formula."

"How?"

"It's complicated to explain right now . . . but the formula was written in code, in the books that Montoyo brought to me in Brazil."

As we walk, I bring Tyler up to date on everything we found out about the Crystal Key – how it's mentioned in the first few pages of the Ix Codex, how it's one of the objects needed to activate the Revival Chamber that Ixchel and I discovered.

"And this Revival Chamber does . . . what?" he asks.

"No clue. It's something to do with stopping the galactic superwave in 2012, though."

I tell him about how the Crystal Key has to be made in zero-gravity conditions, which is tricky. That it seems to be some key to using the ancient Erinsi technology that Itzamna, the founder of Ek Naab, managed to resurrect.

Tyler comments, "And Itzamna got all that ancient technology working again because he's a time traveller, right?"

"At least, that's what I reckon. Hence the Bracelet of Itzamna – a time-travel device. Only it's busted – teleports you in space but not in time. I have to find that Crystal Key. Fix the Bracelet. And then I'll find Blanco Vigores, make him tell me how to use it. Go back in time, save my dad, and none of this will have happened."

This is beginning to sound like a plan I can get behind. I'm already feeling less sickened by my own cowardice.

This is dangerous too . . . but at least it's not suicidal.

"But how will you find your dad? You don't know where he is."

"I can go back to the volcano, way before the avalanche hits. Spend more time helping Dad get his memory back. He arrived on that mountain *months* before we found him near Christmas. Maybe even before I found the Ix Codex in Catemaco? In fact . . . I could take him to the codex. Then Dad will bring it back, not me. My dad will be the Bakab Ix."

I'll be home free.

Tyler does a long, low whistle. "You've really got it all figured out, haven't you?"

"Yeah," I tell him. "That's right."

He stops walking. "And in this new timeline, you and me, we'll never become friends. Right?"

I try not to notice the disappointment in his eyes. "We'll still see each other in capoeira."

"Josh . . . we only became mates cos of what happened to your dad and everything."

I don't hide my impatience. "Ty . . . what do you want me to do? Wait until Montoyo botches another rescue attempt? Let my mum or Ixchel get killed?"

There is one thing you could do. Find a way to give yourself up.

But that thought remains unspoken. Maybe even unthought – by anyone except me.

Tyler shakes his head. "I just dunno. Playing around with time-travel, to sort out your own personal problems. . . I mean . . . is that allowed?"

"Allowed? What do you mean? Do you see anyone making any rules about time travelling? Cos I don't."

"But Josh, where does it end?"

I shrug. "I fix this, and it ends there."

"What if it doesn't?"

"Huh?"

Tyler stops again. We're right in front of the main

173

entrance to the Tec. I look up at the imposing, glass-encrusted building. Next stop – Lorena's lab.

"What if whatever you do doesn't fix things? What if it messes up something else – something you hadn't thought about? Are you going to keep going back in time, trying to change one little thing?"

What Tyler says makes me uncomfortable. He's right – I haven't exactly planned the details.

"This feels right," I tell him. "I'm supposed to go back. My dad as good as said it – his last words to me were *This isn't over*."

"That could mean anything."

Irritated, I say, "*Anything* could mean anything!"

"Josh, hold on, take a minute. You're losing it. One minute you're telling me that your dead sister is texting you from the afterlife . . . the next you're talking about changing time. . ."

My eyes light up. "Yes, and Camila too."

"What?"

"If I change the past, I'll save her too. Tyler – it's the only way. Fixing the Bracelet – that fixes *everything*."

We breeze past the reception desk at the entrance lobby of the Tec. Mind you, so do at least five older teenagers, students carrying books. With an embarrassed reluctance, the guy working the desk sidles out from behind it and catches up to Tyler and me just as we're about to enter the main corridor to the faculties. I'm trying to act like I know what I'm doing because all the place-signs are written in Mayan – meaningless to me. But the reception guy stops us in any case.

"Josh . . . Josh Garcia, yes?"

I nod, trying to look like I've no reason to be surprised that this total stranger recognizes me.

"Uh huh. Carlos Montoyo sent me to meet with the *atanzahab*. Can you tell me the way to her labs?"

The receptionist looks shy, and then once again embarrassed. "I'm really sorry, sir, but . . . Montoyo hasn't notified us. I can't let unauthorized visitors walk right into the *atanzahab's* department."

"Well, maybe it slipped his mind to call," I say, bristling slightly, "cos he's dealing with a serious kidnap situation. My mother and Ixchel – you know Ixchel?" He gulps and nods. "They've been kidnapped by the Sect of Huracan. We have less than six hours to rescue them before one of them is killed. Montoyo sent me to get some supplies from Lorena. Now if you want to delay things, call him out of a meeting and all that, then OK. But no one's going to be impressed."

The receptionist visibly shrinks. I'm amazed that my bluff is being taken seriously, but I try not to show it. He stands to one side.

"Of course, Josh, sir, I'm sorry. I'll call the *atanzahab* and

175

tell her you're on your way. It's the second floor, two turns to your left."

I nod and keep walking.

Tyler hisses. "He's warned her you're coming! What now?"

I guess we'll have to get a little creative.

"I've been to university science labs before," I tell him. "We'll snoop around before we get to her office. We'll say we got lost."

We bypass the elevator and bound up the stairs.

"He called you *sir*," Tyler mutters, impressed.

But there's no time to reflect on how radically the world changes for me in Ek Naab. All I can think about is using the two or three spare minutes we might have to swipe the Crystal Key.

Beyond that, I'm clueless.

Following the receptionist's directions, we quickly reach a department with two sets of doors. Between the two doors is a small sink, plastic bags to put over shoes and an air dryer. There's no one else around. I hesitate for a second and then go through the first set of doors, grabbing a fistful of the blue plastic shoe covers. I pass a couple over to Tyler, then begin to wash my hands with pink liquid disinfectant soap.

"What's all this for?" he mutters. "We gonna be performing surgery?"

"It must be some kind of super-clean area. Just go with it – we need to blend in."

We're through the second set of doors minutes later. Still no sign of anyone in the corridors. I peek behind the glass window of the first door we come to. It looks like a lab. We walk straight past. Then we hear voices. Someone's coming. I grab Tyler and rush towards a big fridge-type door. We're inside just in time.

Inside it's pretty cold but not quite freezing. Metal shelving is covered with boxes of lab supplies, plastic petri dishes filled with cloudy jelly, boxes of test tubes scrawled over with handwritten labels. There is a workbench about two metres wide on which several chunky pieces of lab apparatus sit. Glass plates stand in liquid, with brilliant blue stain across the middle of the plates.

Tyler kisses his teeth in appreciation. "Hey, man, a walk-in fridge!"

"It's a cold room," I say. "My dad's department has one too – for storing specimens. This would be a good place to store the Crystal. . ."

"OK . . . so what are we looking for?"

My heart sinks at Tyler's question. Looking around this slightly messy cold room, I doubt that it would be used to store something quite so significant. Surely Lorena would keep something so valuable somewhere special . . . perhaps in its own fridge?

Then my eye falls on something I recognize. A box of pens – the exact same type of pen that I was given before my mission to find the Ix Codex. An instrument to secretly deliver a dose of a drug. I was supposed to use it to give myself short-term memory loss – in case I was captured by the enemy. But like all the other gadgets they gave me for the mission, I never got to use it.

I grab a handful of the pens. "These could be useful," I tell Tyler. "They inject you with an amnesia thing. . ."

Tyler looks baffled. "Amnesia? What do you want to forget?"

I glare at him flatly. "They're not meant for me, bozo."

I'm still scanning the room when the door begins to open with a loud, clunking noise as the air seal is broken. Hurriedly I stuff the pens into my back jeans pocket. Tyler and I glance at each other wildly for a second.

There's nowhere to hide.

The door opens.

Standing in the opening is Lorena – the *atanzahab*, the chief scientist of Ek Naab. Wearing a stiff white lab coat she looks more imposing than she did the first time I met her, that night I was installed as the Bakab Ix. From behind stern-looking, black-rimmed glasses, she gives me a beady glare.

"Joshua Garcia . . . what the devil are you doing in here?"

21

I lift my hands to where Lorena can see them. "I just wanted to show Tyler a cold room! He's never seen one – he didn't even believe me that they existed."

Lorena looks doubtfully from me to Tyler, who gives a goofy nod. "He reckons there's hot rooms too."

I give Tyler a sharp glare. Hot room – what's he on about? But turns out it's a good guess. . .

"There are," she says coldly. "But the 'hot room' isn't actually hot."

I step forward, looking straight at Lorena, as though nothing in the room could be of the tiniest interest. Innocently I ask, "Why is it called a 'hot room' then?"

Lorena stands aside to let us out of the room. "Because of the radiation," she says, now impatient. "Josh, what are you doing here?"

"Montoyo is organizing a rescue mission to get Ixchel and my mother back from the kidnappers. We thought you

179

might be able to help out with something for weapons, gadgets . . . you know the sort of thing."

Lorena's eyes narrow. "Montoyo sent you? Because I can't get hold of him – he's not answering his phone."

I'm all wide-eyed innocence. "He's in meetings now, planning the rescue. He didn't exactly send me . . . but only because he's got too much to think about right now."

Lorena begins to nod, still a bit suspicious. "There are some things that might be useful, yes. The usual stuff – sedative drugs. . ." Her voice trails off, as though she's not meant to say more. "We have a nice little dart delivery system now."

"Poison darts?" Tyler says. "Why don't you just use guns?"

Her attention turns to Tyler. "Guns? When people are killed there has to be an investigation. A secret like Ek Naab doesn't stay secret very long when it starts murdering people. Look at the Sect of Huracan . . . they're really sloppy. We're picking up news stories linked to them every few months now."

"It's true," I tell Tyler. "My mum showed me one. Simon Madison killed this scientist woman in the Middle East. And he stole the Adaptor from someone in the Middle East, too."

"That's right, from a collector in Beirut," Lorena confirms.

"What's in the Middle East?" I wonder, almost to myself. "Cos Madison keeps cropping up there."

Lorena seems surprised. "You don't know?"

I give her a blank stare. My comment was just offhand – I hadn't expected for a second that Lorena would be able to answer my question. "No, I don't. What's there?"

"I'm sorry." Lorena frowns. "I assumed, with you being the Bakab Ix . . . and the fact that you're the one who found the Revival Chamber. . ."

"Huh? What?"

"There's a second Revival Chamber in Iraq, Josh. Just like the one that you found under Structure X in Becan."

I'm too excited at the news to be angry at yet more evidence of Montoyo's secrecy. "Another one? Wow! How do you know? What does it do?"

"Well . . . we know from the Ix Codex. There were five Revival Chambers, spread throughout the world. One of them was in the ancient city of Eridu, in modern-day Iraq."

"Five chambers! Wow! This is huge!"

"In answer to your second question – we don't know what they do. The one here in Becan is empty."

"Empty . . . what do you mean?" From what I remember, the Revival Chamber was an octagonal stone room filled with what looked like sarcophagi.

"Well . . . we activated it," Lorena continues, still puzzled that I don't know any of this. "All the receptacles are empty."

Now I really do boggle at her. "You activated the Revival

Chamber? You got the Adaptor to work in the Container . . . you have the Crystal Key?!"

They must have followed the instructions in the Ix Codex, succeeded where I'd seen the Professor, Marius and Madison fail. . .

Lorena shrugs. "We didn't need the Crystal Key. The Liquid Key works fine so long as it's used very soon after it is made. The minute we had the amino acid sequence from the Ix Codex, we had it made here in our peptide synthesizer and took it right over to the Revival Chamber."

Then I remember that line from the first few pages of the Ix Codex – the Key is unstable – must be used within sixty minutes. . .

Lorena's words don't fully make sense to me . . . amino acid sequence . . . peptide synthesizer . . . but what I do get is this: Lorena doesn't need the Crystal Key to activate the Adaptor. She can activate it with something that is way, way easier to make.

So if Lorena doesn't need the Crystal Key – maybe she'll let me try it?

I repeat, "You don't need the Crystal Key?"

Lorena frowns. "No, Josh . . . once we cracked the code in the Ix Codex, we realized that the fifteen letters in that sequence represent amino acids. After that it was easy enough."

"So you've just got the Crystal Key sitting there, then. . .?"

Doing nothing. . .

She shakes her head. "We haven't even made the Crystal Key . . . it's actually very difficult to make. We're still some time away from having a big enough crystal. Anyway, there's no need now. The Liquid Key works in our Revival Chamber. Whoever used to be in there . . . has long gone."

"Whoever?"

"Whoever . . . yes. Josh, you need to speak to Montoyo. I don't understand why he hasn't told you these things. Really, it's your birthright."

I feel a wave of such gratitude towards Lorena right then that I regret making plans to steal the Crystal Key from her.

There are five Revival Chambers . . . I guess those ancient Erinsi really got around. I shouldn't have been surprised that one chamber is in Iraq, now I come to think of it. The clues were there all along – the news story about Madison nicking the Adaptor did mention that the object was first found near Eridu in Iraq. Some of the ancient Erinsi stuff is written in Sumerian – the language of ancient Mesopotamia – now mainly in Iraq. Then there's the phrase itself – *Erin si* – ancient Mesopotamian words meaning "People of Memory".

So where are the other chambers? If Lorena expected people to be inside them, then what exactly are we talking about here?

Reviving the dead?

Lorena doesn't want to say any more. She's quietly angry

with Montoyo, I can tell, and bewildered. But even she has her limits. "Go and talk to Carlos," Lorena insists.

I'm angry too, but not surprised. It's typical of Montoyo to keep stuff like this from me. What's almost a million times worse than anything Lorena's telling me is a truth that dawns on me only later.

There is no Crystal Key in Ek Naab. I can't fix the Bracelet.

Ixchel and my mum are going to be slaughtered by those kidnappers. Montoyo will never find them, I know it. He'll never, ever give up his prize Bakab Ix – me.

The Sect of Huracan need me to play some part in their top secret, world-changing plan. Well, so does Montoyo.

The Sect or Montoyo. When it comes down to it, I don't have much idea what either of them have in store for me.

Without the Bracelet of Itzamna, there's nothing I can do about anything. I'm stuck here helpless. Just a kid waiting at home for news from the war.

Lorena gives me a case of stuff to take for Montoyo – the tranquillizer-dart guns and some darts, and also some tubes of a new "greasy glue" made of carbon nanotubes, which she reckons helps with climbing. I can't focus on what she tells us about what's in the case. Tyler at least seems focused on what she's saying, but I just keep nodding. I just want to get out of there. This is no place for me now.

Tyler and I walk back. In my daze, I make a wrong turn and we wind up in the marketplace. It's dense with stalls selling delicious-smelling food. Tyler stops at a juice bar, where a smiling girl in a crisp white apron stands in front of a mountain of fruit. Tyler points to some golden-ripe mangoes and some fleshy guavas. The girl slices up the fruit, throws it into a juicer and pours the pinkish-yellow juice over ice in two glasses.

We take our drinks and sit at one of the tables at the side of the square. I watch rocks of ice clink against the edge as I nervously push the glass around the table. Try as I might, I can't help but think back to that night on the beach at Natal. Ixchel with her goblet of frothy juice, me with the purple grape. How much it stabbed at me to see her laughing and dancing with Benicio. What an idiot I was not to give her a proper hug and kiss hello.

I take a sip, try to swallow, almost choke.

I think about the time Ixchel fell asleep against my chest in the bus to Tlacotalpan last December. Long moments of actually holding her. In my memory, I can still feel her breath ruffling the hairs on my arms. Just before she woke up properly, she squeezed me. I hadn't dared to move.

Why didn't I think about this at the time? It's like some horrible time-delay bomb. As if every detail was logged that day by a secretive part of my mind. It's being slowly released into my system, like poison, to torture me.

Every time I touched her, or looked into her eyes, or even more heart-stopping – every time she touched me. It's all flooding back. Now that I can't see, hear or touch her. Now that she might be about to die.

When I remember that as well as Ixchel there's my mother, my stomach lurches.

I wonder then – is this what Montoyo is going through? Is he thinking about my mum the way I'm thinking about Ixchel? I actually feel sorry for him for a minute. I wouldn't wish this on anyone.

I was so horrible to Mum, to Ixchel, that day on the sand dunes. What if that's their last memory of me?

Tyler says very quietly, "What's wrong?"

I lift my eyes to meet his and actually can't speak.

"Ixchel," he pronounces, watching for my response. I nod miserably, feeling my eyes fill with tears. Tyler looks at me for a few seconds and then he nods too. "Figures."

Not for the first time, I ask him, "What am I going to do?"

Tyler doesn't have an answer to that one. But I can feel the answer forming inside me. It's not as easy as I thought to be a coward, interested only in self-preservation. It takes more nerve than I've got to hold out.

All this and it's only been a few hours. How will I get through the rest of my life, knowing that I let one of them die instead of me?

We finish our juice and wind our way back to the apartment where Montoyo's thrown my stuff. I can't think of it as "my place" yet. But being the one who leads Tyler around Ek Naab – even if I do make a couple of wrong turns on the way – makes me feel strangely at home.

No one tries to talk to us. Sometimes when people don't think I'm looking I notice them staring at us – especially me. It makes me wonder what sort of information is out there about me. What have they heard?

Back at the apartment I open my suitcase and take out the two books by John Lloyd Stephens that Montoyo gave me. Tyler has been asking me about how I solved the code with the chemical formula of the Crystal Key. I show him how the cipher works, and talk him through the solution.

"So that's it, then, is it? Them fifteen letters?"

"Lorena said 'amino acids'. That's some kind of chemical,

isn't it? We did it in biology. I guess each letter means a different amino acid."

"But why? Why is Arcadio putting that in this book?"

I shrug. Right now I'm off the whole idea. If Lorena – with all her labs – can't make the Crystal Key, what hope do I have? "I dunno, Tyler. I don't even know who Arcadio is."

But Tyler won't let it go. "He's written this same thing in all those other books? That's what Montoyo said, yeah?"

I nod. Tyler looks down, touches the final page of the book where Arcadio's scrawled the quotation.

"And he's got a quote, yeah, from this Calvino bloke, from 1979?"

"'*I would like to swim against the stream of time. . .*' That one, yes."

"But what this says, yeah, is that he wants to go back in time and change something, something that went wrong. But new things keep happening in his life . . . and things change. And he can't work out which is the moment he needs to go back to . . . the zero moment . . . the point in time where . . . ."

". . . where his fate changes," I finish. "Yeah . . . that's what he's saying."

It's not the first time those words set off a tingle inside me. Interesting that Tyler should notice something, too.

"So he's talking about time travel, innit? This Arcadio – he's another time traveller!"

I nod. "It looks that way."

"You think he's actually . . . Itzamna?"

"Great minds think alike, mate," I tell him with a slight grin. "That's my theory, anyway. Arcadio disappears, we know that much."

"Disappears?"

"Uh huh. Susannah St John met Arcadio when she and him were both young. They had a 'thing'. Then one day, he never came back."

"What would happen, Josh, if that Bracelet thing broke? If the crystal got bust. You'd get stranded in time, yeah?"

I feel a crackle of excitement. "Unless. . ."

Tyler looks as excited as me. "Unless you could make a new Crystal Key. And to do that. . ."

"You'd have to keep the formula handy."

Tyler looks doubtful. "But writing it in a book. . .? You could lose a book."

"Yeah, it would make more sense to, like, tattoo it on your body. Like in that film about the guy who keeps losing his memory, *Memento*."

Then Tyler says something truly brilliant. "Maybe Arcadio never saw that film? Or had other reasons why he couldn't write everything on his own body. So he wrote it in these books. Maybe other places too. All in code. . ."

"Someone must have been after Arcadio," I say suddenly. I can understand how that might feel – pursued through

189

time and space by the Sect of Huracan. You'd need every trick in the game to stay ahead.

"But then he disappears," Tyler says, closing the book. "Arcadio takes off one day and . . . that's it."

We stare at each other. A stranded time traveller from the future? Sounds a lot like Itzamna. . .

I sigh deeply. What's the use in sitting around an empty apartment, discussing the identity of Itzamna? It's not going to help anyone. Even now the superwave is on its way through space, the end of civilization in 2012 and everything. But compared to the fact that in just a few hours my mother or Ixchel might be killed, it might as well be happening in *2112*. It doesn't seem relevant at all.

I stare despondently at the blank wall next to the kitchen. That's when I remember my phone, and the text from *Camila Call Me*.

I take the phone out, show it to Tyler again.

"This is from your sister's moby, yeah? What happened to it?"

I never found out. It was with Camila when the car went into the swamp next to Highway 186. "Maybe the police found it?"

"They could have dried it out. Someone else has it now."

I scowl. "Someone in Mexico . . . is sending me texts in English? About visiting a grave?"

Tyler raises an eyebrow, smiles wryly. "What are you like?"

"Huh?"

"Your life is madness, man. Here's you thinking you've got a text from a dead person . . . you don't think that's insane?"

"It would be typical of Camila to mess with my head like this. She finds a way to get a message to me from the spirit world, and all she does is make a dig about how I visit Dad but not her. It's not like she's telling me something useful like *I know where the kidnappers have your mum. . .*"

The instant the words are out I stop talking. My mouth freezes, open.

"It's not like she's telling you that. . ." Tyler says slowly. I can see that he's on the same train of thought.

"But . . . what if she could?"

I leap to my feet. Why didn't I think of this before?

Camila. The buzzing phone . . . was she trying to contact me back in Brazil, even before the kidnappers struck?

Was Camila trying to warn me?

Tyler smirks. "*Someone is trying to get in touch with you.*" He waggles his fingers mysteriously in front of his eyes. "Woooo! From the spirit world, maybe. . .?"

This is all a joke to him.

Trust your instincts, Blanco Vigores told me. *Ignore nothing.* I was so busy getting wrapped up in the fixing of the Bracelet, the secrets of the Ix Codex and even

191

Arcadio's book cipher, I totally ignored the chance that this Camila thing might be real, not some weird hoax or coincidence.

Tyler thinks I believe everything and anything, but the truth is – I'm not sure that I do. Even now I wonder: was it really the ghosts of those teenage lovers from Ek Naab, Chan and Albita, that saved Ixchel and me when we were lost in the labyrinth under Becan? The subconscious mind can do amazing things with information you think you've completely forgotten. Just as Vigores said. So it feeds back the information through a dream – what's the difference?

But, *what if*? What if Camila really could contact me from beyond?

It's got to be worth a try.

"We've got to get hold of Montoyo," I say. "I need to get out of Ek Naab, go visit my sister's grave."

From my left jeans pocket I take my Ek Naab mobile phone and call Montoyo. It rings only once.

"Josh! It seems I can't leave you alone for a minute. Lorena called to say you have something for me, yes?"

Looking at the cardboard box of objects that Lorena gave us for Montoyo, I say, "We just wanted to make ourselves useful."

"Good work. We're about to take a break in the planning here. I'll come over and meet you boys for lunch."

I take a deep breath. Then I ask Montoyo for something I

can hardly believe he'll allow – an escort out of Ek Naab and down to Chetumal. As I expect, he's not happy.

"Please," I insist. "We'll be gone less than two hours."

"I can't spare the Muwans," Montoyo explains. "We need them all on standby in case we get a chance to make an early rescue."

"Have you found out where the kidnappers are?"

There's a momentary silence. "Not yet."

"Then get me a driver! There must be a way out of Ek Naab from the surface."

Montoyo pauses again. "There is. It's a tiny private road, mostly. Takes over three hours to Chetumal."

"Forget lunch," I say angrily. "I want to visit my sister's grave. Is that too much to ask?"

His voice grows cold. "Right now, yes. I'd expect you of all people to understand that. Josh, I'm going to send Benicio. This is tough for all of us. I'm doing everything I can."

Without another word the phone goes dead. I'm left staring at it in my hand. I've heard Montoyo speak to people like this – his minions. Now I've been given the same treatment. Surprisingly, it really hurts.

Benicio turns up within twenty minutes. His face is drawn, pinched. He can hardly meet my eyes.

He's really angry.

"OK, Josh, babysitter's here," he says sardonically. "What would you like to do?"

"You can get lost with that attitude, mate," Tyler tells him. "We didn't ask for you."

"I want to go to Chetumal," I tell him. "To visit my sister's grave."

Benicio shakes his head. "Why?"

What can I possibly tell him? That I've had another crazy hunch? But, what else?

"I think Camila's been trying to contact me."

I tell him the rest of the story. Benicio rolls his eyes. "This is far-fetched."

I nod once, slowly. "Yeah."

He stares at me for a second. Far-fetched it may be, but Benicio's not a complete sceptic. Living in Ek Naab has taught him that there are places in the world where just about anything can happen.

And then, as if it only just this minute occurred to him, Benicio asks, "What will you do if your sister tells you where they are?"

My answer is every bit as spur of the moment as his. "We'll go straight there. And I'll give myself up. They promised us one hostage in return. You can bring back Ixchel."

The atmosphere intensifies. I can see from his eyes that Benicio doesn't share Montoyo's attitude to my safety.

At least not when it's a matter of my safety versus Ixchel's.

194

Benicio starts to breathe quickly, eyes flickering around. Thinking. He places his hands on his hips and stares at me for a long time.

"You'd do that?"

I'm defiant. "Said I would, didn't I?"

Tyler's said nothing so far. He puts the box he's carrying on the floor. Like Benicio, he looks into my eyes.

"You're mental. You know that?"

I laugh. I'm literally laughing in the face of danger. It feels scarily good – makes my skin buzz, makes the hairs on my arms stand on end.

"Then I'm coming too," Tyler says. "Benicio can fly the Muwan. And I'll watch out for *you*."

The grin drops from my face. I bite my lip, hesitating, then throw an arm around Tyler. Fiercely, he hugs me back.

"Thanks, Ty," I mumble. "You're the best."

23

Benicio walks us straight to the aircraft hangar, where blue-suited engineers are making final checks to the entire fleet of Mark I and Mark II Muwans. Benicio goes over to one of the guys and has a few words. Then he comes back to us.

"There's no way we're getting out of here without someone noticing. The best thing is just to go for it, nice and calm, no fuss. I've told him that your buddy Tyler wants to see the inside of the cockpit. So just climb in like this is no big deal."

With that he leads the way to one of the Mark IIs. I guess if we're pursued – either by pilots from the National Reconnaissance Office with the stolen Muwan technology, or even by guys from Ek Naab – the Mark IIs give us the best chance of getting away.

We climb in, strap up. Benicio takes the pilot's seat, roughly fits a headset and eyepiece over his face. The anti-gravity engine starts up. From outside I hear a couple of shouts.

"Hold on," Benicio says grimly. The Muwan rises, hovering only metres above the air. A brilliant streak of sunlight opens in the ceiling above us. The Muwan lifts even higher, hovers just under the opening skylight until it's wide enough. Another couple of seconds and we're through.

Then we're above the canopy of the Campeche jungle, skimming just metres above the trees.

Classic UFO style.

My mobile phone buzzes. I go to answer it immediately – another text.

Hey, hotshot, still waiting for you down by Highway 186.

Reading it, I gasp. "Wait!"

Benicio doesn't hear me so I yell louder, beating on the back of his chair.

"Not Chetumal! I made a mistake! She wants to meet on Highway 186!"

The place where the car came off the road, shot by Simon Madison. Where Camila and I crashed into the dark swamp; where Camila died.

Benicio seems irritated. "This gets stupider. I can't believe I listened to you."

He's annoying enough to make me spit out what's been on my mind since he agreed. "Why *did* you listen to me?"

It bursts out of him. "Because Montoyo is nowhere on

this. I've never seen him so panicked. Who do you think he'll let them shoot first, Josh? Not your mum, not Eleanor. Never her." Benicio pauses and breathes out, shakily. What he's admitted has shocked even him. "Who knows if your hunch will pay off? But when *you* are finally convinced that there's no other way. . ."

Benicio really wants me to give myself up to the kidnappers. He's expecting it.

He's doing this to save Ixchel.

Tyler and I stare at Benicio in stunned silence. It takes me several seconds to recover the power of speech. "Just get me to Highway 186!"

"Do you even know where? It's a long road."

"About an hour before Becan . . . a big swamp."

The Muwan changes direction in a long, smooth sweep. Within five minutes I see Highway 186 ahead, a bold asphalt-grey slash in the green forest. As we approach the road Benicio takes us up high, so high that no one could observe us from the ground. He hits a button and the air before me bursts with light – a holographic projection. It's something I've never seen in a Muwan. Tyler breathes out in appreciation.

"Man, that is cool. . ."

It's an image of the terrain beneath us. "Touch the top right to zoom in . . . the top left to zoom out," Benicio informs us. But touch what? Experimentally I poke my finger into the air around the top right of the image. Immediately the image narrows its focus on the ground. I keep touching it until we can see a small patch of the road below.

"Find me your swamp," Benicio says.

The field of vision is too small and changing too quickly for me to focus, so I zoom out until we can sweep enough of the ground at once.

Then I see it – the biggest swamp we've seen so far, but it's still much smaller than I remember.

"That could be it," I admit. "It seems small, though. . ."

"You were here in the rainy season," Benicio says. "It's the only time of year that you could drown in these swamps. Usually they're not deep enough to swallow a car."

I look at the image, feeling a stab of sorrow. So if it had all happened a few months earlier – or later – Camila wouldn't have died. "Then that's it."

Benicio takes us down in a wide spiralling movement, making it difficult for any observer to track our landing. He lands the Muwan in a meadow behind a thick wall of trees.

"Your swamp is around five minutes' walking – in that direction," Benicio says, pointing. "I'm gonna stay here and guard the bird. Tyler, go with him and see he doesn't get into trouble. Hurry, or we'll have Montoyo's people to deal with."

Tyler looks into the box of tricks from Lorena. "We should take something from here, just in case."

I unbuckle. "In case what?"

Tyler picks up what looks like a tiny, silver-grey handgun. "This one shoots tranquillizer darts, Lorena said. That should be enough, right?"

I don't answer. It's actually started to hit me what a crazy escapade this is.

I'm on my way to a meeting with a ghost.

Until now it's all seemed like a sort of fantasy. Once the reality of what might happen actually sets in, I start to shiver. Uncontrollably.

Tyler notices. "You're shaking."

Pressing my lips together, I nod.

"What, Josh . . . you afraid of a ghost?"

Tyler's lazy attitude actually makes me laugh.

"And you're not?"

Tyler climbs out of the cockpit. "If only, man! Practically wetting my pants. But you gotta do what you gotta do, right?"

We make our way through the dry, scrubby vegetation, through a tangle of lean trees, and finally emerge near the edge of the swamp, right next to the road. A haze of warm air wobbles above the hot tarmac, like a mirage. In the far distance there's the whine of an approaching car.

Under the dazzling mid-afternoon sunshine the swamp is utterly unrecognizable. I can hardly believe that I've been here before. Behind the reeds the water is as black as treacle, its surface littered with insects, tiny leaves and pollen. Small frogs rustle, hopping in the grass. There's a background chorus of tiny, high-pitched croaks.

All signs of last summer's car crash have disappeared. I glance to my right, see the beginning of the thicket into which I plunged, right after the crash. Even by day it looks daunting, dark, impenetrable.

There's a constant drone as mosquitoes hover around us. Absent-mindedly I slap at an itch on my neck and face. I walk to the road, gaze in both directions. It's empty and straight as far as the eye can see. Up and over hills; a horizontal line across the state, slicing through the jungle.

We stand fidgeting under the bright glare of the sun. The road surface hums as a vehicle approaches. The engine's roar shatters the air as the car shoots past. Within seconds we're back to the crackle and buzz of insects and frogs. A cloud of yellow butterflies hovers around us for a second or two before moving towards the road.

Time passes.

Tyler shuffles closer, looks down for a moment, uncomfortable. When he looks up he seems surprised.

"There's blood on your face."

I look down at Tyler's raised hand. I'm puzzled, then confused, then kind of appalled.

"Stop pointing that gun at me."

His voice seems to come from far away. "What gun? I'm not holding the gun."

"That gun, the dart gun," I say, wiping my brow. I can't understand why Tyler's messing around like this, pointing the gun. "Put it away. There's no one here but us."

His reply, when it comes, is confused. His speech is slurred. "Mate, I'm not the one with the gun . . ."

I turn back to face the road. It's empty apart from the yellow butterflies. They float around the edge of the road, like a single creature made of fluttering autumn leaves, dipping in and out of the foliage.

Sweat trickles down my neck. A sense of desperation builds within my chest.

No one's coming.

This has to be rock bottom. Let's face it – I'm clutching at straws.

I'm on the point of admitting that it's all been a waste of time; I'm actually opening my mouth to say the words. Then I look closer at the butterfly cloud. No more gaps between the yellow, only a solid block of colour.

It's coming closer, purring. Seconds of confusion pass. I realize that I'm no longer staring at the butterflies, but a car.

A yellow car: a VW Beetle. It draws up alongside me. The driver's window slides down.

"Come on, baby brother, get in the car."

I have to grip the edge of the car to stop myself from staggering.

"Camila. . .?"

She nods, the woman, the ghost. I don't see how she can be a ghost when there's nothing even slightly ghostly about her. She looks exactly as I remember her that day – the only day I ever saw her. Glossy dark hair falling straight down her back, a sleeveless lime-green top, skinny white jeans. Lots of jewellery and lipstick.

I force myself to tear my gaze away from the all-too-lifelike apparition of my dead sister. Where the heck is Tyler? But he seems to have vanished.

"Your friend," Camila says with a jab of her manicured finger, "has fallen asleep. Right there."

I follow her pointing finger and see to my astonishment that she's right. Tyler is fast asleep, nestled just out of sight beside the swamp.

"How long have we been here?" I say aloud, but mainly to myself.

The ghost shrugs. "Your guess is as good as mine, sweetie."

We stare at each other. "So you *are* a ghost?"

She doesn't answer, but purses her very real-looking lips. "Jump in."

Somehow I do, without any serious thought for Tyler.

The next thing I'm aware of is that we're driving. We're far down the road, the swamp long behind us. I gradually notice that the air is filled with Brazilian jazz. I know this song – it's another of my dad's favourites, by Tom Jobim.

"*So close your eyes, for that's a lovely way to be*
Aware of things your heart alone was meant to see."

I hear my own voice say clearly, "What's going on?"

The ghost doesn't take her eyes off the road.

In a soft voice she says, "How did you think this was gonna work, hotshot?"

I'm even more confused. "How what was gonna work?"

"*Hermanito*, there are no happy reunions here."

"But you are Camila. . .?"

I'm actually still not sure. She looks and sounds so real. . .

The ghost says, "I'm an echo; a last breath. A sigh."

"Why am I here? Why are you here?"

"Because there is something I need to show you."

"My mother's been kidnapped!" I yell, only now remembering. "And my friend! Do you know where they are?"

It's amazing, but for a few long moments, I'd actually forgotten all about them . . . and Tyler. There's something very wrong with my thought processes, but I can't tell what.

"All I know is that I need to tell you something. Something I should have told you that day. . ."

Even the ghost seems to have trouble talking about the day Camila died.

"So now, well, now it's time to tell you."

"There's something you want to tell me from that day? But why now?"

"Actually . . . I don't know," she tells me thoughtfully. "It never even occurred to me to wonder."

"What do you mean?" I ask. "Where are you taking me?

205

What about Tyler? And . . . who are these people walking along the road? They look like. . ."

Then I flinch in horror. I've only just now realized that the people we pass every so often, limping along the road with arms and legs at strange angles – are the walking dead.

Zombies.

"The worst thing about all this," Camila's ghost tells me, "are the ones who don't know they're dead. Believe me, they're everywhere. You can't imagine what a pain they are."

I want to scream. The more I look around, the more I see them. Crawling out from the edges of the roads, sometimes staggering around in the middle of the carriageway. At least one every five hundred metres. Sometimes she has to swerve to avoid them.

"They can't hurt you," Camila says grimly, "except maybe by boring you to death. You'd think they'd get over it, but no. Telling you all the details of how they got hurt, asking you to take them to the hospital, every detail of their tragic lives."

I stare at her in horror. When I look very closely I notice that she's got a thin stream of blood trickling from her head.

"You're dead."

"It's kind of rude to remind me."

My own voice sounds hollow when I ask, "Where am I?"

I can't even tell if she heard the question, because she

keeps talking. "I was so happy to meet you that day, Josh. All I wanted to do was to look at you and talk to you and hear about our daddy. But we had that mystery to solve . . . can you understand how I was torn?"

Before I can answer, we suddenly arrive at a junction, which seems to have appeared out of nowhere. There are more people wandering. I watch as one obvious road accident victim stops to buy a bag of fresh pineapple from a street vendor. But the vendor just ignores him, until the zombie starts to wave his arms in despair.

"He can't see him. . ." I say. "Why doesn't the dead guy know he's dead?"

"Road accident spirits," she says, "are the worst ones for not knowing they're dead. Must be the shock."

I look around in steadily mounting horror. The road does seem unusually crowded.

"How many of these people are dead?"

"Oh . . . as many as half," Camila says.

I want to be sick. My skin actually crawls with revulsion. My lips move but no sound emerges.

I am so not cool with this.

We turn off the main road and down an isolated side road. The trees open out in front of us to reveal a long expanse of shimmering water stretching to the left and right as far as the eye can see. So many shades of blue – everything from midnight blue to aquamarine.

"What is this place?" I ask, unable to drag my eyes from the impossibly blue water.

"It's Lake Bacalar," Camila says. "Quite popular for real estate. It's become fashionable to own a nice lakeside property."

Slowly I ask, "Why are we here?"

"It's like I said, Josh, there's something I should have told you the day we first met. That guy in the blue Nissan – I'd seen him once before. I'm pretty sure I told you he was stalking me . . . but until the day I met you, I just thought he was a regular stalker, you know? The kind that wants to date you."

I struggle to grasp what she's saying. "You're saying you met Simon Madison before?"

It's not clear that she's even heard me as she continues, "I showed him around a house. On Lake Bacalar. Well, to be accurate, him and a woman. A woman he called 'Professor'."

"Madison and *the Professor* looked at a house? A house, around here? A house near Becan?"

"Lake Bacalar is less than two hours from Becan," she says. "A few weeks before he chased us off Highway 186, that blue Nissan guy was about to rent a house."

She slows the car to a crawl outside a broad, carved mahogany gateway polished to a gleaming finish.

"It's right here," she says. "Don't you think I should show you?"

Then we're walking up an empty driveway. Me and my super-glamorous sister.

My dead sister.

We've been together for what – an hour? I've started to see dead people. And the strangest thing is happening: it's all starting to feel almost normal.

Camila opens the main door without a key. The house is a large two-storey villa, pure white with narrow pillars, arches on the balcony. There are high arched windows in every wall. A wide stretch of deep green lawn leads to the edge of the water, where a wooden jetty extends deep into the clear azure waters of the lake. Inside, the house is almost unfurnished, a grey marble floor with a few pieces of white furniture. The walls are also white, decorated with an occasional piece of abstract art.

Camila leads me to the second floor, the heels of her golden shoes clicking on the marble. We pass open doors that lead to yet more scarily white rooms containing only beds (made up in white bedclothes) through to a room that looks like an office. The arched window looks out over the back garden down to the lake. It's a stunning view, all those shades of blue against a stretch of unspoilt green wilderness on the opposite bank.

The desk is clear except for a pad by the (white) phone. There are three numbers written there. All begin with 55.

I look up from the desk. "This is the Professor's office?"

She shrugs. "Go figure. None of this was here when I showed them the house. But you can be sure of this – that 'Professor' woman is the one in charge. I thought maybe the guy was her son."

I run a finger along the top of the flat screen monitor. Not a trace of dust.

"He works for her," I say. "His name is Simon. He's an idiot."

She allows herself a smile. "I knew you'd get the better of him. Good for you, lil' bro."

I force myself to look straight into Camila's eyes. That's when I know for sure that she's not alive. When she looks back at me I see nothing – no depth of expression. It's like gazing into a hard, frozen space. After a second I can't bear to look.

Why has she brought me here? If this isn't about finding my mother and Ixchel . . . then what?

A horrible thought occurs to me. Hesitantly I ask, "Do you need me to . . . get revenge for you?"

She shakes her head with an ironic grin. "Oh, you think you're Hamlet now? Of course not."

I breathe a sigh of relief. I'm not sure what she means with the Hamlet thing, but I know this: I can't handle a revenge quest on top of everything else.

"Then . . . why bring me here?"

"Those numbers, Josh."

I stare at the numbers by the phone. "What. . .?"

"Remember them."

"Huh?"

"Memorize them. Now."

"Why. . .?"

She stretches out a hand. Gently she says, "Will you let me touch you?"

I freeze. The ghost withdraws her hand. "I'm sorry, kiddo. Some impulses don't completely go away."

I feel suddenly cold, as if the air conditioning just kicked in.

I stare at Camila's ghost. When I speak, I can actually see my breath in front of my face. "If you're just an echo, then where's Camila?"

She takes a deep breath. "Josh . . . this is only one part of existence."

"I miss Camila," I blurt. "And my dad, too."

The ghost's eyes glisten, brimming with expressionless tears. She backs away.

"The numbers, Josh. Remember."

I force myself to look down at the numbers, obediently memorizing the digits.

When I look up again, I'm all alone. Yet somehow I'm very calm. My fingers trace the numbers on the pad by the phone. I can still hear the strains of jazz from Camila's car stereo.

211

"So close your eyes, for that's a lovely way to be,
  Aware of things your heart alone was meant to see,
  The fundamental loneliness goes whenever two can
dream a dream together."*
I'm still hearing it when I wake up.

I'm lying in the scratchy undergrowth, face up, no shade. Tyler is next to me, still snoozing. It takes me a full thirty seconds to realize that Benicio is stabbing at me with his shoe.

"You idiots!" he's saying. "Wake up, wake up now! Montoyo's guys are gonna be here any minute. What's wrong with you, what kind of stupid game were you playing?"

I sit up, still woozy. "Game?"

Benicio shoves the tranquillizer-dart gun into my face. "Playing with this. You shot each other! Idiots!"

He pushes Tyler hard until, like me, Tyler struggles to his feet.

"What's going on, hmmm?"

"Less talking, more moving," Benicio says. He leads the way back to the Muwan, hurrying. I follow in silence, thinking. Mainly about numbers.

"Did you shoot me?" Tyler asks. He doesn't sound angry, only fascinated.

"I might have," I admit.

I open my palm to see a streak of blood there. My last clear memory is of wiping my cheek, where a mosquito was gorging itself on my blood.

Truthfully, I don't know or remember who shot who or why. But like Tyler, I had a tiny tranquillizer dart in the back of my hand when I woke up.

Numbers.

When we get back to the Muwan, Benicio calls in to Ek Naab. In the background of my thoughts, I hear him telling Montoyo that he's very sorry, that I made a big fuss about the Camila thing, that we'd be back in a bit.

"Can you check a number for me?" I tell Benicio the second he finishes the call.

"Can I *what*?"

I tell Benicio the first number. "Just check it. Does it mean anything?"

He doesn't even bother to type it into his computer.

"It's a telephone number. In Brazil."

I struggle to keep my voice calm. "Can you tell where in Brazil?"

"Of course."

"Benicio. Check it."

He's silent, tapping the numbers into his keyboard. "It's a place called Gesolo. Never heard of it."

"There's another number," I tell him. He checks that too. "Gesolo, again."

The third number is for somewhere in Natal.

Without a trace of doubt, I say, "They're in Gesolo."

Benicio looks at me hard for what seems like ages. Then he says, "You saw your sister."

I nod.

"She gave you these numbers?"

"She showed me a house she sold to the Sect. On the shore of Lake Bacalar. The numbers were by a phone."

"Bacalar. We knew the Sect had to have somewhere local. All that time they spent visiting the Revival Chamber under Becan. . . We never found it, though."

"I know where it is. I could take you there."

Benicio considers this. "That's a good idea. But it's a little soon. Would be smarter to wait. To let them believe their house is still a secret. Anyhow, Montoyo wants you locked up until this kidnap situation is over."

I say nothing, too stunned by the idea that Montoyo would actually do that.

"Are you still willing to trade yourself for Ixchel?"

I can't speak, so I just nod.

Benicio looks thoughtful. He takes his pilot's seat properly. "Then let's go to Gesolo."

I lean back into my chair as the Muwan takes off. It takes some effort to avoid Tyler's anxious stare. I really try, though. I want to be alone to think. This might be my last hour of freedom.

215

Eventually Tyler breaks his silence. "What's he mean – you saw your sister?"

"I dunno how, Ty, but she came to me. It was like a dream. But it felt totally real."

He groans. "Pure madness. Your sister's ghost spoke to you in a dream?"

"It was pretty messed up," I admit. "Like in that film, *The Sixth Sense*. I could see dead people. They were just wandering about among the living people. Most of them didn't even know they were dead."

Tyler hesitates, then, voice heavy with doubt, he says, "You're never giving yourself up to those Sect people. For real, I mean?"

I stare out of the window, watching as the craft plunges deep into the stratosphere. In a tiny voice I say, "What choice do I have?"

Tyler glances in Benicio's direction. His voice drops to a whisper. "We could try to rescue them."

"How?"

"Just you and me, man," he breathes. "With Benicio as the getaway guy. We've got these tranquillizer darts. We've got your memory-wiping injection pens. We've got this climbing-nanotube stuff from Lorena – she said you put it on your hands and it forms some rubbery bond thing with walls. Plus, if we have to, Josh, we use our capoeira."

Now I can't help staring at Tyler. "Are you serious? You're walking around with a three-inch gunshot wound and, like, fifteen stitches."

Tyler lowers his voice. "Look . . . what's the worst that can happen? The way you want to run things, they're already getting *you*."

I gasp. "It can get plenty worse. You could get caught too. They might not keep their promise to free Ixchel."

"Think it through, Josh. They're after *you*. Once they have you, we're no use to them."

"Yeah – what if they kill you all?"

"I don't think so. Why? They haven't done much killing so far, have they?"

I'm indignant. "My sister? My dad?"

"Your sister and dad – they both died by accident. At least the way you explained it to me. Madison could have killed you, plenty of times."

"I think they *have* killed people," I tell him. "There was a story in the paper about this scientist from Oxford – from the same college as my dad. They killed her."

Tyler takes a deep breath. "Look, mate. If you think I'm just going to let you hand yourself over. . ."

We exchange an angry glare.

"You agreed."

"No, I never. Benicio's the one who wants you to walk in without a fight. Not me."

What can I say? I can't believe a friend would risk his own life for me. Do I have the right to stop him?

Then he leans close to me and hisses, "You don't fool me, anyways; I know you want to rescue them. You were glad that Montoyo wouldn't hand you over – I saw it in your eyes. You want to be free to help with the rescue. Then she'll *like* you, right?"

Astonished, I stare at Tyler.

"It's only natural," he murmurs, stretching as he settles back into his seat. "If my mum and my girl had been taken, no one would stop me getting them back."

Just then a map of Brazil appears in the air before us. The image zooms in on a region near the centre, by the border with Colombia and Peru. A thick stretch of river dominates the area.

The Amazon?

The zooming continues as detailed satellite images layer through the air. In the middle of dense green jungle a tiny town appears. I can't even see any roads leading to or from it. The town itself is nothing more than one street, a picturesque square and a few houses. Including one large hacienda-style mansion set in a lush tropical garden.

"Nice little town, this Gesolo," comments Benicio. "Very pretty to be so off the beaten track. My guess is that the owners of that hacienda run the whole town. Nowhere will be safe. You'll need to get right into the hacienda."

"Is that where they're being kept?"

"The numbers you gave me trace to phone lines on the hacienda estate. If you're right, Josh, that was some amazing information you got from that house at Lake Bacalar."

"What was it like to see your sister again?" Tyler asks. "Was it like in a dream?"

I consider. "It wasn't really her. I could tell. Something missing in her eyes." A heavy sigh escapes me. "She was like an echo. Not like a dream."

What had been missing was in me, just as much as in the ghost-Camila. I'd felt numb around her. Cold, distant – no more alive than a ghost.

Seeing Camila, I'd felt nothing . . . not like when I saw my dad again on the volcano.

"We'll be in Gesolo in thirty minutes," Benicio announces. "It should be dark when we get there – it's two hours ahead. I'm gonna find somewhere to land in the jungle nearby. We'll use headsets to communicate. I'll guide you to the hacienda. Once you're in there, guys – you're on your own. I have no clue where they're being held."

Benicio overheard our plans.

Puzzled, I ask, "So . . . you're with us on the rescue plan?"

From the cockpit comes Benicio's languid voice. "You win, Josh. You get to be the hero – or be captured trying. So

219

long as we get our friends back."

My mind is already thousands of miles away, in Gesolo. I'm helping Ixchel into the Muwan. I'm climbing in after her, flying away. There's only me and Ixchel.

In my mind, she's clinging to me, filled with gratitude.

From way above the clouds, Benicio lets the Muwan drop into the jungle. It's over so quickly that we don't see anything but a rush of fluttering greenery lit by the craft's landing lights. We ruffle leaves all the way down. Amazingly, Benicio's used the satellite navigation system to locate a tiny clearing in the jungle. Still, it's not much more than the width of the Muwan.

This isn't a rainforest jungle like in Mexico; it's fully tropical with broad-leaved, enormous trees and a canopy so thick that underneath it's almost pitch-black, even with the last rays of sun still glowing purple in the sky. In a few more minutes the real dark will set in. I check my watch – there are just two hours left from the deadline to agree to hand me over.

Two hours to rescue Ixchel and my mum.

We can do this.

When Tyler and I clamber out of the Muwan, we're hit by a wall of sound – rushing water. Benicio checks his map.

"Guys . . . I'm sorry about this. Looks like there's a stream you gotta cross."

Tyler and I follow the sounds of water through some trees and find the source of the noise. We flash our torches over the water. It's not a stream – more of a whitewater river, at least three metres wide and running very, very fast. We walk back to the Muwan, guided by its faintly glowing lights.

"You have to put us down on the other side of that river. There's no way we can swim across."

Benicio sounds annoyed. "You think I didn't think of that? There is literally nowhere to land on the other side. Unless you want me to put you into the garden of the hacienda?"

I pause. "That's actually not a bad idea. Not that garden, though – they'd see us there. But how about the roof?"

Benicio nods. "That could work . . . to get you in. I could turn all the Muwan lights off, go in on stealth mode. Even in the dark, they might still spot us. I won't be able to stay long – would have to be a lightning drop."

Tyler says, "So how would we get out?"

"You'd have to meet me somewhere. Right here. We're almost exactly due east of the house – no more than one kilometre. Take a wrist compass – look in the panel under your seat. Without a compass, you'll never find your way through that jungle."

Tyler leans into the Muwan and rummages in the drawer.

He pulls out a compass on a cloth wristband and velcro fastening, starts wrapping it around his wrist. "And the river?"

"I'll hover . . . you can all climb on to the rope ladder and I'll fly you over here so you can climb in properly."

I frown. "Sounds dodgy. It's a lot to ask of Ixchel and my mum . . . running a kilometre through the jungle . . . in the dark, probably being chased. And then to dangle from a rope. . ."

Tyler remarks, "I'd say it beats where they are right now."

We climb back aboard. I like the idea of the lightning strike. I'd kind of like an option for a lightning getaway too. But with just one Muwan, our options seem limited.

Have I made a huge mistake by not handing this whole mission over to Montoyo?

I push the thought out of my head. At least my plan has the backup possibility – if we get caught, I hand myself in. Something that Montoyo would never do.

Benicio flies us in low above the trees. The hacienda is just visible under the glow of light from the windows and a few ornamental lamps in the garden. He lands as softly as a feather, on the flattest part of the tiled roof. When we climb out, we realize that the Muwan's landing gear can adjust to a sloping surface, but of course we can't. We immediately struggle to stay upright.

Just then a huge beam of light appears in the garden. It's

a searchlight. It swivels into the air, sweeping the sky. Tyler and I hold our breath as Benicio lifts the craft two metres into the air and then shoots off vertically. The searchlight sweeps the empty air a fraction of a second later, only metres above our ducked heads.

I'm elated by our narrow escape – but at the same time horrified that we were almost caught so early into the rescue.

Got to stay positive. We can do this.

I adjust my headset. In the earpiece I hear Benicio say, "OK, gentlemen, I'm clear. Now get going. Your window is on the lower roof level. So long as there's no guard there – that's your way in."

Tyler and I sidle carefully down to the edge of the roof. About two metres below is another level of sloping tiles. About five metres along there's a window. From our vantage point, we can see that there are two guards in the front garden. I can just spot them under a low coconut tree that's lit by a string of blue fairy lights. They're carrying semi-automatic rifles slung casually over their shoulders as they chat.

All it would take is a single torch beam in our direction. But their attention is focused outwards – towards the entrance of the property. Meanwhile the searchlight continues to criss-cross the sky, a dramatic sword of light in the darkness.

I guess they anticipated that someone from Ek Naab might just drop by. . .

East is behind the house, I note. So when we hightail it out of here, we'll be headed for the back garden. It backs right on to the jungle. Presumably there's some kind of fence to keep wild animals out? I try to push away worries about how we're going to escape – for now.

First we have to get in.

Tyler and I easily lower ourselves to the window. It's slightly open – a trivial job to get in. We're in a bedroom with an ensuite bathroom. Silently, I indicate to Tyler that he should almost close the window, the way we found it. Just then I hear the sound of the toilet flushing. Tyler and I bolt towards the main bedroom door. We escape just before the bathroom door opens.

Then we're in a corridor. This house is huge. I realize now how hard it might be to find them.

Voices approach – two guys. It sounds like one of them is ordering the other around. We hunt for somewhere to hide, and duck behind a carved wooden shrine covered with votive offerings and a statue of the Virgin Mary.

They're muttering away in Portuguese. After the time we spent in Brazil I've finally started to tune into the language. It's sort of like Spanish spoken through some weird filter – once you get the phase shift, it's possible to catch the gist of what people are saying. I can just understand enough to

225

figure out that the younger guy has been asked to take food to the prisoners.

The second they're out of sight, we follow. They make their way down the main staircase and then keep going towards the basement.

But we're stalled at the ground floor level – there's an armed guard by the front door.

"Reckon he could do with a nap," Tyler whispers. He takes careful aim from behind the banister. The guard barely even reacts to the sound of the tranquillizer dart flying through the air before he collapses in a heap. We're down in an instant, taking his weapon. We can't leave him, though – in the middle of the entrance hall he'll be discovered any minute now. So we drag his crumpled body into the cloakroom and stash him inside.

"Lorena reckons it lasts for ten minutes, no more. We'd better move," Tyler says, prising a pistol from the guard's fingers.

We descend the last flight of stairs, Tyler carrying the guard's pistol, me with the tranquillizer gun. Stealing a gun wasn't part of the plan, and I find myself wondering if Tyler would really be able to use it.

Any minute now we're going to find Ixchel and my mum. It's the first time the reality of our situation has properly sunk in.

The stairs lead to a corridor that was clearly once the

servants' quarters. In contrast with the heavy wood and freshly white-plastered walls of the rest of the house, the walls are bare concrete and we're stepping on brick-tiled floors. There's no sign of anyone in the corridor, but we hear voices in a room filled with the noises of laundry equipment. In the far end of the corridor there's a door slightly ajar. As we pass the laundry room, one guy emerges, shortly followed by another, from the doorway at the end of the corridor.

They see us right away and call out in shocked voices.

Before I'm aware of what's happened, I've shot the front guy in the leg with a tranquillizer dart. He stares at me in amazement, then down at his leg, then he topples over in front of the other guard.

"Don't move," Tyler shouts. He points the pistol at the remaining guard.

The second guard slowly lowers his gun. Aiming at his thigh, I shoot him full of a dose of the tranquillizer.

Then, chillingly, we hear another voice, this time from inside the room.

"Whoever you are," the woman says, speaking English with a heavy Brazilian accent, "you're gonna drop your weapons and come in here with your hands up. Or I'm gonna shoot one of the hostages."

We both stand absolutely still.

In our headsets we hear Benicio say, "She's bluffing. If

she's just a foot soldier, she doesn't have the authority to shoot a hostage."

But what if she isn't just a "foot soldier"?

I get an idea. Using hand signals, I send Tyler along the corridor so that he's right next to the door. Pressed against the wall, he'd only be seen once someone was all the way out of the room.

"I'm Josh Garcia, come to give myself up," I announce. "I'm alone. But Carlos Montoyo doesn't know I'm here with his rescue team. They're outside right now, taking out your guards in the garden. If I don't see my mother and Ixchel right now, I'll give the signal."

There's a pause and then a chuckle.

"I just spoke to the guards on my radio. They're fine."

Then I hear Ixchel, loud, almost hysterical. "Josh, she doesn't have a. . ."

Abruptly, Ixchel's voice is muffled.

What was she going to say? *She doesn't have a gun?* Or *she doesn't have a radio*?

I guess that the guard does have a gun – or else why would Ixchel and Mum even stay quiet?

But maybe, no radio. She's cut off, for now.

I step forward. "I'll give myself up, right now. But you need to bring them both out, Ixchel and my mum. I want to see they're OK."

"Josh, think I'm an idiot? If you want me to come out, it's

so you or one of your team can shoot me. You have five seconds to come in here or I'll shoot the girl."

"Get in there, Josh," Benicio hisses over the headset. "Distract her; then Tyler, you follow. And shoot the guard. Don't hesitate."

I stride over to the doorway, being careful to avoid a sideways glance at Tyler. Standing there, I see the three of them – a dark Brazilian woman in her twenties with thin hair in a ponytail. She's pointing a gun at my mother. Mum and Ixchel are tied to chairs, both hands behind their backs. Their eyes light up for just a second when they see me, but both looked exhausted and scared.

"Drop your gun," the woman says.

I let the tranquillizer-dart gun clatter to the floor. My eyes sweep the room as discreetly as possible. It's a small room, hardly more than three metres square. Hard to think of any distraction I could create in here. . .

"Step forward," she says, slowly moving away from my mother. She raises the gun, now pointing it at me.

Then commotion breaks out – the woman cries out as Ixchel kicks her hard in the shin. She staggers for a second, still vaguely pointing the gun at me. But I drop into a *ginga*, shifting my body from side to side. Tyler slots into the gap between me and the door.

It's just enough to distract the guard – for one second her attention flits from me to Tyler. In that split second I use a hooking *gancho* kick to knock the gun out of her hand, then a low *ponteira* kick to floor her. Then Tyler is standing over her with the tranquillizer gun. He shoots a dart into her leg. We watch as her eyes close.

Without a word we start cutting Mum and Ixchel free. They look dishevelled, still scared, but incredibly relieved to be free. I'm not prepared for the rush of emotion I get when I see them both. It's actually pretty hard to speak. Even though I'm dying for a chance to hug Ixchel, there's no time to talk, or even say hello. I pick up the second gun.

"Where's everyone else?" Ixchel says hurriedly, glancing at the door.

"It's just us two," I say.

A mixture of bewilderment and dismay crosses their faces. I'm horribly aware that we've already used two or three of our ten minutes before the first guard comes round from the sedative.

We have less than seven minutes to get out, and at least a kilometre of jungle to get through. And on top of everything else, whatever dangerous wild animals we might encounter out there, prowling around in the dark.

Tyler leads the way out, tranquillizer gun in his right hand. Mum and Ixchel follow; I'm at the back, with my own dart gun. Both Tyler and I have the guards' pistols in our back pockets too, just in case. I guess we're all scared, but there's no time to think about that. Time is running out; every second counts.

"We're on our way out," I tell Benicio over the headset.

"Go carefully," he replies. "You're a long way from safety."

Approaching the laundry room, I'm grateful for the heavy thumping noise from the equipment. So far, it seems to have saved us from discovery.

Just as we're past the door, it springs open. Two dark-skinned, muscular guys in their late teens rush towards us. I try to turn and take aim, but before I know what's happened, the nearest one has thrown himself into a handstand, his feet aiming right at my shoulder.

231

With one swift and deadly capoeira move he's knocked the gun out of my hand. I bend to pick it up; he follows with a sweeping *queixada* kick to block my path. Tyler moves back to protect Mum and Ixchel from the second laundry guy. They clash in the middle of the corridor, a high kick meeting Tyler's blocking movement. Then with his left fist, Tyler punches him in the face. The guy reels for a second, dizzy. Tyler follows up with a tranquillizer dart to his chest. His opponent is out cold.

The guard attacking me throws a punch. I duck, grab him around the waist and throw my full weight on to him, pushing him to the floor. We land almost two metres from the others.

Tyler manoeuvres around to get a clear shot at the guy underneath me. He fires the tranquillizer gun.

Nothing. Struggling to hold my opponent down, I glance up to see Tyler pulling the trigger over and over.

"I'm out of darts, man!"

"Get mine!"

Ixchel, Mum and Tyler all scramble for my discarded tranquillizer gun. Tyler reaches it first, aims at the guard's leg and shoots. Two seconds later the guy stops struggling.

We all breathe a massive sigh of relief, still shocked by the encounter. I check my watch.

"The first guard is going to wake up in four minutes."

We file out of the basement, up the stairs and through

the empty entrance lobby, looking for a way out round the back or side of the house. We stay as close to the walls as possible, treading lightly, but even so we make some noise. Following the corridor through the east wing of the hacienda, we come finally to a door. There's no light from under the door – it's empty.

Tyler pushes it open. There's a large room, sparsely furnished with a round table and some chairs of dark, heavy-looking wood. Against the wall is a small bar counter and a shelf full of bottles.

"The windows," he says, and makes straight for the opposite wall.

I close the door behind us and follow Tyler and the others to the windows. They're already opening them, pushing back the wooden blinds behind the glass. I stick my head out. It's a short drop to the grass below. Tyler swings himself through the window with one smooth leap. I help Mum and Ixchel out, listen to them land softly in the garden. Then I follow.

We're on the east flank of the garden. To the east, the edge of the jungle begins more than seventy metres away, across an almost-clear expanse of lawn. All the larger trees are lit.

Due east is way too risky.

Behind the house, I can see from the encroaching darkness that the perimeter is much closer.

"We need to cross the fence behind the house," I whisper. "And make our way through the jungle."

"We'll lose lots of time," Tyler says.

I point across the lawn. "We'll never make it without being seen."

Mum and Ixchel glance from me to Tyler.

Mum says, "Josh, where's the rest of the rescue team?"

"Benicio? He's waiting in the jungle."

Ixchel says, "Tell him to come get us!"

I hesitate. But the searchlight keeps streaking across the sky.

"He can't land without being seen."

Ixchel sounds annoyed. "Then we head for cover. Don't you boys know anything?"

Before I can stop myself, I say, "I know . . . that's what I said!"

She starts moving towards the back of the house. "Well, let's get going!"

Mum and I follow, staying low and away from the light spreading from the house and trees.

Tyler hangs back for a second, and then he too follows.

As we pass a window, there's an exclamation from inside. We rush past, but inside I hear scrambling for the door and window. When I turn my head to check, I see the shadows of two figures leaping out of the window and sprinting straight towards us.

Behind the house, the fence beckons, less than ten metres away.

Tyler rushes forward, throws himself at the fence. He screams in agony. Thrown backwards, he lands on his back, groaning.

"It's electrified," Ixchel says.

"Oh no," Mum murmurs, her voice quaking.

I take aim in the shadows. The first shot misses; the second dart hits the closest guard just as he's about to leap at me. When I fire a third time, my gun is empty.

"I'm out," I say, tossing the gun away.

Tyler is momentarily shaken but starts to struggle to his feet. I reach into my back pocket and take out the pistol. I aim it at the second guard.

"Shoot him!" Tyler yells.

I hesitate and then fire at the ground. As the gun goes off in my hand, everyone seems to leap. It's so loud that I almost jump too. The second guard doesn't stop running, though. He pulls out his own gun and shoots. I hear a bullet whistle past me, somewhere close to my left ear.

His voice comes from out of the shadows. "Drop the gun."

Ixchel draws a rapid breath. "That's Gaspar," she whispers. "He's in charge."

Behind me I sense Mum and Ixchel shrinking further into the darkness near the fence.

I shout, "Take another step and I'll fire again."

Gaspar laughs, still walking towards me. He's almost completely in shadow and slightly silhouetted too, by the faint glimmer from lights on a tree about thirty metres away. I can't see clearly if his arm is raised or not. "Not a good idea to take shots at each other in the dark, Josh."

I let rage flood into my voice. "Stop moving! If you think I'm gonna let you hurt my mum or my friends, you're wrong."

I fire again, this time aiming into the air only slightly above his head.

He stops, less than four metres away.

"Relax! I've stopped moving. I could kill any of you from here, Josh. And you know it."

I point the gun straight at him. "Better make sure it's me, then. Or it'll be the last thing you ever do."

Gaspar chuckles. "Tough talk from a boy. Ollie told us you were brave. And Madison will never admit it, but I think he's a little afraid of you, Josh. You got him into a *lot* of trouble."

"He's flattering you, Josh," Mum warns. "Be careful, he's good at that."

He mentioned Ollie and Madison. These Brazilian guys really are part of the Sect of Huracan.

I tighten the grip on the pistol, trying to psych myself up to shoot.

"How do we get over that fence?"

"You don't. Face it, you're stuck. Put the gun down and we'll talk. We only need you, Josh. I'm still happy to trade."

"There are concrete supports," Tyler yells from behind me. "We'd have to use Lorena's climbing grease . . . but I think we can get over."

In the darkness, I nod. "Do it." There's a rustle as the three of them head for the fence.

In a low voice Gaspar growls, "Drop the gun, Josh. Or I'll shoot them."

"No," I say. "You and me, we're gonna stand right where we are. Until they're over. Maybe a bit longer too, until I'm sure they're safe."

There's a long pause. I can't make out anything but the silhouette of Gaspar's shape: tall, well-built; but standing perfectly still, I aim my gun at his chest.

"You won't shoot me," Gaspar says. But he doesn't sound too sure. "You're just a boy. What do you know about killing?"

I'm silent, not moving.

Gaspar tries again. "You'll never make it out of here."

I say nothing.

Somewhere behind me, Mum and Ixchel gasp with effort as they climb over the fence. I hear one, then another, land heavily in the thick jungle beyond.

"We're over," calls Ixchel.

"They're bluffing," Gaspar says. "I heard only two. . ."

"That's cos I'm here, muppet," yells Tyler. He emerges from the darkness from where he's doubled back and crept up behind Gaspar. Gaspar swivels and shoots. He shouts as Tyler tries to disarm him with an upward kick.

I falter. I'm scared to shoot now in case I hit Tyler. In the gloom, there's no way to be sure which of the two grappling shadows is Tyler and which is Gaspar.

They're wrestling, a close hold. I hear Tyler shout, then gasp for breath, wincing in agony. Gaspar must have jabbed Tyler in his gunshot wound. I leap in closer, swing for Gaspar's head with the pistol.

I connect with the back of his head. He gasps for a second or two, then grabs my gun arm and yanks my hand all the way to the ground. He's freakishly strong, holding both Tyler and me at bay. Gaspar twists my wrist until I'm forced to drop the gun. My right leg is close enough to get near the gun; I slam the back of my heel into the pistol and kick it far away.

Meanwhile Tyler and Gaspar are still struggling over the weapon in Gaspar's right hand. I try to reach it – it's impossible. With his free arm, Gaspar has my right arm in such a painful hold – one twist and my wrist will snap.

All three of us breathe painfully. I can hear more guards approaching from the east side of the house.

This is not going well.

Into my headset I mutter, "Benicio . . . you gotta help us. There are too many guards. . ."

Abruptly, I relax so that Gaspar falls against me, carried by his own momentum. Just as he's about to crush me, I move away, a classic defensive roll. In the confusion, Gaspar drops his gun. In the dark it's impossible to see where it's fallen. Before Gaspar can reach for it, Tyler kicks him hard in the abdomen.

Gaspar releases us both, rolls away and leaps to his feet. His shadowed figure takes up a *ginga* stance. I hear the smile in his voice. "Come on now, boys. Show me your moves."

We're thrust into the capoeira fight of our lives.

28

Gaspar flies at us, head low to the ground, legs swooping through the air. His raw power and speed are devastating. I duck and dodge but not before his foot catches me hard in the back of the thigh. A second kick rips away my radio headset. Tyler manages to sidestep; he follows up with a series of rapid *queixada* kicks, whirling round and round like a dervish between each one. But Gaspar's moving so fast, he's no more than a shadowy blur. I throw myself into the melee, aiming *ponteira* kicks, dodging low, rolling. Nothing but the most basic moves. Zero elegance.

This is capoeira, street-fighting style. It's more my style, too. Elegance easily escapes me, but survival, I can do. Whatever was missing at the tournament, I've found it now.

The other guards are close now, less than ten metres away. In the sky, there's a loud humming from the east. Instinctively, I glance up to see two sizzling red beams streak across the sky towards us. The ground between the guards and Gaspar, Tyler and me explodes – clods of soil, lumps of grass fly in every direction.

Benicio's here – giving us laser-fire cover from the air.

We don't stop fighting – we're all arms and legs and energy. Every so often someone lands a kick and there's a yell or a groan. But with adrenaline roaring through me, I don't feel any pain beyond the first blow. For the first time ever, I know what bloodlust is.

I want to get Gaspar. I want to land a kick that lays him out cold, or even breaks a bone.

The laser fire stalls the guards for a second, but then some of them turn and start firing at the Muwan. Benicio's zipping all over the place, it's dark. . . I can only hope it's enough to keep the Muwan from serious damage.

The Muwan fires two more bolts. A guard falls screaming to the ground.

Hearing that, Gaspar's energy seems to double. It dawns on me that Tyler and I can't take him.

I need an advantage. On my next dodge I roll to the ground. From my back pocket I pull one of Lorena's drug-delivery pens. Meanwhile Gaspar flies at Tyler with a cartwheel attack. Tyler manages to duck, so Gaspar sails right over him and crashes to the ground right in front of me.

I roll the pen in my fist, preparing to surprise him with a stab.

As I'm getting up and he's landing, I swing back, then hurl myself at Gaspar: a high kick followed up by a tremendous punch as I throw my whole body round, leading with the pen.

It lands against the hard muscle of his shoulder. Gaspar gasps in shock as the spring-loaded needle punctures his skin. His momentum carries him forward, but by now he's out of control. He reels, falls against me, drags me to the ground. Holding my pen arm hard against the ground, he tries to punch me in the face. But his aim is off, his reactions are slow, and I easily dodge the punches. Then Tyler comes up from behind Gaspar, lands an immense kick to the guy's ribs.

Groaning slightly, Gaspar slides to one side, a hand clutched to his shoulder. He slumps on to all fours, more disoriented by the second.

The Muwan's lasers are still walloping into the ground between us and the guards. Benicio isn't trying to kill them – he's just holding them off. I hear Tyler mutter into his headset, "We're going for the fence. Hold them off a bit longer, then meet us at the rendezvous."

Tyler grabs my arm and pulls me towards the fence. We stop in front of a smooth concrete support post. It's about three metres high and no more than fifteen centimetres wide.

"Give me your hands," Tyler urges. When I open my

palms in front of him, he squeezes two dollops of Lorena's grease from the small tube he's been carrying. Then he applies some to his own hands. "You have to slowly peel your hand away from the surface," Tyler mutters, trying it out. "Like this. Don't just yank it away." I watch, breathless with urgency and seriously relieved that Tyler actually paid attention to Lorena's instructions, unlike me. I slide my palms along each other in upward strokes. I place both palms as high as I can reach on the concrete post, taking care not to touch the electrified wire.

It works. I can hold my whole weight on my palms. The skin on my hands stings and stretches with the effort, but it holds me. I peel one, then another, palm off the post and slap it on a few centimetres higher. It's incredible. When my hands are actually in contact with the post, I can't imagine that anything will unstick them. But after a second or two I can feel the glue weakening – after just enough time to move along.

Moving up the post like that, I'm over in a just over a minute, and so is Tyler. We land on the rough ground beyond, under a thick canopy of leaves. From the shadows, deeper inside the jungle, I hear Ixchel calling out to me.

I throw a last quick glance to the guards on the other side of the fence. They can't climb over. But they're not going to stop. Someone else is barking out orders: "*Shut down the electric current.*"

Any minute now they'll be chasing us. I reach inside my pocket for one of the slim, powerful torches Lorena gave us. I shine the light into the trees until I pick out Ixchel and my mum. They're dazzled by the beam. Tyler and I join them and then we're all running – due east.

Around five minutes later, we hear the buzz of the Muwan flying overhead.

Five minutes is a good lead. But the jungle is so dense in places that it's slow going. We're about as quiet as a herd of elephants. Between that and the flashes from our two torches, I can't imagine we're hard to locate.

The only thing for it is to reach the rendezvous first. Then Benicio can throw down the rope ladder, we can all hang on and he'll fly us to safety.

Amazing. Me, Tyler and Benicio will have done what Montoyo couldn't: rescued everyone.

I'm flushed with confidence as we make our way through the jungle. Ixchel doesn't need any help at all. Just as she was the very first time we met, when she guided me through the rainforest to the ruins of Becan, she's nimble and agile. I'm relieved that this time I'm less of a liability – back then I was soaked through, terrified and nursing a snake bite in my ankle.

I can already feel a few nasty bruises from Gaspar's heavy capoeira kicks . . . but other than that, for once – incredibly – I'm in good shape!

What worries me, as we keep crashing through low branches and thick undergrowth, is Tyler. I can hear it in his breathing – he's in agony. Gaspar caught him more than once in the stitched wound. I can guess how painful that is, remembering my own bullet wound.

I slow down to wait for Tyler. He's bringing up the rear, lighting the way for Mum. He pauses for a second, leaning against a tree. Ixchel stops too. She turns around.

Agitated, she cries, "Don't lean against the trees!"

Tyler pulls away in alarm.

"There can be snakes hanging from trees," she continues anxiously.

From behind us there's a scream. It's just a shocked yell at first, the kind you might make when you trip and fall. But it's followed by the most blood-curdling scream of terror I've heard for a long time. . .

Abruptly as it started, the scream stops.

Tyler, Ixchel and I stare at each other, horrified.

Mum.

We race back, flashing beams of light all over the foliage. When we see her, we stop hard in our tracks.

She's on the ground, tussling among dry leaves. Three thick, muscular coils of a giant snake are wrapped around her. Mum's eyes are wild with panic but she hardly makes a sound above a whimper.

Ixchel says in a loud but steady voice, "Eleanor . . .

breathe shallow . . . try not to struggle. It's gonna be OK, we'll kill it."

I'm not so calm; I push past, throw myself on to the snake and grab its head. With the sharp end of one of the drug pens I stab it in the throat, dragging the tip of the pen down in a slicing movement to tear open its flesh. I grit my teeth the whole time; I don't flinch when the snake's blood spurts out on to my hands.

I've never wanted to kill something so badly.

The coils are still rock-hard for several seconds, until finally they begin to slacken. I pull the beast off my mother and pick her up, hugging her tightly. Not surprisingly, she's still shaking.

Me too. The violence of what I've just done takes me by surprise.

Ixchel puts a hand on my shoulder. "Josh," she urges. "We really need to go."

I wipe the snake blood on to my shirt and take my mother's hand in mine. She grabs a few deep breaths and gives a flustered laugh. "Jesus, Mary, Joseph and all the saints . . . I thought I was dead for sure," she says, which makes me laugh too.

I love it when Mum's Irish side comes out.

We press on, slower now, being even more careful to check everything in our path. It's nerve-racking to make such painstaking progress, knowing the kidnappers are only a

246

couple of minutes behind. I keep pausing to listen for any signs of them. But every time I stop, all I can hear is my own heart, pumping fit to burst.

Every now and then I steal a glance at Ixchel. It's weird, being with her again yet managing not to look at her or think about her (much). I've somehow blocked the thoughts I was having about her – I have to, if I'm going to get through the next five minutes alive. But now I'm confused. Maybe I don't like her so much after all? Maybe she's just a girl running through a dark jungle beside me, again?

The next few minutes are pure concentration as we manoeuvre through a tangle of trees, creepers and leaves. With who knows what gross kinds of insects and spiders underfoot. . .

When we hear the rushing water of the river, we begin to breathe more easily.

Tyler speaks to Benicio, tells him to get the Muwan ready. We're sticking like limpets to the compass bearing. Any minute now we'll break through the jungle, on to the narrow riverbank. Anxiously, I look at my mother. She's hardly said a word, not even glanced at me since the anaconda. Is she scared? Or still angry with me for what I said that day on the dunes?

I mean, she can't still be angry. Can she?

We arrive at the riverbank. We're just in time to see the Muwan being slowly lowered to a few metres above the river. A rope ladder hangs from the side. I've no idea how we're all going to fit inside the craft – there are only two passenger seats.

I guess Ixchel and I can share one. . .

Under the blue-white landing lights of the Muwan, I spot another problem – Tyler. He's bent double with exhaustion, barely able to stand. His side is soaked in fresh blood – just looking at it makes me shudder. He's fading fast.

From about thirty metres upriver, there's a sound: the rustle of leaves. Then footsteps. I flash my torch to see four men rushing towards us. Gaspar's among them – I catch the glint of his fair hair in my torch beam.

One of them begins to shoot.

We break out in panic. Mum leaps up, grabs the end of the rope ladder. Tyler tries to reach but staggers and Ixchel has to catch him.

"That's it, Tyler, get over here," Mum instructs. I watch her in amazement. Despite the fact that she's hanging from a rope for dear life, Mum's voice sounds pretty steady.

"Get your arms around my neck. Properly now. Hold tight. Now don't you worry, I'll hang on for the both of us."

If Tyler even thinks about grumbling, he doesn't. My mum can be pretty tough to argue with.

The guards are almost upon us. Bullets zing into the river and trees around us. Benicio's already starting to float the Muwan away. There's only enough room on the ladder for one more pair of hands. I grab hold and tell Ixchel, "Do like Tyler. You hang on to me."

Rushing footsteps tell me that the kidnappers are almost here. Ixchel wraps her hands tightly around my neck, clinging to me as the Muwan begins to climb. Glancing up, I'm dazzled by a stream of light. I can see the effort in Mum's face as she struggles to grip the ladder. And Tyler looks ready to drop.

Just a few more seconds.

Then there's confusion. Ixchel's grip becomes a bone-breaking tug around my neck, a deep pain in my shoulders. Ixchel screams. I can feel her fingers loosening around my neck. I clench my jaw, trying not to yell from the effort of keeping my neck muscles rigid. My head's bending from the weight: Ixchel's being tugged hard from below. I lower my eyes, terrified. There are two guys grabbing each of Ixchel's legs, pulling her back down to the riverbank. With Ixchel, me.

The Muwan lifts slightly, wrenching another agonized scream from Ixchel. Mum and I are yelling at Benicio to stop lifting the craft.

There's one last, wrenching cry from Ixchel.

Then her fingers unravel, sliding over my neck and shoulders.

Ixchel drops.

She drops and I'm still hanging in mid-air. I'm yelling at

the top of my voice, back for one terrible second in the chill of that moment, gripping the ice claw, feeling the weight of my father's body suddenly vanish as he falls to his death.

Below us, something unbelievable is taking place.

One of the guards grabs Ixchel and holds her, screaming with terror, at the brink of the river's edge. I glimpse flashes of white water under the lights – the river crashing over her feet.

A voice shouts in the darkness, staccato words, like gunfire. It's Gaspar. "The girl goes into the water, Josh. Unless you let go. Now."

"No, Josh, no," Mum shouts desperately. "Please. . ."

I stare directly ahead. Then slowly, down.

My fingers slacken. There's a tight ache in the knuckles. I open my hands, head ringing with Mum's imploring cries.

I can't let them hurt Ixchel. That would be simply . . . impossible.

So I drop.

Arms catch me, hands muffle me. There's a cold bite of pain – a needle slamming into my arm.

A drowsiness washes over me. I sway, trying to catch sight of Ixchel.

The last thing I see before my eyes close is the silhouette of my mother and Tyler, dangling from the rope ladder. Around them, a halo: the glowing lights of the Muwan.

They sail lazily upwards, like a hot air balloon. I can't hear them any longer – there's a roaring in my ears. Even the air slows down.

Everything fades.

I open my eyes from what feels like a long night of broken sleep. There are flashes of dreams left in my memory – but nothing that makes any sense. For the first few seconds of being awake I'm aware of fading images of people carrying me, of smooth, curved metallic walls, of an almost deafening roar. Another needle is pushed into my arm the minute I open my mouth to scream.

I was drugged. We were taken somewhere – where? I woke up at least once, I'm fairly sure of that. But now there's no sign of Ixchel. The last I remember seeing of her is her drugged body, tied up and next to mine in . . . where were we?

Then the image-memory makes sense to me. We were in the freight section of an aeroplane.

Now I'm alone in a room – looks like a hospital room. Could be anywhere. I seem to be wearing a hospital gown. I try to sit up and immediately, something chafes hard against my wrists. With steadily mounting terror I realize that I'm strapped to the bed. I can't move either arm.

The second I realize that, I begin to struggle. I don't care how much it hurts. There's something absolutely electrifying about being strapped to a bed. I struggle, I yell for help.

Within minutes, the door opens. A nurse strolls calmly towards me, totally ignoring the fact that I'm making a racket. She grabs my shoulders and forces me to stare into her eyes.

"Josh Garcia. Yes? Be quiet now. You won't be hurt. The Professor is on her way to see you. Try to remain calm."

The woman speaks with a French accent. She has short red hair and pink cheeks – she doesn't look much older than me. But when she talks to me, she's expressionless. I gaze back at the woman, silenced by her words.

"Where am I?"

"I can't tell you."

I have an idea, though – a terrible idea. As time passes, I'm starting to remember things, put everything together. The Professor – the woman from the Sect of Huracan. The one Camila told me was in charge . . . the woman who Ixchel and I spied on in the Revival Chamber in the tunnels under Becan.

"The Professor. . ." I repeat. "What's she doing here?"

For the tiniest second, the nurse's bland expression changes – she almost smiles. "Ah . . . so you do know who she is. . .?"

Before I can answer, someone else comes through the door. A woman, probably in her late forties, very elegantly dressed in soft fabrics in grey, black and white. Her hair is shoulder-length light brown with amber highlights. All very stylish. She looks like one of the mums who pick up kids at the posh private schools near my house, in their massive cars. Good-looking, I suppose, for a woman that age.

Yet definitely familiar. *I've seen her before.* But where? Immediately, I start racking my brain.

She sidles up to the edge of my bed. She actually smiles.

"Josh," she says softly. "It's good to meet you properly. We didn't get a chance for a real introduction that day in the tunnels."

It's the Professor – the scientist who was with Marius Martineau the day that Ixchel and I stumbled across the Sect in the ancient Revival Chamber.

I scowl. I kind of doubt that meeting her is good for *me*. But I daren't say anything cheeky. I mean, you don't. Not when you're strapped to a hospital bed.

"Where's Ixchel?"

The Professor makes a shushing sound. "She's fine. She's done what we needed, led you to us."

"If you've hurt her. . ."

"I don't blame you for being angry with me," she drawls in her American accent. It's definitely *her* – listening to her voice, my memory goes right back to that morning in the

Revival Chamber. "After all, I did bring you here against your will." She gives me a meaningful stare. "I doubt you'd have volunteered, though, would you? Even in the interests of science."

I return her gaze with as much hostility as I can muster. But still I say nothing.

Then, to my surprise, she removes something from the pocket of her flowing grey cardigan.

The Bracelet of Itzamna.

Her eyes meet mine. "You were wearing this on your arm," she says lightly. "What is it?"

I roll my eyes. "As if I'd tell you," I say, after a long while.

"Well, sure, I didn't expect that you would. Even if you actually knew."

I feel sweat break out on my forehead. My breathing quickens.

She's not going to torture me for information about the Bracelet – is she?

The Professor rolls the Bracelet around her wrist for a minute or two. "It's Erinsi, isn't it? The ancients who were really behind the Books of Itzamna and all that incredible technology in Ek Naab."

I'm about to say something vague, when she continues, "Don't bother to lie, I can see perfectly well for myself that it *is* Erinsi. I've seen this kind of writing before. And you know where, don't you?"

Slowly she regards me, as if sizing me up. For a second or two I remember Blanco Vigores's words about the Bracelet being activated by accident. I fantasize that the woman before me will suddenly vanish into a wormhole in space and be zapped into the molten centre of a volcano.

But it's not that easy. I've had the Bracelet for months – never yet managed to activate it accidentally.

"I wonder how much you saw in that Revival Chamber," she muses. "Do you even know what the Chamber is for?"

I shake my head. It's the truth – I really don't.

"If you saw as much as I think, then you'll remember this: my colleagues and I in the Sect have been hoping to get your help with some experiments. For as long as we've known about you, in fact. It's not that we're short of males with the Bakab genes. As you must have realized by now, Josh, you're not unique. Except in Ek Naab, where they've been throwing away one of their greatest resources for hundreds of years."

"I don't know what you're talking about," I tell her stubbornly.

She smiles. "Josh, don't be silly. I know that you do. Your friend Ollie told me – you had quite a discussion with her about the Sect, didn't you? And she told you that all but the first-born Bakabs were eventually exiled from Ek Naab, before they grew old enough to learn the secrets of the city."

I find myself wondering if this woman has any idea how

secretive Ek Naab really is. I doubt that even the Bakabs who stay really get any idea of the big picture.

I know I don't.

"What kind of society does that, Josh, to *children*? Can you imagine what those boys have gone through, throughout the ages? Being sent away when their older brothers became the Bakab? Do you think anyone in Ek Naab ever asks themselves what becomes of those boys and their families?"

She's confusing me on purpose. No one in Ek Naab's ever told me that it happened like that. I don't want to believe her.

"Well, they come to us; to the Sect. *I've* found them, their descendants. I'll tell you all about it if you survive the genetic modification, Josh."

If I survive?

She stares once again at the Bracelet, and then at me. Carefully, she puts it down on my bedside table. "You'll get this back, don't worry. Then perhaps you'll be kind enough to tell us how it works."

"I've got no idea," I tell her.

The Professor looks deep into my eyes. "You might be telling the truth, I suppose," she says absent-mindedly. "I guess we'll see."

Who is she?

It's seriously starting to annoy me. There's no doubt that

hers is the voice that I heard in the tunnels under Becan that day with Ixchel. But when I look at her face, my mind keeps thinking of Oxford, strangely enough.

"Don't I know you?" I say.

For the first time she looks slightly disconcerted. Like something might not be going according to some great plan.

"I doubt that. We hardly move in the same circles."

She's lying, I can tell. She's been in Oxford. I concentrate hard, trying to remember. It's something to do with my dad, and Oxford. Somehow, amazingly enough, there's a connection.

I remember. "You're Melissa DiCanio," I blurt. Too late, I realize my mistake. Her mouth hardens into a straight line.

She's Professor Melissa DiCanio – that scientist from Oxford who runs the pharmaceutical company in Switzerland. The one from the news story: I recognize her from the photo. She's supposed to be dead – killed by Simon Madison.

Her voice a low, menacing purr, she almost whispers, "Well, no one is as free as the dead. . ."

The Sect faked her death. Now she can do anything she wants.

She pauses, gazing at me with an unmistakable air of threat. "You've got lovely eyes, Josh. I hope they're as fetching after the experiment."

The blood drains from my face.

What are they going to do to my eyes?

I pull against the wrist straps again, even though I know it's useless. DiCanio keeps watching me, interested to see my reaction but entirely without pity. As if I were just some lab rat.

I'd love to reply with some tough talk but I can't find my voice. The sheer ludicrousness, the horror of the situation is nauseating. It's like some nightmare James Bond thing . . . I literally can't believe it's happening to me. Yet there's nothing vague, weird or dreamlike about anything. It's all too starkly cold and real.

"I can't deny it's a risky procedure. . ." she admits. "If you hadn't come along, we might have been forced to try it on one of our own people." Her eyes twinkle dangerously. "But imagine how unpopular that would make me in the Sect."

Finally, I bring myself to say it. "What are you going to do to me?"

DiCanio inhales deeply. "Nothing less than this, Josh: the genetic procedure will change the course of your destiny."

I wait, but she says nothing for a long while. I'm desperate to ask *Will it hurt? What are the chances of it going wrong?* But I don't. She's not getting the pleasure of watching me dissolve into tears like a terrified kid.

Eventually she concludes, "When you wake up, Josh, all being well . . . I believe you'll be more than happy to join us in the Sect."

259

Are they going to brainwash me – from inside my DNA?

It's a struggle to keep my voice from shaking, but I do it. "I will never, never help you, no matter what you do to me. Not after what you did to my dad, to my sister, to my mum and my friends."

DiCanio leans in close, puts her mouth next to my ear. "We had *nothing* to do with your father's disappearance. But you're right to fear me, Josh; I'm relentless. The fate of the planet is at stake. I won't let a teenage boy stand in my way."

She pulls away and stares down at me, her expression dark and fathomless.

I look back at her but can't answer.

There's a taste like ashes in my mouth when I wake up. For several seconds I have the strongest sense of déjà vu. I'm alone, strapped to a bed in a barely furnished hospital room.

Did any of that stuff with the Professor woman actually happen? Or did I dream it? The last thing I remember is that redheaded nurse approaching me with a syringe. I was literally rigid with fear.

I tug at the straps.

Amazingly, my wrists slide right through them. The straps have been unbuckled.

I'm free.

But who unbuckled them and why? I'm entirely alone. The room is exactly as I remember it. Even the Bracelet of Itzamna is precisely where I remember DiCanio leaving it – on my bedside table. I pick up the ancient relic and slide it on to on my left arm until it won't go any higher.

In no time at all I sense the familiar surge, a sizzle of

energy between my skin and the Bracelet.

It's definitely a specific thing, this weird electricity between the artefact and me. The Professor didn't seem to experience anything similar when she touched the Bracelet. At least – she didn't mention it to me.

But then I guess she might not tell me anything . . . who knows?

Slowly, I climb off the bed and test my legs. They seem fine. I'm still wearing the hospital gown, but when I glance towards the end of the bed I notice a heap of blue and green clothes and trainers. They're mine.

Needless to say, they weren't there before.

Someone has tried to rescue me. Were they disturbed before they could wake me?

I remove the gown and give myself a quick once-over. Pretty much as expected, my chest and ribs are covered with bruises from Gaspar's capoeira blows. But apart from the bruising, I seem to be OK. There's a plaster taped on the inside of my left forearm – when I pull it away there's a blood-soaked dab of bandage.

OK, so needles have been plugged into my arm . . . but that seems to be all. Whatever they did to me, it doesn't seem to have caused any obvious damage.

Unless they haven't started yet. Or maybe the changes are inside me – something I won't know about until I eat or drink or talk?

I test my voice, quietly. It seems OK. I check my face with my fingers. That seems OK too. Then I remember that she mentioned my eyes. I blink a few times. My vision seems unaffected. I don't seem to have x-ray vision or anything cool. . .

So what was DiCanio on about?

Quickly, I get dressed. The door to my room has a small glass window. I peer through into the corridor before opening it. It's empty. I nip out and walk down the corridor until I come to what I recognize as the door to a cold room similar to the one in Lorena's research department in Ek Naab.

I can't resist taking a look inside. I found some pretty useful stuff in Lorena's cold room. Who knows what I might find in here?

Inside, I'm shivering within seconds. I don't seem to be able to handle the cold as well as I used to. Is that a side effect of the genetic treatment?

Fear twists my guts. Is this how it's going to be for the rest of my life? Every time I feel some new or strange sensation, wondering whether something is going wrong inside me? Waiting and wondering when and how my body is going to betray me?

My gaze passes over some metallic shelving, on which sits a large glass case with a sliding door. I catch my reflection in the glass and metal, just for an instant. That's when I glimpse it for the first time.

There *is* something odd about my eyes.

I focus; stare hard at my reflection in the shiny aluminium. It's such a simple thing but even so, it takes me seconds to work it out.

My eyes have turned *blue*. Nothing too distinctive; not a deep or violet shade. Just everyday pale blue.

Carefully, I poke a finger into my right eye. I force myself to touch the eyeball. There doesn't seem to be a contact lens there.

My eyes are *actually* blue.

Now that's a proper change. Just as I'm starting to feel elated that it isn't something grim, I wonder what else they've done. The Sect wouldn't have gone to all that trouble only to change the colour of my eyes – would they?

Suddenly it's all shockingly real. They've changed the inside of me – altered my DNA. But *what* have they done? Will I ever really know?

It's a bombshell. I blink rapidly, now incredibly aware of my eyes. Leaning against the glass case on the metal shelving, I slowly focus on the contents – a bunch of plastic tubes with blue screw-cap lids, in a rack. Each one has a long label, handwritten in black marker pen.

I stare at one of the labels. Once my brain registers what I'm looking at, it's unmissable.

AGYLIHRPPREIKGR

The fifteen-letter sequence of the Key. Is the Sect still working on making the crystal version?

Very gradually, I begin to work out where I must be. The newspaper story mentioned that Professor Melissa DiCanio ran a pharmaceutical company. I can't remember the name, but it was definitely in Switzerland. That must be where they would store the Crystal Key – in the company's top-secret labs.

So I'm in Switzerland, not the jungle of Brazil. That explains the aeroplane. If I can only find Ixchel, maybe we can break out of this place, escape.

Switzerland: organized, efficient. How hard could it be to get around such a country?

I'm on the point of turning away and leaving the cold room to look for Ixchel, when I turn back. I stare long and hard at the tube with the label **AGYLIHRPPREIKGR**.

Could it be that the actual Crystal Key is in there? The object I've been searching for, obsessed with during the past months – what if it's actually here, just centimetres away?

With a hand that trembles not only from the cold, I pick out the tube and unscrew the lid. Inside is a coin-sized piece of polystyrene foam. I pluck it gingerly between two fingertips and pull it away.

Underneath, lying on a further wedge of foam, there it is.

It's beautiful.

They did it; the Sect actually did it. They managed to grow the Crystal Key.

A crystal: not particularly shiny like a diamond, yet definitely a crystal. It's about as big as a garden pea and roughly diamond-shaped, but with at least eight faces of different sizes.

I roll up my T-shirt's sleeve to expose the Bracelet of Itzamna. Holding my breath, I pick out the crystal with utmost care and position it over the dimple in the Bracelet. It's going to fit – more or less. But I've no idea how I'm going to keep the crystal in place. I'm still holding my breath when I push the crystal into the depression on the Bracelet.

I gasp. The metal of the Bracelet seems to melt around the edges of the crystal. Some of the symbols light up from some hidden power source. I didn't realize that the Bracelet has moving parts, but from the vibrations through my skin, I sense that it does. Parts of the outer casing slide over each other, revealing a smaller panel covered with symbols that start to flash. Another symbol, which seems to be made of what looks like mercury, actually changes shape before my eyes.

There's a scarily steady rhythm to the shape-changing. Like seconds counting down.

With a jolt of dread, I register the fact that the roaring

noise in my ears isn't just my own fear. From outside the cold room, there's a steady noise like a klaxon. Somewhere in the labs, an alarm has gone off.

I've triggered something – maybe when I took the tube holding the crystal, or opened the glass case that contained it. Either way, I'm about to be toast. Judging from the commotion outside in the corridor, the security guards just sprang into action.

In a kind of fascinated horror, I stare at the Bracelet on my arm. It's counting down to something – but what? The newly exposed flashing symbols keep cycling through the same series of flashes. Am I supposed to press something?

The Bracelet of Itzamna can be activated by accident.

This must be what Blanco Vigores meant. He said it happened to him too, when he first found the Bracelet. The Bracelet of Itzamna is active now; it's going to transport me somewhere in time and space. Maybe I need to press some of the symbols . . . but I'm way too scared of making a mistake to risk it. Desperate, I try to unclip the Bracelet.

The release catch has vanished into the inside of the device. I can't shift the Bracelet.

I'm trapped – going wherever the Bracelet of Itzamna decides to take me.

The door to the cold room clunks heavily, opened from

the outside. Harsh voices reach me from the corridor.

"There's someone in here. . ."

I feel the rise of panic. This is unstoppable. Let's hope I don't end up inside a mountain. . .

There's no blinding flash or anything. It's as though a tear appears in the world around me, like a mask ripped off to reveal the true features underneath. The cold room vanishes, torn away in one gigantic sheet. Instead, I'm in a long, bare corridor, a concrete floor, walls of bare rock. Faint strains of music drift from somewhere down the corridor. I can't hear much more than the soft, steady rhythm of a snare drum. Dim electric lighting flickers unsteadily overhead. I take a few steps forward and see a heavy metal door. It's slightly ajar. I push the door gently and peer inside. The music gets louder.

I know this song – but what's it called? Something about the tune drills deep inside my head. There's a sense of a dream half-remembered. It feels like something connected with my father, but also . . . with Camila.

I shiver from the sheer impossibility of what's just occurred to me. This really can't be happening . . . can it?

Not again. . .

I'm staring into a prison. Most of the room is separated off with floor-to-ceiling bars. There's a man sitting in a cell about ten metres square. He's wearing an orange-coloured jumpsuit, sitting on a wooden stool facing away from me, reading a book.

He doesn't have to turn around for me to recognize him. I know my father from this angle – his head in a book, cool jazz on the stereo.

I clear my throat quietly. "Dad."

I try my best to stay calm when he turns around, but don't quite manage. He turns around and meets my eyes with an expression of such joy that a lump forms in my throat. He leaps up, drops his book and rushes to the perimeter of his prison.

"Josh! Josh!" He laughs, incredulous, hands gripping the sides of his face. Then I'm against the bars and hugging him, feeling his beard against my cheek. When I look at him again, he's so thrilled that tears have come to his eyes.

"*Hijo*, Josh, what" – his eyes roll with amazement – "what are you *doing* here?!" He laughs again, more dazzled by the second, throws his head back. "This is incredible! Do you have any idea how much I've dreamed that I'd see you again? That somehow you'd just walk through my door one day? And now you have? God, it's unbelievable!"

Dad's joy is infectious. But I can't quite give myself over to it. I need to understand what's just happened. Because if my dad's alive, then. . .

I've gone back in time.

"Dad, Dad . . . where are we?"

He looks puzzled. "You don't know?"

I shake my head.

"Inside Area 51," he explains. "In a deep underground military base. But if you didn't know that . . . how did you get here?"

Silently, I roll up my sleeve and show him the Bracelet. That instant, his expression changes completely. He looks at the Bracelet for a long time, not touching it. Then, carefully, he runs a finger around the depression which holds the crystal. And looks back at me.

"The Bracelet of Itzamna."

I nod. "I fixed it – I found the Crystal Key! Now I'm going to get you out of here. You know how to use it, don't you, Dad?"

He takes a deep breath. "Yes, I do."

We both gulp, moved by the utter seriousness of what I'm suggesting. Instead of getting on with it, Dad takes a step back, his chin in one hand. He looks me up and down slowly, as if seeing me for the first time.

"You're older. Taller. Your arms, your chest, they're bigger. Even your face – you're getting a square jaw. . ."

"I'm fourteen," I tell him.

"But . . . there's something else . . . something very different about you. . ."

"My eyes," I say. "They're blue. From a genetic experiment. Long story. . ."

If he's surprised, he doesn't show it. In fact, he seems to be thinking deeply. Bluntly, he says, "You're from the future, aren't you? When did you get here?"

"Less than a minute ago."

My dad is speechless, just looks at the ground, shaking his head.

"You found the Crystal Key . . . and fixed the Bracelet? When?"

I shrug, puzzled. What's he getting at? "Right before I used it."

Dad's expression intensifies. "No one used the Bracelet since you found it?"

Now I'm frowning. "Well, no. It was broken."

Dad starts muttering to himself. "He found it . . . fixed it . . . ended up here . . . which means. . ."

"We have to send you back into the past," I interrupt, pushing my face against the bars. "And stop the NRO from capturing you . . . and bringing you here."

But when Dad looks up again, there's a sad smile on his face. "Why?"

"Because unless we do, bad things happen."

"'Bad things'? You look to be in pretty good shape, Josh. How's your mother? I miss her so much, you've no idea."

I swallow, nervously thinking of what my mother went through when my father first disappeared, and then when he really died. How can I tell my dad any part of that? I decide to stick to the bare bones.

I don't want to have to tell my dad that unless we get him out of here, he's going to die.

"Mum? She's OK – now. It's been hard for her . . . really hard."

He nods thoughtfully. "I wish we had more time, Josh. But we don't. If I'm right . . . and I think I am . . . we have probably five minutes."

"Before the guards come?"

"Before I use *my* Bracelet."

Now he's completely thrown me. "What?!"

My dad lifts up his right arm, pulls back the orange sleeve to reveal the Bracelet on his forearm. "Your Bracelet is mine – but from the future. If you just used it a few minutes ago – that means that it was last used to leave this place about five minutes from now."

I stare at him blankly. "Huh?"

"You don't know how to use the Bracelet, do you, Josh? So listen carefully now. I'm serious. Your life and the lives of millions of others may depend on it."

Anxiously I lick my lips. "What? No. You have to use my *fixed* Bracelet to escape. And I'll use the old Bracelet . . . to get to wherever it's going."

Which, I now realize, must be Mount Orizaba. Dad's broken Bracelet would zap him from here to the slopes of the volcano.

Well, not in my new timeline. This is the *zero moment*. From here, everything changes.

I stretch an arm through the bars, trying to reach my father's wrist. "Give me your Bracelet. Show me how to use it. I'll be fine – come and look for me on Mount Orizaba. Dad, can you remember that? Orizaba."

My dad steps back. "Don't you know you can't trust your memory when you use that device?"

I falter again. "Memory?"

"Amnesia . . . is a risk with the Bracelet. That's what Vigores told me. Use it and you risk losing your memory. Even worse, you risk ending up inside a mountain – or in space. There's only one safe way to use the Bracelet – that's the default."

"How do I do that?"

"It's simple. Press hard on the crystal. It triggers the safety mechanism."

I stare in astonishment. "Safety mechanism?"

"You just used it, Josh. It takes you back to the same place, ten minutes before you last used it."

"Ten minutes?" I'm so baffled by everything that I can't quite follow or believe what my dad is telling me.

My dad points to his own Bracelet and the empty crystal chamber. "You said you fixed the Bracelet. You used it and it brought you here. That means that the Bracelet returned you to the place and time it was last used. Don't you see, Josh? In a few minutes I'm going to use this Bracelet. . . If I don't, then you wouldn't be standing here."

I push forward, my voice urgent. It's all beginning to make a horrible kind of sense.

Amnesia.

"Not you, Dad, me! Take your Bracelet off . . . give it to me!"

He looks sad. "I can't. It's locked into position. When the NRO captured my Muwan, I panicked. I started the countdown . . . and then I stalled the countdown. The Bracelet is locked on my wrist now until it's used to transport me."

"You stalled the countdown?"

"Well, it was kind of a crazy thing to do in the first place. To use the Bracelet without the crystal is practically suicide! Without the time-control circuit, the most likely thing is that you get zapped into space!" He grins ruefully. "I decided to take my chances with those NRO bastards. So yes, I stopped the countdown."

275

I stare at my dad in sheer frustration. "Dad! You have to get that thing off your arm! It's not safe. . ."

Now I get it: if my dad uses the Bracelet, he's going straight to Mount Orizaba . . . he's losing his memory and everything will unfold just the way it did.

My plan will be ruined.

My dad gazes at me curiously. "Where did you say to meet you, Orizaba? You don't want me to use the Bracelet to go there. . . Yet somehow you believe it's safe for *you* to go to Orizaba. . .?"

I start to shake my head. "Don't use it." I've changed my mind – maybe the best thing is not to use the Bracelet at all. We'll both stay, tackle the NRO together, change the timeline a different way. . .

Dad echoes, "*Don't* use it. . .? Josh, what's going on here? Who sent you . . . why are you here?"

"No one sent me. I'm here because I want to save your life. And Dad. . ." I stare at my father, dreading what I have to tell him. "If you go to Mount Orizaba, you're gonna die."

That doesn't faze him as much as I'd expected.

"I've faced death a few times since we last saw each other, Josh," he says, leaning forward suddenly.

He's no idea how literally true that is from where I'm standing. . .

"Death doesn't worry me," continues Dad. "But you . . . you do. What's been going on? Why are you involved?"

"I found the Calakmul letter," I say bluntly. "I found Camila. I found Ek Naab. I found the Ix Codex."

He staggers slightly, a smile spreading across his face. "You . . . you did all that?"

"It should have been you, Dad. Take my Bracelet and get out of here. I'll find another way out of this place."

"Josh," he laughs, "this is Area 51! They will *never* let you out of here!" He faces me with grim resolve. "No. This is how it's going to be: I'm going to use my Bracelet – complete the countdown. I'll go to Orizaba and everything will pan out just the way it did. You'll use your Bracelet – to go right back to where you came from." He winks once. "Except . . . ten minutes before you set out. Safety mechanism, OK?"

I shake my head in desperation. "No . . . Dad, NO! I came back here to save your life! To change the past . . . to stop everything from going wrong. . ."

"You think I'm going to risk the life of my own son to save my skin?" He shakes his head. "Josh, you don't know me very well." He grips my shoulder hard, makes me look him right in the eyes. "How do you know I die on Mount Orizaba?"

I stare back at him, lips trembling. "Because I was there. I saw it."

He nods. "But you didn't die."

"No, Dad," I whisper. "You died saving me."

That silences him. For a second or two we just stare at each other. Dad's stereo is still playing the same song. It breaks across our silence, tugging at some part of my memory.

My dad takes a step forward, stretches an arm through the bars. An expression of fierce pride crosses his face. He pulls me close, presses his lips against my forehead. "That's good enough for me," he breathes.

After a few seconds he releases me, a quizzical, faraway sort of look in his eyes. "You look so different with blue eyes. You remind me of someone I knew . . . a long time ago."

I stare at him . . . hardly able to believe what I'm thinking.

"I remind you of someone. . .?"

He nods. "You do. A guy I knew when I was not much older than you."

My voice drops to a whisper. "Was his name . . . Arcadio?"

It's as though someone hit my dad in the face – he looks that stunned. "Josh . . . no . . . it can't be."

Am I Arcadio?

Dad keeps shaking his head. "No . . . no, Josh, please. That can't be your life. It's too dangerous."

"What . . . what's going to happen to Arcadio?"

I'm not getting through to my dad. He's still reeling from the implications of what I've said, talking frantically to himself.

"Arcadio . . . you? No . . . it can't be. . . You?" And finally he stops pacing the cell and stares at me. "It's true. You remind me of Arcadio. How do you know about him?"

Where do I begin?

"Dad . . . is Arcadio a time traveller?"

Dad presses his lips together, deep in thought. Then he says something that astonishes me. "Promise me you'll only use this Bracelet once – right now. Promise me!"

I'm dumbstruck. "What . . . Dad . . . why?"

Dad is becoming more serious and thoughtful by the second. He doesn't speak again for several seconds. Then urgently he says, "Give me your arm, Josh."

Baffled, I stretch my left arm through the bars. He grabs a pen from his bed and then takes hold of my arm, scrawling something into my inside wrist. When he lets go, I stare at what he's written.

I am Josh Garcia from Oxford, England, son of Eleanor and Andres.

"Use the Bracelet just this once, Josh. Go back to where you came from. Then never use it again!"

I'm about to answer when there's a sound from somewhere down the corridor. Hurried footsteps, and they're on their way to us. Frozen, I stare at my dad. His eyes widen; he grabs my arm.

"OK. This is it."

My mouth drops open. "What. . .?"

With his other hand, my dad ruffles my hair. He smiles, eyes shiny with emotion. "Goodbye, Josh."

I'm too astounded by the speed at which things are moving to take his words in. "Dad, don't go, please."

With a nod, he steps back. "If it's meant to be, we'll see each other again, Josh. Don't worry."

The footsteps are right outside the cell. I'm paralysed, watching as my dad presses something on his own Bracelet.

"Press on the crystal, Josh," he murmurs. "It'll take you right back."

The door to the cell opens, but I can't take my eyes off my dad. A surge of white light emerges from the Bracelet and envelops him. For just a second he glows like some unearthly apparition. And then all that light seems to contract, as if it's suddenly been sucked down a plughole.

He's gone – to Mount Orizaba. To a life fractured by a lost memory, a few months living like a hermit and then to that final, fateful day of the avalanche.

Where he'll save my life by giving his.

When the three uniformed soldiers barge into the cell, I hardly even give them a glance. They all train their guns at me.

"Get your hands up where we can see them," barks one of them, aiming a semi-automatic rifle at my head. Then he screams, "Now!"

I sigh despondently, shake my head and raise my arms slowly. Another soldier steps forward to search me.

"What just happened to the prisoner?" shouts the first soldier.

I sigh again. "You know what. . ." Then I reach one arm behind my head and through my sleeve, press hard on the crystal.

"Stop moving! Get your hands back in the air!"

It's too late. Already the soldiers are being ripped out of my field of vision. Instead, the surrounding air fills with the nearby walls, shelves and lab equipment of the cold room.

Just like my dad said, I'm back where I came from – the mysterious labs where the Sect took me and Ixchel after Brazil. Except that according to Dad, it's ten minutes in the past – ten minutes before I first used the Bracelet.

Well . . . ten minutes? In ten minutes you can change the world.

32

At a time like this, you need a watch. But I don't have one. I can almost hear the seconds ticking away in my head as I search the cold room for something that might help.

Ten minutes from now, the past version of *me* is going to walk through the door of this cold room. I don't know much about time travel, but that sounds a lot like *time paradox* territory. . . I'm pretty sure I want to avoid being here for that.

On one of the metal shelves I find what I'm looking for – a grey plastic stop clock, like a kitchen timer. I set it for nine minutes. Not taking my eyes from the clock face, I begin to think.

Dad didn't have time to show me how to use the Bracelet properly. But I can use it in safety mode. If I hit the crystal again, I'll go right back to Dad's underground prison . . . and probably meet myself!

But that's not what actually happened. I know because I was there. If I do try to go back, I guess I might even cross over into a parallel reality where I do meet myself. Yet another paradox. . . My head hurts just thinking about it. I can't risk something like that.

As I start to think through the possibilities, the potential power of this Bracelet begins to make me feel dizzy. I mean, it's incredible.

Time travel!

It was just a dream before. Now it's real. And I don't know how to control it.

Just one press of the crystal will buy me ten extra minutes with my dad.

Eight minutes to go before past-me comes crashing through the door.

In the past, Dad's in a secret base in Area 51. In the present, he's dead and buried. He died saving me.

For the first time, a shadow falls across my plan.

Past-me is going to come through this door. But only if someone frees me.

Ixchel is somewhere in this building. If I could find her, we could escape together. Right now, no one knows I'm free – for all they can see, I'm still lying in a hospital bed, until someone unbuckles the straps which tie me down. Until someone frees me – someone thoughtful enough to bring my clothes.

My heart begins to sink. It's me – I'm the one. Who else?

I'm the one who sneaks in and unties myself.

If I don't do it, I won't find the crystal. I won't fix the Bracelet. I won't get a chance to go back in time to see Dad. I won't even be here wondering what to do.

Seven minutes.

The way I see it, I don't have a choice. If I don't . . . this timeline might just disappear right now.

So I leave the problem with Dad to one side. I have problems to solve in the here-and-now. Like – where do I find the clothes to leave at the end of my hospital bed? How am I going to get out of this building?

Leaving the cold room is a tense moment. Behind that thick fridge-style door, there's no way of knowing if someone's in the corridor. Grabbing hold of the timer, I close my eyes, hold my breath and push. When I see the corridor outside is empty, I exhale.

There are some lockers a few doors further down. I dash up to them, try opening doors until one gives way. My clothes and shoes are heaped up in a pile. As I pick up the jeans, I notice some extra weight and bulk. In the back pocket is one of the drug pens I took from Lorena's lab. My Ek Naab and UK mobile phones are in the front pockets.

Bonus!

I stash the drug pen and phones in my own pockets. Then, holding the clothes and shoes, I rush back to the room where they performed their experiment.

I'm inside the room in the next few seconds. I drop the clothes at the end of the bed, exactly where I remember finding them. I have to get this just right. No mistakes – or who knows what will happen. . .

I unbuckle the wrist straps, trying not to look at the sleeping body on the bed.

My own sleeping body.

That was me, about six minutes ago. Or even less. It strikes me then – this sleeping version of me still has to wake up, get dressed, find the cold room, fix the Bracelet.

All in less than six minutes. A heart-stopping thought hits me. Did I really do all that so quickly?

I have to wake myself up now!

I put my mouth right next to my own ear and whisper loudly: "*Josh – wake up! Go to the cold room down the corridor. Find the Crystal Key, repair the Bracelet.*"

Anxiously, I stare at the closed lids of my own eyes. There's an agonizing second or two whilst nothing happens. Then they begin to flicker.

I glance at the timer. Five and a half minutes.

Time to leave.

I race down the corridor towards a group of doors.

Something's pumping through me; it feels exactly like adrenaline but it's just a single word, an idea.

Freedom.

It's so close that I can taste it. I only have to find Ixchel and we are out of here. For the next five and a half minutes it's as though I don't exist: I'm off the radar.

Passing the elevator lobby, I see I'm on the fifth floor of five. A lift is on its way to this floor. I dive into the nearby stairwell.

Time to make a choice. Where would they be keeping Ixchel?

Some companies put their restaurants on the highest floor – but not this place. I guess that a secretive pharmaceutical company puts its most secure facility on the top floor.

My guess is that Ixchel is somewhere on the fifth floor, too. But there are so many doors. . .

I take a deep breath. There's nothing for it but to try every possible door. I peer from behind the glass in the stairwell door, waiting for the lift to arrive. Two passengers step out; both are wearing white coats. They're deep in conversation. I don't recognize either. I watch as they disappear down the corridor, then push the stairwell door open. I'm just in time to see them vanish behind a door about halfway down the corridor.

A door only metres away from the one where by now *past-me* is awake and getting dressed. . .

That could have been a close shave. . .

I stride to the door nearest to the stairs, which are at the extreme end of the corridor. It's a solid door, no glass window. There's a red light beside it, which isn't lit up. I open the door to find a room full of camera equipment and trays of vinegary-smelling liquids. A photographic dark room.

The next door leads to a small lab – I can see that much by looking through the window. Looks like it's unoccupied right now. The next door is solid, with a name plate. Someone's office? I decide to give it a miss.

The next door is also solid. But there's no name plate. I push it open slightly.

Amazingly, a voice I recognize says, "Who's there?" Someone yanks the door wide open.

It's Ollie. Now that I see her I'm not totally surprised – I guess she goes where the Sect sends her. Still, it's a bit of a jolt – for Ollie too. Seconds tick past on the clock as we stand, frozen, gaping at each other.

"Hi Ollie," I say, trying to sound cool. Ollie stares at me as if she can't decide whether to yell for help or not. Her eyes and mouth are doing that whole *You? Here? Really?* kind of thing.

"Your eyes. . ." she says, gazing at my face with an expression of wonder. "It works!"

She's obviously confused. The idea that I could have escaped seems simply impossible to Ollie. So I decide to play along. "The Professor told me to come to you. She wanted you to be the first to see."

Ollie gazes at me, now obviously moved. "She . . . she wanted me to be the first to see. . .? So she's not still mad at me?"

The Professor was mad at Ollie. . .?

Ollie takes a step forward. She looks older than I remember. Her hair isn't as blonde or lustrous; her face seems less rosy. I guess she's stopped making an effort to look sixteen – her clothes certainly look more grown-up: brown jeans, a white blouse, a long blue woollen cardigan. She's still pretty but looks tired and a bit drained. All that confidence that used to burst out of her – it seems to have vanished.

Looking at her now, I don't fancy her even a bit. In fact, I wonder what I ever saw in her.

"Josh," she says, touching a hand to my hair. "Still so cute. Blue eyes suit you!"

I struggle not to push Ollie's hand away. For some reason she's in the doghouse with the Professor – I'll have to find a way to use that.

"What about the other genetic changes?" Ollie asks suddenly. "Have they worked too?"

So there are other changes. Anxiety surges through me again, like a wave of nausea. What have they done to me? So far I seem to be OK. Is that going to change? Soon? Or do I have years to wait, worrying?

I just nod. "It looks like it, yeah. The Professor sent me down here to get you."

"She's going to make the announcement. . .?" Ollie asks, eyes round, hopeful.

If you say so. . .

I keep nodding. "Uh huh." I reach into my back pocket for Lorena's drug pen.

"And I'm invited?" Ollie continues with a smile of amazement. I try to smile, concealing the pen behind my wrist. I step forward, in what I hope is a friendly way.

"And Ollie, I just wanted to say . . . the Professor told me to say. . ."

I put a matey hand on her shoulder. Ollie's face is a picture. The Professor's approval really seems to mean something to her.

"No hard feelings, Ollie, OK?"

Yeah, right.

Behind Ollie's back, I slide the pen into position. Just as I'm going in for an all-friends-again hug, I jab it against her neck, feeling the spring-loaded mechanism burst inside. For one still moment, Ollie's eyes stare directly into mine, with a look that's half shock, half betrayal.

She collapses through my arms, slides to the floor trembling as she falls into unconsciousness. I watch her drop and can't feel any pity at all.

Softly I mutter, "But now I reckon you're really gonna get it. . ."

I'm standing in a windowless room which has floor-to-ceiling bookcases against every wall. Rows of bound science journals cover the shelves. In the middle of one wall is a door. I try the handle but it's locked. From behind the door I sense movement. I lean against the door, put my mouth close to the surface. In a low voice I call, "Ixchel. . .?"

There's a pause, then an amazed reply. "Josh. . .?"

For a second, relief washes over me. Then I'm looking around for a way to open the door. From behind the door Ixchel says, "Ollie has the key, Josh. . ."

Right – of course she does. As Ollie lies sleeping on the floor, I go through her pockets until I find the key. I open the door to find Ixchel standing before a window through which sunlight streams. For a second I can't move. Luckily for me, Ixchel doesn't hesitate. She rushes forward and hugs me tight. After a second I squeeze her back. Over her shoulder, I gaze at the view.

A blue-green river glistens like a slug trail in the sun, right in front of the building. To the left, the river snakes off into a lake. Across the river a field of mountains rises from the ground, surrounding the lake. In the distance they're jagged, crooked, white.

"Switzerland," I breathe, releasing Ixchel.

Ixchel freezes, staring at me. I'm getting that look again – the one when someone I know first sees my eyes. A half-smile. In Ixchel's case it's followed up with a frown.

"Blue eyes," she goes. "Uh oh. . ."

Before I can ask her to explain, she continues, "So, hotshot, do you have a plan this time?"

I give her a sheepish grin. "Um . . . nope. . .?"

Ixchel pretends to sigh. "Well, your eyes may be different . . . but you're the same old Josh."

I *do* have a plan! It goes something like this: run down the stairs, get out of the building, keep running. . .

Oh yes, and somehow find time to stop and call Benicio. Not sure exactly how he's going to get me out of this, though. Switzerland is a very long way from Ek Naab. Even with a Muwan.

We make it to the stairwell. We get all the way to the third floor when the commotion hits. An alarm goes off, followed by all kinds of running noises and shouting. I'm guessing that someone has found Ollie and the open door

292

with Ixchel missing. Maybe even my own vacant hospital bed?

Which means that by now *past-me* is hiding in the nearby cold room, about to discover the Crystal Key, about to activate the Bracelet of Itzamna, about to zap back through time and space into the underground military base in Area 51.

About to meet my father.

I get a little shiver thinking of that. For me, that's all in the past, but past-me is about to get one of the shocks of his life. Of *my* life.

I've experienced the past ten minutes of time *twice*. Is this what they call a time paradox, or a time loop? It doesn't seem paradoxical to me, though. Just like some more stuff I did to get out of a tight spot.

I stepped outside of time and helped myself to escape. Weird but true.

Some of the guards are heading in that direction already. I heard them when I first lived through this moment in time. There could be others, too. There usually are. . .

I've caught up on myself – my ten minutes are up. I can't help grinning as we almost tumble down the stairs.

I bought ten extra minutes. Reckon I spent them pretty well.

At the bottom of the stairwell there's a fire exit. It only opens one way – to the outside. It isn't guarded at all. I guess they built the place with the idea of stopping people getting in – not out. Ixchel and I push heavily against the fire door and we're into the company car park.

At least I assume it's the company car park, which is already packed. I spot at least two signs as we dash past: Chaldexx BioPharmaceuticals.

Yep – that rings a bell. It's the name of the company from that news story.

The Professor definitely *is* Melissa DiCanio. I'd say she's in pretty good shape – for a corpse.

From behind us, I hear the sound of the fire door being opened again. I risk a tiny glance over my shoulder to see two security guards racing towards us. They're led by a fair-haired, dark-skinned figure that I recognize.

Gaspar.

I flinch. Even in that split second I've seen enough to realize that Gaspar is very, very mad with me.

"Faster," I say to Ixchel.

She gets just one word out as we pelt away from the building and down towards the riverbank. "Where?"

I can't answer that. Mainly because I have no idea. The river? There's nowhere else.

"Look for a boat," I yell, speeding ahead of Ixchel.

Staying to fight isn't an option. No more drug pens . . . and I don't imagine that Gaspar will let me slither through his fingers a second time.

There's a line of trees on the riverbank. We bound through them, desperate to get some cover in case Gaspar and pals start shooting. Then it's along the riverbank, towards a nearby kink in the river. After that there's a small harbour lined with about ten leisure boats.

With Gaspar and his men less than fifty metres behind us, we can't risk slowing down. I put my head down and run harder, pulling even further away from Ixchel.

I only hope she doesn't think I'm abandoning her. One of us needs to get to a boat and get it started up – and fast. As the harbour comes into view, I start hunting for a boat that might not be locked.

I don't know what time it is, but my senses tell me that it's morning. There aren't too many people out on the boats. Over on the river I can just see the edge of a big cruise steamer heading for the road bridge. Beyond that the river runs clear to the lake.

Scanning the line of white speedboats, something catches my eye. At the far end of the mini-harbour, a man is guiding his boat in between a dinghy and another speedboat.

Over my shoulder I call, "Ixchel . . . gonna head for that boat. . ."

If he sees me coming, the guy doesn't get suspicious until the last second; he's too busy turning off his engine and steering his boat. By the time I get close enough to jump for it, the boat owner is already fiddling with the moorings.

I leap off the edge of the pier and land smack in the centre of his deck. The guy is so stunned that he hardly reacts – at first. Once he's realized that I'm actually daring to try to nick his boat, he makes a grab for my shoulder and starts to punch. He's in his late forties or so, quite a bit taller and heavier than me. When that first punch lands near my ear, the whole side of my face rings with pain. In fact, there's definitely something wrong with my right arm – it feels weak and slightly tingly. No time to wonder why, though – so I concentrate on ducking to avoid his follow-up punch. A tirade of what sounds like German streams out of his mouth. I recognize at least one swear word.

Well, yeah. I'd be mad too, if some scruffy teenager tried to nick my boat.

I twist free of his grasp and drop into a low defensive roll. There's just enough room to swing to my feet and fly at him with a couple of rapid *queixada* kicks. I land blows to his chest and gut. The second kick winds the guy, who is clearly out of shape. As he's doubled over, I shove hard and then high-kick him. Staggering in stunned bafflement, he topples and falls overboard into the river with an almighty splash.

I turn around just in time to see Ixchel flying through the air towards me. I don't even have time to step aside – she crashes straight into me, almost knocks me to the deck. Gaspar and his men are close. They've almost reached the harbour.

We have one chance to get this boat moving. I've never driven a speedboat before. But Ixchel has. . .

I don't have to ask her to get started – she pushes past me, goes straight to the engine and yanks on something. The boat jerks into motion. Seeing that we're about to move out of range, Gaspar puts on a final spurt of energy. He leaps into one of the nearby boats and then jumps from boat to boat. We're still moving slowly, trying to navigate the other boats. He's only one boat away by now. . .

"Pull away!" I yell as Gaspar jumps from the last boat in the row. Our boat moves away just in time to watch Gaspar crash into the edge. He lands in the water but grabs on to the boat, gripping, and tries to swing his legs up on to the deck. I push all my weight against him and shove a hand into his face, pushing him back. We struggle for a few seconds, him trying to climb aboard, me leaning my whole weight against his face. The boat picks up speed, wobbles as we turn towards the lake.

With a final shove I push Gaspar off the boat. By the time he hits the water we're already away.

But we still have a problem. The other two security guys from Chaldexx seem to have found another boat to commandeer. It's pulling out from the mini-harbour and

297

sluicing around towards Gaspar. I gaze down the river towards the lake, trying to think.

The big river cruiser I spotted moments before is turning slowly, just ahead of the road bridge. In fact, if we don't make it to the bridge pretty soon, we're going to have trouble squeezing past the cruiser. Ixchel has seen it too – I can tell by the way she's leaning forward, urging the engine to go faster. But it just won't. Our boat has a top speed of . . . something not very fast.

I can't tear myself away from the front of the boat, staring out over the windshield.

"We've got to go faster. . ." I say, feeling helpless.

"I know, I know, you wanna try?!" Ixchel says, exasperated.

I make myself look back, past Ixchel and towards the second boat. I almost freeze in panic when I see how fast it's moving. I guess they've picked up Gaspar by now. . .

The space between the fat paddle steamer and the road bridge narrows. The steamer doesn't seem to have any problem with taking up all the space on the river and making the smaller boats wait.

"We have to make it to the road bridge!" I yell.

"I know, Josh . . . hold on tight. . ."

Briskly, Ixchel steers the boat, almost toppling me in. We bank hard to the right and then make a headlong rush for the last remaining gap under the road bridge. I can see it getting smaller by the second.

"Keep going!" I urge. The second boat is gaining, no doubt at all.

The last few seconds are pure nervous energy. I'm helpless to do anything about it. Ixchel just stares ahead, her features tense with concentration. We head for the gap, the second boat now less than ten metres behind. I think we might just about make it . . . but will they get through too?

If they do, we've had it.

We spring through the gap with what seems like less than half a metre to spare between us, the boat, and the road bridge. As we pull through, I'm aware of a small crowd of people watching us from the deck of the steam cruiser. They look cross and hugely disapproving, some of them actually shaking fists and wagging fingers at us.

The second boat has decided to abort the attempt – it stalls with a crazy spin, sending a huge wave crashing into the air. Spray rains down on the deck. There's a chorus of outrage from the tourists.

We're clear to the lake. That river cruiser has bought us a few precious minutes. Even as I take out my Ek Naab phone to call Benicio, I can't help fretting.

Will we have enough time?

"Hey, Josh, what's going on?"

Benicio sounds deliberately cool. I'm a bit surprised, given that I might have been dead and everything. His voice changes then, becomes urgent. "Is Ixchel with you?"

"Yeah," I reply, a bit miffed at his reaction. "She's driving the boat. I can hardly hear you cos of the engine. You're gonna have to shout, OK?"

"What?"

I have to bite my lip to stop myself from yelling angrily down the phone. This is a very bad time for Benicio and me not to make ourselves clear.

"We're in Switzerland," I tell him slowly, shouting.

"I know that, Josh, I can track your phone when it's on, remember? You're on Lake Brienz."

"Where?"

"Go to Interlaken," he says. "It's a city behind you."

"We're running away from there!"

"Oh . . . damn."

There's a silence. Ixchel and I look at each other, exasperated.

"What's he saying?" she calls from the back of the boat. I shrug dramatically and then point back from where we came. "He says that's Interlaken."

"Can you stop the boat?" Benicio says. "I can't hear you very well."

"Can't stop!" I yell. "We're being chased! The Sect took us to Chaldexx BioPharmaceuticals."

Benicio goes quiet again. "What are you doing?" I ask, getting annoyed by the silences.

"I'm trying to find a place for us to rendezvous. My ETA in Interlaken is thirty minutes. You're lucky – we knew you were in Europe, so I've been flying around here. Someone must have turned your phone on at some point."

"Benicio," I tell him, now really shouting, "we can't go back to Interlaken! They. Are. After. Us."

"Cool it, buddy; I know. OK. I've got it. You're on a boat, yes? You need to get off the lake and on to the road. Find a car."

"Find a car. . .?" The idea of racing through the mountains sounds pretty cool, but I have to admit I've never handled a car in traffic. . . "Mate, I don't drive!"

"Of course not," he continues smoothly, "but Ixchel can. At the end of the lake is the town of Brienz. Find a car. Take the left fork on the road after Brienz. Keep going to Lake Lucerne. I'll find you, got that?"

"Brienz," I repeat. "Lake Lucerne. Got it."

I close the phone, slip it back into my pocket and look back at Ixchel. For the first time since I rescued her, she smiles at me.

"Is he coming for us, Josh? That's so great – we did it!"

I nod, try to smile and say, "He's coming, all right. But not for a while. We have to keep moving."

Behind us the paddle steamer has well and truly blocked the river under the road bridge. It's too far away to see what's going on, but I imagine there's probably something of a row with Gaspar and his men. The people on that steamer seemed pretty irate at our stunt . . . looked like they were keen to hand out a mighty telling-off.

Under a milky sky, our boat cuts a deep white V into the clear green depths of the lake. Forested mountains on either side of us create a dark, brooding atmosphere. In the distance to the right is a spectacular expanse of high, snowcapped peaks. There's a suggestion of mist on the lake, thickest near the bank to our left. Past the beach I can see a small town: a few stylish old buildings nestled amongst a cluster of log-cabin chalets.

Brienz.

Looking around, Ixchel says, "Josh, this place is beautiful!" She beams at me.

"Stick with me, babe," I tell her. "I'll take you to all the best places."

Wow. I can't believe I actually said that. But it's too late to take it back. I try to look like I'm concentrating on something else, but secretly watch Ixchel for a reaction. She just smiles a bit and says nothing for a while.

"Well, life sure is a lot more interesting when you're around," she eventually says.

I turn away to hide my grin.

She likes me.

Behind us, the paddle steamer has finally cleared enough space to let Gaspar's speedboat through. I brace myself to watch them bursting free and ramping up the chase. But they're nowhere to be seen. I search the lake and river behind the steamer for any sign of them – but they really seem to have gone.

"Have they given up?" Ixchel asks. I guess she can sense that I'm puzzled.

"Can't believe it. . ." I say. "But where are they?"

For now, it looks like smooth sailing all the way to Brienz. Anxiously, I eye the lakeside road, where a steady line of traffic zooms by.

Out here in the middle of the lake, we're not exactly hard to spot. The sooner we get to Brienz, the better.

"Josh," Ixchel begins, "how did you get free?"

I've been wondering when she'd ask that. . . I've realized

that there's a limit to how much I want to tell Ixchel about the Bracelet – for now.

"The Bracelet," I say. "I fixed it, went back in time by ten minutes and freed myself."

She fixes me with an even look. "You did *what*?"

"I fixed the Bracelet. The Crystal Key – the Sect have it! They made it – it's in their labs. I woke up in the bed after the experiment . . . I'd been untied. I picked up the Bracelet, sneaked into the cold room nearby . . . and found the Crystal Key. Then I put the crystal into the Bracelet . . . I went back in time by ten minutes. I freed myself – ten minutes in the past." I pause, realizing that I'm breathless with excitement. "That's when I came to find you."

Ixchel stares at me in wonder. "You worked out how to use the Bracelet?"

I grin. For several seconds Ixchel says nothing, staring out over the water, seeming to concentrate on getting the most out of the speedboat's engine. I'm surprised that she isn't more delighted, but for some reason the news seems to have put Ixchel into a deep think.

"How did you work out how to use it?"

I need to be careful – I'm not ready to talk about what happened in Area 51 with my dad. I don't want Ixchel knowing that I might be Arcadio . . . that's way too complicated. I mean, Arcadio gets together with the young Susannah St John . . . which is too weird for even me to

304

get my head around just now, let alone remind Ixchel about.

But it's tough to keep something this important from her.

Cautiously I say, "I didn't work out anything. I just pressed the crystal into place and . . . bam! There I was."

"There you were," she echoes doubtfully, "ten minutes in the past?" Ixchel lifts her eyes to mine for a long moment and then turns the boat to avoid another boat coming the opposite way. The sudden movement sends a fine drizzle of spray into my face, but I don't wipe it away.

"Well, that's amazing. . ." She stares up at me again. "You travelled in time?"

"I didn't know what was going to happen," I say. At least that part is true. . . "I just wanted to see if the Bracelet could be fixed. But it must have some sort of default mechanism. . ."

"A what?"

"A fail-safe," I suggest. "Maybe to use in emergencies. I guess if you're in danger . . . it's always safe to take you back ten minutes. . ."

"I guess," Ixchel says, but she doesn't sound entirely convinced.

Of course, even safer is to take you to *where* and *when* the Bracelet was last used. I can't imagine how the Bracelet knows where it is – I can only guess that it has some kind of GPS, like a satellite navigation system. Only – with the added power to bend time.

Is there some ancient Erinsi satellite in orbit around the planet? Have I just activated a mechanism that hasn't been used for centuries? Did my dad activate it when he used the bracelet? Or is Itzamna, the original time traveller, still wandering around the space-time continuum, getting up to who knows what?

No use worrying about it now, though, because unless we manage to get to Lake Lucerne before Gaspar and his goons catch up with us . . . we'll end up right back with the Sect.

This time, I imagine they'll be quite forceful about getting information regarding the Bracelet.

I peer towards the distance at the cars streaming along the lakeside road. Gaspar's in one of those cars. And there's not a thing I can do about it.

The town of Brienz rises up ahead, dwarfed beneath a rocky mountain face that drops sheer into the blue-green waters of the lake. Dark-timbered chalets and yellow-and-cream-painted buildings cling to the mountainside, their balconies decorated with baskets of red flowers. A red railcar chugs along a steep slope. There's a promenade at the edge of the lake and beside that a little harbour of water that's crystal clear to the rocky bottom.

"So I've been meaning to ask," Ixchel begins. "What's that writing on your arm?"

I blush. "Nothing."

Ixchel gives me a curious glance. "It's not *nothing*. In fact, I've seen it . . . I just asked to know why. Why did you write your name on your arm, Josh?"

I sigh. There's no easy way out of this. "Because when you use the Bracelet . . . you can lose your memory. Like my dad when we found him on Mount Orizaba. Remember?"

She's silent for a bit. "You really used the Bracelet, then," she muses.

"Said I did, didn't I?"

To that, Ixchel says nothing. As we get closer to the town, a high rustle of tinkling bells carries across the water towards us. It doesn't seem to be coming from the red-roofed church spire . . . this sounds like lots of little bells ringing at random.

Ixchel stands up for a better view. "Now what?"

I take a deep breath. "Well, now, we have to steal a car."

"Steal a car," she says casually. "Is that all?"

I eye Ixchel closely to see if she's kidding – she's good at keeping a straight face.

Ixchel switches off the engine as the boat floats into the harbour. She looks up at me and for a moment, we share an uneasy smile. I try not to think about the stress of what is about to come. Just twenty minutes or so . . . and we'll be meeting Benicio on the banks of Lake Lucerne.

If we manage to steal a car.

If the Swiss cops don't jump on us.

If Gaspar and his men don't catch up.

The way I see it, that's three big *if*s. I'm starting to get a really bad feeling . . . twenty minutes is stretching into a painful length of time.

The side of the boat clunks against the pier. A few bystanders throw us suspicious looks. Two young teenagers on their own in a speedboat may not be your everyday sight for the people of Brienz. Then there's the fact that we don't look very Swiss. Nervously, I help Ixchel tie the rope to the mooring. The bell-tinkling noise is much louder now. I keep looking around to see its source, but so far there's no sign.

An elderly woman pauses as she walks by. She fixes first Ixchel and then me with a glare. Then comes a garble of sharp-tongued German. I don't understand a single word.

"*Französisch?*" Ixchel replies hopefully. If it's possible, the old biddy eyes us even more beadily.

"*Que vous faites?*" she says in a guttural accent.

Ixchel answers her with a stream of perfect-sounding French. I just gape. "How many languages do you speak?" I mutter.

"Languages . . . are what I do. . ." she replies under her breath, still gazing sweetly at the Swiss lady. "You didn't notice?"

Whatever she said to the woman – it worked. She carries on her way and we climb out on to the pier.

"I told her I was parking the boat for my father," Ixchel explains as we scurry towards the main street.

Finally I can see the source of the bell-tinkling. The streets are filled with cattle. Huge, long-haired beasts coated in toffee-coloured fur, with their little cream-skinned calves. Brass bells hang around their necks, swishing back and forth as they walk, led by young cowherds.

I have to catch my breath. All the traffic is stalled – cars paused where they stand as the cattle navigate around them. Pedestrians and drivers look on admiringly at the animals. Some people stop to take photos. The town is at a standstill.

How are we going to get out of here?

Ixchel turns to me. Outwardly she looks calm, but I'm beginning to wonder if it isn't something else: resignation.

In a flat voice, she says, "OK, what now?"

"Don't give up on me, Ixchel," I say softly. "We *are* going back to Ek Naab."

With a tiny shrug, Ixchel turns away. I can sense that she doesn't believe me. My heart sinks. How can I blame her? This is the third time I've tried to rescue Ixchel. The idea that we'll get caught again is an almost choking fear.

I look once more down the cattle-filled street. The cows are processing through the main part of the town and then up a side street. Firmly, I grab Ixchel's hand.

"Let's go."

I probably look a fair bit more confident than I actually feel, striding along the narrow lanes of the lakeside town. Yet it's looking like we might be trapped in Brienz . . . and that's hitting Ixchel pretty hard. I have to do something to cheer her up; something to make escape seem possible.

A moment later we're in one of the side roads and away from the cattle procession. As carefully as possible, we start trying the doors of the parked cars.

All locked.

A woman driving a small white Peugeot car almost knocks us down as we dive across the road. She gets out in a rush, her face flushed with anger, hardly even looking at us as she dives into a nearby door marked "Arztespraxis" – something to do with a doctor's surgery, I'd guess, from the green cross.

Ixchel's eyes follow the woman and then trail back to her car.

"She didn't lock it."

Something tells me that this is our only chance. I dash across the road and test the car door – Ixchel's right, it's open. If the car is an automatic, I've half a mind to insist on driving. One glance dashes that idea. Manual gears – no chance!

But there's also some very good news – the keys are still in the ignition.

"I guess that lady's in a hurry," I say, helping Ixchel into the driver's seat.

I'm just belting up in the passenger seat when the woman reappears.

Ixchel starts the car and swerves out into the road, speeding towards the main street. Behind us, the owner's expression turns into outrage and astonishment. I can hardly believe my eyes as we approach the main street. There are still some cows straggling through; the traffic is still stalled. Ixchel drops the car into a lower gear, makes it mount the wide pavement. Even through the windows I can hear the angry shouts from pedestrians as they leap out of the way.

With all the lunatic driving I've made people do these past few days, it's a wonder I haven't killed anyone. . .

"You're . . . crazy," I say, impressed. "How come you drive so well?"

"Never really driven in traffic before," she replies, eyes fixed to the road. "Only around the ranches above Ek Naab."

One of the stalled cars we pass suddenly roars into action. I turn around to watch as it turns clumsily in the middle of the road, narrowly missing a couple of huge cattle in the process. Then, like us, it mounts the pavement and heads out of town, against the traffic.

Chasing after us.

"It's Gaspar," Ixchel says. I can hear the tension in her voice.

I close my eyes, trying to think. This does not look good. We haven't even made it out of Brienz and we've already got Gaspar and his thugs on our tail. The Swiss police can't be far behind either.

Once we've passed the cattle we join the main road. Luckily there's not much traffic in the out-of-town direction. Ixchel speeds up to a hundred kilometres an hour. I glance behind to see that Gaspar's car – a red Mercedes – has also speeded up.

"You need to go faster," I urge Ixchel.

She hesitates for just a second and then slams her foot down. The engine roars as we approach a hundred and sixty. I have a sudden flashback to being in the car with Camila on Highway 186, just seconds before we crashed. For a brief moment, I can't breathe.

A signpost zooms up ahead – a fork in the road. Before I can open my mouth, we've followed the road round to the right. As we flash by, I notice the word "Luzern" on the sign.

"Erm. . ." I begin, then look over my shoulder. Gaspar's car is approaching the signpost too. In the distance I can hear a siren.

Ixchel says, "What?"

"I think . . . we should have turned left there. . ."

Turn left after Brienz . . . that's what Benicio said. I can't believe I forgot.

In disbelief she says, "Turn left?"

"You didn't see the road sign. . .?" I say mildly. "To Lucerne?"

Ixchel explodes. "No, Josh, I'm the one driving the car . . . didn't you notice?"

There's no way around this. We can't turn around – not with Gaspar and now maybe the police behind us.

There's a slow-moving tractor up ahead, pulling neatly stacked bundles of chopped wood. Our car swings out as we overtake. Ahead, an oncoming car squeals noisily, honking its horn – but Ixchel slots the car back into the carriageway just in time.

I murmur, "Nicely done. . ."

We approach a curve in the road. Ahead the sky fills with towering, snow-capped peaks. I check behind us – no sign of Gaspar. I guess it might take some time for them to get around that tractor.

I take out my Ek Naab phone and try Benicio. But there's no answer.

"Well. . .?"

I swallow. "We may have a problem."

Ixchel resumes her stony silence. We churn through another few kilometres, zooming through a forest of pines. I stare ahead, feeling pretty useless. I can't tell if Ixchel is angry with me, too scared to talk, or just concentrating on driving. All I know is that we need to stick together through this. Ixchel needs to know she can count on me – but I've already messed up.

Maybe I should be the one driving – if I could actually drive – because it looks like I'm useless at navigating. I need to come up with something new, and fast. We're racing headlong towards a wall of mountain, cutting off any easy way to escape. Any minute now Gaspar is going to overtake the tractor. In that big Mercedes, it won't take them long to catch up.

There has to be a solution. One glance at Ixchel is enough to tell me that she's using up everything she has just keeping this car on the crazy mountain roads. It's going to have to come from me.

I don't know where this road plans on taking us, because we're running out of ground. A sign up ahead reads "Sustenpass".

Softly I say, "A mountain pass."

"There's nowhere else to go," Ixchel says, "except up."

In the rock face that looms above, I catch glimpses of cars moving sluggishly, zigzagging back and forth. They're practically in slow motion.

"Oh no," Ixchel breathes. "We really are in trouble now."

So far there's still no sign of Gaspar's car. That tractor must have held back quite a tail of traffic because for a long way behind us there's no sign of a car.

We slow down, approaching a hairpin bend.

"Don't brake on the turn," I suggest. "Or we'll skid. And accelerate as soon as you're straightening. . ."

Ixchel shoots me a questioning look. "Thought you couldn't drive."

"I know the theory," I say.

"Sure, and I'm the one behind the wheel."

I flush. "Just trying to be helpful."

Ixchel says nothing. She's gripping the steering wheel so tightly that her knuckles have gone white. She takes the first few hairpins so slowly that I'm starting to get nervous. At this rate Gaspar won't have much trouble catching us.

To take my mind off it, I try calling Benicio again. Still nothing.

Surely he's close to Lake Lucerne now? Why isn't he phoning me?

I put a hand on Ixchel's shoulder. "You're doing really well."

The encouragement seems to work, because she takes the next bend a bit faster. And the next two. In fact, by the fourth, my stomach is starting to lurch. Then I make the mistake of looking over the edge of the road.

It's a sheer drop of several hundred metres.

"Don't look down," I warn Ixchel.

"Think I'm mad? I'm looking right ahead . . . and nowhere else!"

My hand moves to my mouth, hiding a smile. Ixchel is even cute when she's scared.

At the next bend I look down again. That's when I see the red Mercedes. Gaspar and his men are only two bends away from us.

"OK. . ." I tell her. "I want you to stay calm. . ."

But there's an unmistakable edge of panic to her reply. "Gaspar?"

"Yeah. Just keep driving. You're doing brilliantly."

"Josh. . ."

"Yeah?"

"Look at the petrol level. . ."

I follow Ixchel's paralysed stare. The arrow is in the red zone. We're almost out of petrol.

"Oh, you have got to be joking. . ."

I gaze back over the road. We're most of the way up the mountain face, overlooking a forested valley cradled by mountain peaks. At this altitude there's snow piled high at the edge of the road in stacks as tall as me. The temperature outside drops. The car windows begin to mist.

Perilous mountain roads, an inexperienced driver, low on petrol and now we're having trouble seeing through the windows. . .

At that moment my Ek Naab phone rings. I almost leap out of my seat.

Benicio shouts down the phone, "Where the hell are you?"

"We're on the Sustenpass. . ."

"I know that! What are you doing there? I can't land in these mountains."

"We're almost out of petrol, Benicio. The guys chasing us have almost caught up."

Benicio swears quietly a few times. Exasperated, he says, "What do you expect me to say? Keep going as far as you can. I'm getting a good lock on your location . . . I'll stay close. At the top of the pass there's a small lake at the base of a glacier . . . if you can make it that far, I can land around there."

"OK . . . what if we don't. . .?"

He's silent for a second. "Keep going. I'll call you when you're close to the lake."

But as I snap the phone shut, it's already too late.

The red Mercedes has just pulled around the last bend in the road. It bears down on us until I can see Gaspar's eyes in the mirror. He looks triumphant, winks and gives us a little mock-salute.

Then their car rams ours from behind. We skid slightly; Ixchel pushes harder on the accelerator. They speed up, catch us at the next bend and slam hard into the rear right flank. Our car goes into a tailspin. Looks like we'll twist too far to make the turn.

I shout, "Hit the accelerator – not the brake." The car straightens just in time.

My phone rings again. "There's a place I can land up ahead!" Benicio yells. "The next hairpin bend, there's a little place for stopping. I'll be waiting!"

We hit the first long stretch of straight road, thickly lined with snow and deep-green pines.

"Put your foot right down," I urge.

"I'll kill us both!"

But when the Mercedes creeps up behind us again, she doesn't think twice. Even so, they match our speed and then pull out to overtake.

"Don't let them overtake! We have to get to the rendezvous with Benicio!"

There's nothing to be done. Gaspar's car is already drawing level in the opposite carriageway. It starts to snow: a drizzle of thick, wet flakes. I flip the windscreen wipers into action.

Ahead, a lorry trundles around the corner, heading towards our position. For a second the Mercedes pulls even further ahead, daring to go for the overtake. Ixchel screams as the lorry hurtles straight at Gaspar's car.

"Don't let them in!" I shout, grabbing hold of the wheel.

At the last second, Gaspar chickens out. The Merc's brakes squeal as it drops back in line behind us. The lorry whizzes by close enough for us to feel the rumble of its wheels. As soon as the lorry has passed, Ixchel swings our car out to block the Merc overtaking. I check the petrol level. It's right at the bottom.

Our car, the Merc and the lorry: we all shoot past the

stopping place. I guess not one of us gives a second glance to the Muwan parked there. . .

Ixchel wails in despair. "Josh . . . what are we gonna do?"

"Don't let them overtake, Ixchel, keep driving . . . let me think. . ."

After the next bend, the terrain changes. The road clings to the edge of a slope, drops off steeply to a forested valley on the right. There are hardly any trees up here, just snow-coated scrub. The snow falls more thickly. Heavy mist hovers over the road ahead. To the right we can finally see across the valley from which mountains rise. They dominate the entire field of vision now, rising like an apparition out of the clouds: snow-smoothed peaks over ashen rock.

I check the petrol gauge. It's practically empty. We're running on vapour.

In the distance, I spot a pool of milky-green water. Behind it there's a long trail of grey ice flowing from somewhere high. It must be the lake and glacier Benicio mentioned . . . but I can't see a way down to it.

Our car enters a cloud slung low across the valley. We're enveloped in grey, damp mist so thick that we can't see more than a few metres ahead. Ixchel slams on the brakes. The Merc finally shoots ahead of us.

Then she groans, "Oh no. . ." We're almost at a standstill. Ixchel pumps away at the accelerator, but nothing happens.

"We're out of gas!"

Through the mist, I can just make out that the Merc has pulled off to the side of the road.

"We have to get the car off the road, Josh . . . or someone will crash into us. . ."

Eyes glazed, we both stare ahead at Gaspar's car. One of their doors opens; a shadow appears at the side of the Merc as someone climbs out.

Our car comes to a halt. I look across at Ixchel. Her hands are still gripping the wheel. Violently, she begins to shake, her teeth chattering.

I put a hand on hers. Her muscles are locked rigid.

Gently, I say, "Ixchel . . . let go . . . we need to get out of the car."

Actually, we need to run for it. I have no idea where. We're almost out of options.

The grey figure of Gaspar walks through the mist towards us, slowly. From behind us there's another sound – a third car enters the cloud. It speeds just beyond our car and screeches to a halt.

The cops.

Two uniformed policemen spring out of their car, making a beeline for us.

I unwrap Ixchel's fingers from the wheel and squeeze her hand.

"It's OK, Ixchel . . . we're safer with the police than with the Sect. . ."

She can't stop trembling. The stress of the car chase has finally slammed into her. Ahead, Gaspar has stopped moving.

Both doors are yanked open. One of the cops starts shouting at us in German.

"I think they want us to get out. . ." I whisper. Ixchel nods slowly, still shaking. "Come on, Ixchel," I tell her. "It's gonna be OK now . . . we'll just let them arrest us. . ."

We're both about to step out of the car when from the direction of Gaspar's car there's a muffled, almost squeaky sound – a shot being fired. The cop at my side of the car slumps to the ground, stone-cold dead.

Lightning-fast, the second cop ducks behind our car. A second later he pops up again. This time he fires a round into the fog. It's followed up by a barrage of bullets in our direction. Some of them hit the car, shattering the rear windscreen, bursting a tyre.

Ixchel and I cower in our seats, bent double, clutching our heads.

My Ek Naab phone rings. My own hand trembles slightly as I answer it. The gun battle isn't letting up. A bullet explodes into the back of my car seat – I almost jump out of my skin.

"You have to get out of there!" Benicio's voice screams against my ear.

"Oh, ya think?" I reply. "*Where are you?*"

"I'm right next to you, buddy, I'm right here. I'm hovering under the road, at the edge of the mountain."

I gasp. "Hovering. . .? What do you expect us to do?"

"Jump," he says firmly. "Move in a straight line from your car to the edge of the road. Jump off. I will catch you."

In this fog, there's no way I can check whether Benicio is right or not.

"Benicio is here. We have to run for it," I tell Ixchel. "Get over to this side . . . we need to crawl out together."

Ixchel hesitates for a second, then slides across my knee. We both squirm around until we're both lying across the front two seats with both our heads next to the passenger door. We're completely squashed together, but thankfully Ixchel doesn't seem too bothered by that.

Of course I'm not bothered about it either, not one bit. . .

I raise my hands above my head, getting ready to push on the door.

Right then, the front windscreen shatters. Crumbled glass rains down over us, scatters across the floor of the car.

My eyes meet Ixchel's. "It's gonna be OK. . ." I murmur. "On the count of three, crawl out, stay low, get to the edge of the road. You'll see Benicio there. He'll catch you."

Silently, she nods.

"One . . . two. . ." I push the door open, hard. "Three!"

We both drop to the ground, slithering out of the car on

our bellies. The edge of the road is only a metre or so away – and we have the shelter of the car.

We crawl within centimetres of the dead body of the first policeman. I almost throw up when I see what the bullet did to his head. He's dead because of us – because he chased a stolen car.

The soggy air is filled with the sound of gunfire. One person has died because of us . . . and the second one has no hope against Gaspar's men. We have to do something to help this guy. I can't leave this place with two innocent deaths on my conscience.

We crawl under the railing that lines the edge of the road. The lights of the Muwan greet us, glowing white and blue behind the mist, hovering about three metres below the road.

Benicio – he really is here.

The cockpit opens and Benicio stands up. He's less than two metres away from the edge of the road. I can't quite make out his face, but I can see him stretching out both arms.

He calls, "I'll catch you. . ."

I nudge Ixchel forward. "You go first. Jump out as far as you can, and put your arms out so that he can grab you."

We look at each other one more time. With one smooth movement Ixchel gets to her feet and leaps off the edge of the slope, arms outstretched . . . flying. The Muwan dips slightly when she lands smack-dab in Benicio's arms. I hear her relief as she tumbles into the passenger compartment.

Behind me the gunfire is relentless. Abruptly, the cop stops shooting. Gaspar's men yell something . . . I hear them rushing forward, towards the edge of the road.

They start shooting on the Muwan.

"Give up, Josh," calls Gaspar, his voice coming from somewhere close. I'd guess he's just behind the car. "Hand yourself over, boy. How many people have to die?"

I watch in dismay as the Muwan drops out of sight under the cloud. When I look around again, Gaspar is right next to me. He gives me a smug grin.

"OK, Josh. Game over."

Before I can budge, Gaspar grabs hold of my left wrist
and twists it hard, into an armlock. I'm opening my
mouth to gasp when he pulls me against him fiercely,
wrenching my arm even further. An agonized yell leaves
my throat.

He pushes me down to my knees, presses his foot against
the back of my neck. Slowly, he forces me to bend all the
way to the floor.

"I could snap your neck right now, you know that, don't
you?"

My eyes water from the pain. I just nod.

"I'm not going to end up like Simon and that girl,
Ollie . . . doing only the stupidest jobs. After all their
training! No. The minute they put me in charge of hunting
you down, boy, I told them: no problem. OK? With Gaspar
on the case, you got a deal. You cannot fight me, boy, I will
always win. Hear me?"

I nod again, my face stinging as he pushes me harder against the gravel.

He shouts, "You got that, Josh Garcia?"

"Yes!" I groan in reply, voice muffled.

"You're gonna work for us now. You're a miracle of science, you know that? A walking Nobel Prize for DiCanio. You should feel honoured!"

"What did she do to me?" I manage to ask.

He repeats, "What did she do. . .? Man, what *didn't* she do? The whole nine yards. You've got it all, kid. You're wayyyy too valuable to lose now."

Behind us there's a sudden crunching sound – a body rolling on the ground. Then a single gunshot, then a scream of pure agony. Loud, uninterrupted groaning follows – I get a terrifying vision of pain. Gaspar turns away for a second, evidently shocked by what he's just heard.

Sounds like someone is dying. But is it Gaspar's man? Or the cop?

Gaspar loosens his grip just enough for me to get some wriggle room. In another second I'm out of the armlock, attempting a dodge roll. His attention returns with laser-like focus. He sweeps a foot into my ribs – it's like being kicked by a horse. I'm so winded that I can only lie motionless, gasping like a fish tossed on to the deck.

There's another gunshot; the bullet whizzes past above Gaspar, who stops moving. I tilt my head slightly for a better view. Like a ghost emerging from behind a veil of gauze, the figure of the second Swiss policeman appears. He holds his arm rigid, straight, the gun and he merging into one shadowy killing machine. In the distance, the groans subside, replaced by an occasional pitiful whimper.

"In my country," the cop begins in halting, heavily accented English, "we do not tolerate child killers."

I whisper a prayer of thanks. Gaspar says nothing.

"Move away from the boy," says the cop.

Gaspar hesitates, then takes one step away from me. I finally manage to catch my breath and suck in a few freezing-cold gulps.

The grey shadow-cop waves his gun slightly. "Further away."

Gaspar takes two more steps away from me. I struggle to my feet, still slightly unsteady. Gaspar and the cop stare at each other for a few seconds.

"Take out your gun," the cop orders, "and throw it to the ground, over here."

"I'm no child killer," Gaspar says slowly. "The boy is a runaway. Look what he did – he stole a car."

"You killed a police officer. My partner. This we also do not tolerate."

"It was an accident. If I wanted the boy dead," says Gaspar, "he would be."

But still Gaspar won't obey.

I can hear the policeman's breathing quicken. He takes aim and points the gun straight at Gaspar's head. "Boy . . . get behind me."

I shuffle around until I'm behind the cop. Another groan from Gaspar's man shatters the silence.

"Your friend is going to bleed to death," the cop tells Gaspar. "I shot him in the belly – not a nice death. Throw down your gun and I'll handcuff you; we'll take your friend to the hospital. Maybe he'll live. As for your other pal. . . A life for a life."

Gaspar doesn't move.

In my pocket, the Ek Naab phone buzzes.

"If you answer that phone," Gaspar seethes at me, "I'll kill this cop."

The policeman bristles. "Silence!"

I breathe quietly through my mouth. This cop has no idea how fast Gaspar can move. He might get one shot off before Gaspar's on top of him. Or Gaspar will throw himself into a wild, unpredictable capoeira move.

One thing is for sure: the longer these two blokes keep staring each other down, the less I can believe that the cop is ever going to shoot Gaspar.

Chances are, Gaspar senses it too.

My decision's made. I bolt away, back towards the cars. The cop's gun goes off and then I hear two voices, yelling. I keep running hard along the mountain road, past the cars, further into the thick cloud. I can't see anything now but mist; mist and the solid line of tarmac beneath my feet. I'm running full pelt, the sounds of my footsteps squelched in the damp air, blood thundering in my ears, no sound but my own heartbeat.

Against my thigh, the Ek Naab phone buzzes again. I feel like yelling with rage at Benicio – *I'm a bit busy now, think you could call back later?!*

Through a haze of adrenaline, I become aware of a sound behind me.

Footsteps, hard and swift, twice as rapid as mine. They're chasing me, coming closer. It can't be long now; any second. Fear surges within; I squeeze a last effort from my legs.

Then, to my right, there's a mist-muffled voice.

"Josh! Jump! I'm right with you, buddy . . . got a lock . . . just jump . . . I'll catch you."

Run off the edge off the mountain – without even looking first? The idea fills me with terror. I keep running. Even to change direction would be too risky now. Gaspar is mere steps behind me – I'd run right into his grasp.

"You're coming to a bend in the road, Josh," Benicio calls. "Keep going! Jump! Jump right out!"

I put my head down for a final spurt. Without warning, I burst free of the cloud. Sunlight explodes around me. I can see everything – the road, the valley, the mountains. The sheer drop to the bottom of the valley.

Hovering in mid-air, just beyond the road, is Benicio's Muwan.

Immediately before I hurl myself at the road's fence I hear Benicio shouting, "Josh . . . trust me!"

I grab the fence with both hands and spring off into a handstand flip. The valley spins around me as I turn in the air. I fly across the divide, the Muwan directly below.

The cockpit is open, but I don't quite make it. With a thud I land just short of the opening, clutching at the edge of the cockpit, scrabbling for a firm hold. For a few breathless seconds I hang one-handed over the edge. With a gasp, I swing my other arm over and grab hold with both hands. When I gaze up, it's straight into Ixchel's eyes. For once, they're filled with admiration.

"You did it, Josh. . ."

Benicio lowers the craft all the way to the floor of the valley. I relax my grip and crumple to the ground. From the front of the Muwan, Benicio's triumphant voice yells, "Nice flying, Batman!"

All the fear and tension vanishes, replaced by a surge of euphoria. We made it. Me, Tyler, Mum, Ixchel – we all escaped the Sect.

About fifty metres above I catch sight of Gaspar leaning over the edge of the road. He stares down in disbelief. I grin and give him a little wave.

Hasta la vista, baby.

BLOG ENTRY: SLEEPING IN A CITY THAT NEVER WAKES UP

Well, turns out that I'm not done with the blog. I'm back where I started, with a whole bunch of things I can't talk to anyone about.

Most of the way flying back to Ek Naab, I was semi-sleeping. I was thinking; couldn't stop. More than anything I wanted to talk to Ixchel.

What is it about that girl that makes me want to tell her just *everything?* Yet every time I open my mouth to speak about anything really serious, I choke on it.

Benicio being up in the front of the Muwan didn't make things any easier. He doesn't know about the Bracelet, so that topic is out of bounds. Luckily he didn't seem to notice my dad's writing on my arm. More than once, I caught Ixchel staring at it.

Was she wondering if it's my handwriting?

So much happened in the last couple of days, it's one big jumble in my head. The dream-visit from Camila, the genetic treatment they did on me, finding the Crystal Key, fixing the Bracelet. Meeting my dad again in Area 51. Having the power to travel through time.

Tyler and Ixchel kept making me explain what had happened in the Chaldexx labs, how I went back ten minutes in time and rescued myself. It's almost as if they sensed I wasn't telling them the whole truth.

"I just don't get how that thing works," Tyler concluded. "Why does it take you ten minutes into your own past as a safety setting? Isn't that just gonna send you right back into the same problem? And how come when your dad used the Bracelet he wound up on that volcano? It doesn't add up. . ."

Well, I agreed with him, of course! What else could I do?

Tyler was also a bit bemused about the idea of two versions of me in the same place.

"You saw yourself on that bed? You rescued yourself?"

I told him I did.

"What happened to that other you, the one you woke up?"

"He's me, don't you get it? I'd already been him. I woke up, went to the cold room, found the Crystal Key, fixed the Bracelet and . . . bam! I travelled back in time. All that happened was that I got to see myself from another viewpoint. I went back on myself and then caught up."

I even drew a loop in the air with a finger, explained all about the time-loop thingy, just like Dad explained it to me.

Tyler still seemed a bit doubtful. "Seems to me that's got to happen quite a bit, with the time travelling. How do you know it hasn't already happened? Maybe you've already met your future self – you know, yourself, but, like, older."

At which point I started to think about Arcadio again. In case Ixchel started to wonder about Arcadio too, I changed the subject.

Anyway. There may well be bad news waiting for me. Lorena and Montoyo are eager to find out what genetic changes the Sect introduced into my DNA.

It's kind of worrying . . . to say the least.

Benicio told me right away that Tyler had been rushed back into

334

surgery when he got him back from Brazil. His wound had opened up again. All that fighting had made it worse. By the time Tyler reached Ek Naab, they even had to give him a blood transfusion.

Mum was fine – scared out of her wits about me and Ixchel, of course. If I was a better son I'd probably worry more about putting Mum through all this stress.

It's not as if I go looking for trouble. I just want a quiet life.

Is that too much to ask?

Maybe I'll enjoy life in Ek Naab, after all. From what I've seen, it's pretty darn quiet.

I'm writing my blog on a brand new laptop in my own room in my very own new apartment in Ek Naab. Tyler lies resting. I insisted on getting a bed. Hammocks are all well and good, but sometimes you need a proper bed.

There's a polite little knock on the open door. It's Montoyo. I turn around and meet his eyes. There's a half-smile there, but he's looking solemn.

"Josh," he says with a nod. "It's time."

I snap the laptop shut, follow him out of the apartment and into the street. Trying not to give away how nervous I am. I don't like blood tests at the best of times, so yesterday's session with Lorena wasn't much fun.

Today I get the results.

Today I find out what Melissa DiCanio really did to me. Apart from changing the colour of my eyes to blue . . . which I wouldn't mind, except that the one person I want to like the new colour is Ixchel. She doesn't seem that pleased.

"What were you writing in your blog?" Montoyo begins. "Your deepest, darkest thoughts?"

I try to chuckle. "Something like that."

"Ha! I wish we'd had blogging when I was a youngster. I think I'd have enjoyed having a secret diary."

"What stopped you?" I ask. "I mean, you had pen and ink, right? Or would that be a quill and parchment?"

Montoyo looks slightly irritated for a second. "Sure, I could have written a journal. I just always seemed to have other things to do. Scribbling away in a book . . . would have seemed kind of . . ."

". . . girly?" I offer with a grin. "I kind of felt that way too."

Montoyo laughs and shakes his head. "Not at all! I was going to say . . . earnest, serious. Very, very serious."

"That sounds like you, all right."

"Earnest and serious?" He seems surprised. "Not when I was a young man, believe me."

I look up at him. "What changed you?"

He turns away, shrugging. "So many things happen at your age. Don't you find?"

"Well, to me, yeah. . ." I say. "But all I want is a quiet life."

Montoyo guffaws. "Absolutely not true! It's as I told you, Josh; for men like us, happiness comes at a cost. We're only truly happy when we're living life at the edge."

"Not me," I say, objecting. "I've got the soul of a poet, man!"

Montoyo laughs even harder. I'm enjoying myself now, despite my anxiety. I decide to take it further. "I could have been another Alex Turner! But instead I have to go on all these crazy missions for you. . ."

"Who's Alex Turner?"

I can tell he's being serious. Well, OK. Even my mum might not know.

"Only the coolest guy on the planet. He's a singer – a rock star."

Montoyo arches an eyebrow. "A singer? I'm sure he's making a tremendous contribution," he says. "But he's gonna have to leave the important work to people like you and me." Then he frowns. "Anyhow, when have I ever sent you on a mission? As I recall, I forbade you from getting involved in rescuing your mother and Ixchel. Or have you forgotten?"

I haven't forgotten. Remembering how protective Montoyo was of me, I'm suddenly uncomfortable about deceiving him. The Bracelet is back in my bedroom, safely stashed in my luggage amongst my clothes.

"You sent me after the Bracelet," I tell him in a quiet voice.

He gives a dramatic sigh. "Ah, yes . . . the Bracelet of Itzamna. Since you raise the subject, Josh, I was thinking that we should have a conversation about that."

He stops, turns to face me. In that instant I see it.

He knows.

I pause, then try to continue walking. Montoyo grabs hold of my arm. Staring deep into my eyes, he twists my arm so that the inside wrist faces upwards. I've showered since arriving from Switzerland, but my dad's handwriting is still there – faintly.

"You wrote this," Montoyo says, his eyes boring into mine. "You wrote this because you used the Bracelet."

Hotly I reply, "I *so* did not!"

"I met a man once," Montoyo says, his expression now deadly serious, "with a tattoo on his forearm – the exact same place. Can you imagine what that tattoo said?"

I shake my head nervously. There's something about his tone that I don't like.

Montoyo's grip on my wrist tightens. "It said *Incidents II JLS 195*."

I struggle to return his gaze. A tattoo like that – it can only mean one thing. It's a reference to that book by John Lloyd Stephens. To *that* page of *that* book – the one with the coded message, the formula of the Crystal Key.

I can only think of one person who might tattoo that on to his arm.

Which means that Montoyo has met Arcadio.

I whisper. "Where did you meet him? When?"

But Montoyo brushes off my questions. "Surely the real question is *who is he*?"

I breathe, "Arcadio. . .?"

"Precisely. Blue-eyed Arcadio Garcia, the forgetful time traveller. Now here you are . . . mysteriously, *miraculously* escaped from the clutches of our deadliest enemy, your eyes blue, your name inscribed on your arm . . . *in case using the Bracelet makes you forget.*"

He continues, and I'm almost pinned to the spot under the intensity of his gaze. "A strange thing to have tattooed on one's arm, wouldn't you agree? I thought as much back then when I met him. Imagine my surprise to find Arcadio's name in a book with the title *Incidents of Travel in Yucatan, Chiapas and Central America* by a Mr John Lloyd Stephens."

He's right; it's a strange thing to have tattooed. Montoyo's not the first person to have that idea. It's like I said to Tyler about Arcadio: why didn't he tattoo the formula on to his body like that guy in *Memento*?

Well, maybe he did.

Montoyo and I stare at each other in silence. Citizens of Ek Naab stroll by, giving us a wide berth. Everyone knows who we are. Everyone would love to listen in, I'll bet. But nobody, nobody dares to give away the tiniest hint of curiosity.

He walks away a few paces, sits down on a bench next to a small fountain. I listen to the water gurgle up and splash over the blue ceramic tiles. His shoulders slump slightly; he's exhausted from a long day's work. "You have to give me the Bracelet, Josh," Montoyo says, a tad sharply. "Time travel is not a thing to be trifled with."

He's right, I know. I haven't forgotten that my dad tried to make me promise never to use the Bracelet again. But I don't want to accept it.

"If I'm Arcadio," I say quickly, licking my lips, "then it stands to reason – I keep the Bracelet. Don't I? One day in the future, I must figure out how to use it. And then I use it to travel in time. So I can't give it to you," I tell him, warming to my argument. "Or that would change the timeline. Wouldn't it?"

Montoyo laughs again, this time cynically. "A nice try! But Josh, see it from my point of view: you think I can leave a teenage boy running around with the power to change time itself?"

I ask him flat out: "Am I Arcadio?"

Montoyo shrugs. "Maybe."

"Do I look like him?"

He studies my face closely for a long time. "The truth is, I don't know." He sounds sincere. "It was a long time ago. I didn't exactly take a photograph."

I remember how Susannah St John once told me that Arcadio didn't like to have his photo taken. Was he trying to avoid leaving evidence – a hostage to fortune?

I say, "How can I find out?"

"We can ask Blanco Vigores."

"Vigores?"

"He found the Bracelet of Itzamna, Josh. He knows more

about it than anyone," Montoyo says with a sigh. "Don't pretend you don't know that."

"If Vigores tells us I can keep the Bracelet," I say, thinking rapidly, "will you let me keep it?"

Montoyo hesitates. "If you give me the Bracelet today," he says, "then you have my word: when we talk to Vigores, he can decide who keeps it; you or me."

"What if he wants it for himself?"

Montoyo shrugs. "He has the authority to do that. You and I, we had a deal. Remember?"

"That's right," I say with a touch of sarcasm. "My secret mission for you."

"I'll owe you, Josh. Don't dismiss it out of hand – many in Ek Naab would enjoy having me in their debt."

I know immediately the "favour" I want to ask Montoyo.

Stay away from my mother.

BLOG ENTRY: BLUE-EYED BOY

Mum was the first person to meet me when we arrived in Ek Naab from Switzerland.

The minute she saw me, she burst into tears. Later she said it was because of my eyes.

"The day you were born, Josh, the first thing I noticed about you was your eyes. Dark brown, just like your father's. That's rare, you know? Babies are usually born with blue-grey eyes. Yours were brown, from the very first minute."

I just stood there, blinking. It was hard to believe what she seemed to be saying. She gave birth to a brown-eyed boy. Now they're blue.

I remember how my voice shook when I told her, "Mum, it's still me."

But is it? Deep down I've got a nagging suspicion that the Sect have changed something important about me; something that will make sure that whoever I am from now on, it's not Josh Garcia.

At least, not quite.

Mum was already with Lorena when Montoyo and I rolled up at her office. It was just getting dark outside and the lights from the Tec poured over the quadrangle in the middle of the building. I stared through the window, watching the students – some of them the same age as me. They shuffled around, laughing and talking. I got a little stab of pain in my chest when I remembered mucking about in my own school, hanging out with Emmy, chasing classmates through the circular cloister.

I'll never go back there. That life is over for me now. Looking down at those Ek Naab teenagers, I knew instantly that I'll never fit in.

Not properly. The Bakab thing will always keep me apart.

I noticed Montoyo looking at me. He flashed me a quick grin, as if to say "hang in there". Then he took my mother's hand and squeezed it. Mum's cheeks flushed a little.

For a second or two I couldn't tear my eyes away from their linked hands. I felt pretty uncomfortable. I thought about my father in that Area 51 cell. It didn't matter to me that it really happened months

343

ago, or that he'd died since then.

Lorena sat down. She smiled at me, then at my mother. You didn't need to be psychic to see that they were both nervous. It took all my self-control not to start shaking. I dragged down a couple of long breaths and held them there, releasing the air slowly through my mouth. Just the way they showed us in capoeira.

Lorena cleared her throat. "From what I can tell, Josh, the news is good."

My mother began to sob with relief. I leaned over to hug her. Montoyo watched us, his expression unreadable.

I closed my eyes so that I didn't have to look at him.

Tyler, Ixchel and Benicio are hanging around in the lobby of the Tec. When we come down the stairs from Lorena's office, they turn anxiously.

I break into a grin. All three of them rush forward, Tyler and Ixchel hugging me at the same time.

"You're all right?" Tyler asks, breathless.

"Probably," I tell him.

"So, what did they do to you?"

I take a deep breath. "I've got all four Bakab genes now; not just the Ix gene, but the other three too."

Ixchel and Benicio are wide-eyed with amazement. "You have the abilities of all four Bakabs. . .?"

I nod. "Yep."

Benicio frowns. "Kind of worrying, that the Sect can do that."

"The good bit is that they don't know for a fact that it worked. They didn't do any tests after I woke up. So hopefully they'll still have to test it on someone else."

Benicio shrugs. "Still . . . it's only a matter of time."

I'm actually pretty cross at his attitude. Sure, it's not great news all round – but at least I'm not being turned into some genetic monster super-warrior. . .

Ixchel gestures at my eyes. "And the eye colour? Do they have some Aryan fantasy of repopulating the world with blue-eyed specimens?"

"Some *what*?"

"Like Hitler," she says.

I dart a look at Ixchel to see if she's joking. I guess she really doesn't like my eyes like this . . . and I'm starting to wonder why.

"Lorena reckons it was the 'positive control'," I tell them. "The Sect used their genetic technology to change my eye colour – an obvious change that they could see. If that worked, if that was 'positive', then there would be a good chance that the other genetic changes also worked."

"So you're a four-times Bakab now," Benicio says. "Hmm, wonder what the other Bakabs will feel about that?"

I don't mention the other change that Lorena spoke about. That's something that I still have to come to terms with, something that Lorena's going to be working on.

"They put something else into you too, Josh," Lorena told me, back in her office. "A gene which makes the Key peptide."

"The Key . . . you don't mean. . .?"

"The substance which makes up the Crystal Key . . . yes. It can be produced by your own cells now. And isolated from your blood."

I have the Key inside me. It's just like Arcadio wrote in those postcard messages.

WHAT.KEY.HOLDS.BLOOD.

Arcadio knew. I feel sick just thinking about it. Something else he knows about my future.

"Why?"

Lorena shook her head. "I have no idea. Aside from activating the Adaptor in the Revival Chamber, we don't know what the Key does."

"But you can find out, right?"

Lorena smiled then, quite gently, first at my mother, then at me. "Sure, Josh. Finding things out – that's my speciality."

Montoyo and my mother follow me down the stairs. Benicio and Ixchel still appear shaken by the news about the genetic changes that DiCanio and the Sect have made to my DNA. In fact, they've gone fairly quiet.

It's not the first time I've had to face up to the fact that something I did has helped the Sect.

At least I made it back to Ek Naab. More importantly, so did Mum, Tyler and Ixchel. So long as we're all together, I feel as if I can tackle any problem.

Tyler draws a breath. "The Sect have a leg up now, no

doubt. But you're back alive, innit? That's what really matters."

For a second or two I can't speak; then I nod a couple of times and say, "Thanks, Ty."

As he passes me, Montoyo taps my shoulder.

"Josh. We need to speak."

He motions me outside the lobby and past the huddle of students crowding the front of the building. There's a consistency to the air that's unusual in Ek Naab. It feels almost powdery. I glance upwards and realize that above the surface, it's raining. But this rain stops at the ceiling mesh. Only a very fine mist descends, almost imperceptible.

"It stops the rain. . ."

Montoyo nods. "Things are different here. But you'll adapt." His expression becomes sterner. "Now, let's get this done. The Bracelet of Itzamna – you're going to give it to me for safe keeping."

It's a struggle to hide my resentment. "OK. It's at our apartment. But what about Vigores? You said we'd talk to him. . ."

"Yes, Vigores. I've been trying to get in touch with him. No luck. His assistant says he left a few days ago."

"Left . . . for where?"

"He had business outside the city. That's not unusual for Vigores. He travelled widely in his youth – he still has many friends in Mexico."

"He does. . .?" For a few seconds I just stand in silence,

348

gazing at the ground. Slowly it's dawning on me how little I know about the daily lives of any of the people who have so much influence over me.

What do Montoyo and Vigores *do*; what were their childhoods like? Did they ever have normal jobs? Girlfriends, wives? Any kids? Montoyo seems to be forever on the go: putting in appearances in the Yucatan University in Merida where he's supposed to be a lecturer, fixing financial deals for all the technology in Ek Naab. Vigores lives in his mysterious apartment in the middle of an underground labyrinth and famously disappears for weeks at a time.

One thing is for sure – the members of the ruling Executive of Ek Naab, like Montoyo, Vigores and Lorena, seem to have way more freedom than other citizens.

Or maybe that's just my impression? After all, Ixchel was allowed to run off to live as a maid and waitress in Veracruz – when she was only fourteen. More freedom than any fourteen-year-old I know would be given. I wonder then if it's something to do with the fact that she lost her mother so young. She never told me the details of that. But I'm willing to bet Benicio knows all about it – another advantage he has over me. I stare over Montoyo's shoulder, watching Ixchel through the glass. She and Benicio still seem tense.

I need to learn more about these people.

"Can you help me to get to know people here?" I say suddenly. Montoyo peers at me. He looks more surprised by the minute.

"Anything I can do, Josh, of course."

"People my own age," I tell him firmly. "I want to meet them first. If I'm going to stay here, I need some friends. More people like Ixchel and Benicio."

Montoyo nods, but now looks a little wary. "OK. Yes, I can see that. All right; why don't you have a party?"

I consider this. "Like, a house-warming party?"

"Yes, Josh. Exactly like that."

"I guess . . . it could be cool."

BLOG ENTRY: BLINDED BY NOSTALGIA

Tyler asked me, "So you still keeping up with your blog?" And I replied, "As if. . ."

There's no point having a blog that people you know are going to read. Where's the fun in that? If your friends – or your enemies – are reading it, you can't be truthful.

Since there's not a person alive I can be truthful with, I'll have to stick with the secret blog.

Tyler and Mum help me to get the apartment ready. Mum
buys paintings from the market, and vanilla-scented candles.
We make the living room feel really inviting. Tyler and I make
fruit punch and Benicio slips us a bottle of tequila to give it
some oomph. The baker delivers hot *empanadas* – tasty little
cheese, pork, and chicken pasties.

I plug in my dad's iPod and select some jazz. Tyler
wrinkles his nose. "You're kidding, yeah? It's like
Summertown Starbucks in here. . ."

Well, why not? I could do with a reminder of home. It's
sad to think of someone else living in our house. At least
Mum is only renting it out. I'd like to think I could go back
there, one day.

As we're waiting for the guests to arrive, Tyler says, "You
didn't tell us everything about the Bracelet, did you?" I try to
avoid his eye but he just grins. "It's all right, man; you don't
need to tell me the details. Me, I reckon you used it to go

back in time, further than ten minutes and not just to rescue yourself from that hospital bed. You'd never let Montoyo have the Bracelet . . . not unless you'd already done what you wanted. Unless you'd found your *zero moment*."

I point out that Montoyo didn't exactly ask – he basically laid down the law. That I didn't know how to control the Bracelet, so it was a non-starter.

I haven't told anyone about going back in time and meeting my dad. If time travel is risky, then it stands to reason that talking about it might be risky too. Maybe what happens in the past should stay there.

Tyler's comment about the *zero moment* stays with me, though. Was that it, I wonder – meeting Dad in the underground base in Area 51?

Things are different since that, it's true. I don't have the same drive to change the past any more. Not when the future seems so uncertain – and so exciting.

In less than eighteen months I'll be sixteen; a member of the ruling Executive. It's a lot to prepare for . . . and I'm starting kind of late in the day.

People begin to arrive, the first bunch with Benicio. Some faces I recognize from the Tec. Benicio himself acts very laid back, introducing me to everyone as his "cousin Josh from England", not as the Bakab Ix, which is a relief. I wonder then how Benicio feels about the way Montoyo keeps ordering him around the world. Is he bothered that he isn't going back to Oxford? It doesn't look like it. In my apartment that night, Benicio doesn't seem to have a care in the world.

Then Ixchel arrives with four or five girls. They're all wearing dresses and skirts, much more tidily, formally dressed than any girls I know would be for a party. None of the girls are as pretty as Ixchel.

It feels like a dream, sitting in my new apartment, entertaining friends. Like a scene from a movie. The playlist reaches the Brazilian jazz numbers – a familiar tune by Tom Jobim, one of Dad's all-time favourites.

This again.

It's a different recording to the one I heard in the dream with Camilla, or in Dad's cell; this time the singing is in Portuguese. But I'd recognize the tune anywhere. Now I think of it, this was playing in Brazil too, the night we sat in that restaurant on the beach.

Standing by the window, I stare at the title of the song. Then I smile. There's nothing else I can do.

Ixchel wanders over, giving me a quizzical look. "Something funny?"

If only you knew.

My mind goes back to that first night in Brazil. If I could use the Bracelet to time travel, that's when I'd go back to. Forget Arcadio and the galactic superwave; if I had to pick just one moment to revisit, I'd want another shot at that evening on the beach in Brazil.

This time I wouldn't let Ixchel go straight to Benicio. I wouldn't play it so cool; I'd let her see how excited I was to see her again.

But really – would that have changed anything? After all – what did Arcadio write to me, the quotation from that writer Borges – *Time is a river which sweeps me along, but I am the river*?

And a river flows only one way. . .

I think of the Bracelet, now locked away in Montoyo's office. I don't think I'll ever totally get rid of the urge to "swim against the stream of time". If I really am Arcadio – that sounds a lot like a warning from my future self.

Wonderful idea – but it can't be done.

Whatever purpose time travel serves, I guess Tyler and Ixchel were right. The Bracelet of Itzamna isn't a tool for solving my personal problems.

Ixchel continues to stare at me, her puzzlement turning into a grin. "So . . . what? Why are you smiling, Josh?"

"This song," I tell her, "is called 'Wave'."

"'Wave'. . .?" she echoes.

"Yeah. 'The wave is on its way.' Kind of like . . . the superwave, don't you think?"

She's still slightly puzzled. "I guess that's funny. . ."

"Yeah, a bit."

"I like it," Ixchel says, thoughtfully. "It reminds me of that night we arrived in Brazil. Portuguese sounds so great there, doesn't it? Really must learn to speak it."

She's thinking about that night too.

I raise a glass of fruit punch to my lips, hiding my face. She starts to look a little nervous too; she lowers her eyes.

"I never really got to thank you. . ." she begins.

I stare in disbelief; I get butterflies in my stomach.

Still not properly looking at me, Ixchel continues, "I always knew you'd come back for your mother. But by that river, in Brazil." She looks up. "You could have got away. You didn't have to come back for me."

"It's OK," I mumble. "Course I had to. That was the point – to get you all back."

Ixchel smiles. "Well . . . I'm grateful."

Then, as if she's just thought of it, she leans over and kisses my cheek. For some reason I can't make myself move.

Say something. Say anything. Now.

But all I can do is nod, smile a bit and take another sip of my drink. There's a lump in my throat the size of a plum.

After all the stuff I've been through, why is *this* so hard? Truth is, it's impossible. I don't know where to start. Might as well try to speak Japanese.

Warm air wafts in from outside. It smells of the rain-drizzled blossoms that fill the lanes and alleyways of Ek Naab. Ixchel stands centimetres away from me, facing the crowd of her friends from the Tec. The silence between us lengthens, becomes awkward. I pretend to glance away but out of the corner of my eye I watch her twist her ponytail between two slender fingers. Then Ixchel turns and I follow her gaze.

She's looking over towards Benicio. She just stands there, waiting for him to notice.

Ixchel is the one person I would love to tell everything. But I can't bring myself to do it. I can't say anything; not a word.

Acknowledgements

Eternal thanks to Team Joshua at Scholastic Children's Books UK, especially my new editor, Polly Nolan, who joins us mid-series, and to Jessica White, Alyx Price, Alex Richardson, Sarah Lansbury, Elaine McQuade and Hilary Murray-Hill for continued energetic support. To Elv Moody for a brilliant suggestion when we first discussed the plot. To my agent, Peter Cox, for being generally wonderful. To Matt Barnard, barista and manager at Summertown's Starbucks, for providing me with such a wonderful "office", and to fellow children's author Susie Day for sharing long hours and laughs at the "office". And mostly to my husband, David, for always supporting me, letting me take the family to Brazil, and for jumping on the manuscript as soon as it's finished and not putting it down until he's read right to the end.

Desperate to know what happens next? Turn
the page for a sneak preview from Joshua's
fourth adventure,

DaRk ParALLeL

DaRk PaRALLeL

"I think I'm losing my mind," I tell Lorena, the second she closes her office door behind us.

A wry grin flickers at the edge of Lorena's mouth. Her serious brown eyes twinkle for a second, but she remains calm. "I suspect not."

"Can you do a brain scan or something?"

"To see if you're losing your mind? Possibly. It depends how you're losing it."

"Do a brain scan," I say firmly. "Please."

With a pencil, Lorena taps the desk between us. "Josh, talk to me. What's wrong?"

"Remember a few months ago, when my mum and Ixchel were kidnapped in Brazil?"

Calmly she nods, blinking slowly. "Naturally."

"I came here to your labs. You found me in your cold room."

She smiles at the memory. "Yes."

"Who was with me?"

"No one."

"You don't remember a guy called Tyler?"

"Tyler?" Lorena frowns. "No. You were alone."

"And you ... you told me all this stuff, remember that? About Montoyo."

"I did?"

"Yeah, and about the five Revival Chambers, and the Crystal Key…"

"The five Revival Chambers?"

I pause, glancing up at her. "Yes. The one here in Mexico, in the Depths near Becan. Then you said there were four others in Iraq, China … Pakistan … I can't remember the fifth one. Oh yeah, Australia."

Lorena frowns, gazing deeply at me from over her black-rimmed glasses. "Josh … we just know about one Revival Chamber. The one that you and Ixchel found."

"But they're written about in the Ix Codex…"

Lorena sits back, now totally bewildered. "Josh … the Ix Codex is mostly blank."

"Mostly blank?" I can't do anything but echo.

"Apart from the first few pages." Lorena nods vigorously. "It's as if the book was torn into pieces and the first few pages grafted on to a blank manuscript. A fake, made to look like the genuine article by someone who got their hands on the first few pages of the real thing." She looks at me curiously. "But everybody knows this. We've known since you returned the codex from Catemaco."

I sit in silence for a few moments, aware of a deepening ache in my lower spine and wrists, and a slight numbness. The hard day of bike riding has taken a lot out of me. If only I could forget about all of this and just get some rest.

I wouldn't sleep, though, not with this worry.

"Then you'd better do that brain scan," I tell her. "Cos that's not how I remember things."

THE JOSHUA FILES

And catch up on the beginning of
Josh's story with these stunning
new paperback editions. . .

THE INTERNATIONAL BEST-SELLER

M.G. HARRIS

THE JOSHUA FILES

ICE SHOCK

THE INTERNATIONAL BEST-SELLER

M.G. HARRIS

THE JOSHUA FILES

INVISIBLE CITY

MAYAN MYSTERIES of 2012
A Young Person's Guide

Some readers of *The Joshua Files* have been asking if there is any truth in the "2012 prophecy" which features in Josh Garcia's adventures.

In fact, the Mayan calendar end date really is 22 December 2012.

But don't worry – the rest of the details of 2012 in *The Joshua Files* are fiction, based on some of the more entertaining theories about what might happen. There is no proof that there's really any danger at all.

Fact or fiction?

FACT:

• The ancient Mayan civilization existed in countries we now call Mexico, Guatemala, Honduras and Belize.

• Between 500 and 900 A.D. they enjoyed a "golden age" of city-building and writing.

• Mayan astronomers made remarkably accurate observations and used their Long Count Calendar to commemorate historical and astronomical events.

• Like the Gregorian and Julian calendars, which start with the presumed date of Jesus of Nazareth's birth, the Long

Count Calendar (the Haab) has a start date.

• Unlike those calendars, however, the Haab also has an end date.

• The Haab start date is August 11 3114 B.C.

• The end date of the Haab is thirteen baktuns later ... which translates as 22 (or 21) Dec 2012.

If the start of a calendar commemorates the most important event a society can remember, what might the end date of a calendar commemorate?

FICTION:

• The Ix Codex and the Books of Itzamna are fictional.

• Josh Garcia's adventures happen in a fictional world where the 2012 threat is real.

What the ancient Maya wrote about 2012:

Almost nothing. Pretty surprising, don't you think? If they really did believe it was the end of the world, you'd expect many mentions of the date. But in the Mayan books and temple inscriptions that survive, there's only ONE reference to 13 Baktun – 22 Dec 2012. That inscription is known as Tortuguera monument 6. Mayan writing expert Professor David Stuart translated the inscription.

Here's his translation:

"The Thirteenth 'Bak'tun' will be finished
(on) Four Ajaw, the Third of Uniiw (K'ank'in).
? will occur.
(It will be) the descent(?) of the Nine Support(?) God(s) to the ?"

As you can see, it's not clear at all what the "2012 prophecy" actually says or means. Which means we can use our imaginations. Most of what you'll hear about 2012 is just that – pure imagination.

If you'd like to know more about the Maya or the mysteries of 2012, please visit a website on the topic written by M.G. Harris.

www.mayan2012kids.com

BLOG ENTRY: JOSH NEEDS YOU!

Help Josh solve a murder!
Enter **www.thejoshuafiles.com** to join the
  Alternate Reality Game
Plus:
Watch exclusive trailers
Enter competitions
Win cool prizes

BLOG ENTRY: THE COUNTDOWN HAS BEGUN!

Is the world really going to end in 2012?
Where did this all come from?
Is there any truth in the stories we're hearing?
Find out more at **www.mayan2012kids.com**

Keep up with M.G. Harris at:

www.themgharris.com – M.G.'s website
www.mgharris.net – M.G.'s blog
www.facebook.com – join the official *Joshua Files*
Facebook group
www.youtube.com/user/mgharrisauthor – visit
M.G.'s author channel on YouTube

M. G. HARRIS

M.G. Harris was born in Mexico City but moved to England as a young child. Before becoming a writer, M.G. worked as a scientist and ran an Internet business.

On regular visits back to Mexico, M.G. became fascinated by Mayan archaeology and made several trips to Mayan ruins in Yucatan and Chiapas. One such trip planted the seed of the idea for *The Joshua Files*. While recovering from a skiing accident that resulted in a broken leg, M.G. began writing *Invisible City*, the first book in the *Joshua Files* series, on a laptop next to the bed. Joshua's next adventures, Ice Shock and Zero Moment, followed soon afterward.

When not wandering around the exotic settings for *The Joshua Files*, like Mexico, Brazil and the Swiss mountains, M.G. and family live on a quiet street in Oxford.

THE MERMAID'S SCREAM

Kate Ellis

piatkus

PIATKUS

First published in Great Britain in 2017 by Piatkus
This paperback edition published in 2017 by Piatkus

1 3 5 7 9 10 8 6 4 2

A CIP catalogue record for this book
is available from the British Library.

ISBN 978-0-349-41311-2

Typeset in Baskerville by M Rules
Printed and bound in Great Britain
by Clays Ltd, St Ives plc

Papers used by Piatkus are from well-managed forests
and other responsible sources.

Journal of John Lipton

12 April 1884

Today the puppets have come to town.

Mr Gunster's marionettes attract the crowds wherever
they appear with their tales of bloody murder, and today
is no exception. I see little ones watch with mouths
agape, their tiny fingers clutching their mothers' hands as
the marionettes dance and stab and strangle.

Today in Tradmouth's Market Square I witness
a small wooden William Corder ending the miserable
life of a small wooden Maria Marten in a miniature
Red Barn, all to the audience's rapt delight. How I
marvel at people's appetite for death and suffering as
they feast on cruelty and violence like beasts of prey.
Mankind, I think, must be most wicked species on this
earth.

If I were given to imagination, I would fear Mr
Gunster's puppets with their hard painted faces. There is

something evil about them and I dislike Gunster with his avaricious, glinting eyes.

I walk round to the back of his booth and watch Gunster and his son as they control the puppet's strings. The scenery before which the puppet's murderous deeds are enacted is as well painted and elaborate as that in any theatre. I have heard Gunster has a daughter who paints the backdrops with great skill, although at present she is nowhere to be seen.

It must be a family business for Mrs Gunster collects the money from the assembled crowd. Gunster's wife is pale and unsmiling like a ghost. I can't help but wonder if she is afraid of her husband and her son.

1

Zac Wilkinson had read the opening passage from *The Viper's Kiss*, Wynn Staniland's best-known book, so many times that he almost knew it by heart.

"'I can hear the mermaids screaming,'" he began. "'They sit each day on the rocks at the foot of the cliff, throw their heads back and scream at the waves crashing by their glistening tails. I am afraid of the mermaids. I fear that one day their screams will turn into a song and they'll lure me into the sea with all those poor dead sailors whose souls they have claimed over the centuries.

"'Because the dead never leave you. The dead are there whenever you glimpse a vague shape in the shadows, caught for a moment then gone. Never forget the dead because they never forget you. What you do to the dead in this life matters more than you can know because they haunt you forever with blessing or vengeance, like the mermaid's song.'"

3

As always he ended his talk with these familiar and disturbing words and, as always, there was an uneasy pause between his silence and the polite applause, as though the mention of the dead had left the middle-aged and predominantly female audience temporarily stunned.

Once the reading was over they asked the usual questions. 'Have you met Wynn Staniland? What does he think of the biography you're writing? Does he mind having his dirty linen washed in public? Is he ever going to write another book?'

Zac's answers were well rehearsed and noncommittal. Yes, he'd met Wynn Staniland. He'd visited the author and his daughter at their home, Addersacre, on a number of occasions. And yes, Wynn was happy to cooperate with the biography. But it had been made quite clear to Zac that one subject was strictly off limits and that was the death of Wynn's wife. This was quite understandable, Zac said. A biographer shouldn't be in the business of resurrecting painful memories just for the sake of selling a few more copies of the book (which, incidentally, will be out next spring, published by Bream and Seager, priced at £18.99).

Zac's reply to the audience's final question had been more vague. Wynn hadn't altogether ruled out writing another novel, but that's all he was at liberty to say for the moment.

As the last stragglers trickled out of the room, Zac tidied his papers and returned them to his leather shoulder bag before complimenting the librarians who'd organised his talk with their customary efficiency. They hadn't been sure how many people to expect but, as it turned out, the subject of Wynn Staniland had attracted quite a crowd, all fascinated to get the lowdown on the reclusive author's private life and to find out why, after five award-winning books that had taken the literary world by storm, Wynn Staniland had suddenly turned his back on fame and chosen to live the life of a recluse. Zac, reluctant to spoil the revelations in his book, had dropped tantalising hints but he'd been careful to give little away.

After saying his farewells he stepped into the night, aware that he needed to go over the latest draft of the opening five chapters first thing the next morning. Since he'd taken on the biography there had been draft after draft to be pored over like some precious, sacred tome. Then of course Wynn would want to give it his nod of assent or otherwise, adding ideas and taking others away. Zac's previous subjects had never been so particular, but then they'd been sportsmen, TV personalities or actors, happy to go along with anything he suggested. Writing about Staniland, the author he'd admired so much during his teenage years, had seemed like a dream when he'd first gained the great man's approval for the project. It couldn't feel less like one now.

Zac walked straight back to the tiny cottage near the town centre he was renting for the duration. It was up a steep, narrow street – a one-in-three hill. He took a deep breath before attempting the climb, contemplating the bottle of single malt waiting for him on the coffee table. His reward for a hard day's work.

When the cottage came into view he stopped to catch his breath for a few moments, suddenly reluctant to carry on. With everything that had happened over the past days, the cottage had ceased to be his haven. A serpent had crept in, curling itself round the foundations, slithering over his sleeping body. He had the sensation of being watched, but every time he looked round there was nobody there.

Although he told himself it was all in his imagination,

the question always nagged at the back of his mind. What if somebody had discovered the truth about who he really was? He'd been assured it could never happen but those promises were starting to seem hollow. He felt vulnerable. More vulnerable than he'd felt since he'd been reborn as a new creation.

As he approached the cottage he took his key from his pocket. Then he saw the damage: splinters of wood around the lock as though somebody had taken a chisel to it. For a brief moment he contemplated calling at the neighbouring houses to ask whether anybody had seen or heard anything suspicious. But his front door stood down a small side passage, invisible from the street.

His heart pounded as he unlocked the door, and when it swung open he hovered on the threshold for a few moments before flicking on the light switch.

As far as he could see, nothing had been disturbed which meant that whoever had tried to break in hadn't succeeded. Either that or they'd gone about their business with neat professionalism.

His hands were shaking as he took his phone from his pocket, wondering whether to report it to the police. It took him a few moments to decide that he'd need a crime number for the letting agency's insurance and, besides, he'd done nothing wrong. This time.

Farming was tough these days and, from bitter experience, David Gough knew you had to diversify to survive. His father had bought the field overlooking the sea in more prosperous times and while the ten static caravans he'd put there a couple of years ago didn't bring in a fortune, every little bit helped – just like the time he'd sold those strange old puppets he'd found in the barn for a tidy sum to some weird man who ran the Dukesbridge Arts Festival.

His wife, Joan, had moaned when he'd spent money on the new fencing in the caravan field but he'd got it done cheaply. No problem. Although at times David wondered whether the caravans were worth the effort of all the maintenance. But, since he'd handed over the day-to-day running of the farm to his sons, they'd become his responsibility.

A couple of weeks ago a family from Birmingham had complained about the smell of slurry. But nothing could be done about the slurry pit when the wind was in the wrong direction. Now someone else had called him with another complaint and as he opened the gate to the field, shutting it carefully behind him, he rehearsed his excuses.

At least the rain had stopped; there was nothing like rain to put the holidaymakers in a foul mood. As he trudged across the damp grass in the darkness, he could see the glow of the moon through ominous clouds. If the sky had been clear there would have been a fine display of twinkling stars. The visitors often commented on the lack of light pollution here.

The latest complaint had been made by the man in caravan three and, after Gough had had a terse word, he approached the caravan in question and sniffed the air. He knew the smell of slurry only too well and this wasn't it.

Caravan five stood at the end of the field by the new fence, slightly apart from the others. Lights blazed behind the thin floral curtains, suggesting someone was at home. But as Gough drew nearer he saw that the windows were alive with moving black dots. It took him a few seconds to realise they were flies.

He gave three sharp raps on the door. According to the

man in caravan three, the occupants hadn't been seen for a couple of days and the curtains hadn't shifted. When Gough knocked again all he could hear from inside the caravan was the faint buzz of insects and he had an uncomfortable feeling that something was very wrong.

The man from caravan three, a nosy character with a shiny bald head and an officious manner, was still watching. Gough unlocked the door and as it swung open the buzzing grew louder and he put his hand to his nose as the odour of decay hit him.

He forced himself to look at the two people inside. The woman lay on the floor, fully clothed, her arm outstretched as though she was trying to reach for help. She wore a yellow sun dress that seemed quite inappropriate in that grisly tableau.

Beyond her a man was slumped on the tweed banquette seating, reaching for the half-empty champagne bottle on the table as though spoilsport Death had caught him before he could help himself to another glass. The man's other hand rested on the woman's hair. A touch of farewell before their world turned dark.

Gough heard the man from caravan three's voice behind him.

'We should call the police.'

David Gough hesitated then took his phone from his pocket. It looked like he had no choice.

2

DI Wesley Peterson watched his wife as she sipped the tea he'd just brought her. Since her spell in hospital that spring after her breast cancer had been diagnosed, he'd become quite the devoted husband. Sometimes she scolded him for fussing, but he knew she'd prefer this to the alternative.

The clock on the mantelpiece told him the ten o'clock news was about to begin and he felt unusually tired. Perhaps it was the oppressive weather, warm and dull with regular showers to add to the humidity. Or perhaps it was the constant worry about Pam's health.

When he told her he was going to bed, she said she intended to watch the news headlines before finishing the next chapter of her book. She'd be up later. It was something she'd read years ago but was rereading for a book group she'd recently joined. The central theme was the impact of a woman's suicide on a small rural community. When Wesley had read it himself he hadn't particularly enjoyed it.

The antihero in Wynn Staniland's *The Viper's Kiss*, the

man who'd driven the woman to take her own life, was, in Wesley's opinion, amoral, charmless and unworthy of anyone's sympathy. When he'd shared his thoughts with Pam she'd teased him for being reactionary, blaming the strictly moral way he'd been raised by his God-fearing Trinidadian parents. He'd felt obliged to counter her argument, saying his upbringing had been loving and secure. He was tempted to compare his family to Pam's self-centred mother, Della, but erred on the side of tact and kept quiet. He'd always regarded it as a miracle that Pam had turned out as well as she had. He presumed she'd inherited her down-to-earth nature from her long-dead, long-suffering father.

Wesley knew *The Viper's Kiss*, Staniland's second book, was generally regarded as a masterpiece and, like its predecessor published the year before, it had won numerous awards. After this the author had produced three further novels before withdrawing completely from the literary scene, no doubt disappointing his publisher but making himself a legend in the process.

Staniland lived in the locality and had a long-established reputation for being a recluse. Journalists who'd tried to invade his privacy had always been given short shrift but, after decades of shunning publicity, the author was now allowing his biography to be written. Pam speculated that he might be running out of money and needed to boost his book sales by bringing himself back into the public eye. Wesley suspected her cynical observation was probably true. Even recluses have to make a living.

Tradmouth's library-cum-arts centre happened to be next door to the police station and Wesley had seen posters advertising a talk by Staniland's biographer – a man called Zac Wilkinson – who promised to reveal the secrets of the great man's life. Although when Pam had attended the talk earlier that evening she'd come back with the feeling she'd been cheated, since none of the alleged secrets dangled so temptingly in the publicity blurb had been revealed and the speaker had told the audience they'd have to buy the book to find out more. To Wesley this seemed like an underhand trick. But he'd encountered worse deceptions in the course of his career.

He was about to head upstairs when his phone rang, setting off a frantic search until he located it behind a cushion on the sofa.

'Wes.' He recognised DCI Gerry Heffernan's voice with its distinctive Liverpool accent at once. When Gerry called at this time of night it usually meant trouble.

'Sorry to spoil your evening but we're needed at Stoke Beeching – Cliff View Caravan Park. Two unexplained deaths.'

For a few moments Wesley didn't speak. Pam appeared to be engrossed in her book but he sensed she was pretending, hoping he wasn't about to leave her alone again. She went to great pains to convince everyone around her she no longer felt fragile and vulnerable but Wesley knew her too well to be fooled. Reluctantly he told her he had to go out, but promised he'd be back as soon as he could.

It began to rain heavily as he drove out to Stoke Beeching – a front of low pressure had been stuck over the West of England for the past day or so. He switched on his windscreen wipers and they swished to and fro with a hypnotic rhythm as he steered the car down the snaking road. There were streetlights in the villages but once the houses petered out, the world was plunged into darkness. When he'd transferred from London to Devon all those years ago he'd hated driving down these roads at night. He still didn't like it but it was something he'd had to get used to.

Half a mile outside the village he spotted a sign in the beam of his headlights: the words CLIFF VIEW CARAVAN PARK in faded letters below a smiling seagull pointing the way with its wing. In his experience seagulls were never that cooperative in real life. He followed the directions and soon found himself at a reception area which was little more than a shed beside a farm gate. However, he could see that the shed had lace curtains. A touch of class.

After driving through the open gate he spotted a brace of patrol cars parked next to an unmarked police car at the end of the field. Some keen constable had already sealed off the caravan in question – a medium-sized static standing slightly apart from its neighbours – with police tape. Wesley saw light streaming from the open caravan door.

He left his car at the top of the field and as he walked towards the action he saw faces at the windows of some of the other caravans – rubbernecking neighbours who would have to be interviewed at some point. If it wasn't for the rain, he guessed they'd be outside gawping, enjoying a bit of holiday excitement.

He put up the hood of his waterproof coat and hurried towards Gerry, who was standing just inside the caravan door. But before he could utter a word of greeting, the scene manager handed him a package containing his crime scene suit, the white overall that was de rigueur on such occasions.

He sheltered in the back seat of one of the patrol cars to undertake the undignified procedure of pulling it on over his clothes. The car smelled strongly of body odour and he was eager to get back out into the damp fresh air, until he neared the caravan and caught a whiff of something even more unpleasant, a faint smell of rotting meat. He stepped over the metal plates the CSIs had put down and began to climb the caravan steps.

'Wes, let's talk outside,' Gerry said, coming down the steps to join him. He sounded relieved, as though Wesley had lifted some great burden from his shoulders. Gerry Heffernan was a large man with a chubby face and grizzled hair, not especially tall but certainly carrying more weight than the medical profession would approve of.

Gerry turned his head and looked at the half-open door behind him. 'Colin's in there doing his stuff. I came out. Couldn't stand the smell.'

'What have we got?' The smell of decay was stronger now.

'Man and woman. They've been dead a couple of days, according to Colin, but with the heat . . . ' He wrinkled his nose in disgust. 'They rented the caravan in the name of Mr and Mrs Lombard; gave David Gough who owns the site an address in Leeds. We've notified their local police.'

'Suspicious?'

'Colin's first thought was poison. He reckons it could be a suicide pact. Or a murder then suicide. It happens.'

Wesley bowed his head. In the course of his career he'd encountered a few cases of someone killing a loved one then taking their own life. It was usually an act of fury – or sometimes desperation.

'If it's poison do we know how it was administered?'

'There's a half-empty champagne bottle on the table and two glasses. Looks like they decided to go out in style.'

Wesley sneaked a look at his watch. It was after eleven. 'Are you sure we're needed here?'

Gerry shrugged his shoulders. 'No, but we can't take any

13

chances.' He walked back up the steps and pushed the door open. 'You ready?'

Wesley nodded, took a deep breath and followed his boss into the unknown.

3

When Zac Wilkinson reported the attempted break-in at his rented cottage he was told not to touch anything until someone called round. He waited up for the police until two in the morning then, when nobody arrived, retired to bed in disgust.

A constable finally turned up at ten o'clock the following morning: a stocky middle-aged man in a bulky stab vest who wore the bored look of someone who'd seen it all before, which he probably had. With no apology for the delay and only a cursory examination of the damaged front door, he doled out a crime number for the landlord's insurance company.

'Did they manage to get in? Is anything missing?' he asked, taking his notebook from his pocket.

'I don't think so.'

'You here on holiday, sir?'

Zac hesitated. 'No. I'm a writer. I'm down here to work.'

'A writer, eh?' The constable scribbled something in his book. 'What kind of books do you write?'

Zac swallowed his impatience and told him.

'Wynn Staniland? I've heard that name. Doesn't he live round here?'

'Yes. Er . . . there's something else.'

'What's that?'

'I think someone's been following me.'

'And what makes you think that, sir?' the constable said as if he was humouring a child.

Zac suddenly regretted saying anything. 'Not sure. Just a feeling.'

The expression of amused scepticism on the constable's face told Zac the man considered him the over-imaginative, arty type.

'This is the only attempted break-in round here so far this season. Why pick on you? Do you think he was after something in particular?'

'I don't know.'

Zac saw the constable give him another sceptical look. This wasn't going well. And if the man knew the truth about him, things would get even worse.

Dr Neil Watson of the County Archaeological Unit felt a tingle of anticipation as he headed for the village of Whitely. It was only two miles from Tradmouth and the proximity reminded him that he hadn't seen his old friend Wesley Peterson for almost a month. Every time he'd contacted Wesley there's been some excuse not to meet and he wondered if this had anything to do with Pam's illness. Wesley had been uncharacteristically subdued since her diagnosis, as though he'd caught a brief glimpse of the gloating, skeletal face of the Grim Reaper and it had shaken him more than he'd cared to admit.

Neil had been busy himself. Over the past month he'd been in charge of a rescue excavation near Exeter city centre, finding out what was under the ground before work started on a new block of flats. It was an interesting site, producing a good selection of medieval and Roman finds, but within the next few days he was due to hand it over to the developers who'd been circling impatiently like hyenas round the corpse of a wildebeest, waiting for the lions to have their fill.

Neil had been intrigued when he'd received a call from Giles Billingham, Tradmouth Council's conservation officer. Newfield Manor – or rather the ruins of Newfield Manor – had been on the Buildings at Risk Register for a number of years. Now, however, according to Giles, the Manor had a new owner who was anxious to develop the property, which meant there'd need to be a full archaeological assessment of the building and the site before any work went ahead.

Neil turned the car down the narrow lane, lined each side with hedges high and impregnable as castle walls, and when he finally reached his destination he saw that both ivy-clad gateposts guarding the entrance to Newfield Manor were slumped against the crumbling wall at a drunken angle. He turned into the drive and proceeded slowly over the potholed ground, fearing for his exhaust. The shadows cast by the overgrown trees leaning over the drive forced him to turn on his headlights and when he suddenly emerged into the dazzling sunlight he saw the shell of a building rearing in front of him, vegetation sprouting from the windows and what little remained of the roof.

He switched off the engine and sat for a few moments before leaving the car and when he slammed the car door shut the noise echoed like a gunshot. Crows shrieked and cackled in the surrounding trees and an unexpected shock of fear passed through him, as though something malevolent didn't want him to be there. He studied the house, noting every feature, each stone lintel, each brick and each remnant of fallen roof slate. The windows were blank and glassless like the dead eyes of a corpse and the stonework showed signs of scorching as though there'd been a fire at some point in the building's history.

He was relieved when he heard a car engine approaching. Giles to the rescue, he thought, feeling stupid for letting the place spook him. He watched Giles emerge from his vehicle. He was in his thirties, with prematurely thinning hair and the look of a benevolent medieval clerk. Always prepared, he wore a waterproof coat over his local government jacket and tie, and also wellingtons, in case of rain.

'Strange place, isn't it?' Giles said once greetings had been exchanged. 'I've been here a few times but it still gives me the creeps.'

'I know what you mean. What can I do for you?'

'The farmer who used to own the place sold it a few months ago to an American, name of Karl Banville. Mr Banville wants to undertake a complete renovation – which might be good or it might be bad.' Giles had always been cautious by nature.

'What does he plan to do with it?'

'So far there's been no application for change of use so I suppose there's a chance he wants to live here.' Neil heard a note of disbelief in Giles's voice. 'But I have heard mention of a hotel. We'll have to wait and see.'

Neil looked at the wreck of a building in front of him. 'He must have money to burn,' he said, half envious. Still, if he'd wanted to be a rich man he'd never have chosen a career in archaeology.

'No doubt he has fancy plans for it. Let's just hope they'll be plans I can approve. Before he makes any planning application I'd like a detailed archaeological report on the fabric of the building so we can monitor any future development. You know the routine.'

'I certainly do.'

Giles hesitated. 'The new owner asked me if I knew how to arrange a proper excavation in the gardens. He says he's willing to fund it.'

Neil's eyes lit up. It sounded as if it might be his unit's lucky day.

'How long's the house been in this state? What's the story?'

Giles looked around before replying, as if to check that nobody was eavesdropping. 'There was a murder here in the eighteen eighties. Quite a notorious case. After that it changed hands many times but nobody stayed for long. A fire in the nineteen forties destroyed one wing completely and after that the house was abandoned and most of the land sold to a neighbouring farmer.' He paused for dramatic effect. 'I know it's nonsense but there's a story that nobody wanted to live here because the murder victim never left. They say she's still here.'

Zac Wilkinson knew the chances of the police finding whoever tried to break into the cottage were virtually zero. Usually they were useless. But they'd succeeded once and he'd paid the price.

He didn't own a car. Living in London, it was easier to rely on public transport to get around. But this hadn't been an option in rural South Devon where buses were regarded as unpredictable and rarely glimpsed creatures, so he'd hired a small VW for the duration of his stay. He'd left the car on Crossbones Hill, the nearest parking place though precipitously steep. When it came into view he was relieved, as always, that the handbrake had held in his absence.

He had an appointment with Wynn Staniland to get his approval for the revised chapters. He also needed to ask him more questions about his time at Oxford because before when he'd broached the subject the answers had been tantalisingly vague. Zac had been a great fan of Staniland's writing in his younger days when he'd had plenty of time to read but he was finding the reclusive author increasingly prickly and evasive. The adage 'never meet your heroes' was one he increasingly thought was true. He promised himself that in future he'd stick to sportsmen or semi-literate celebrities, even if they insisted on taking the credit for authorship themselves.

As he turned the corner onto Crossbones Hill he saw a dark figure in a shabby hooded sweatshirt standing a few yards away from his car. When he began to approach, the person slid off down the path leading to the allotments where the locals grew their vegetables on steep, terraced plots.

The stranger vanished into the trees and Zac told himself it was probably some local thug trying car doors. He'd always thought places like Tradmouth were virtually crime-free but it was beginning to look as though he'd been wrong.

He was about to unlock his car door when he saw something on the windscreen, a single sheet of dirty paper tucked beneath the wipers.

And when he unfolded it he saw five words printed there in childish capital letters: I NO WHO U ARE.

The Journal of Mary Field

12 April 1884

I had heard the servants talk of how Mr Gunster's marionettes re-enact the dreadful murders on the Ratcliffe Highway and I yearned to see this spectacle for myself. I took the carriage to Tradmouth with Sarah and found a place at the edge of the crowd in the market square. I laughed when Sarah squealed in horror, yet I felt nothing but excitement at the sight of that innocent family's slaughter.

When the performance ended I expressed a desire to examine the new bonnets in the draper's, but before we reached the High Street a young man bid me good day and asked how I had enjoyed Mr Gunster's show. He introduced himself as John Lipton and he was considerably more handsome than William Banville, with black curls and eyes of deepest blue. He assured me we had met before at Sir James Merryweather's ball in the spring, although I do not know the truth of this for I am certain I would have remembered.

Mr Lipton says he has a great interest in cases of murder and the dreadful deeds Mr Gunster's puppets portray. He himself has started to amass a collection of a most macabre nature. I was eager to point out that I share his interest and when we parted at the Butterwalk he said he hoped we would meet again as he has gruesome delights he wishes to show me. The death mask of a hanged man and a snuffbox created from timbers from the dreadful Red Barn itself, stained with the very life blood of the unfortunate Maria Marten.

4

On the rare occasions when Dr Colin Bowman, the Home Office pathologist, hadn't been available during an investigation, Gerry Heffernan had never felt comfortable dealing with his replacement, clinging to the familiarity of his old friend's presence like a child clings to a comfort blanket.

Today, Wesley noticed a spring in the DCI's step as they entered the swing doors of Tradmouth Hospital mortuary. Colin was presiding and there would be tea and biscuits afterwards in his office so all was well with Gerry's world. Colin was a genial man and Wesley often wondered why he'd chosen to work with the dead rather than the living who would appreciate his affable nature. One day perhaps he'd ask him. In the meantime he had the grim spectacle of the postmortem to face.

Colin offered the customary vapour rub to dab on their nostrils to mask any unpleasant odours and he chatted as he worked, conducting the Lombards' postmortems one after the other – first the woman and then the man – noting how they'd lived their lives as well as how they met their deaths. Frank Lombard was in his mid to late fifties, Colin calculated, and his wife – if she was his wife – probably several years his junior and she'd taken better care of herself than he had. She had wavy shoulder-length brown hair and Wesley thought sadly that she must have been an attractive woman in life. He noticed a heart-shaped birthmark the size of a fifty pence piece on the top of her left arm. If it hadn't been for the colour he might have taken it for a tattoo.

After Colin had weighed the various organs with earnest concentration, he enquired about next of kin and Wesley had to admit that they were still looking. The police up in Leeds had sent an officer to the address provided by David Gough, but the house had been empty and none of the neighbours had been able to provide much information.

Wesley found the likelihood that the couple had taken their own lives unsettling. Dying like that in a field so far from home seemed such a sad end and he wondered whether the location held any particular significance for them. Did they choose to end their days there because of some sentimental connection? He was curious to find out what had led to their fatal decision. Or had only one of them desired oblivion, and the other been tricked or coerced into following their partner into death?

'They were certainly poisoned,' was Colin's final verdict. 'But I can't tell you what the substance was until I've had the results of the toxicology tests from the lab. They'd both eaten a light meal several hours earlier – possibly lunch – and they appeared to have consumed a quantity of champagne shortly before death.'

'A champagne bottle was found at the scene,' said Wesley.

24

He watched as Colin studied the steel bowl containing Frank Lombard's stomach contents and wrinkled his nose.

'Double suicide then?' Gerry asked hopefully.

'There's no signs of violence on either body so I don't think they were forced to ingest whatever it was,' said Colin. 'So yes, Gerry, my guess would be a suicide pact. Last sip of champers, then lights out.'

'They often choose to do it away from their home turf,' Gerry observed philosophically.

Once the postmortems were over, Colin led them down the corridor into his office and switched on his own private kettle.

'That's that then,' said Gerry as he took his first sip of tea. 'Suicide. Or murder–suicide. Either way we're not looking for anyone else.'

Wesley said nothing. He was still thinking of those two individuals dying unnoticed in that field amongst strangers. And wondering what could have driven them to commit such a heartbreaking act.

Neil returned to Exeter as soon as his meeting with Giles Billingham was over, thinking of Newfield Manor with increasing excitement. A lost house, virtually reclaimed by nature; a Sleeping Beauty's castle ready to give up its long-dormant secrets. And the possibility of a funded dig dangled before him like a juicy carrot.

That night he thought of little else, trawling through the internet to see what he could find out about the house. When he resumed work at the site in Exeter the next morning Newfield Manor was still on his mind.

He blamed his budding obsession on the absence of Lucy Zinara. Lucy had come to Devon at a time of family crisis after spending most of her career working on archaeological sites in Orkney and, for the past year or so, she'd been sharing his life. Neil had hoped she'd decide to stay in Devon for good but the lure of Orkney's rich Viking heritage had proved too much and she'd returned there for the summer to supervise a new excavation. She'd promised to be back as soon as the bad weather forced her to abandon work but Neil hadn't told her he was counting the days to her return, checking the Orkney weather forecast in the hope of violent storms. Playing things cool had become a habit over the years.

The dig that morning had been productive, but Neil knew they needed to be out by the end of the week so the bulldozers could move in and destroy their painstaking work, which served to dampen his excitement.

He was examining the latest finds when his phone rang. The caller's number was unfamiliar and he was tempted to ignore it but, after swearing under his breath, he passed the finds tray to one of his colleagues and answered.

'Am I speaking to Dr Watson?' The voice was male, confident and American.

Neil answered in the affirmative.

'My name's Karl Banville. I've been speaking with Giles Billingham from the council. He says he called you in to have a look at Newfield Manor. Can we meet at the Manor? Say seven this evening?'

Neil had been longing to get home and soak in a hot bath but he didn't argue. 'OK. See you then,' he heard himself saying.

Then when the phone went dead he stared at it for a while, wondering why he felt uneasy.

5

'Has the champagne bottle been sent for analysis?' Wesley asked when he returned to the CID office on the first floor of Tradmouth Police Station.

DS Rachel Tracey was sitting next to the large window overlooking the river and as he spoke his eyes were drawn to the view outside. Boats scurried across the water and, being the height of the season, tourists meandered through the Memorial Gardens. He watched a couple stroll by the bandstand, eating fish and chips, unaware that predatory seagulls were eyeing their alfresco meal. They were around the same age as Gina and Frank Lombard, the couple he'd just seen in Colin Bowman's mortuary. Life and death: he'd learned over the years there was only a fine line between the two.

'Bottle's at the lab,' Rachel said in reply. 'But the results won't be back for a few days. How did the PM go?'

'Colin thinks they were poisoned. Probably a double suicide.'

'Their phone and bank records haven't come through yet and there's no word from Leeds about next of kin,' she said, anticipating Wesley's next question.

'I'd like to take another look at that caravan,' he said. 'Want to come with me?' he added on impulse. He didn't fancy being alone there.

Rachel hooked her cardigan from the back of her chair. The sky outside was now clear blue dotted with fluffy clouds, but she knew from long experience that a chill breeze often blew in off the river.

Wesley sat in the passenger seat as Rachel drove out to the caravan park. He lacked her confidence on the narrow, single-track roads. She was a farmer's daughter, brought up in the area, and she'd been tearing down them since she'd passed her test shortly after her seventeenth birthday.

'How are your wedding arrangements going?' Wesley asked, breaking the amicable silence.

'Not bad,' was the noncommittal reply.

Rachel had been injured in the line of duty earlier in the year so her wedding to a local farmer had been postponed until the autumn. Wesley and Pam had received their invitation, along with most of his colleagues, but there were times when the prospect made him uncomfortable. He had been attracted to Rachel once and they'd hovered on the brink of a liaison that had never quite happened. Pam's health problem had shocked him out of the reckless temptation he'd felt. In his darkest moments it had felt almost like a punishment.

The caravan park looked considerably more attractive in today's sunshine. The police tape still fluttered around the scene of the Lombards' deaths while holidaymakers sat outside the neighbouring caravans enjoying the weather.

Wesley ignored their stares as he climbed out of the car. The thought of them regarding the recent tragedy as holiday entertainment made him angry for a moment, then he told himself that it was human nature to be curious. He'd probably feel like that himself if his day job didn't involve dealing with the reality of violent death and its aftermath.

When they reached the Lombards' caravan Wesley noticed a car parked in its shadow; a ten-year-old Vauxhall. No doubt Uniform would deal with it in due course.

Once inside the caravan he left the door open because the odour of death still lingered in the stale, warm air. He stood at the entrance, scanning the interior which looked quite different in the daylight: shabby, abandoned and a little sordid. The corpses of flies littered the floor like currants spilled by a careless baker.

'I'm not sure what we're doing here,' said Rachel, who was standing behind him. 'If it's suicide, surely we can leave it to Uniform.'

Wesley ignored her and made for the bedroom. It was small with beige walls and, to Wesley's surprise, the bed was neatly made and Gina Lombard's lotions and cosmetics were lined up in order of size on the little dressing table. The living room was a mess because things had been knocked over as the couple struggled with the agonies of death, but everything was different here – neat and ordered. The knowledge that Gina had been a tidy woman somehow made her seem more real; a living, breathing human being.

'What are we looking for?' Rachel asked.

Without answering Wesley began opening drawers and the flimsy fitted wardrobes that occupied one end of the room, concluding that the Lombards had travelled moderately light.

Rachel started to search the bedside drawers, attached to the headboard and covered in the same wood-effect beige plastic as the rest of the fittings. Caravan standard issue.

'Look what I found in the drawer.'

Wesley stopped what he was doing and swung round to face her. She was holding up a hardback book, an old edition from the look of it. Wesley recognised the name of the author.

'It's by Wynn Staniland.'

Rachel passed him the book and he looked inside.

'It's been signed but there's no dedication.'

The signature was an untidy scrawl but he could just about decipher it. As he flicked through the pages of the book a scrap of paper fell out. On it were directions, printed in a sloping hand: *Ferry to Queenswear; road to Bloxham; take turning to Fishwick; turn right at Adder's Cross. After two miles turn left. Three hundred yards on right.*

He read them out to Rachel. 'Ring any bells?'

'Not really, but it should be easy to find out. Do you think it's relevant? The Lombards killed themselves, Wesley. Did anything in the postmortem suggest otherwise?'

'No,' he admitted. 'But we don't know what they took yet ... or how they got hold of it. I haven't seen any sign of—'

'What did you expect to find? A big bottle with a skull and crossbones label saying POISON. DO NOT DRINK?'

'They didn't leave a note.'

'Suicides don't always leave one, especially if they have no close family. I can't see anything here that suggests a more sinister explanation. Can you?'

'I still want to know more about them. Did they have children? Siblings? Parents?'

Rachel stared at him, exasperated. 'Let it go, Wesley. It's up to the police in Leeds to fill in the gaps. They were only down here on holiday.'

'But why choose this particular place to die?'

'Perhaps they came here on holiday in happier times. Perhaps they just liked the sea. Does it matter?'

Wesley knew her patience was wearing thin. She'd accused him before of having an overactive imagination. But even when he'd studied archaeology at university he'd felt a strong urge to discover all he could about the dead he excavated: how they'd lived and how they'd come to meet their end.

They continued their search in silence and he knew Rachel thought they were wasting their time. Undeterred, he carried on searching through the drawers before turning his attention to the pair of small suitcases on the unused bed in a tiny second bedroom. There was nothing inside that told them anything about the Lombards or their lives.

'When the tox report comes through and Forensics do their stuff with that champagne bottle, we might make some progress,' he said as he made for the door.

Rachel rolled her eyes. 'If you say so.'

The woman with the brown ponytail stood outside the police station while the gulls wheeled through the air above her. She was used to seagulls in her native Liverpool so she hardly noticed their frantic cries. She had other things on her mind.

She'd never visited Tradmouth before and had only heard about the place in passing. It was nice, she thought: a picturesque port clinging to a hillside, packed with painted houses and narrow winding streets. The river was almost as busy as the Mersey with yachts and tourist boats plying up and down. There was a little town on the opposite bank and, further inland, the river was lined with thick woodland. From the esplanade she'd noticed a castle guarding the entrance to the river. Liverpool didn't have a castle – not any more.

The man she was looking for was called Gerry Heffernan and she knew he was a policeman: a detective chief inspector. When her mum knew him he'd been a sailor but some people can make a new start. She wished she had the chance to do the same.

Her stomach was churning. She'd come all this way – over six hours on the train – so it was too late to change her mind.

Taking a deep breath, she stepped through the glass door that separated the police station from the outside world.

This was the moment that could change her life.

6

After grabbing a pizza from a takeaway near his flat, Neil drove to Whitely, going over everything he'd discovered about Newfield Manor in his mind.

He'd consulted the internet during his tea break in the site hut that afternoon, only to discover that Giles's hints had some substance behind them. Newfield Manor had a bad history; so bad that it had never been rebuilt after the fire that destroyed one wing back in 1946. Most of the stuff on the net mentioned the place was haunted by the ghost of a murder victim but Neil knew this was nonsense. He'd worked on hundreds of historical sites and he'd never yet met a ghost ... and he wasn't expecting that to change in the next hour or so.

Even so, as he drove up the pitted drive, he couldn't shake off the sensation that something didn't want him there. He was a man of science who didn't live in the realm of the imagination but the feeling was definitely there, buzzing away inside his head like an irritating fly.

As he pulled up he saw a sleek black SUV parked in front of the house and he assumed it belonged to Banville, although there was no sign of him. Then he saw a man emerge from the undergrowth at the side of the ruined building. If this was Banville he was older than Neil expected; probably in his sixties with neatly cut grey hair and a smooth olive tan. His clothes wouldn't have looked out of place on an expensive yacht and his hands were thrust casually into the pockets of his pale-blue chinos. As the man strolled towards the car he looked completely at home in that abandoned place.

Neil got out and greeted him with a wave of his soil-stained hand – the ingrained dirt was an occupational hazard.

'Dr Watson. Not brought Sherlock?'

It was a joke Neil had heard so many times before but he forced himself to smile as though this was the first.

'Sorry, he's busy.'

'Karl Banville,' the man said, offering a manicured hand.

'Neil Watson. What can I do for you?' If there was a chance of Banville financing a proper excavation of the site, he was going to be on his best behaviour.

Banville studied the ruin for a few moments before answering.

'I don't know how much Giles Billingham's told you . . .'

'Not much.'

'I've always taken a great interest in Newfield Manor because of a family connection. I'm going to rebuild it. Return it to its former glory. It'll be an exclusive hotel and I intend to emphasise the history of the place in the marketing material. That's where you come in.'

'Giles said something about you funding an excavation.'

34

'Too right. I need you to excavate in the garden ... and while you're at it, I want you to find out all you can about an incident that took place here in 1884.'

'I'm not a researcher.'

'But you know the right people. I'll pay well.'

Neil raised his eyebrows. It wasn't often he heard those words in his line of work.

'But I expect results.'

'Of course. What happened in 1884?'

'A murder.'

'Giles did mention something.' Neil paused for a few moments. 'What exactly are you hoping we'll find if we excavate, Mr Banville?'

'Will you do it or not?' Banville said, suddenly impatient as though he suspected Neil of wasting his time.

Neil saw a movement out of the corner of his eye but when he looked round all he could see were the blank, glassless windows of the old house. However, he was as sure as he could be that somebody had been there behind one on the first floor. Which was impossible because when he'd looked inside the building there had been no floor up there.

The misspelled words of the note he'd found the previous day echoed in Zac Wilkinson's head. I NO WHO U ARE. They were the words he'd dreaded hearing for years. They meant the past had caught up with him, something he'd hoped would never happen. In the intervening years he'd put that terrible time behind him and become a new person.

In the meantime he had work to do. At eight o'clock he was due to deliver a talk at Neston Library about the life and work – mostly the work – of Wynn Staniland and the process of researching his biography. Once the talk was over, he'd have to come straight home and carry on going through the latest draft of the book – incorporating the changes Staniland had demanded during their meeting the previous day. Delivery date was looming and he didn't want to disappoint the publisher. He had his hard-earned professional reputation to think of. Besides, work would take his mind off his problem . . . albeit temporarily.

He checked his watch. If he set off now he'd reach Neston very early but he could have a look round the town before he made for the library. The tickets they'd issued had mentioned refreshments and he hoped that meant wine. Even though he was driving and could only have a couple of glasses, he needed something to dull the shock of finding that note.

As he walked up the hill to the car he glanced round every so often to make sure nobody was following. He rounded the corner of Crossbones Hill and saw the car there just as he'd left it with no new note on the windscreen. Perhaps it had been someone's idea of a joke but, if so, that joke had certainly hit home. How could anybody know the truth when so much care had been taken? It was impossible.

He pressed the remote control and the door locks clicked open.

Then he heard a voice behind him; a voice that sounded vaguely familiar; an echo from a half-forgotten, long-rejected past.

'I thought it was you.'

Zac swung round and found himself facing a man of about his own age. His hair hung in greasy strings and there was a film of ingrained filth on his clothes and flesh. It took Zac a few moments to recognise him and as soon as he did, he caught his breath, fighting the urge to turn and run. Precautions had been taken. This shouldn't be happening.

'What do you want?'

'I'm in trouble, mate. I need help.'

'You've got the wrong man.'

The other man froze for a second as though Zac's reaction had thrown him. Then a knowing smile spread across his face and he took a step forward. 'It's me ... Callum. Remember? Looks like you've done well for yourself. Nice clothes.' He looked at the car. 'Nice wheels.'

'It's a hire car. It's not mine.' Zac felt foolish as soon as he'd said it. This man wasn't interested in technicalities.

'Get my note?'

Zac didn't answer.

'I could make a lot of trouble for you.'

'I don't know what you're talking about.' It was a desperate lie and he knew it sounded unconvincing as soon as it left his lips.

'Liar.'

'Was it you who tried to break into my house?'

'Tried to?'

'Yeah. You damaged the front door.'

The man grinned, showing crooked, yellow teeth. 'Sounds like an amateur. If it had been me I'd have been in, no problem, and you wouldn't even know how. Are you going to help me or what?'

Zac could smell the odour of his adversary's body – foul, as though he hadn't washed for some time – and he saw the determination on his pinched face.

He knew when to give in.

*

The light had started to fade by the time Neil finished examining what was left of Newfield. Karl Banville had dogged his footsteps the whole time, following him everywhere, asking questions.

'It's going to take a hell of a lot of work to get this place habitable,' Neil observed.

But Banville seemed unworried by the prospect. 'You can't put a price on a dream,' he answered. 'If my plans work out, it'll pay for itself ten times over.'

'Have you got planning permission?'

'It won't be a problem. Giles'll be only too glad to get it off this Buildings at Risk Register he goes on about. And a hotel will bring jobs to the area. Councils can never resist that, can they?'

'New hotels don't always succeed.'

'This one'll be unique. Never underestimate the public's appetite for murder and mystery. And with your research to add historical background . . . This place dates back to the Middle Ages, doesn't it?'

'The present building dates to the seventeen hundreds but there's probably been a house on the site for centuries. I'll be able to tell you more when I've had a more detailed look at the building. First of all I'll need all the vegetation cut back, then we'll have to discuss costs.' Neil thought it was worth making some demands of his own.

All of a sudden he heard an approaching engine – something bigger than a car. A minibus appeared, driving towards the house at a stately pace. To Neil's surprise Banville began to run towards it, waving his arms, and stopped defiantly in front of the vehicle, blocking its path. Neil watched with interest as a young man in his late teens alighted from the front passenger seat. The newcomer strolled towards Banville with a look of tolerant amusement on his face. He was tall with neatly cut hair, lips that formed themselves into a slight sneer and a load of confidence. Unusually, he was wearing a top hat and a long black cape.

Neil was too far away to hear what was being said but he saw the newcomer retrace his steps and summon the other passengers out of the bus. There were eight in all, a motley assortment of ages and sexes, but all wore the same expectant expression, as though they were anticipating excitement.

Then Banville raised his voice and Neil could hear quite clearly. 'This is private property. You're trespassing.'

Neil edged forward until he could read the logo on the side of the minibus.

Jones's Ghost Tours, it said. *The only genuine ghost tour in the South-West. Sightings guaranteed.*

He thought it was time he left.

Neston was rightly proud of its brand-new library, state of the art and flooded with light during the day. It was the sort of library authors were keen to visit and Zac Wilkinson had accepted the invitation to talk about his forthcoming biography of Wynn Staniland without hesitation. At ten past seven the library staff were putting out chairs in anticipation of a large audience because Wynn Staniland was a legend. The fact that he lived locally too added to the attraction.

At seven fifteen Zac Wilkinson called to say he'd been delayed but he still hoped to make it on time. And by seven thirty-five people were beginning to arrive, accepting the offered glasses of wine (or orange juice for the drivers and those of a more sober nature) and bagging their places.

By five to eight Zac Wilkinson still hadn't made an appearance and at eight o'clock Julie Shepherd, the librarian who'd arranged the event, rang his number, fearing he'd been held up in traffic. When there was no answer she left a message, reminding him gently that they were waiting for him.

She kept trying but had no luck and by eight thirty the audience began to disperse, their angry muttering fuelled by second glasses of wine.

Julie tried for a last time but there was still no answer.

Zac Wilkinson had either suffered some grave misfortune or he had let them down very badly indeed.

Journal of John Lipton

12 April 1884

When I return to the Market Square after walking
Miss Field and her maid to the Butterwalk, the show is
over and the crowd dispersed. I watch the small murderer
and his victim being returned to a rough-hewn crate
large enough to accommodate the entire wooden cast.
Both the victim and her murderer have eyes that are shut
in death while the little hangman wears an expression of
smug satisfaction.

Mr Gunster's son loads the crate onto the cart but before
he can move away to help his father dismantle the booth, I
approach him. I must get to know this boy with his hard,
cruel face and dead eyes. I think he is the very one I seek.

I learn his name is Enoch and he listens politely when
I introduce myself and explain that I have harboured a
life-long interest in the subject of murder, hoping this will
allay any suspicions he might have and gain his trust.

I ask him where he performs his shows and he names markets and inns in different parts of the county, most of which are unfamiliar to me. Then I enquire whether he and his father ever perform in private houses and I see the light of avarice in his eyes.

'At a price,' he says before naming his fee.

7

As soon as Gerry Heffernan arrived at the police station the following morning he disappeared upstairs to bring Chief Superintendent Noreen Fitton up to date with developments. The chief super was an angular woman with an immaculate uniform and the capable air of an old-fashioned hospital matron but Gerry always found himself feeling a little sorry for her. She was stuck permanently in her office buried under paperwork, forced to endure endless meetings about policy and budgets and, as far as Gerry was concerned, that wasn't what the job was about. He'd never chased further promotion because he liked to get his hands dirty and catch criminals. He had to face enough mountains of irritating paper as it was. Most of it he filed in the bin, hoping the powers that be wouldn't notice.

It was another fine August day and when Gerry returned to the CID office he gazed out of the window for a while, longing to be out of doors taking his yacht, the *Rosie May*, for a spin on the river. But self-indulgence wasn't an option on a working day so, as the lab results for the Lombard case hadn't yet come back, he went to his desk, intending to catch up on some long-neglected routine matters. Just as he sat down he heard a knock on his open door.

He saw DC Rob Carter standing there. With his open face he looked, to someone who didn't know better, like a schoolboy who was reporting to the headmaster to be punished for some minor misdemeanour. But Gerry was aware of a hardness in Rob's eyes. He was a young man who couldn't hide his ambition to climb the promotion ladder and eventually sit in Gerry's executive leather chair, now scruffy with wear and sagging under the DCI's weight.

Gerry greeted him with a scowl. 'Unless the lab results on that couple in the caravan have come through or riots have broken out in the Memorial Gardens, I don't want to be disturbed.'

'We've had a call from a lady called Julie Shepherd; she's a librarian over at Neston.'

'Why? Is there a body in the library?'

Rob shook his head, not connecting with Gerry's attempt at humour. 'An author was due to give a talk at the library last night but he didn't turn up. Name of Zac Wilkinson.'

Gerry rolled his eyes. 'So he got cold feet or he forgot.'

'He rang her to say he might be delayed but he said he'd definitely be there.'

'Perhaps he was taken ill.'

'She tried to get in touch with Wilkinson several times over the evening but he didn't answer his phone. She lives in Tradmouth so she decided to call at his address this morning on her way to work because she was worried about him. There was no answer.'

'I don't see what it's got to do with us.'

A look of frustration passed across Rob's face, as though Gerry was being deliberately obtuse. 'She's wondering whether to report him as a missing person.'

'Does he live with a partner? Anyone else she can contact?'

'He told her he lives alone. He's down here writing a book so he's renting a cottage in town. He's doing a biography of that writer – what's his name?'

'Not Wynn Staniland?'

Rob gave Gerry a look of grudging admiration. 'That's the one.'

Gerry said nothing for a few moments. His mind was working overtime. It was probably a coincidence that Staniland's name had already come up in connection with the Lombards' deaths but there was always a remote possibility that something more sinister was going on.

'Leave it with me, Rob,' he said, peering into the outer office to see if Wesley was there. He needed to share this new piece of information with somebody – and that somebody wasn't Rob Carter.

Rob moved to leave, then stopped and turned. 'I was talking to Nadia on the front desk earlier. She said someone came here looking for you last night. A woman with a Liverpool accent.'

'Name?'

'Didn't give one . . . sir. Would you like me to go and have a word with this Wynn Staniland?'

'Let's not jump the gun. Have you seen DI Peterson?'

'Don't think he's in yet.' Gerry heard an edge of disapproval in the words.

'Oh yeah, I asked him to call in somewhere first. If you see him before I do, tell him I'd like a word.' Wesley was late but since Pam's operation Gerry had made allowances, and he certainly wasn't going to give Rob Carter the satisfaction of knowing his superior officer had bent the rules.

He wondered whether it was worth speaking to Wynn Staniland and hoped Wesley would turn up soon. He needed his opinion.

Over the past few weeks the criminals of Tradmouth and district had been unusually indolent, which meant Wesley had been able to arrive home at a reasonable time. However, if his niggling suspicions about the Lombards' apparent suicides came to anything, this happy situation would change rapidly.

That morning he left Pam resting in bed. The radio-therapy had left her tired and, in spite of her insistence that she was returning to work once the school holidays were over, he'd told her she should allow herself longer to recover. He'd expected her to argue but she'd accepted his misgivings with uncharacteristic meekness.

He was about to leave for work but Amelia and Michael were still in their pyjamas, making the most of the school holidays. As he opened the front door he turned and saw that Michael had followed him into the hall.

'Will Mum be all right?'

Michael and his sister had appeared to take Pam's illness in their stride, so much so that Wesley had assumed they hadn't absorbed the seriousness of her diagnosis. Now he saw that he might have been mistaken.

'The doctors are really pleased with her,' he answered quickly. 'She'll be fine,' he added with a confidence he couldn't quite feel.

'I heard you telling her not to go back to work?'

Wesley retraced his steps and put a comforting hand on the boy's shoulder.

'The more she rests the quicker she'll get better. Don't worry.' He was doing his best to sound cheerful but he guessed Michael could see through the act.

'Harry's asked me to go over to his house tomorrow.'

'Who's Harry?'

'From school.'

'Where does he live?'

'Burston – not far from school. I'll be with Nathaniel. I'll be OK.'

Wesley realised his son was growing up. He was twelve, almost a teenager. But a child is never quite old enough to strike out on his own without a parent's imagination working overtime. As a policeman he knew the chance of anything untoward happening was statistically remote but he couldn't stop himself imagining all kinds of vile scenarios, from his precious offspring slipping into the river and drowning to him falling prey to a crazed killer. He forced himself to smile and offer a lift there and back, work permitting. When Michael shook his head and said he'd make his own way, he felt a little hurt ... and suddenly old.

He arrived at work late and felt a nag of guilt as he made his way up to the CID office, even though Gerry had given his approval. The DCI was in his office, a space in the corner separated from the main office by a flimsy glass partition, talking on the phone. As soon as he spotted Wesley he made a beckoning motion. Gerry was a man who found it hard to hide his emotions and when he ended the call Wesley could tell he had important news.

'That was Leeds on the phone,' Gerry said as he sat down. 'They've been having a chat with the Lombards' neighbours and work colleagues. The usual thing neighbours say in this situation is that they were a lovely couple and they can't believe they'd do something like that. But instead they said the Lombards "kept themselves to themselves" and rarely spoke to anyone, which is neighbourspeak for downright antisocial.'

'Perhaps they were just private people.'

'You were brought up in London, Wes. This is the north we're talking about. Neighbours tend to pass the time of day even if they don't nip in and out of each other's houses borrowing cups of sugar.'

'I'll take your word for it. What about their work colleagues?'

'Frank Lombard worked in an insurance office and his colleagues said he was pleasant but he didn't socialise and rarely talked about his private life. Gina worked in an antique shop. Same story there: quiet, reliable employee who gave very little away about her life outside work. All her colleagues knew about her was that she lived with Frank, had no kids and liked reading.'

'Anything else?'

'The Leeds police are still trying to trace relatives.'

'Good luck to them,' said Wesley with a heartfelt sigh. If there was one thing he hated about his job it was breaking bad news to relatives; whenever possible he left it to someone else.

'They did say something interesting.'

'What?'

'When they went through the house they found a folder of press cuttings about Wynn Staniland. And there was that signed book in the caravan.'

Wesley raised his hand. 'Hang on, I want to check something.'

He rushed from Gerry's office and opened the notebook he'd left on his desk. In it he'd written down the directions he'd found in the Lombards' caravan tucked between the pages of Gina's Wynn Staniland novel, and now he consulted the Ordnance Survey map on the wall of the outer office, tracing the directions which led to a house called Addersacre. When he looked the name up on his computer he discovered that Addersacre was the home of Wynn Staniland and had been for years.

'Well well,' said Gerry when he broke the news. 'So the Lombards knew where he lived.'

'He might be a recluse but it's no state secret.'

'They might have gone there. Harassed him.'

'If they'd caused any problem, surely he would have reported it.'

Gerry wasn't giving up. 'Wonder which one was the fan? Gina or Frank?'

'I'd say Gina but I could be wrong,' said Wesley.

'Maybe she knew him – or Frank did. He'd signed that book.'

'It was an old edition. It might have been signed years ago, before he shut himself away from the world. There was no dedication so one of them might have bought it from a book dealer. Any news from the lab yet?'

Gerry shook his head. 'My old mum always used to say patience was a virtue but she never had to deal with our Forensics people. Staniland's name's come up in another context too. An author who's writing his biography was due to give a talk at Neston Library last night – only he didn't turn up. One of the library staff's been trying to contact him but she's had no luck.'

'And they reported it to us?' Wesley asked, a little surprised.

'She went round to his address this morning and there was no sign of him.'

'What's his name?'

'Zac Wilkinson.'

Wesley raised his eyebrows. 'He might have forgotten to put it in his diary. Or he might have been called away unexpectedly and couldn't let them know.'

'He rang the library to say he might be delayed. He didn't forget.'

He returned to his desk, thinking of Wynn Staniland. Did something about the author, something he'd done perhaps, drive the Lombards to take their own lives? It seemed unlikely but there was only one way to find out if there was a connection and that was to ask him, or if that proved impossible, to talk to Staniland's official biographer; the one who'd failed to keep his appointment at Neston Library the previous evening.

From what he'd discovered on the internet, Addersacre had once been famous – or notorious, depending on your point of view. In his younger days Staniland had over-indulged in alcohol, held wild parties and dabbled in drugs, and scandal had led to the tragedy of his wife's suicide. Then there was the mystery of why he'd produced five brilliant award-winning novels before plunging himself into reclusive retirement at a relatively early age.

All of a sudden he wanted to meet the man for himself. And he had the perfect excuse.

8

The incident with the little band of ghost hunters at Newfield Manor the previous evening left Neil with the uncomfortable feeling that maybe there was something Karl Banville hadn't shared with him.

He received another call from Banville while he was supervising the back-filling of one of the Exeter trenches and he wondered whether the man would make unreasonable demands on his time just because he was footing the bill. Some people thought they could buy you – body and soul.

'Neil,' Banville began. 'We need to talk.'

'I said I'd have another look at the Manor as soon as I've organised the Exeter post-excavation work. It'll take a few more days and then I'll be free and so will my team.'

Banville didn't appear to be listening. 'Sorry about those crazies last night. Let's meet again this evening. Same place.'

Neil was about to say he was too busy to drive all the way down to Whitely again after a day's work. But the urgency in Banville's voice aroused his curiosity. 'Yes, but—'

'There are things you need to know.' He paused. 'About me. I'll see you tonight.'

Neil heard the dialling tone. It looked as though he'd committed himself, and he wasn't sure how he felt about it.

Gerry had received a call from above, as he put it, meaning that Chief Superintendent Fitton wanted another word. This meant Rachel was going with Wesley to visit Wynn Staniland in his place.

She didn't say much as she steered the unmarked police car down the A road, passing the sign to Bloxham. Since her recent brush with death she'd been quiet – or perhaps the prospect of marriage was weighing heavily on her mind. Being a bride, so Pam informed him, had become quite a burden in recent years, what with so much to arrange and choose. Even so, he wouldn't have expected the strong-minded Rachel he knew to succumb to any pressure that wasn't to her liking.

'Pam'll be jealous,' Wesley said, breaking the silence.

'Why?'

'Wynn Staniland's a literary legend.'

There was no reply.

One advantage of having Rachel with him, Wesley thought, was her total indifference to the talents of Wynn Staniland. She said she'd read a couple of his books in her teenage years and found them pretentious, verbose and, frankly, boring. And there were invariably terrible crimes tucked away in the plot somewhere: sick murders; incest and sexual obsession. Rachel had always preferred Agatha Christie. Her books were easier to read and had a proper puzzle.

Wesley couldn't help smiling to himself at Rachel's

damning literary criticism. Staniland was generally regarded as one of the greats.

Rachel turned off the main road and carried on until the lane narrowed into little more than a track. Grass and weeds grew on the sparse tarmac, suggesting that few vehicles passed this way. The hedgerows too were overgrown. It looked like the road to nowhere.

Rachel swore under her breath as the car bounced out of a pothole.

'You sure this is the right way?' Wesley asked.

'Course I am.'

He knew he could trust her local knowledge so he stayed silent as she drove on slowly, looking for any sign of Addersacre. He wondered whether the directions he'd found in the Lombards' caravan had ever been used. Had they come this way? If so, what welcome had they found at the end of their journey?

Suddenly Rachel brought the car to a halt and backed it up a little. To his left he saw a gate, tall with spikes at the top, and on the left gatepost there was a metal panel with a speaker attached. The people who lived on the other side of the barrier didn't encourage unexpected visitors.

Wesley hated the contraptions but he got out and pressed the button. After a few moments he heard a female voice, tinny and distant.

'DI Peterson and DS Tracey, Tradmouth CID. Can we have a word with Mr Staniland, please?'

'He's resting,' came the reply and the line went dead. Wesley tried again, explaining patiently who he was and why he was there. This time the tactic worked and the gate began to open frustratingly slowly, inch by inch.

Rachel revved the engine. Her impatience didn't speed

things up but Wesley could tell it made her feel better. Soon the gate stood fully open and a dark, winding gravel drive stretched out before them, well worn and dotted with weeds. Rachel took her time driving over the unpredictable terrain.

'You'd think he'd get this drive seen to,' she muttered as the house came into view. 'He can't be short of a bob or two.'

Wesley didn't reply. He was too busy looking at the house ahead of them, taking in every detail. It was a low stone house – a large cottage the size of a country rectory; a classic Arts and Crafts building, unpretentious and beautifully proportioned with leaded mullion windows and an oak front door. The windows were dull as though they hadn't been cleaned in years and the place had the air of neglect he'd seen before in houses lived in by elderly people who'd become overwhelmed by the maintenance of a large property.

He marched up to the front door and pressed the bell push at the side. After a while he heard footsteps ringing on a stone floor.

He and Rachel had their IDs at the ready and they held them up for the woman who opened the door to examine.

Wesley guessed she was in her late forties or possibly older; it was hard to tell. Her wavy dark-brown hair, sprinkled with grey, reached her shoulders and she wore a long, ethnic print skirt with a white T-shirt turned grey with much washing. She was thin but her jawline had begun to sag and there was a web of fine lines around her eyes.

'Mr Staniland's resting,' she said softly, rubbing the material of her skirt with nervous fingers. Her voice sounded tense and there was a vagueness in her manner that gave the impression of vulnerability. 'Then perhaps you can help us, Ms . . . ?'

'Staniland. Perdita Staniland. I'm his daughter. I look after him.'

When Wesley stood his ground and gave her an expectant smile, she eventually stood aside to let them in. She led them through a door to the left of the passage into a spacious room with a low ceiling, oak-panelled walls and a stone floor covered by a large Turkish rug, and invited them to sit on a threadbare sofa.

'What's this about?' she said as she perched on the armchair opposite, watching them anxiously.

'A couple called Gina and Frank Lombard were found dead at a caravan park near Stoke Beeching.'

'What's that got to do with Father?'

'Probably nothing but we're tracing their movements while they were down here. Directions to this house were found in the caravan where they died.'

There was no mistaking the relief on the woman's face. 'We sometimes get people coming here to gawp. They press the intercom but we never let them in.'

'Has this happened in the last week or so?'

'A couple of times I suppose.'

Rachel took photographs of the Lombards from her bag. They'd been taken after death but the police photographer had done his best to make them look acceptable. Even so Perdita Staniland winced when she realised what she was seeing.

'Sorry. I don't recognise them,' she said, handing the photos back as though they were contaminated.

'Perhaps your father ... ?'

Before she could answer the door opened and a man walked into the room. Wesley guessed he was around seventy, tall with abundant white hair. His thin face and aquiline nose gave him the look of a watchful bird of prey. Wesley recognised Wynn Staniland from the author photograph on the jacket of Gina Lombard's book even though it had been taken when he was in his prime. His first thought was that he didn't look like a frail invalid. He saw Rachel shift in her seat as though she'd sensed some charisma about him and felt a little embarrassed about it.

Wesley stood up and introduced himself; Staniland shook his hand limply before taking a seat. He appeared relaxed but Wesley suspected it was an act put on for their benefit. 'How can I help you?' he asked quietly, fixing his eyes on Rachel. He smiled at her and Wesley saw her cheeks redden a little.

When Wesley handed him the photographs of the dead couple he saw the colour drain from the man's face.

'You recognise them?'

It was a few seconds before Staniland answered. 'I'm sorry, I've never seen them before in my life.'

'There was a book signed by you in the caravan where they were found.'

'At one time I signed a lot of books but that was a lifetime ago. There are probably hundreds of them around.' Wesley thought he could hear a note of sadness in his voice.

'Father's right,' said Perdita. 'I don't understand what this has to do with us.'

Wesley smiled. 'I take your point, Ms Staniland. But we have to follow every lead.'

'This couple,' Staniland said. 'I presume their deaths were suspicious or you wouldn't be asking these questions.'

Wesley hesitated, wondering how much he should reveal. 'It's possible the victims took their own lives but their deaths are unexplained so we have to find out all we can about them.' He caught Rachel's eye. 'We're sorry to have disturbed you. If you do remember anything, please get in touch.' He handed Staniland his card and rose to leave. But as soon as he reached the door he turned round. 'By the way, do you know a man called Zac Wilkinson?'

'Of course. He's writing my biography. Why do you ask?' Staniland's words sounded guarded. His gaze was still focused on Rachel and she looked away.

'He was due to speak at a library last night but he didn't turn up. You don't know where he is by any chance?'

Staniland shook his head. 'I can't help you. Sorry.'

There was something final about his words and Wesley knew they were being dismissed.

'Let us know if he shows up here, won't you?' he said as Perdita stepped forward to show them out.

'I think you made an impression,' Wesley said when they were halfway down the drive. 'Mind you, they were in a hurry to get rid of us.'

Rachel gave a secretive smile. 'I was thinking exactly the same myself.'

Callum now had cash, courtesy of Zac Wilkinson as he was calling himself now. The pressure was off for the time being but the money wouldn't last long because he needed to buy food and decent clothes. And if he didn't get out of Devon fast there was a chance they'd come looking for him.

Callum could tell Zac had been scared when he'd confronted him. That was why he'd handed over the cash so readily – only fifty quid, all he had on him. When Callum suggested he go to the cashpoint to get more, Zac had made the excuse that he didn't have time because he had to be at some library. Then he'd taken a phone call that had made him excited and he'd hurried off in the direction of the town, promising Callum he'd be back later. But he'd done a runner, which was a big mistake. He couldn't escape from his past that easily.

Callum had knocked on Zac's door at ten o'clock, hoping he'd be back from whatever he was doing at the library, but there'd been no answer. However, there was a solution to every problem. The old supermarket loyalty card in the lock trick had worked like a dream and when the door clicked open he'd given it a push and darted inside.

The place had been silent; the heavy silence of an abandoned house, and there'd been no sign of Zac. Zac – why had he chosen to call himself that? Jamie had always been a pretentious prick, even though he'd been transferred from a secure unit. He'd thought he was cleverer than the rest of the lads on the wing just because he'd once been to a posh school, but he was scum like they all were. He wouldn't have been there otherwise. And Jamie was the worst scum of all because of what he'd done. The rest were thieves and thugs but none of them had borne the mark of Cain like Jamie.

After drawing the curtains Callum sat waiting, alert for Jamie's return. He was sure nobody had seen him go in. It wouldn't have mattered even if they had because the street was full of holiday lets and weekend homes and those sort of people tended not to be too curious. Besides, if anyone challenged him, he could always say he was a friend.

Callum had slept in Jamie's spare bedroom; the first time he'd had a proper bed in ages. The sheets had been cool and smooth and they'd smelled clean so before he'd gone to bed he'd stripped off his clothes and stepped into Jamie's shower, lathering his body with expensive shower gel and watching the filthy, foaming water disappear down the plughole.

Since he'd climbed into the back of that Transit, unaware

of what awaited him, he'd lived a half-life of helpless fear and he kept going over the events in his head, cursing himself for being so trusting. Now he was free at last and relishing the heady sensation of liberty.

He'd slept better than he had in months and that morning he'd been awoken by sunlight streaming through the thin blind and a polite tapping on the front door which he ignored because he knew opening the door to visitors wouldn't be a good idea. He lay staring at the snow-white ceiling, wondering if this was what heaven was like; savouring the comfort and listening for sounds from Jamie's room in case he'd come back during the night. But all he heard were seagulls, crying like souls in torment, and the buzz of passing conversation in the street below.

Eventually he went into Jamie's room and when he found he hadn't returned he had another shower, standing beneath the spray of warm water for ages just because he could.

Once he'd dried himself he chose something from Jamie's wardrobe and dressed, delving into the drawer to find a belt to hold the trousers up because he'd lost so much weight over the past year. Even though Jamie was hardly a big man, his clothes hung loosely off Callum's skeletal form. The clothes were designer; must have cost a fortune. But Jamie had always been a man of taste . . . and means.

As soon as he'd collected up his own stinking clothes and stuffed them into an old carrier bag in the backyard, Callum's next thought was food. Then as he made for the fridge he heard another knock on the door, echoing through the cottage like a portent of doom.

Maybe staying there was too risky. Maybe it was time to go.

9

'The results have come back from Forensics,' said Gerry as Wesley walked into his office. 'The Lombards were poisoned with aconite. It was in the champagne bottle and the glasses.'

'It could still be suicide,' Wesley said, wondering why Gerry looked so excited.

'The only fingerprints found on the bottle were Frank Lombard's. Bottles are handled by lots of people before they're sold and people leave prints. This bottle was perfectly clean apart from Lombard's. It had been wiped before they drank from it.'

Wesley thought for a moment. 'I take it the cork and the foil are in the exhibits store?'

Wesley didn't wait for a reply. He left the room and headed straight for the exhibits store in the basement, taking the stairs two at a time. He searched the shelves and once he'd found what he was looking for he returned to Gerry's office carrying two plastic evidence bags containing the champagne cork and the foil that had covered it. He placed them on Gerry's desk, pulled on a pair of crime scene gloves and extracted the contents of the bags with great care.

'Got a magnifying glass?'

'Those went out with Sherlock Holmes,' Gerry muttered as he delved into the cluttered depths of his drawer, finding a magnifying glass at the back which he'd almost forgotten was there. 'But you're in luck.'

There was a long period of silence while Wesley examined the objects closely. Then he looked up.

'I can see a tiny pinprick in the foil, barely visible to the naked eye. I think someone's put a needle through it. It's not easy to tell with the cork.'

Gerry caught on fast. 'Are you saying someone injected the poison through the cork?'

'Forensics should be able to confirm it.'

'Maybe Frank Lombard poisoned the bottle intending to kill his wife and then himself.'

'So why wipe it clean?'

Gerry gave a deep sigh, anticipating a dramatic increase to his workload. 'If you're right we'll have to start treating it as a double murder. How did you get on with Wynn Staniland?'

'He denied knowing Gina Lombard. Said he used to sign hundreds of books back in the day. He also said they often have unwanted visitors pressing the intercom by their gate but his daughter just tells them to go away. If Gina Lombard had called, Staniland wouldn't necessarily have known.'

'Did you believe him?'

Wesley considered the question for a few moments. 'Yes. His daughter's very protective and I can't see the Lombards gaining admission even if they made it as far as the gate. We hardly received a warm welcome when we turned up unannounced.'

'That make you suspicious?'

'Not really. Staniland values his privacy,' Wesley replied. 'Even so, I'd like to find out more about him. He's a bit of an enigma. Struck me as the charismatic type and switched on the charm as soon as he saw Rachel. But he suddenly stopped writing and shut himself away from the world. I'd like to know the full story.'

'It's strange that his biographer's gone AWOL, don't you think? I presume he's not turned up?'

'It's far too early to treat him as a missing person just because he chickened out of giving a talk. Perhaps something cropped up. Perhaps he got a better offer. He's a grown man.'

'Or he had a hissy fit and went off in a huff.' Gerry rolled his eyes. 'Arty types.'

Wesley smiled to himself. 'Rachel said someone was looking for you. A woman? Did she find you?'

'Never left her details so there was nothing I could do about it.' He grinned. 'Probably a grateful customer – some tart I arrested years ago who saw the error of her ways, started her own business or married a millionaire and now she's come back to thank me.'

'You can dream, Gerry,' Wesley said with a laugh. 'Look, I'll send that cork and foil to the lab but in the meantime are we treating the Lombards' deaths as murder?'

Gerry sighed. 'If you want to do away with yourself you might want to enjoy a last drink of champers . . . but you'd put the stuff straight into the glass, not mess about getting it into the bottle. No poison container was found at the caravan and you'd hardly go to the trouble of wiping off fingerprints. I'd lay odds on it being murder, wouldn't you, Wes? Only someone would like us to think otherwise.'

Wesley couldn't disagree. So much for a peaceful summer.

When Callum risked looking out of the window to see who was calling he was almost relieved to see a uniformed policeman standing on the doorstep. There were far more frightening people around than the fuzz. He'd met quite a few of them in his time. He wondered if this was the second call they'd made that morning, but the previous knocking had been timid and, in his experience, the police didn't do timid. Neither did the people who'd be out looking for him.

The constable at the door glanced up at the bedroom window just as Callum shot back into the shadows. After a second knock the officer gave up and walked off down the street. Result. At least it meant he wouldn't have to move on immediately.

He was probably safe there. For now.

Rachel Tracey knew the dislike she'd taken to Wynn Staniland and his daughter was irrational but she couldn't help how she felt. She'd come across their type before. They were the sort of people who either patronised the farming community she'd been a part of since birth or, alternatively, romanticised the tough, backbreaking rural way of life to a ridiculous degree. Either way, they hadn't a clue about real life and struggling to make ends meet.

But some memory, some association from childhood was emerging from her subconscious and she closed her eyes as it returned slowly, fragment by fragment. A half-remembered conversation; her parents talking about Staniland in a context which had nothing to do with literature. Something that had happened a long time ago; a tragic death. If only she could remember the details.

She typed Staniland's name into Google and waded through pages of book reviews until she found what she was looking for.

'Wesley, have you got a moment?'

Wesley was at his desk, deep in thought, but as soon as he heard Rachel's voice he looked round. 'What is it, Rach?'

'I've been looking up Wynn Staniland on the internet.'

'And?'

'First of all Perdita's his stepdaughter, not his daughter. Her mother was his late wife. Father unknown.' She paused. 'And thirty-four years ago his wife killed herself. She drowned herself in a sea pool not far from the house.'

'Wasn't it suicide?'

'That was the inquest verdict but, according to the internet, there were rumours flying around at the time that she was murdered.'

Gerry had watched a lot of police dramas where the chief investigating officer swept in dramatically and ordered his devoted team to 'listen up'. But after his conversation with Noreen Fitton he didn't feel like taking such a gung-ho approach. She'd babbled on about budgets and asked him whether he was a hundred per cent certain they were dealing with murder rather than a double suicide. He'd stood his ground though. It was murder all right. He felt it in his bones. And once Forensics got their fingers out and examined the foil and cork, he'd know for sure.

Gerry Heffernan's first rule of detection was that to know your murderer, you have to know your victim so, ideally, he'd have liked to travel up to Yorkshire the next day to make a thorough search of the Lombards' house. He was still waiting impatiently for the couple's mobile phone records and he wanted to talk to everyone in their address book – everyone over a certain age has an address book. Now, with the chief super advising caution, he feared their trip would have to wait.

The delay meant his mood was subdued as he addressed his team in the CID office. In all probability, he announced, Gina and Frank Lombard had been murdered. Poisoned with aconite, a poison obtained from the plant monkshood. When Rob Carter commented that poisoning was a woman's crime Gerry told him not to jump to conclusions. It was early days and, so far, they had no suspects.

By five o'clock Gerry was hungry so he told Wesley he was going out to get some fish and chips, saying that a growing lad like him couldn't survive on sandwiches alone. Wesley had mumbled something about healthy eating before ordering a chicken wrap from DC Paul Johnson, who was taking the orders. With the new developments it could turn out to be a late night.

Gerry slouched out of the police station, his hands in his pockets, lost in thought. Had the Lombards brought the champagne with them down from Leeds? Had they bought it themselves or had they been given it? The answer would make all the difference and he'd put DC Trish Walton onto finding it. And why were they drinking champagne anyway? Were they celebrating something? There was so much to discover that he suddenly felt overwhelmed.

He didn't hear the footsteps coming up behind him and he wasn't aware of the woman's presence until she spoke his name.

'Is it Gerry Heffernan?'

He swung round and saw her. She was in her thirties, medium height with brown hair tied back in a neat pony-tail, and her accent suggested she came from his native Liverpool. She had freckles and there was something famil-iar about her, although he couldn't think what it was.

'Yes, love. What can I do for you?' Then he suddenly remembered. 'Have you been asking for me?'

She blushed. 'That's right.' She hesitated, suddenly nerv-ous. 'I think you knew my mam.'

'What's her name?'

'She was Donna McQuail ... before she married me dad.'

Gerry frowned in an effort to remember. There had been a lot of girls in his Liverpool youth. He'd been at college studying navigation, working towards his mate's ticket, and he'd been a bit of a lad back then. Afterwards when he'd gone to sea he'd lived up to the traditional sailor's reputa-tion of having a girl in every port. That was before he'd developed appendicitis and been airlifted from his ship to Tradmouth Hospital. Kathy had been nursing him and he'd fallen in love. They'd married and he'd come ashore, joined the police and his life had changed forever.

'Oh yeah?' Although he really didn't have time to rem-inisce, he always liked to hear news of his native city. Yet try as he might, he couldn't remember a Donna McQuail.

'Thing is ... er ... Gerry, before she died, me mam said you and her ... '

Gerry suddenly had the feeling that this might not be an easy conversation. 'The thing is ... well, she said you're me real dad.'

10

To Callum's relief the police hadn't been back. He lay on Jamie's – or rather Zac's – spare bed and grinned to himself. He'd eaten half the contents of the fridge and unless Jamie returned he knew that sooner or later he'd need to venture out to buy in more supplies, although now he'd found this cosy bolthole he was reluctant to leave it. They were still out there somewhere and if they found him . . . He knew what they did to runaways.

He levered himself off the bed and stared at his reflection in the dressing-table mirror. He'd done his best to make himself look respectable. It's hard cutting your own hair but he reckoned he hadn't made a bad job of it. He'd shaved and put on some of Jamie's smarter clothes and now he felt he wouldn't merit a second glance in the streets of Tradmouth. He was a new man. And, with any luck, the men who were after him wouldn't recognise the filthy, half-starved creature they'd kept in that locked outhouse like an animal awaiting slaughter.

Besides, would they be looking for him in Tradmouth? They'd expect him to be holed up in the countryside, in a derelict barn or outhouse – not that there were many of those left since it became the fashion to convert them into desirable homes.

Callum knew that others had been found and brought back but he was determined that he'd be the one who got away.

He was weighing up his next move when he heard a sound downstairs: the click of a lock. Jamie was back. He froze, wondering how to play it. Jamie would be shocked to find him there – angry maybe – but he had to persuade him that helping him was in Jamie's best interests. Callum knew who he really was and he knew what he'd done.

He waited for Jamie to go into the kitchen; to switch on the TV; open the fridge; to do the other normal things people do when they arrive home. But whoever was down there wasn't making much noise.

Callum hovered at the top of the stairs, straining to hear, unsure what to do. Someone was opening drawers with the stealth of a thief and, even though the front door had been unlocked with a key, Callum was as sure as he could be that this wasn't Jamie. He had to act before the intruder decided to try upstairs so he crept down into the hall and dashed on tiptoe past the half-open living-room door.

Then, wearing Jamie's clothes, hair washed and clean shaven, he slipped out into the street.

On Saturday morning Neil took a break in the site hut and poured himself a coffee from his flask. He'd been examining the medieval pottery from the final trenches, wishing they weren't under so much pressure from the developers who couldn't wait to cover his site with concrete. But the winding up of the Exeter dig wasn't the only thing on his mind.

The County Archaeological Unit was chronically short of funds and an interesting project bankrolled by a generous benefactor was something he'd long fantasised about. So why hadn't he said yes to Karl Banville right away instead of saying he'd think about it? He felt the need to talk it over with someone he trusted so he called Wesley's number.

'What can I do for you, Neil?' His friend sounded distant and preoccupied and Neil sensed he'd called at a bad time.

'Are you at home today?'

'I'm in work. Why?'

There was a short silence before he answered. 'I've been asked to excavate a site near Whitely but I've got a bad feeling about it.' Now he put it into words it sounded foolish.

'Why's that?' To Neil's relief Wesley suddenly sounded interested.

'Giles, the local conservation officer, called me out to an at-risk building. It's been bought by a wealthy American for redevelopment but before planning permission's granted Giles needs a report on the fabric of the building and an assessment of any archaeology that might be on the site. Routine stuff.'

'What's the problem?'

'The new owner asked to meet me in private.' He hesitated. 'It was a bit weird.'

'In what way?'

'I felt he had an agenda – something he wasn't telling me. He wants the Unit to carry out an excavation of the gardens. And he's willing to foot the bill.'

'That's good, isn't it? Sorry, Neil, I'm in the middle of something here.'

'Look, is there any way of checking out the new owner? His name's Karl Banville. He's American but he's been living over here for a few months.'

'What does the conservation officer think?'

'Giles hasn't got a suspicious bone in his body.'

'OK. I'll keep my ears open but I can't promise anything.'

'Thanks. How's Pam?'

'Not too bad.'

Wesley's reply was automatic, as though the subject was one he'd rather avoid. Neil didn't enquire further; he'd wait until they were face to face.

As soon as Neil ended the call his phone rang again. He recognised the voice on the other end of the line immediately. It was Karl Banville and he sounded excited.

'Neil, there's someone I want you to meet. How about later today? You name the time.'

Neil's first thought was, how can I get out of this? But Banville had asked him to name the time so he couldn't think up an excuse on the spur of the moment. He heard himself saying it was fine. He'd meet Banville at four o'clock at Newfield Manor.

Wesley could tell something was bothering Neil and, in all the years they'd known each other, he'd rarely been worried by trivialities. Curious, he made some discreet enquiries about Karl Banville but nothing untoward was known about him. On the contrary, according to Google, he was a businessman who'd made his pile in a hi-tech industry in California, the nature of which Wesley didn't quite understand. He listed his place of birth as Ohio and his interests as heritage and genealogy, which to Wesley seemed both endearing and understandable.

He called Neil back to tell him the good news, saying that hunches belonged in the more clichéd variety of detective fiction and he could embark on his new, subsidised dig with a clear conscience.

Wesley was feeling satisfied that he'd done his good deed for the day when Gerry appeared in the doorway. The boss had left the office an hour ago without saying where he was going. Wesley couldn't help wondering what he'd been up to, especially when, instead of doing the rounds of the desks as he usually did on his return to ask whether anything new had come in, he vanished into his office without a word. Wesley decided to follow him and was greeted with a curt nod, as though the DCI's mind was elsewhere.

'Everything OK, Gerry?'

'Why shouldn't it be?' The DCI sighed and slumped down into his seat. 'Anything new?'

'I've just heard from Forensics about the champagne foil and cork. As I suspected, there's a tiny hole in the foil and traces of poison inside the cork. Whoever killed the Lombards injected the stuff into the bottle. You wouldn't do that if you were committing suicide.'

'Double murder it is, then,' Gerry muttered. 'Just what we need.'

'I wish Leeds would hurry up and get back to us. If they brought the bottle with them from home it means the killer lives up there. We need to find out who wanted them dead.'

'What about that Wynn Staniland?'

'So far there's no suggestion Gina Lombard was anything but a fan.'

Gerry grunted. 'So seeing him was a waste of time?'

Wesley shrugged. 'It was interesting to meet him. And it's something to tell Pam. She's reading one of his books at the moment.'

Gerry didn't comment. Instead he stared at the paperwork piled on his desk.

'Is something wrong, Gerry?'

When Gerry shook his head, Wesley left the office and returned to his own desk.

At midnight Callum summoned the courage to return to Jamie's cottage, being extra careful in case the intruder was still around. To his relief he found the place empty and apparently undisturbed.

It was hard to tell what, if anything, was missing but he was sure some of Jamie's papers weren't there any more. He had no idea what was in them because he found reading difficult. Not that he couldn't read; it just took him more time than it took other people and the remedial classes he'd been given in prison hadn't helped much.

As well as the files, the laptop on the sideboard had disappeared so perhaps it had been a burglar after all, a common thief just like himself.

First thing the following morning he ventured into Tradmouth and when he walked down the street wearing Jamie's clothes nobody batted an eyelid. He shopped for food in the little Co-op near the waterfront but Jamie's fifty quid hadn't gone far. He needed more cash and until Jamie came back, he wasn't sure how to get any. There was always thieving, of course. At one time he'd been good at it – but not quite good enough, which was why he'd landed in trouble.

He'd found a spare key to the cottage in a bowl near the

front door so at least he had the means to get in and out without arousing suspicion. When he returned from the shops he used the key as if he owned the place, knowing that if you went about anything with enough confidence, nobody asked questions. It was something Jamie told him once and he was absolutely right.

The identity of the previous night's intruder was still bothering him. There was a chance it was someone from Jamie's past. What if they came back and mistook him for Jamie? He'd heard Jamie had powerful enemies; dangerous men. That's why he'd become Zac.

Callum weighed up the pros and cons of staying there and eventually convinced himself that if the intruder hadn't found Jamie there he wouldn't bother coming back and Callum would probably be safe for the time being. And the people from the farm would never think of looking for him there.

He was starting to feel more confident so he decided to conduct a search of his own. So far he'd been interested only in the necessities of life, food and clothes, but now he wanted to find out what else the cottage had to offer. He started in the bedroom, reckoning Jamie would keep anything of value in his most private room. At first he found nothing but when he slid his hand under the mattress he found a passport. He read the name inside, mouthing the words – Zac Wilkinson; the name Jamie was using in his new life. He put it back where he'd found it, thinking it might come in useful someday. However, it wasn't until he went down to the living room and searched the cupboards that he found what he was really looking for.

The credit and debit cards were in a small leather holder, smaller than a wallet, hidden away behind a pile of crockery: Jamie's answer to a safe. It was lucky, Callum thought, that he hadn't taken it out with him – and even luckier that the intruder hadn't stolen it, especially as the scrap of paper tucked in beside the cards bore four digits that Callum guessed was his PIN number. A gift to a thief, but some people never learn. Callum had always been a lot better with numbers than he was with letters. There was a beauty, a logic, about numbers so if the PIN number didn't work first time, he'd try all the different combinations.

Now he had the cards perhaps he could find a way of helping Ivan, Ivan who coughed all night and whose flesh looked grey, like a dead man's.

Journal of Mary Field

26 April 1884

Although Mr Gunster's puppets have made no further appearance in the town, I am attracted there by the prospect of meeting John Lipton for he shares my fascination with the macabre. I sometimes think we are twin souls, fashioned for one another by fate.

Sarah relays our messages and I can rely on her discretion. I think perhaps I am in love.

John has thought up a plan so bold it takes my breath away. He says he loves me and will ask Father for my hand but first he intends to provide an entertainment that cannot be surpassed in the district. He has persuaded Mr Gunster to give a private show at the Manor for my parents' delectation. How can they fail to appreciate his thoughtfulness?

11

Wesley could see Gerry through the glass wall of his office, staring into space.

He'd never seen the DCI like this before, not even in the darkest times they'd shared together. He gave a swift token knock on Gerry's door.

Gerry looked up. 'What can I do you for, Wes?' The jocular question was half-hearted, as though his mind was elsewhere.

'If West Yorkshire don't get back to me soon about the Lombards, I'm going to give them a call. See what's going on.'

As Gerry grunted in reply, the phone on Wesley's desk began to ring. Normally the boss would leap up to see whether the call would push the investigation forward. Instead he remained in his seat, lost in his own world.

Wesley's caller turned out to be a sergeant from Leeds and he listened carefully to what the woman with the pronounced northern accent had to say.

'The Lombards lived in a close of little semis, the sort of place where everyone knows everyone else's business,' she began. 'But the neighbours didn't tell us much, apart from the old lady next door. She saw Mrs Lombard in the garden the day before they went away.'

Wesley pressed the phone to his ear, holding his breath.

'She said Mrs L – Gina – had hardly said a word to her before, but that day she seemed excited. On edge, was how she put it. She said they were going down to Devon for a caravan holiday.'

'Anything else?'

'No, that's all. We've found Frank Lombard's next of kin – a brother who lives in Roundhay. We've been there to break the news to him and he was upset as you'd expect. He said him and Frank weren't particularly close but they did see each other once a month or so. They met up last week just before Frank and Gina went away. According to the brother, Frank said something strange.'

'What was that?'

The sergeant paused, as though for dramatic effect. 'He said him and Gina were going to Devon to get rich.'

Pam Peterson didn't want to be regarded as an invalid for any longer than necessary. Her treatment was over and she was feeling much better so she'd called her headteacher that morning to say she'd work three days a week instead of the promised two when the new term started in September. But she hadn't shared this with Wesley because she knew he'd warn her not to do too much. She wasn't sure whether to be annoyed with him for interfering or glad that he cared.

It was the weekend – the time most families spent together – but Wesley was at work, investigating the case of the couple from up north who'd been found dead in a caravan three miles away. She thought it sounded like a tragic suicide pact but, even so, it meant Wesley wasn't there with her. And neither was Michael.

Her son, having reached the age where independence is the newly achievable Holy Grail, was spending the day with a school friend who lived across the river. The fact that she knew nothing about this new friend or his family made her uneasy but she told herself Michael was almost thirteen now and she couldn't keep him close and protected forever. He had to explore the world and make his own judgements and mistakes even though these mistakes and their possible consequences frightened the hell out of her. When he'd told her about Harry's invitation she'd forced herself to smile and agree, as had Wesley. And Michael would be with Nathaniel, a sensible boy she'd known since he and Michael were at nursery school together, so it was bound to be all right.

With Michael away she'd been looking forward to sharing the day with her daughter, Amelia. Her plans had gone awry, however, when one of the other mothers offered to take a group of Amelia's school friends to the cinema in Morbay to see a film featuring some clone cartoon princess. Amelia had nagged to go until Pam, yielding to the inevitable, had agreed so now she was spending the day alone with her thoughts and the Wynn Staniland book she was obliged to reread for the next meeting of her monthly book group.

She had just settled on the sofa to read when the doorbell rang. Reluctantly she uncurled herself and answered the front door.

'I thought I'd come and keep you company,' Della said, sweeping past her into the living room. Most mothers would have offered to put the kettle on but Della wasn't most mothers. Instead she produced a bottle of Prosecco from her canvas bag.

'Bit early for me,' Pam said.

'The sun's always over the yardarm somewhere in the world. Fetch some glasses.'

Della flopped onto the sofa Pam had just vacated, spreading her long ethnic skirt out and adjusting her scarves. She'd dyed her long hair blond, claiming that blondes have more fun, but she couldn't disguise the havoc time had wreaked on her face, those deep lines radiating from her eyes and upper lip. Della had talked about Botox but hadn't got round to it yet.

'What are you reading?' Della asked once she'd opened the bottle with a satisfying pop.

Pam held up her book for her mother to see. '*The Viper's Kiss*. Wynn Staniland. Bit depressing.'

But Della wasn't interested in Pam's literary opinion. She was leaning forward, waving her half-empty glass in excitement. 'We tried to get him but he wasn't playing ball.'

'We?'

'The Dukesbridge Literary Festival. I'm on the organising committee this year. If we'd managed to get Wynn Staniland to speak it would have been a real coup but he's a bloody hermit. Won't leave his house.'

For a few moments Pam said nothing. Then she spoke quietly. 'I don't like his books. I find the violence ... prurient. It's as though he's trying to shock.'

'Surely that's the whole point of literature – to shock people out of their complacency.'

'I'm sure Jane Austen wouldn't agree with you,' said Pam. 'I think the point is to hold a mirror up to society and make people think about what really goes on around them – the funny quirks of people's behaviour and the reasons we do what we do.'

Della muttered something Pam couldn't quite catch, except she did manage to make out the word 'outmoded'. Della liked to be fashionable in all forms of thought and opinion.

'You haven't asked me how I am,' Pam said, pouring herself a second glass of Prosecco to numb the nagging irritation of her mother's presence.

'If you weren't OK you would have told me by now,' was Della's response. 'I've been reading about Wynn Staniland. Thought I'd do a bit of homework when we tried to get him for the festival. Mind you, we've got his biographer which is the next best thing, I suppose. Staniland's had a tragic life, you know. No wonder he became a recluse. His wife drowned herself in a pool near their house and the strange thing was, when they found her she was sitting bolt upright in the water.'

'So how could she have drowned herself?'

'She weighed down her pockets with pebbles, walked into the pool until it was deep enough to drown her and sat down. Mind you.' Della pointed to the book Pam had been reading. 'She took the method from the plot of *The Viper's Kiss*. The ultimate revenge on her husband, don't you think?'

Pam glanced down at the book lying beside her on the sofa and gave an involuntary shudder.

Callum had been running out of food but, with the help of the cards and PIN number Jamie had been foolish enough to leave around for anyone to find, he'd managed to remedy that. Recent events had robbed him of the little courage he once had but the triumph he felt when he saw the money roll out of the cash machine outside the bank gave him a new glimmer of hope. Maybe things would go his way from now on.

Jamie still hadn't come back. Callum couldn't think of him as Zac. Zac was someone else – an unfamiliar new creation that had nothing to do with the man he used to know; the man with whom he'd shared so much. When he'd first spotted Jamie in Tradmouth, he'd planned to take advantage of what he knew about his true identity. But now he was beginning to worry. Why had Jamie vanished without a word? Callum knew he was clever – he wrote things for newspapers and books about people's lives – but was he involved in something he couldn't control? Or had he left because Callum had turned up – a face from a past he'd rather forget?

Callum put one of the ready meals he'd bought in Jamie's microwave, taking care to read the instructions slowly and carefully. As he watched the black plastic container spinning on the glass turntable, he couldn't help thinking of Ivan. There had been a time when he'd thought the hard years had killed any softness inside him; but the image of Ivan burned bright in his mind. Ivan in chains coughing uncontrollably, his scrawny body filthy with sores. Ivan being beaten with the lengths of rubber hose they liked to use. Some of the others in the barn were in a bad way but Ivan was the worst. For the first time in his life, Callum felt a strong urge to help another human being.

He put on the coat he found hanging by the front door. The coat had an expensive label, was slightly too big and far, far too warm for the August weather, but Callum liked the feel of it. It made him look like someone.

Although he hadn't driven for a while he'd found Jamie's car keys in the pocket of one of his coats and he knew the car was parked up on Crossbones Hill, there for the taking.

When he reached the car he unlocked the door and slipped inside, sitting in the driver's seat for a while, getting used to the long-forgotten feeling of being in charge of a vehicle. He was about to turn the key in the ignition when he had an idea. Had Jamie left anything in the car that might be of use to him? Or that might provide a clue to where he'd gone?

He got out again and unlocked the boot. Inside he saw a holdall and when he unzipped it he found a couple of blank notebooks and an iPad, slim as a picture frame. He was surprised that Jamie had one of these as well as his laptop – now missing – but he supposed a writer needed more than one option. It was a piece of technology that was no use to him but he reckoned he could flog it in a pub if he ran out of funds. He wondered whether to take it back to the cottage but there was always a chance the intruder might return – or maybe Jamie himself. He knew somewhere they'd never look so he carried the holdall along the lane to the allotments and deposited it in what he thought of as his shed, hiding it underneath the old sacking that had once served as his bedding. If he ran out of resources the iPad would be there, like an insurance policy.

The car started first time but, faced with the controls, his initial confidence began to slip away. Still, if he didn't drive it would mean walking down to the waterfront to catch the bus out of town so he took a deep breath and set off.

It wasn't easy manoeuvring the unfamiliar vehicle down the cramped streets and his heart pounded as he crashed the gears. By the time he'd found the main road out of town he was getting used to driving again and after a couple of miles he looked out for familiar landmarks. He'd studied the name on the sign carefully: Stoke Beeching. If he could find the village, he was sure he could find the right place.

He drove slowly down the narrow road and parked in a wide section just before the sign that welcomed travellers to the village, pleased with himself that he'd managed to recognise it. After locking the car against thieves he started to walk. He'd discarded his own shoes, swapping them for a pair of Zac's, which were only half a size too big and fairly comfortable. He hoped that even if his captors saw him they wouldn't recognise him now he'd cleaned himself up and clothed himself in borrowed respectability.

He walked past a few well-kept cottages that might have been holiday homes, head down, trying to look inconspicuous. When he'd last been there it had been dark and he remembered seeing a warm glow from the pub windows as he'd limped past, his mind focused solely on escape. Then he'd walked all the way to Tradmouth and found shelter in the disused allotment shed, rummaging in bins behind the town centre restaurants for food.

He'd lived like that for three days, staying in the shadows. Then he'd spotted the photo of Jamie in the library window. As far as he could make out the poster said he was giving a talk, although Callum wasn't quite sure what he'd be talking about – not his past, that was for certain. And he was using a different name – Zac Wilkinson – but a change of name was hardly surprising, given what he'd done. Besides, it had all been official; done by the authorities so he could start a new life. Not everyone in that place had been so lucky.

On the night of the talk Callum waited in the alley beside Tradmouth Library and followed Jamie home to a little cottage on a steep street at the heart of the town. It was near the allotments, which was a lucky coincidence, and when Callum found out that Jamie parked his car up there on Crossbones Hill, he hadn't been able to resist leaving the message on the windscreen, just to tease.

Now, however, he had more urgent things to think about than Jamie and his disappearance; he needed to get Ivan out of that hell and take him to a doctor. Looking after number one had always been his mantra but when he'd escaped he'd promised to rescue Ivan from that place before he died like the others he'd heard talked about in whispers.

He was beyond the village now, walking down a lane that looked familiar, although he couldn't be sure. On the night of his escape he'd just had the silver sheen of the moon to see by and the only sounds had been the wind in the trees and the shriek of an owl as it homed in for the kill. It would have been useless going back there at night because as soon as darkness came the men were usually locked in. His best hope was to find them while they were working and their captors let down their guard.

He walked until he came to a gate he thought he recognised. It was new and padlocked – they liked padlocks – and the hanging sign next to the gate was one he'd seen before when he'd first been taken there. The man had caught him and his mate outside the hostel and offered them work with good pay and accommodation and they hadn't hesitated. They'd picked up their things and climbed in the back of the Transit with the sunny optimism of a pair of holidaymakers, only when they reached their destination the adventure turned dark. When they weren't working for nothing they were locked up and their erstwhile benefactor's kindness turned to cruelty as the threats and beatings began.

Now he was back there the fear returned. If they found him there he'd be punished, and those who were punished were sometimes never seen again. But he had to find Ivan.

He was about to climb over the gate when he noticed a CCTV camera on a pole and he dodged out of the way, hoping the camera hadn't picked him up. There might be other cameras nearer the house, he thought. This wouldn't be as easy as he'd hoped.

Then a shot rang out, sending the screaming crows rising from the surrounding trees. To Callum, that sound meant only one thing: death.

12

Michael Peterson tried to ignore his mother's warnings as he left the house. Take care. Keep away from the railway line. Don't go near the river bank because the currents are treacherous. Let me know when you get to Harry's and call to tell me what time you'll be back. She thought he was still a kid.

His dad had gone off to the police station at eight thirty even though it was the weekend. Sometimes Michael hated that police station because his dad spent more time there than he did at home, but at least it meant he wasn't on his case all the time; not when he was on someone else's.

Michael had lied to his mum. He'd said Nathaniel was going with him to Harry's but that wasn't true. Nathaniel hadn't even been invited so Michael travelled to Burston on his own, taking the passenger ferry to Queenswear and walking the half-mile to Harry's house once he reached the far side of the river. And now he was having a good time with Harry and his older brother, Archie. Archie was cool and he'd spent the first half of the morning dispensing words of wisdom; the wisdom of an experienced eighteen year old who's seen it all and done most of it.

Archie was taking a year out before going up to Oxford and he was using his time profitably by organising ghost tours. He and a mate drove the punters around to local sites that were reputed to be haunted and scared the pants off them, Harry told Michael with a smirk. The tourists loved it.

After an hour Archie left to meet some girl but Michael hadn't really minded. It was Harry who was his new friend and, like all new friends, he had a gloss of mystery and excitement about him lacking in his old mate Nathaniel whom he'd known nearly all his life. Nathaniel was tarnished by long familiarity whereas Harry possessed an edge of danger. His parents let him stay out late; they allowed him to explore places Michael's own parents wouldn't approve of.

Harry's mother was stick-thin with long pale hair and a nervous smoking habit and his dad had a golden tan, tattoos and a shiny black Porsche SUV. Neither asked where they were going that day. Pam and Wesley always asked, which was a pain.

Twenty minutes after Archie's departure Harry announced that they were going to explore the woods at the back of his house. To Michael they looked dark and impenetrable. A place of possibilities. Harry warned that there were a lot of walkers at this time of year so they'd have to stay off the tracks and keep to the hidden places. Michael said he was up for it.

When they'd been walking through the trees for ten minutes, to Michael's surprise Harry started talking animatedly about wildlife and he realised they weren't there traipsing through the ferns and sharp twigs in search of adventure but to see what birds and wild creatures they could spot. He knew he should be disappointed but, strangely, he felt relieved and soon found himself swept up with his new friend's enthusiasm. The cool, disdainful Harry who'd made such an impression at school had transformed before his eyes into a boy just like himself and Nathaniel and soon they were on the lookout for adders. You had to watch out because they were poisonous which, of course, increased their allure.

Armed with the long sticks they carried like staffs of office, the young countrymen ploughed through the green ferns. Every so often they heard voices in the distance; walkers, usually very old, with their sturdy boots and backpacks. But the intruders didn't bother the boys. They were on the trail of adders. Vipers, Harry called them knowledgably; evil things but fascinating. He had seen loads of them in these very woods.

Harry was walking ahead, sweeping the undergrowth ahead of him with his stick. Then suddenly he stopped and held up a warning hand.

'Is it a viper?' Michael whispered, straining to see beyond Harry's back.

Harry didn't reply. Instead he crept forward and Michael shuffled after him. Whatever Harry had spotted, he could tell it was interesting.

Then Harry stood aside and he saw it clearly: a shoe, and attached to that shoe was a leg encased in denim. A bush concealed the rest of the body but something told Michael the owner of the shoe and the leg was dead.

It was Michael who stepped forward to investigate

further and when he was a couple of feet away from the body he could see the exposed flesh of the dead man's hand was dark – livid as a bad bruise. He stared at it, torn between terror and excitement.

'I'd better call my dad,' Michael said, making a great effort to sound casual, as though this was something he faced on a daily basis. But he was aware of the tremor in his voice.

'Why?'

''Cause he's in the police,' he said. This was the first time he'd made this confession to Harry. 'He's a detective,' he added, hoping this would add a touch of glamour to his parent's occupation.

At first Harry said nothing. Then he tore his eyes from the corpse and looked Michael in the eye. 'Do you think that's a good idea?'

Michael watched in horrified fascination as his new friend knelt by the corpse, inserting his searching hands into the clothing, tugging at the thin black jacket until all the pockets were accessible. He turned to Michael and told him to help but Michael hung back. He knew what Harry was doing was wrong but the hard determination on his companion's face told him that any word of protest would mean he'd be called chicken, and it would get round the school that he was a coward. Even so, he couldn't bring himself to touch a dead man, especially one who smelled like that.

Harry pushed the foliage further out of the way until Michael caught sight of the man's face, discoloured like the flesh of the hand, with empty orbs where the eyes should have been. Michael's first thought was that it looked like something out of a zombie movie. Only this was real and he felt sick.

'We'll have to tell the police about him,' Michael said as Harry washed his hands in a stream flowing down from the hillside because he'd complained that they smelled of death.

'Why? He'll be found soon enough.' Harry held up the wallet he'd taken from the dead man's pocket in triumph. 'Sixty quid in here. Want some?'

Michael shook his head. It felt like blood money.

'Go on.'

Before he could object Harry was thrusting grubby notes into his hand and when he made a feeble attempt to give them back Harry shook his head.

'Here, have this.' Harry passed him a card.

'What is it?'

'Driving licence. It's ID to buy fags and fireworks. It'll get you into pubs and everything.'

'It's got a photo.'

'You cover that with your thumb.'

'Don't you want it?'

'I've already got a fake one,' Harry said smugly. The nature lover had gone now and a hard teenager had taken his place.

Michael was about to refuse, but Harry was walking away so Michael started to follow, half running to keep up. He thrust the licence and money into the pocket of his jeans, out of sight, trying to forget.

When they reached the main path again, Harry swung round to face him. 'What's the matter with you? I've done you a favour.'

'Nothing's the matter,' he said as he caught up, assuming a swagger he didn't feel. 'But I still think we should tell someone.'

'Not now we've taken the money. We'll have left finger-prints and that.'

'You mean you've left fingerprints. I never touched him.'

'You were there. That means you're as guilty as I am.'

As Michael walked back to Harry's house, the words sank in. He'd just robbed a dead man.

At four o'clock Neil kept his appointment at Newfield Manor as arranged and he was relieved to find Karl Banville was already there. He hadn't fancied waiting in that strange place alone with the crows mocking in the surrounding trees.

Banville was leaning on his car, enjoying the sunshine, and Neil still couldn't throw off the feeling something was watching from the windows of the derelict house.

'Dr Watson, thanks for coming,' Banville said, shaking Neil's hand heartily. 'There's a guy I'd like you to meet. We'll go in my car.'

'Who is he?'

'He's an expert on local history. His name's Raynard Bishop.'

He tilted his head and looked at Neil enquiringly, as though he expected him to recognise the name. But Neil had never heard it before.

They drove off and five minutes later the car came to a halt outside a double-fronted stone house tucked away in the side street leading to Whitely church. It was a substantial house, the kind that might once have housed a local lawyer or gentleman farmer; trees had grown up tall around it, cutting out the light. The little front garden was overgrown and the windows were grubby as were the net curtains that obscured the interior.

Banville raised the door knocker which, Neil noticed, was in the form of a hideous face, twisted in a tortured grimace like some evil guardian spirit. They waited half a minute and when the door opened Neil saw a bearded man standing there. Raynard Bishop was dressed entirely in black and had unusually small eyes and a sparse fringe of grey hair around his bald pate. When Banville made the introductions, Bishop assessed him as though he were some exotic specimen brought there for his entertainment.

Then another man appeared at the top of the oak staircase, pausing for a moment before coming down to join them. He was thin, probably in his late sixties, with grey hair long enough to reach the collar of his faded denim shirt. He wore jeans and a row of wooden beads around his scraggy neck and had the unworldly look of a former hippy. Nevertheless Neil sensed a sharp intelligence behind his assessing gaze.

'Let me introduce you to Peter Walsingham,' Bishop said. 'He's staying with me.'

Walsingham gave a small nod of acknowledgement and followed the party into a room off the panelled hallway, bringing up the rear. It took Neil's eyes a few seconds to adjust to the gloom. Like the hall, this room was panelled in dark oak which seemed to absorb all the available light. Neil sat down as instructed and it was only when he began to look around that he realised they weren't alone.

A group of figures, around two and a half feet tall with stiff wooden limbs, hung in the corner furthest from the window: puppets with the strings clearly visible. The wood they were made from was darkened with age and their clothes were frayed and faded. Some had faces of exaggerated sweetness but a few wore an evil, gloating look. Neil's eyes were drawn to them, especially the malevolent ones. He counted nineteen in all, a mixture of sexes and ages. To their left a pair of booths were set against the wall, elaborately painted with curtains drawn across each little stage. Stacked beside the booths were what Neil at first took to be paintings, frameless canvases, until he realised they were painted backdrops, elaborate scenery for the little theatres.

'I see you're admiring my collection,' Bishop said proudly while his house guest, Walsingham, watched in silence. Neil thought he'd probably heard all this before.

'How old are they?' Neil asked.

'Mid to late nineteenth century. Puppet shows were a popular form of entertainment in those days. Let me show you something.'

A glass-topped display table stood beneath the window. Bishop lifted the top and took out what looked like an ancient book which he handed to Neil. 'It's a script used by a man called John Gunster who operated a puppet show in this area. Gunster's speciality was the re-enactment of famous murders and the booths belonged to him, as did the puppets. I was fortunate enough to buy the whole lot a year ago; a farmer was selling the contents of a barn near Stoke Beeching once owned by Gunster himself.'

'Tell us about the puppet shows,' Karl Banville said. He'd been so quiet that Neil had almost forgotten he was there.

Bishop, gratified by his interest, picked out one of the puppets, unhooking it from its resting place. It was a young woman in a faded blue gown with an innocent, almost simple, expression. A victim rather than a killer.

'This is Maria Marten. She was murdered at Polstead in Suffolk in 1827 by a man called William Corder and buried under the floor of the Red Barn where she died. Corder was

93

hanged on the eleventh of August 1828 at Bury St Edmunds and his body was dissected.'

Bishop replaced Maria and picked out another puppet, a man this time, with beetling brows and an expression of pure evil. 'This is John Williams. He slaughtered Timothy and Celia Marr and their baby along with their apprentice James Gowan at a draper's shop on the Ratcliffe Highway in London in December 1811. He also murdered three people in a tavern called the King's Arms on New Gravel Street. The murders were particularly brutal and Williams was hanged for his crimes and buried at a crossroads with a stake through his heart.'

Neil looked at the puppet dangling there and shuddered at the possibility of it suddenly coming to life with the manipulation of a few fragile strings. To his relief, Bishop returned it to its resting place. Then he selected another, a young woman in what must have been a rich Victorian costume, now reduced to tatters.

'And this is Mary Field,' he said proudly. 'This show was particularly popular about these parts,' he said with relish. 'Quite a cause célèbre. She was murdered by William Banville in 1884. Allegedly.'

Neil turned to Karl Banville. 'Any relation?'

He saw Banville and Bishop exchange a glance. Then Banville took a deep breath.

'He's my goodness knows how many greats uncle. That's why you're here, Dr Watson. You're going to prove his innocence.'

13

'Report of a shotgun accident at a farm near Stoke Beeching, Sarge. One fatality.'

The constable's words made Rachel Tracey's blood freeze. Farmers and shotguns. Accident and suicide. She had known quite a few victims of the latter; men who'd succumbed to despair over falling prices, harsh weather, diseased livestock and isolation. During the last foot-and-mouth outbreak she'd feared her own father might fall victim to temptation. She'd been living at home at the time and she'd watched him as the carcasses of his beloved cattle burned in the field. To the casual observer he'd seemed to take the tragedy with remarkable stoicism but she and her mother had been worried by his subdued silence. Disaster had been averted back then but she was always aware of the possibilities. Now she was due to marry a farmer herself and she knew she'd always be watchful; on the alert for any signs that things weren't right. After the wedding her life would never be the same.

She recognised the name of the shooting victim. David Gough was the owner of the small caravan park where the Lombards died and she knew Wesley would wonder whether there was a connection, although she was sure he'd be wrong to be suspicious. According to the constable she'd spoken to there was no sign of foul play. All the indications were that David Gough's death had been a tragic accident.

When she'd told her parents about the caravan deaths they'd said things hadn't been going well for the Goughs in recent years. People in the farming community tended to know each other – and look out for each other – but the Goughs shunned all support and kept their affairs private.

Someone would have to call on the family as a matter of routine and Rachel was sure they'd appreciate somebody who understood their world.

Gerry Heffernan's office was empty so she went and perched on the edge of Wesley's desk. 'Remember David Gough, the farmer who owns the caravan site where the Lombards were found?'

'What about him?'

'He's been shot – looks like an accident.'

Wesley raised his eyebrows. 'You sure it's not suspicious?'

'The FME's pretty certain but Dr Bowman's been called out and Uniform thought CID should be informed because of the Lombard connection. My parents know the family vaguely so I thought I should go over and ... '

'Yes, of course.' He stood up. 'I could do with a break from this paperwork so I'll come with you. Any idea where the boss is?'

Rachel shook her head. Gerry had sneaked out of the office without a word about twenty minutes before. It was a mystery.

*

Gerry Heffernan hadn't told anyone where he was going, which was unusual when they were embroiled in a murder investigation. The inquiry into the poisoning of Gina and Frank Lombard wasn't progressing as well as he hoped. All they knew for sure was that Frank had told his brother they were going to Devon to get rich; but how they intended to do that was a puzzle they were nowhere near solving.

In the meantime he had a problem of his own and he wasn't sure what to do about it. One moment he felt nervous – more than nervous, terrified – and the next he experienced a strong desire to see Alison O'Neil again and to discover everything he could about the woman who was claiming to be his daughter. Alison. He'd always liked that name.

So far he'd managed to keep quiet about her insistence that she was the product of a long-forgotten liaison between himself and Donna McQuail, even though it was at the forefront of his mind. He'd lain awake the previous night wondering whether the whole thing was a mistake – and, if it did turn out to be true, how he was going to break the news to his children, Rosie and Sam. And how he was going to tell his partner, Joyce.

He'd arranged to meet Alison at the Jolly Kettle and sure enough she was waiting for him. The Jolly Kettle was a traditional tearoom with lacy tablecloths, bone china crockery and not a tea bag in sight. It was run by Sebastian and his partner, Malcolm, both of whom were keen on maintaining high standards, specially blended leaf tea and the freshest of home-made scones. Gerry knew of the tearoom's high reputation but he had never actually set foot in there before. However, today was a special occasion. He was having afternoon tea with a daughter he hadn't known existed.

Once they were seated he saw a mixture of eagerness and fear in her green eyes which were so like his own. She gave him a nervous smile.

'What do I call you?' she asked as he caught the eye of Sebastian, who was hovering near the kitchen entrance.

'Gerry, I suppose.' It seemed far too early to commit himself to 'Dad', especially as he still couldn't place Donna McQuail. He had vague memories of a Donna who'd hung round the pub he'd drunk at for a while when he was at college but he couldn't recall having any sort of relationship with her. If he'd fathered her child, his failure of memory seemed somewhat sordid. But he'd been a different person back then – a wild lad. His son Sam's adolescence had been remarkably staid in comparison.

'You said your mum's dead.'

'She passed away in May,' she said. 'Cancer. Like I said, she told me about you just before she died and I've been wondering what to do ever since. I asked a private detective to track you down. It didn't take long.'

Gerry took a sip of the tea Sebastian had just brought to their table. He found the idea of being traced by a private detective bizarre. That was usually his job and it was strange being on the receiving end.

'I was worried how you'd react … especially when Mr Smith – the detective – found out you were a policeman.'

Gerry didn't reply. Instead he pretended to study the menu, hardly registering the words. 'What do you fancy to eat? I've heard they do a mean afternoon tea here; dainty little sarnies and all.'

'Welsh rarebit,' she said after giving the menu a cursory glance. 'That was always me mam's favourite. Do you remember?'

Gerry didn't answer. He couldn't even remember what Donna McQuail looked like, let alone her culinary preferences.

'So tell me about yourself, Alison. What do you do?'

'I work at a dress shop in Liverpool One – you know, the big new shopping centre.'

Gerry nodded. Liverpool had changed an awful lot since his day and he didn't get back up there as often as he'd liked, but he'd heard of Liverpool One. 'You didn't tell me where you're staying.'

'At a B&B in Connaught Road. But I can only stay another night because they're booked up after that. I'll have to go home. Where do you live?'

'Baynard's Quay. It's not far from here. Overlooking the river. I've ... er ... got a partner. Joyce. She lives there too.'

'You mentioned kids ... '

'Yeah. Rosie's a music teacher and Sam's a vet. All grown up now.'

'Can I meet them?'

He hesitated. 'I'll have to think about it, love. There'll be some explaining to do.' Rosie and Sam were adults who shouldn't be affected by the discovery of a previously unknown half-sister. But adult children, he knew, are bothered by things like that and they can react in unexpected ways, especially Rosie who'd always been sensitive; highly strung from early childhood.

He had the uncomfortable feeling that things were hurtling out of control, and he wasn't sure how he felt about it.

Over lunch she revealed that she'd never got on with the man she'd always supposed was her father and hadn't seen much of him after he and her mum split up a couple of years ago. She was an only child and she'd been brought up in the Aigburth area, somewhere Gerry knew well. She'd not been to university because her stepdad hadn't encouraged it. When Gerry told her about Rosie and Sam's academic achievements he immediately regretted what must have sounded like a veiled criticism.

'Would you ... er, like to go for a meal ... tonight if I can get away in time?' he asked after he'd paid the bill.

'Thanks, Gerry.'

They parted at the tearoom door and Gerry hurried back to the police station. Maybe he'd been too hasty. Maybe he should have kept his distance until he'd found out more.

On the way to White Pool Farm Rachel explained to Wesley that farms were dangerous places where accidents can easily happen and he listened in silence, bowing to her superior knowledge.

David Gough had been out shooting crows in woodland next to the far field and, if what they'd already been told was correct, his death was a tragic accident; just another statistic. Even so, the whole panoply of police investigation had been set in motion until it was confirmed that nobody else was involved in the farmer's death.

When they arrived Colin Bowman assured them that the angle of Gough's wound fitted the theory that the farmer was aiming a shot at the offending crows when he tripped on a protruding tree root and dropped his shotgun which went off accidentally. He'd come across similar accidents before and he was sure it wasn't suicide which, he said, would be a small comfort for the widow.

Joan Gough was a plump woman in her sixties with unnaturally blond hair and a thin slit of a mouth. She looked the sort who could deal with most things but today she looked shaken. However, Rachel was a good person to have around in a crisis and she sat opposite the woman, leaning towards her attentively like a priest in a confessional.

It was a while before Wesley felt it appropriate to butt in. 'Mrs Gough, I'm sorry to have to ask you this but was your husband upset about the deaths of those two people in the caravan?'

Joan Gough compressed her lips. 'Not upset. It wasn't as if he knew them, was it? But it was a nuisance. Meant he had to have the van cleaned before it could be let out again.'

'Did you ever meet the couple who died?'

'No. David dealt with all that.'

Before he could ask any more questions a man entered the room. He was stocky with a shaved head and he stared at Wesley and Rachel with barely disguised hostility.

'You OK, Mum?'

Joan nodded and turned to Rachel. 'This is my son, Barry.'

'We're very sorry for your loss,' Wesley said quickly.

'Have you finished?' said Barry, putting a protective arm around his mother's shoulder.

Rachel took the hint and stood up. 'We're sorry to have bothered you. If there's anything you need . . .'

Joan Gough gave her a gracious nod.

As they were about to leave Mrs Gough spoke again. 'You want to talk to Jack Proudfoot at Red Water Farm next door. The far field's next to his land. There's all sorts of odd things going on in there.'

'What sort of things?' Wesley asked, suddenly alert.

'Jack took over the farm a year ago after his father passed away. He's always been a bad lad – gave his parents no end of trouble.'

'You think he might have had something to do with your husband's death?'

'I'm not accusing anybody. But if you find out it wasn't an accident, that's where you should start looking.' She sniffed and turned her head away. She'd said all she had to say.

'Maybe we should have a word with Mr Proudfoot,' Wesley said when they reached the car.

Rachel didn't answer.

Michael arrived home earlier than Pam expected and he rushed upstairs to his room before she had a chance to ask about his day. Then she heard the shower going so she went up after him to find out what was going on. Even though her son had taken to showering more frequently in recent months, doing so at that time of the day was unprecedented. She presumed he'd covered himself in mud during a day of innocent boyish activity but when she picked up the clothes he'd thrown into the linen basket, they didn't seem unusually dirty. She took them downstairs anyway and prepared to shove them in the washer. Wesley always joked about money laundering whenever she accidentally left coins in any pockets so, out of habit, she made a quick search.

When her fingers came into contact with something that felt like a credit card she took it out and studied it. What was Michael doing with a driving licence? And cash: a twenty-pound note and a tenner.

When she saw the name on the licence – Zac Wilkinson – she dropped it as though it was a venomous snake.

14

Callum sat in Jamie's small living room watching daytime TV. In spite of the intruder the other night, this was the safest and most comfortable refuge he had. Jamie's credit and debit cards made life a lot easier too, as did the unlimited access to his wardrobe.

He'd searched the farm as best he could, flattening his body against the walls of the outbuildings and praying his captors were elsewhere. They usually took the men out in the windowless van during the day – but if anybody was left there he'd hoped the noises of the animals in the sheds would mask the sound of his footsteps on the stinking concrete ground. He hadn't been able to find the windowless outhouse with the padlocked door where they'd slept but he wondered if he'd recognise it if he did see it again. On the night of his escape, when he'd managed to slip out before the door was secured, he'd been in too much of a hurry to take in his surroundings. Nevertheless he was sure it was the right place because he remembered seeing the sign: Red Water Farm.

He'd left as soon as he'd made the search, terrified he'd be spotted and the nightmare would start again. But he'd got away safely and, now he was back in Jamie's cushy bolthole, it was time to make plans. He needed to rescue Ivan – if he was still alive.

Rob Carter visited Red Water Farm with a uniformed constable but he came back with little to report. He'd spoken to Jack Proudfoot, a taciturn man who'd greeted him with a barking dog at his heels and a shotgun broken over his arm. Proudfoot claimed he knew nothing about his neighbours. And as for hearing the shot that killed David Gough, everyone round there used shotguns to control vermin.

Wesley asked if he'd looked around the farm but Rob shook his head. Proudfoot wasn't exactly welcoming and he hadn't wanted to push it.

'Do you think he's hiding something?' Wesley asked. Although the two of them had never really got on, Rob was intelligent and ambitious so he had his uses.

'Not sure. These farmers are a breed apart, aren't they?'

Wesley glanced in Rachel's direction, hoping she hadn't heard.

'He never said much about his neighbour dying,' Rob continued. 'I mean, most people go through the motions, don't they? David Gough owned the caravan where the Lombards were found. Think there might be a connection?'

Rob had asked the question that had been on Wesley's mind ever since he'd learned of Gough's death. Checks had already been made but, apart from the caravan rental, no connection had been found so far between the Goughs and the Lombards, although that didn't mean none existed.

'Until we find evidence to suggest otherwise, we can probably assume it's a coincidence,' Wesley said.

As soon as Rob returned to his desk Wesley checked his emails. There was still no word on the origins of the champagne bottle that killed the Lombards. DC Trish Walton had been chasing up all the shops stocking that particular brand and, with luck, they'd eventually be able to trace the sale; maybe even find the purchaser's face on the shop's CCTV. Then they'd make some progress.

Gerry entered the incident room and hurried to his office with no word of greeting. Wesley followed and Gerry looked up as he entered, but instead of offering his usual grin of welcome he looked like a man who'd just received bad news.

'Something the matter?' Wesley asked.

Gerry sighed and fidgeted with a pen on his desk, turning it over and over in his fingers. 'I don't know. Any developments while I've been out?'

'Rob went to Stoke Beeching and spoke to the Goughs' neighbour but he didn't see or hear anything. David Gough's shooting's still looking like an accident.'

Wesley waited for Gerry to make some comment but he was staring at his cluttered desk.

After a few seconds the DCI looked up. 'Shut the door.'

Wesley did as he was asked and it was a while before Gerry spoke.

'I've had a bit of a shock, Wes,' he said. 'A woman came up to me and told me I was her dad.'

Wesley opened his mouth to say something but no words came out.

'She hired a private detective to trace me, would you believe. I've just met her. That's where I've been.'

'What about her mother?'

'Passed away a couple of months ago. Cancer. She made a deathbed confession and that's why Alison's come looking for me.'

'And is she ... your daughter?'

'I've been thinking about it and I'm sure I was seeing a lass called Selina around the time in question.' A faraway look came into his eyes. 'She worked on the perfume counter at George Henry Lee – nice posh department store on Church Street. She always smelled nice as I remember.' He sighed. 'I suppose it could have been a one night stand ... you know ...'

Wesley raised his eyebrows. This wasn't like the Gerry he knew but anyone can have moments of youthful irresponsibility.

'I was a bit of a lad back then, Wes. Young sailor with a girl in most ports. But I really can't remember Donna McQuail. Mind you, Alison does look a bit like me. Poor lass.' For the first time he smiled.

'What are you going to do?'

'Acknowledge my responsibilities. What else can I do? Her mum's dead and there's a stepfather she doesn't get on with so ... She's staying in a B&B and I'm thinking of asking her to come and stay at mine.'

'What about Sam and Rosie? And Joyce?'

Gerry frowned. 'It's Rosie I'm most worried about. Not sure how she'll take a new half-sister turning up out of the blue. You know what she's like.'

Wesley understood. Rosie Heffernan wasn't the most easy-going of young women.

'You'll have to meet Alison,' Gerry said.

The warmth of the statement surprised Wesley. He

hadn't expected the boss would take to playing happy families so readily. 'You are convinced she's who she says she is? Even though you don't remember her mother?'

'Why would she lie, Wes? It's not as if I'm a millionaire and she wants to get her hands on my fortune, is it?'

'That house of yours on Baynard's Quay must be worth a lot.'

'It was dirt cheap when me and Kathy bought it.'

'Things have changed. Incomers pay megabucks for waterfront properties like yours these days. I'm just asking you to be careful, that's all.'

A look of disappointment appeared on Gerry's chubby face as though his dreams of domestic bliss with his long-lost child had been spoiled by Wesley's words of caution.

'You're sure she hasn't made a mistake? There's always DNA and—'

'That'd make it look as if I don't trust her. She's a lovely girl, Wes. And it sounds as if she had a bad time with her stepfather. If I'd known . . .'

Wesley's mobile phone began to ring and he was tempted to leave it. Then he saw it was Pam calling so he muttered an apology to Gerry and answered.

After a short conversation he said, 'Sorry, Gerry, something's come up. I've got to go home.'

Gerry suddenly frowned. 'Pam all right?'

'Yes, it's . . . Look, I'll call you later. It's just something I've got to deal with.'

Wesley barged into the hall and Pam rushed out to greet him, speaking in a whisper.

'He came back from Harry's and went upstairs without saying anything. He got straight into the shower and put all his clothes in the linen basket to be washed. I found this in the pocket of his jeans.'

Wesley recognised the object in her hand as a driving licence.

'Maybe he found it.'

'There was money too.'

'How much?'

'Thirty pounds. I know he didn't have that much. Look at the name on the licence: Zac Wilkinson. I went to that talk he gave last week. Remember? Didn't you say he was missing?'

Wesley caught his breath as she handed him the licence. The picture stared out at him. Wynn Staniland's biographer; the man who'd failed to turn up at Neston Library.

'I'd better have a word with Michael.'

As he made for the stairs Pam caught his arm. 'I think he's upset. Go easy on him.'

Gerry's revelation vanished from his mind as he climbed the stairs. His own son had somehow become mixed up in a man's disappearance and the thought caused a knot of fear in his stomach.

He gave a token knock on Michael's bedroom door before pushing it open. The boy was lying on the bed and as soon as he saw his father, he sat up. Wesley could tell he was doing his best to look casual. But the act wasn't working.

'Mum says something's upset you. Want to tell me what it is?'

When there was no reply Wesley tried again. 'Are you in some sort of trouble? You see that driving licence you had in your pocket belongs to someone we're interested in. How did you get it?'

'Found it,' Michael said, head bowed, studying the pattern on his duvet.

'Where?'

'Walking through the woods over the river.'

Wesley, who was used to detecting lies, thought he was telling the truth, about this at least.

'Was Nathaniel with you?'

Michael hesitated for a moment before shaking his head. 'He couldn't come.'

'So it was just you and Harry?'

The answer was a sniff.

'You found the man the licence belonged to, didn't you? He was dead.' It was only a guess but Michael's nod told him he'd hit the target.

'Why didn't you call the police?'

'Harry said not to.'

'Was it Harry who persuaded you to take the money and the driving licence?'

Michael didn't answer. He wasn't going to grass on a mate.

Wesley sat with his arm round his son's shoulder for a while, unsure whether to be angry and point out the serious-ness of the situation or play the sad, disappointed parent. He felt helpless, numb, but he made a great effort to stay calm. 'Will you show me where you found him? Don't worry, I'll be with you ... and Uncle Gerry.'

Michael took a shuddering breath. 'OK.'

The terrain meant the CSIs had to leave their vehicles some distance away and carry their equipment to the spot Michael showed them. The boy was subdued and even a lift home in a police car failed to raise his spirits.

Wesley's first instinct was to confront Harry himself but he knew it wouldn't be a good idea because he was too involved. Instead he sent Rachel and Trish Walton over to the village of Burston with instructions they were to take Harry to Tradmouth and give him a good talking-to in an interview room with an appropriate adult present.

Wesley hoped the incident would bring his son's association with the boy to an end. But, although Michael was shaken, he still wouldn't admit that robbing the dead man was his new friend's idea. At that impressionable age, friends could exercise more influence than family.

Once the CSIs had begun work and the crime scene tent had been erected, Gerry joined them, still not his usual ebullient self, even when Colin made an appearance.

Wesley took Gerry to one side and gave him a brief account of how the body had been located.

'How's your lad?' the DCI asked.

'I think he's just discovered that he's not cut out to be a hard man. At least I hope he has.' He hesitated. 'Think we should interview him at the station; bring it home to him how serious this is?'

'Maybe a short sharp shock's what's needed. Up to you, Wes.' Gerry put his hand on his shoulder. 'I'll read him the riot act if you like.'

'I think that'd be best. Thanks.'

'What about the other lad?'

'Rach and Trish are taking him in for questioning. I get the feeling it was all his idea although Michael hasn't said as much.'

'Think a caution would do the trick?'

'Possibly. But I never like the idea of kids having something like that on record unless it's absolutely necessary. We all do stupid things when we're young.'

'Too right.' A distant look appeared in Gerry's eyes. 'They're always a worry, aren't they . . . kids.'

They watched as Colin entered the tent to make his initial examination. Although they hadn't looked too closely at the body in case they contaminated the scene, Wesley had pushed the undergrowth aside to have a look at the face and even though it had begun to swell and discolour in the August heat, he recognised it from the posters he'd seen outside the library. This was Zac Wilkinson all right and this meant the subject of his biography, Wynn Staniland, would have to be questioned further. He wasn't sure whether he was looking forward to another encounter with the author but there was a chance he might be able to shed some light on the dead man's last movements.

Colin's inspection of the corpse took longer than usual, or perhaps it just seemed that way because Wesley wasn't in the mood to pass the time of day and take his mind off the wait. Eventually the pathologist appeared, taking off his latex gloves.

'Sorry, gentlemen. I can safely say this is one for you. Blunt force trauma to the head. This poor chap was murdered.'

Journal of John Lipton

1 May 1884

I have arranged for Mr Gunster to give his marionette show at Newfield Manor – a special performance for invited guests only.

I do not know what Sir Cuthbert and her ladyship will make of the show, although I knew it will amuse Mary greatly. She is an eager devourer of murderous tales and I desire to please her above all things.

Now the day has arrived and Sir Cuthbert and Lady Field sit on a pair of red velvet chairs at the centre of the little audience like a king and queen upon their thrones and wait, solemn-faced, to be entertained.

Gunster has set up his booth at the end of the hall and the seats are arranged in a semicircle before it. Mary sits beside her parents, her eyes wide with excited anticipation. I have told her to expect a rare treat and she looks towards me and smiles. She will be mine soon, I know it.

I see her maid, Sarah, seated at the back with the servants and I think how like Mary she is with her fair hair and snub nose. But Sarah dresses in simple black while Mary is clad in purple silk and lace.

William Banville is here, seated at the end of the front row. I had not expected to see him at such a party. He stares at me for a while then I see his gaze travel to Mary's face.

I will watch him carefully.

15

Zac Wilkinson was renting a cottage in the centre of Tradmouth on a six-month lease and September's rent had already been paid in advance. The letting agency reported no problems, apart from damage to the front door from an attempted break-in the previous Tuesday evening. Other than that, Zac Wilkinson had been a model tenant.

Uniform had attended when he'd reported the damage to the door although, as nothing appeared to have been taken, they'd put it down to kids and no further action had been stolen. The incident had been quietly forgotten: a crime number rather than a crime.

The likely murder weapon was found in undergrowth not far from where the body lay. It was a large stone, matted with hair and blood, which suggested to Wesley that the murder had been committed on the spur of the moment.

When Rachel and Trish returned from their interview with Harry Jones it was hard to read Trish's thoughts. But Rachel wore an expression of disapproval and Wesley hoped she'd given the lad a hard time. The more he thought about Harry, the more angry he felt.

Once Zac Wilkinson's body had been removed to the mortuary at Tradmouth Hospital they left the CSIs to their work and returned to the police station where Rachel gave her report on her encounter with Harry.

'That Harry's a cocky little sod,' she said, slumping down heavily on the chair by Wesley's desk.

'I haven't met him.'

'His parents came with him and would you believe they tried to blame your Michael for leading their precious son astray.' She hesitated. 'They referred to him as that mixed-race boy.'

Wesley looked away. The words stung, even though he knew the allegations against his son were lies invented to get their own offspring off the hook.

'Anyway, I told them Michael comes from a good family and he's never been in trouble before.' She grinned. 'Hope I did the right thing. What's happening with Michael?'

'Gerry's going to have a stern word with him at the station and I hope that'll be the end of it. Did you learn anything from Harry?'

'He took money from the corpse – sixty quid. He admitted he gave Michael half the cash and the licence and he said Michael refused to touch the body and wanted to call the police. Don't think his parents were too pleased at his attack of honesty. He also admitted to taking the dead man's mobile phone, although he was very scathing about it – said he had a better one but he took it anyway.' She rolled her eyes. 'The parents didn't seem bothered. They said it was the kind of thing most kids got up to.'

Wesley didn't answer. One moment he felt like a lion

defending its cub then the next he felt like an inadequate parent for allowing Michael to mix with the boy in the first place. Then he told himself that any attempt to forbid an adolescent from seeing an undesirable friend can only make that friend more alluring.

'Were there any house keys in Wilkinson's pockets?'

'Harry said not. Odd that. Most people carry house keys, and car keys. We don't know whether he has a car but if he's been going round the area giving talks, it's highly likely.'

'So the killer probably took his keys. Someone tried to break into his house last Tuesday and failed. If that was our killer perhaps he's had another go now he has the keys – or he's planning to. Have the letting agency given us a spare set?'

Rachel nodded. 'Someone went over to fetch them while we were out.' She shot over to her desk and picked them up, brandishing them in triumph. 'Want to go over to the house and have a look round?'

Half an hour later Wesley was unlocking the front door of Zac's rented cottage, noting that the reported damage still hadn't been repaired. He stepped into the tiny hallway, his ears attuned to any telltale noise, but all he could hear was the familiar heavy silence of an unoccupied building, and the sound of Rachel breathing just behind him.

'Let's see what we can find,' he said, pulling on his crime scene gloves.

They began the search in the bedrooms. Both were in an untidy state and the towels in the shower were damp. According to Colin, Wilkinson had been dead for a couple of days so this suggested someone else had been in there using the facilities. They needed to speak to that person as quickly as possible.

As soon as they'd finished upstairs they headed for the living room. Like the bedrooms it was untidy with takeaway pizza boxes piled on the coffee table beside an assortment of dirty mugs.

'I thought he was supposed to be a writer,' said Rachel, puzzled. 'I can't see a computer, can you?'

Wesley began to search the cupboards, but the only item of interest he found was an empty credit card wallet containing a scrap of paper bearing four scribbled digits that might have been a PIN number.

'Any sign of a manuscript or any notes?' Rachel asked.

'No. We'll get a team over to do a more thorough search but I can't see anything. There's only this.'

He'd found a large white envelope containing a publisher's contract and when he scanned it he noticed that the victim's biography of Wynn Staniland was due to be delivered in three months' time. He knew nothing of the world of publishing but he presumed the biography was still a work in progress, which meant there should be evidence of industry at the cottage as the deadline loomed ever closer. So far he could see none.

'If we find his mysterious housemate, he or she might be able to throw some light on it,' Wesley said.

'It's definitely a he,' said Rachel, wrinkling her nose.

Wesley followed her to the kitchen where the sink was filled with unwashed dishes, even though a dishwasher stood next to it. She unlocked the back door and stepped outside. The little courtyard was neat, apart from an old carrier bag stuffed in the corner behind a plant container. She pulled it out and saw that it was filled with foul-smelling clothes, little more than rags.

She turned to Wesley. 'Wouldn't have thought these were Zac Wilkinson's style. Wonder where they came from.'

'We'll get them sent to the lab. Are you thinking what I'm thinking?'

'The murderer killed Wilkinson, took his keys and has been holed up here ever since. These could be his clothes.'

'The letting agent said Wilkinson had two sets of keys. He'd asked for a spare set in case he lost one. Have you seen another set?'

'No sign of one.'

Wesley put his hand to his nose as the smell from the clothes wafted towards him. 'I want this place searched for fingerprints and DNA. And the victim must have a computer somewhere. At least we've got his mobile now so we can see who he's been in contact with, and the neighbours might be able to describe our squatter.'

'Think he'll be back?'

Wesley considered for a moment. 'Maybe we should keep the search low-key. We don't want to scare him off, do we? No crime scene tape, no patrol cars, no constable stationed outside. With a bit of luck he might not realise we're here and come blundering in. Then we'll have him.'

After leaving Raynard Bishop's house Neil walked the short distance to the pub in Whitely with Karl Banville. The pub had been Banville's suggestion and he insisted on buying the drinks, saying they needed a serious talk.

As soon as the drinks were on the table Banville took a file from his briefcase and passed it to Neil. When Neil opened it he saw that the contents concerned Newfield Manor, in particular the case of Mary Field.

'Mary was the only child of Sir Cuthbert Field and his wife, Emaline, who had inherited a considerable fortune from her industrialist father,' Banville began. 'She was an heiress in her own right, which made her an attractive proposition for any fortune-hunting young man. In 1884 such a young man appeared. His name was John Lipton and he'd worked as second mate aboard a Bristol merchant ship before coming ashore to take advantage of a business opportunity – something connected with machinery for the mines of Dartmoor – and when he met Mary he pursued her with a view to marriage. Mary's parents, meanwhile, were encouraging an alliance with William Banville, a local lawyer who was devoted to their daughter. But Mary chose Lipton and they married.

'On her parents' death Mary inherited the estate and a couple of months later she was found dead in a pool in the Manor grounds. It was assumed she'd drowned, perhaps by accident, until an astute doctor noticed marks of strangulation on her neck and suspicion fell on her new husband, John Lipton, who was set to inherit Mary's fortune. However, John had been in Bristol on business at the relevant time so, as William Banville couldn't be found, it was assumed that he'd killed her in a fit of jealous rage and fled. Nothing was heard of William again; it appeared that he'd escaped justice. Now do you realise why I want you to pursue this?' Banville said as Neil handed back the file.

'Not really,' said Neil.

'Two years after Mary's death Lipton sold Newfield Manor and went up north to start a new life. He married another heiress, built a huge house and became mayor of some town in Yorkshire, not sure which. He did very nicely out of Mary's death.'

'But he was in Bristol when she died. And William did disappear.'

Banville leaned forward and put his face close to Neil's. 'I don't think William ever left. I think he's buried there. The perfect scapegoat. And I want you to find him.'

16

A small team was going over Zac Wilkinson's cottage with instructions to be discreet in case the mystery housemate returned. As far as Wesley could tell from his own perfunctory search, the mystery man had left no clue to his identity, only a trail of empty takeaway boxes and a stash of ready meals and beer in the fridge. Whoever he was, he wasn't the domesticated type.

In his absence Pam had taken Michael to the station for his interview with Gerry. When he returned he was hoping to find Gerry in his office to see how the encounter had gone but DC Paul Johnson greeted him with the news that the DCI had gone out.

Wesley wondered whether the boss's unexplained absence had something to do with his new-found daughter. The thought of the girl turning up out of the blue like that made him uncomfortable and he wondered whether she was lying for some reason that might become clear at a later date. For Gerry's sake, he hoped she was being honest.

They were still waiting for more news to come in about Gina and Frank Lombard and Wesley was frustrated by the delay, especially now they had another murder to investigate. In the meantime he needed to learn more about Zac Wilkinson.

There was no car registered in Wilkinson's name so he told someone to contact the hire companies. Then, with the help of the internet, he soon found that the victim had worked on biographies of several celebrities from the worlds of sport and show business.

Wilkinson's publisher had commissioned him to write Wynn Staniland's biography because the fortieth anniversary of his first award-winning novel was fast approaching and they hoped to take advantage of the occasion. The publishers reckoned everyone was fascinated by the reclusive Staniland's tragic and mysterious life and Zac Wilkinson had been the man chosen for the task. However, when Wesley tried to find out about Wilkinson's private life he hit a brick wall. All he could discover was that, along with millions of other people, he lived in London.

As he scrolled through various websites in search of more information, the officer who'd been given the job of tracing Wilkinson's family arrived at his desk with a puzzled frown on his face.

'Are you sure Zac Wilkinson's his real name, sir? It's not just a pen name?'

'It's the name on his driving licence. Why?'

'I can't find any trace of him. There's a birth certificate for a Zachary Wilkinson in 1983 but when I did more digging I found he'd died as a baby so it can't be him.'

'Perhaps he was born abroad,' Wesley suggested.

'Maybe. But so far all we've got is his rented flat in Notting Hill and the landlord was no use.'

121

'Bank account?'

'Nothing unexpected but there's no record of him having any sort of account before 2006. Do you know, sir, it's as if he's only existed for the past ten years.'

'Let me know as soon as the fingerprint results come back from his house, won't you?'

The officer nodded and departed.

When Wesley awoke the following morning he realised it was Sunday but it wouldn't be a day of rest. The investigation into the death of Zac Wilkinson would soon gain momentum and the Lombard case was still at a relatively early stage too so he'd be working long hours for the foreseeable future. This was just when Michael needed him, he thought, a worm of guilt crawling into his heart. But it couldn't be helped.

Pam reached out to him as he was about to climb out of bed. 'What time will you be back?'

He leaned over and kissed her forehead. 'Not sure. Keep an eye on Michael, won't you?'

'Course I will. He's been very quiet . . . and he said he was sorry.'

'Think he means it?'

'Yes. I think Gerry having that word was just what he needed. Are you sure there'll be no charges?'

Wesley did his best to reassure her. Being marched down to the station for a stiff word with the senior investigating officer, even though he had known him all his life as 'Uncle Gerry', was probably punishment enough. As for Harry, he wasn't so sure but it was unlikely things would be taken further.

'My mother said she'd call in,' Pam said with a heavy sigh.

'How is she these days?'

'Full of this literary festival she's helping to organise.' She paused as if she found the subject distasteful. 'The man Michael found was going to be one of the speakers. His name's on the flyers she's been handing out to all and sundry.'

'You haven't told her about Michael finding . . . ?'

'Of course not. Can you imagine the fuss she'd make? It's something I'd rather put behind us.'

When he reached the police station he was still thinking about Michael's recent experience and hoping the shock had taught him a valuable lesson. Pick your friends carefully and know your own mind.

He made for Gerry's office where he found the DCI discarding heaps of paperwork into his office bin. As soon as he saw Wesley he stopped what he was doing and looked up.

'How's your Michael?'

'Repentant . . . I hope.'

'Good.' Gerry paused. 'I probably let him off a bit lightly but I think he got the message. This has come in.' Gerry put on his reading glasses to study the sheet of paper in his hand before passing it to Wesley.

It was a statement from a couple staying at the Cliff View Caravan Park who'd rented caravan seven for a few days and left the site the morning before the Lombards' bodies were discovered. This was the first time the police had spoken to them and, as Wesley read their statement, his spirits lifted.

'So that's how they came to have the poisoned champagne.'

'Someone left it on the Lombards' caravan step on the morning before they died, like a bottle of milk. It's lucky the other caravanners were honest and no one was tempted to pinch it. The couple from caravan seven went home and thought no more about the champagne until we traced everyone who'd stayed there recently. When we contacted them they remembered it – they'd assumed it had been left as a present for a wedding anniversary or a birthday.'

'I don't suppose they saw who left it.'

'Sadly, no. They say it was there first thing in the morning so it could have been left any time during the night.'

'According to the stockists Trish has spoken to it comes from a small champagne house in Rheims, not one of the big ones, and it's only stocked by a few outlets in this country. Seven in London, five in the Home Counties and a wine merchant in Millicombe.'

'Trish visited the Millicombe shop and was told that it's an old bottle – good vintage, but they haven't sold one recently. With this new evidence we can forget the possibility that the Lombards brought the bottle down from Leeds with them.'

'True. It looks like a targeted poisoning. Who knew the Lombards were there?'

'Someone who'd been watching them. Or perhaps it was meant for someone else and the killer got the wrong caravan. I'll ask Uniform to have another word with everyone on that site – see if the bottle jogs any memories.'

'Any news on the fingerprints in Zac Wilkinson's cottage?'

'Still waiting,' said Wesley. 'But we've had confirmation that David Gough's prints were the only ones on the gun that killed him. His shooting was an accident so we can forget about it.'

'Thank goodness for that.' Gerry began to shuffle the papers on his desk.

'Have you seen any more of Alison?'

Gerry smiled fondly. 'I'm thinking of calling her ... asking her out for lunch.'

'Be careful, won't you, Gerry?' Wesley said, without quite understanding why he'd chosen those particular words.

Being invited for Sunday lunch wasn't something that often happened in Neil's line of work. Karl Banville had called him first thing to say he'd meet him at the Tradmouth Castle Hotel.

With the confidence of the successful businessman, Banville's invitation had sounded more like an order than a request and Neil felt he couldn't refuse. As he'd been tying things up at the Exeter site that morning he was wearing his digging clothes so he had to rush back to his flat to shower and change. Nevertheless he managed to turn up at one as arranged, dressed in the outfit he kept for meetings with council officials and developers.

The restaurant was crowded with well-dressed people conducting hushed conversations over dinner. Feeling self-conscious, Neil made his way over to join Banville at his table by the window, the best seat in the house.

'I have something that might interest you,' Banville said after the waiter had taken their order.

He produced a small book from the bag at his feet. It was the size of a school exercise book with a battered leather cover. As he opened it Neil noticed the pages inside were fragile and yellowed.

'Raynard Bishop lent me this.'

'What is it?'

'A book about the murder of Mary Field.'

'Does it prove your relative's innocence?'

'Not exactly. But it's a contemporary account so I want you to read it and familiarise yourself with the case.' He looked Neil in the eye and Neil found the intensity of his gaze unnerving. He wondered if the man was becoming fanatical; he'd never liked dealing with fanatics.

'Where did Raynard Bishop get it from?'

'Apart from his interest in Victorian puppet shows, Raynard collects old books about famous crimes. He bought this via the internet from a dealer up in Scotland who brought it down himself because he had business in the area. You met him – Peter Walsingham: he's staying with Raynard.'

Neil nodded. He remembered meeting Walsingham at Bishop's house but there'd been no mention of his profession.

Banville pointed a finger at the book. 'I'm hoping it'll give us some clue about where we should start looking. I'm convinced William Banville's buried at Newfield Manor.'

'If you're right. Don't forget Lipton was away so who killed Mary?'

The light of enthusiasm suddenly vanished from Banville's eyes. 'Lipton wasn't there, that's for sure. He had lots of respectable witnesses who vouched for him. That was why William fell under suspicion.'

The meal was delicious but as Neil worked his way through the three courses, listening to Banville's theories, he felt increasingly uncomfortable, as though he was caught in the grip of another man's obsession. At two thirty he said he had to get back to Exeter and offered to pay his share of the bill. Banville wouldn't hear of it and insisted the meal was on him. Neil, unable to make a fuss in the hallowed atmosphere of the restaurant, had no choice but to accept gracefully.

As he reached the hotel entrance he regretted his moment of weakness. He was beholden to the man now, and if the dig at Newfield Manor didn't produce the evidence Banville was hoping for, Neil wasn't sure how he'd react.

Zac Wilkinson's hire car was found parked on Crossbones Hill not far from his rented cottage. And when the fingerprint results from the car and the cottage came back Wesley felt as if he'd been presented with a particularly exciting gift.

He was about to dash to Gerry's office to share the news when he realised the DCI hadn't returned from lunch with his new-found daughter, who'd been only too keen to accept the invitation. In spite of the hard act Gerry put on in the presence of the criminal classes and his underlings in the force, Wesley knew that he was an old softy underneath. Anyone could take advantage of his good nature once they got to know his susceptibilities.

In Gerry's absence he approached Rachel, who was staring at her computer, deep in thought. He needed to share what he'd learned with somebody.

'I've got news,' he said, unable to conceal his excitement.

'Hope it's good,' she said miserably. 'I can't stop thinking of David Gough.'

'It was an accident.'

She shrugged her shoulders. 'Gough's been around guns all his life. He knows how to handle them.'

'Accidents happen on farms. Anyone can trip.'

He saw her shudder. With her background, this was too close to home. He hoped what he had to say would distract her. 'I've just had the fingerprint results back from Zac Wilkinson's cottage.'

'Well?'

'You know we couldn't find out anything about Wilkinson's past and we've had no luck tracing his relatives? That's because Zac Wilkinson isn't his real name. Ever heard of Jamie Hursthead?'

Rachel sat back in her chair. 'The name's familiar.'

'Double murder at a boarding school back in 1996. A twelve-year-old student called Jamie Hursthead was found guilty of killing two of his classmates and sent to a secure unit. After having all the care and rehabilitation the state could provide it was judged that he no longer posed a danger to society, so ten years ago he was released and given a new identity. Only his prints are still on file. And there's more: we have a suspect for his murder.'

'Who?'

'They found a second set of prints in the cottage and in Hursthead's hire car. They belong to a Callum Joy. Twocking, burglary, mugging. Callum's a bad boy.'

'So he killed Zac . . . or Jamie?'

'He's the best suspect we've got. Now all we have to do is find him.'

17

Gerry looked remarkably cheerful when he arrived at work first thing on Monday morning and Wesley wondered whether he'd kept his word and moved Alison into his house. After the morning briefing he walked into Gerry's office.

'Everything OK?'

'Why shouldn't it be?' Gerry's question sounded defensive.

'Has Alison moved in?'

'Last night. She couldn't stay any longer at the B&B and . . . It'll give us a chance to get to know each other.'

'How's Joyce taking it?'

'She hasn't said much but I think they're going to get on OK.'

'What about Sam and Rosie?'

Gerry looked sheepish. 'I'll have to pick my moment to break the news.'

Before he could say any more Trish Walton appeared in the open doorway.

'I've got those details of Jamie Hursthead's conviction you asked for, sir. No wonder they locked him up in a secure unit.'

Gerry leaned forward, eager to learn more.

'Jamie Hursthead was a public schoolboy from a wealthy family,' Trish began. 'His father's Sir Stephen Hursthead, head of Hursthead Engineering, but Jamie was always a difficult boy. He was expelled from three schools for attacking other pupils and staff and he set fire to his bedroom at home, although because of his family's wealth these incidents went unreported.'

Trish looked as though she was preparing to tell a long and eventful tale.

'Jamie was a disturbed child but throughout his life people covered up for him. It was only when things went too far that everything came out. When he was twelve years old he lost his temper during his first fortnight at his new boarding school and killed a boy who'd been giving him a hard time. He knocked him unconscious with a cricket bat in the sports pavilion and set it on fire. There was another boy in there who witnessed the whole thing and somehow Jamie managed to lock him in the changing room. The whole place went up and because of the wire mesh on the changing-room window, the boy couldn't escape.'

Wesley winced. 'So he killed two people?'

'That's right and this time Jamie couldn't wriggle out of the consequences. He was sent to a secure unit with a recommendation that he receive psychiatric treatment. When he was eighteen he was moved to an adult jail where he became a model prisoner. He took a degree and spent most of his time in the prison library. He was released on licence when he was twenty-two and followed a career in journalism. From there he branched out into writing biographies of the rich and famous.'

'What about his family?'

'They washed their hands of him. He had a brother and sister who'd never given their parents a moment's trouble and from the time of his conviction the family pretended he didn't exist. They'll have to be told, of course.'

'Where do they live?'

'Up north. York.'

Wesley caught Gerry's eye. 'Maybe we should pay them a visit. We can take a look at Gina and Frank Lombard's house in Leeds while we're in the vicinity and have a word with Frank's brother – the one who reckons they came down here in search of riches. I never like relying on the local force. With the best will in the world, they might have missed something important.'

'Good idea. We'll square it with their local nick.' Gerry thought for a moment or two, furrowing his brow as he made some demanding mental calculation. 'I'd better stay here and run the show, Wes. You go.'

It wasn't like Gerry to refuse a trip away and Wesley suspected Alison was the reason for his reluctance.

Trish had more to say. 'Jamie Hursthead was given a new identity on his release because the authorities were afraid of reprisals. He became Zac Wilkinson and it seems he's been living a blameless life ever since.'

'Could someone have found out who he was?'

Trish took a deep breath before she replied. 'The father of one of the boys is a major criminal, although he describes himself as a "businessman". He lives in a mansion in the Home Counties and has contacts in the criminal underworld even though he always manages to stay squeaky clean.'

'Name?'

'Kieran State. Not a nice man by all accounts . . . and he swore vengeance at Jamie's trial.'

'Can't say I blame him,' said Gerry. 'I suppose he has to be put on our list of suspects. What about the other lad's family?'

'The boy who was locked in the changing room was called Ben Restorick and his parents live in Cornwall. His father's an architect. Semi-retired.' She bowed her head. 'He was an only child.'

'So they'd have every reason to want revenge,' Wesley said. The Restoricks' pain must have been unimaginable and he wondered how he'd react if he was in their situation. It was something he could hardly bear to think about. 'Jamie Hursthead did a terrible thing. If Zac Wilkinson's true identity became known, he was bound to be the focus of a lot of anger.'

'I'm surprised he had the brass neck to go around doing talks,' said Gerry.

'He probably didn't imagine anyone would recognise him. He was only twelve when it happened. A child.'

'There's something else too,' said Trish. 'Callum Joy was in prison with him. They shared a cell.'

'So they're old friends?'

'Or old enemies,' said Gerry.

Callum had seen the police at Jamie's cottage, which meant that particular bolthole was off limits for the time being. They'd also been crawling all over the car so now that was useless too.

He wondered whether Jamie been up to his old tricks again. In prison they hadn't been meant to know about each other's crimes but Jamie had been too notorious for anonymity. He was no petty criminal, but the real deal: a cold-blooded murderer who'd set fire to his victims and watched them die. Even so, Callum hadn't been afraid of him back then. On the contrary, it was hard to connect the posh boy with his love of reading with the terrible crime he'd committed. When they said Jamie was fit to be released they'd given him a new name, just in case. He'd heard they'd given him the name of some dead kid . . . a whole new identity. If that was true, Callum thought, it seemed a bit sick.

At least he'd got some decent clothes out of Jamie and the cards that gave him access to an unending supply of cash from whatever hole in the wall he chose to use. Then there was the iPad in the holdall he'd hidden in the allotment shed which would give him a source of cash to fall back on if Jamie stopped his cards.

Now he had nowhere to stay he toyed with the idea of checking into a B&B. But the owner might ask questions and he didn't like questions. He'd had to answer too many of them in the course of his life; particularly from the police. After some thought he decided to return to the allotment. The shed was sheltered and dry and not far from the centre of town if he needed money or food.

His last attempt to help Ivan had failed but he was determined to try again. They had guns so there'd be danger. Still, he was used to danger. He'd once shared a room with a killer.

18

Now they knew Zac Wilkinson's true identity, Gerry wanted to speak to Wynn Staniland again. He didn't care who he was, or if he preferred to have no contact with the outside world. The man must have worked closely with his biographer so surely he would be able to tell them something.

After his wife's death he'd withdrawn from public life and produced no more books. But this lack of industry had, ironically, made him a legend; a man of mystery and the subject of endless speculation. Rumours flew around that the books had really been written by his wife and that's why his output had dried up. However, his wife was an artist with no literary pretensions so that theory didn't seem to hold water. Then grief was blamed, which Wesley thought more believable until he learned that the Stanilands' marriage hadn't been altogether happy and he'd had several affairs.

For years the media would forget all about him, then some article in a newspaper or magazine would generate a flurry of interest which would die down again as fast as it had erupted.

When it was announced that Zac Wilkinson was working on the first biography of the man, the publishing world made the most of the opportunity and all Staniland's books were reprinted with flashy new covers and a great deal of publicity. The hype was sufficient to kick-start a new bout of Staniland mania and he was becoming a hot property again, even though nobody had yet been able to coax him out of his self-imposed isolation.

Wesley trawled the internet for further information and at last he found the details of Staniland's wife's suicide in 1983, a lurid story which had delighted the voracious press at the time. Rachel had already given him the bare facts but now he delved deeper into the events of that tragic time.

Rosemary Staniland had been found near Addersacre in a sea pool on a private beach belonging to the house. In the 1920s the pool had been constructed to provide a safe place for the children of the house to swim. It was tucked to the side of the beach and filled up with sea water each high tide and it was here, where she would have played as a child, that Rosemary Staniland had chosen to die. Addersacre had been her family home and she had taken her young genius of a husband – seven years her junior – to live there when she inherited it on her father's death.

Unusually Rosemary had been found sitting bolt upright in the pool with the water just covering her head, her body weighed down by large pebbles in her pockets as though she'd climbed into the pool, sat down and waited for death to come. An analysis of her blood established that she'd been heavily sedated before death but the coroner had concluded the drugs were self-administered and a verdict of suicide had been brought in. It was pointed out at the inquest that her suicide mirrored an incident in one of her husband's books, which raised the possibility that she had chosen that particular method to make a point. As far as he could see, the rumours of murder Rachel had mentioned didn't appear to have much substance.

Wesley then brought up the police report into the incident and it pretty much confirmed what the website said. The drugs Rosemary Staniland had taken were found in her bedroom and, according to her husband, she had been depressed for some time. Statements taken from everyone who was in the house at the time of Rosemary's death backed this up. He looked at the names: Perdita, Rosemary's daughter from a previous relationship, had been almost seventeen – a vulnerable age, he thought. Then there was a housekeeper called Jane Whitsun who had, according to the officer who interviewed her, mentioned that Rosemary and Staniland didn't get on but said little more. She too killed herself a couple of weeks later. Tragedy piled on tragedy.

Shortly after Rosemary's death Perdita left Addersacre, returning a week or so later, presumably in a fit of remorse. Since then both Wynn Staniland and his stepdaughter had lived quietly, saying they wanted to be left alone. United in grief; or wallowing in it. To Wesley, the whole set-up seemed unhealthy.

Now he was armed with this information, he felt ready for another visit and, with perfect timing, Gerry was just finishing a phone call.

'Ready to see Staniland?' Wesley asked, hovering by Gerry's door.

Gerry nodded but he looked preoccupied. 'Might as well get it over with.'

Wesley drove as usual. It was a beautiful day and as they left Tradmouth the river teemed with yachts, their white sails racing across the water. He'd always regarded it as a miracle that they didn't collide with each other or with the numerous ferries that plied up and down, but somehow disaster was always averted.

During the drive Wesley brought Gerry up to date with what he'd learned but Gerry merely grunted in acknowledgement and didn't attempt any further conversation. As Wesley steered the car up Staniland's drive again he couldn't help wondering why the man had stayed there. If he'd had to endure such traumatic events in his own house, he'd want to move well away. It wasn't as if Staniland had a wide social life in the area, friends and family he could rely on for support. He said as much to Gerry, who made no comment. As for Perdita, it seemed she'd sacrificed her whole life to look after her stepfather. Wesley wasn't sure whether this was commendable or sad.

It was Perdita who greeted them and showed them into the living room before hurrying off to let her father know they'd arrived. The room looked even shabbier today with the sunlight streaming through the window, setting the specks of dust aglow as they floated through the still air like snow on a windless day.

As they waited for Staniland to join them, Wesley pictured his late wife's final journey. She would have left the house and made her way through the garden until she came to the path leading down to the beach. She must have taken the pills at home then staggered to the pool, her head swimming as they took effect. He imagined her filling her pockets with pebbles from the sea shore and sitting at the edge of the water as the world began to blur and spin around her, then slipping in just as she was about to lose consciousness, unable to fight back against death, unable to save herself.

When Staniland entered, the surface charm was still there but Wesley noticed telltale signs of strain on his face. Today his flesh looked pallid and the lines around his eyes appeared to have deepened.

'We're sorry to bother you again, Mr Staniland,' he began. 'We need to ask you a few more questions.'

'That's what the police always say,' the author said with a bitter smile. 'You haven't brought that policewoman. Detective Sergeant Tracey, isn't it?'

'Not today.'

'Pity. Look, I can't add anything to what I told you last time. As far as I know I've never seen that couple in my life.'

'We haven't come about them this time,' said Wesley. 'When did you last see Zac Wilkinson?'

'Zac?' He frowned as if he was making a great effort to remember. 'It must have been about ten days ago. He came round to do another interview.'

'You don't sound too happy about it,' said Wesley.

There was a long pause. 'It was becoming rather intrusive to tell you the truth; having to go over the most painful period of my life. I was starting to regret agreeing to this biography but there was always the implication that if I didn't cooperate, it would go ahead anyway. At least if I spoke to him there was a chance I'd have some control over what he wrote.'

'You're speaking in the past tense.'

For the first time Staniland looked flustered. 'The initial work's finished as far as I know. He's past the research stage and he's in the process of actually writing the thing.'

'I'm afraid he was found dead on Saturday.'

Staniland stared ahead and what little colour there had been in his face drained away. Wesley hadn't heard Perdita enter the room. She must have done so silently and now she was standing near the open door listening to what was being said.

As soon as Wesley finished speaking she rushed over to her stepfather and sat down beside him, her hand resting comfortingly on his arm.

'Is this true?' she said, looking from Wesley to Gerry accusingly, as though she imagined they were lying for some unfathomable reason of their own.

'I'm afraid it is,' Wesley said. 'Mr Wilkinson was found in woodland near Queenswear. He'd been murdered.'

'Who'd want to kill him?' Perdita asked in disbelief. 'He didn't seem the kind of man who'd make enemies. He was a hack – a man who wrote to order. Writing about Father was a step up for him but he was little more than a journalist.'

She said the last word as if it was something disreputable, Wesley noticed. Staniland had probably had trouble with journalists in the past. The tragedies in his life had been bound to attract attention of the more prurient kind.

'What can you tell us about him?'

'Not much,' said Perdita. 'Father's publisher contacted us saying Wilkinson was writing a biography and asking whether we'd be willing to cooperate. At first Father said no but then his publisher got in touch again to say they were very excited about the possible publicity . . . and the increase in Father's sales of course. They promised Father's privacy would be guaranteed and encouraged us to see Wilkinson and it went from there. The publisher was right, there has been a lot of interest and Father's been approached to speak at literary festivals already.' She looked at her stepfather protectively. 'We had to refuse, of course. His health's not up to it and all we want is a quiet life.'

Wesley said nothing for several moments as he wondered how best to phrase the next question. 'Mr Staniland, did you talk to Wilkinson about your wife's death?'

Staniland caught his breath. 'I told him I didn't want to talk about it but he insisted. He said that's what people wanted to know about and that if I spoke to him it would stop others intruding. There was some logic to his argument, I suppose.'

'You must have come to know him quite well,' Gerry said.

'I wouldn't say that. He asked questions and I answered as best I could, trying to avoid anything that might cause distress. But of course that's what he was mainly interested in. That and the reason I stopped writing.'

'So there were disagreements.'

'A few – there were bound to be. But I didn't kill him if that's what you're implying, Inspector.'

'The idea's ridiculous,' said Perdita before pursing her lips.

'We're sorry he's dead, of course,' said Staniland. 'But I really don't know what else we can tell you.'

Wesley nodded sympathetically. For a renowned novelist, he thought, the man was fond of speaking in clichés.

'Would it surprise you to learn that Zac Wilkinson wasn't his real name and that he spent his teenage years in custody for killing two boys when he was twelve years old? He was at boarding school at the time and his victims were two of his fellow pupils. The case was quite notorious and when he was released he was given a new identity.'

Perdita stared at him with a disbelief that couldn't be

faked. Then she turned her eyes towards her stepfather, who was looking perplexed. Unless they were very good actors, this was news to both of them.

'I find it difficult to believe,' Staniland said when he'd composed himself. 'The man didn't seem the violent type. Quite the reverse I would have thought.'

'And he never mentioned any of his associates? Anyone he was afraid of? Any plans he may have had?'

Perdita and her stepfather shook their heads in unison. With hindsight Wesley realised it had been a foolish question. The Stanilands and Zac Wilkinson hadn't had that sort of relationship.

'I don't think they can tell us any more,' said Gerry as they got into the car to drive back to Tradmouth.

Wesley didn't answer. He wanted to keep an open mind.

Journal of John Lipton

10 May 1884

I meet Mary in the walled garden when the household has retired for the night. We keep to our secret trysting place because if her father were to suspect, he would lock her in her chamber like a prisoner. She tells me he has done it before.

On the evening of the puppet show he thought me part of Gunster's troupe, a person of no consequence, and I cautioned Mary against presenting me to him in such circumstances. To Sir Cuthbert Field an entertainer, an assistant to a puppet master, is no more than a servant.

Mary comes to me eagerly while Sarah keeps lookout and when she raises her face towards me I stroke her fine fair hair and kiss her. Then I ask how she liked the performance; our little murder played out to the delighted squeals of the ladies. She replies that William Corder *must have been a very wicked man in life and I ask her if she thinks all murderers are wicked. She laughs at my question and says Corder must have been very handsome. She says Corder must have been rather like me.*

19

Della Stannard had been through a terrible ordeal in recent months, or at least that's what she told her colleagues on the organising committee of the Dukesbridge Literary Festival. She'd supported her only daughter through her treatment for breast cancer – she'd had to because her daughter's husband was a policeman and he was never there to look after her. Most people believed Della's glowing version of herself, until they got to know her better.

The change of programme was causing a great headache. Zac Wilkinson had been booked to speak a week on Friday about his upcoming biography of Wynn Staniland. Interest in Staniland never seemed to wane. The notion of the genius shunning the world seemed to appeal to the reading public and there'd been a lot of hype recently about Wilkinson's biography and the secrets it promised to reveal.

But now Staniland's biographer was dead – which Della thought was inconsiderate of him – and the committee was faced with the problem of replacing him. She had suggested approaching Staniland himself but this idea was thrown out immediately. It was well known that the man never gave talks or did book signings, and avoided any form of human contact. Undeterred, Della said there was no harm in trying but her fellow committee members were strangely reluctant.

The committee's extensive discussions about Wilkinson's replacement had resulted in heated disagreements as the various factions vied with each other to promote their own choice. In the end they'd reached stalemate, a situation made worse by the fact that most of the speakers suggested were unable to take part at such short notice.

Having rejected a romantic novelist with a well-known taste for the bottle and failed to hook a prestigious children's author and a local crime writer, the committee was left with no alternative other than to go for something innovative. Something nobody else had thought of.

Della had first met the committee chair, Raynard Bishop, several months ago when she'd spotted a poster in a Neston bookshop advertising a special performance of a nineteenth-century puppet show. The subject of the show was famous Victorian murders and she'd been so intrigued that she'd gone along, choosing to take a man she'd met on one of her many forays into internet dating. She'd thought it might be fun in an ironic sort of way – but that was before she'd actually witnessed the performance in the barn at Tradington that had been converted at great expense into a community arts centre.

The puppets re-enacted a variety of gruesome slaughters and Della had found the content of the show depressing. She'd thought Punch and Judy, with its depiction of domestic violence and death by hanging, was bad enough but the graphic depiction of the murder of Maria Marten in the notorious Red Barn, the bloody Ratcliffe Highway Murders and the sad death of Little Saville Kent, allegedly at the hands of his own sister Constance, had made her feel decidedly queasy.

Bishop had told his stunned audience that the show was a valuable historical exercise and that back in the days of Queen Victoria marionette shows such as they'd witnessed had been a hugely popular entertainment at inns, fairs and market places throughout the land. Murder had been big business, the man said, as were public executions when the culprit was finally caught.

Della had chatted with Bishop afterwards as he'd packed away the puppets and their booth and later their paths had crossed again on the committee.

She'd always thought Bishop a little strange but now he had to be persuaded that his show would be an ideal replacement for Zac Wilkinson's talk at the festival, especially if he was willing to augment it with a lecture about the Victorian taste for murder and death. Della was confident that, if she gave Bishop the full force of her charm, he was bound to agree and, having settled all this in her mind, she felt rather pleased with herself.

On his return from Addersacre Wesley was about to call Pam but before he could do so his phone rang and he saw it was Neil on the line.

Neil came straight to the point.

'Are you free tonight? I need to talk about this dig at Newfield Manor.'

Wesley knew Neil well enough to realise something wasn't right.

'Sorry. I won't be finished here till late; we've had

146

two suspicious deaths in Stoke Beeching and a murder near Queenswear. Another time, eh.' He didn't mention Michael's part in the discovery of Zac Wilkinson's body because he hadn't time for elaborate explanations.

'I heard about the Queenswear case on the news. Who was the victim?'

Wesley decided there was no harm in telling his friend the basics. 'He was Wynn Staniland's biographer but—'

'Wynn Staniland? Didn't his wife kill herself? She was found in a pool sitting upright. Funny that.'

'Don't suppose she was laughing.'

'No, I mean it's similar to the murder of Mary Field in 1884. She was found sitting upright in a pond, the water just over her head. It was said she'd been strangled and taken there by her former suitor, who was sick with jealousy. He vanished straight afterwards so I suppose he must have done it.' He didn't sound too sure of himself. 'That's what my new dig's about. I'm supposed to prove his innocence.'

This captured Wesley's attention. 'How are you going to do that?'

'Don't ask me.'

'I heard Staniland's wife copied her suicide from something in one of her husband's books. Perhaps he got the idea for his book from the Mary Field case.'

'Mary was definitely murdered. Perhaps someone killed Staniland's missus and copied the MO. Made it look like suicide,' said Neil. 'I'd better go.'

Wesley ended the call, uncomfortable about Neil's suggestion that Rosemary Staniland's death might not have been as straightforward as it seemed. If this was the case, there was a chance, slight though it was, that her apparent suicide was connected to recent events.

147

Before he could call Pam one of the constables assigned to his team hurried up to his desk. He was a burly lad with a ginger beard who looked as if he'd be useful on the rugby pitch, but in spite of his appearance he was shy and so quietly spoken that Wesley had to strain to hear what he was saying.

'We've still had no luck finding out where that champagne was bought, sir. It definitely wasn't locally or at any outlet in Leeds. It's not even available to order online.' The young man assumed an apologetic expression. Wesley thought he'd be great at breaking bad news.

Wesley assured him this failure wasn't his fault but, instead of leaving, the officer produced a few sheets of A4 paper stapled neatly together. 'Jamie Hursthead's phone records.'

'No sign of the Lombards' records yet?'

The officer shook his head. 'Different provider. They're taking their time.'

'Have Hursthead's numbers been traced?'

'Most of them are to do with his work: his agent, his publisher, Wynn Staniland, people he interviewed about his book and various libraries. He didn't seem to have many friends,' he added sadly. 'There's only one we haven't been able to trace and that's an unregistered mobile. He received two calls from it on the evening he was supposed to be giving a talk at Neston Library … just before he disappeared.'

'The killer arranging to meet him at the murder site,' said Wesley quietly.

The officer nodded eagerly as if Wesley had made some brilliant deduction. 'You could be right, sir.'

*

148

Gerry felt a little guilty about leaving the incident room early that evening but he promised himself he'd make a special effort to be in early the next morning. After all, it wasn't every day you acquired a new daughter.

He'd arranged to take Alison out for a meal that evening. The Carved Cherub: nothing but the best. He wanted to make up for the lost years, the years he hadn't even known of her existence. The fact that he didn't remember her mother made him feel bad, but she must have been telling the truth: people don't tell lies on their deathbed. If anyone was at fault he was. Besides, Alison definitely had a look of him.

He walked home to Baynard's Quay, the cobbled water-front where centuries ago Tradmouth's trading vessels unloaded their cargoes. Gerry's house stood at the end of the row, dwarfed by its grander neighbours. Wesley was right. It was a desirable spot.

The light was on in the hall – a shady space which was gloomy even on the brightest day – and Gerry took this as a sign that Joyce was home from her job at the Register Office in Morbay where she presided over weddings, birth registrations and the bereaved who came to register deaths. Joyce was good with people – she had to be – and yet so far she hadn't formed much of a bond with Alison. He told himself it was early days.

He found Joyce in the living room watching her favourite soap. Normally she'd greet him with a kiss on the cheek and ask him what he fancied doing about dinner. But today she hardly looked up and he could feel the vibrations of disapproval from where he was standing.

'Everything OK, love?' he said cautiously.

'She's in the bath. Been in there half an hour. I'd hoped for a shower.'

'Sorry, love.'

'She said you were taking her out to dinner tonight. The Carved Cherub.'

'Er . . . You can come too if you like.'

'I've already eaten,' she said before walking away.

20

The next morning Wesley needed to talk to the people whose lives had been devastated by Jamie Hursthead's appalling act of murder. He viewed the prospect with dread because reminding them of that terrible time would be like opening a half-healed wound.

As he sat at his desk staring out at the river his mind strayed back to the events of the weekend. Michael had been unusually quiet since his grim discovery and this made Wesley uncomfortable. He wasn't even a teenager and there were already things he wasn't sharing with his parents. He hoped and prayed they'd seen the last of Harry Jones – although he was in Michael's class at school so he couldn't be sure.

Trying to set his family worries aside, he brought up the details of the Jamie Hursthead case again on his computer screen, searching for any mention of the victim, Ben Restorick, and his relationship with the boy who was to become his killer. But there was nothing in the reports to indicate why Jamie had chosen to kill Ben along with the boy he'd argued with: Jason State – son of the notorious Kieran.

Ben Restorick's family lived over the River Tamar in Cornwall, about an hour's drive away. He asked Gerry whether he wanted to go with him to Launceston and Gerry looked around the office before replying. The morning briefing had been completed and everyone was absorbed in their allotted tasks so, after proclaiming that he'd had enough of paperwork, Gerry accepted the offer.

It was a sparkling day and as Wesley drove, the DCI sat silently in the passenger seat looking out at the bleak beauty of Dartmoor with its rolling grey-walled fields and dramatic rock outcrops towering above the landscape. They had to slow down a few times for ponies who clearly hadn't learned their Highway Code but, apart from that, there were no major hold-ups and they reached the outskirts of Launceston just before lunch.

The town guarded the main route into Cornwall and was dominated by a thirteenth-century castle, a ruined round tower on a high mound. Wesley knew the place had a grim history and was once known as Castle Terrible because so many were hanged, drawn and quartered there in 1548 for the killing of a king's officer who was carrying out the royal policy of desecrating local holy shrines. The remnants of turbulent history lay all around in the region, yet despite all the long-ago suffering Wesley found that focusing on the past took his mind off his coming meeting with the bereaved family. But as he drew up outside the Restoricks' large double-fronted stone house on the edge of the town, he knew it was time to return to the present.

The man who opened the door to them looked grey.

Grey hair, grey polo shirt and chinos, short grey beard. There was even a tinge of grey about his complexion. Brian Restorick's face was expressionless as he led them into the large and immaculate living room where his wife was waiting, perched on the edge of an upright brocade sofa. It was a formal room, like a miniature version of drawing rooms Wesley had seen in stately homes, and it didn't look comfortable. It was hard to imagine a teenage boy in such an environment and Wesley wondered whether the house would have looked the same if Ben had lived.

Mrs Restorick was a thin nervous woman with the look of someone who'd given up caring about her appearance and Wesley immediately felt sorry for the ordeal he was about to put her through. She invited them to sit and Gerry chose an armchair by the window while Wesley opted for a hard upright chair in Mrs Restorick's direct line of sight.

He gave her what he hoped was a reassuring smile. 'We'd like to ask you some questions about your son's death,' he began gently. 'I realise the subject must be painful for you but we'll try and keep it brief.'

It was Brian Restorick who spoke. 'We've been over and over it enough times, Inspector. Once more won't hurt.'

His words were brave but Wesley wasn't sure whether he believed them. He began to question the couple, breaking the news of Jamie Hursthead's death with as much tact as he could muster. Gerry sat watching and said nothing; he knew Wesley was better at this sort of thing than he was.

'I'm not sorry he's dead.' Mrs Restorick spat out the words. It was the first time she'd spoken and her voice was unexpectedly deep. 'He wasn't punished – a few years in a secure unit getting more attention than most children do in a lifetime, being pandered to by every do-gooder. Then he was given a new identity. Why? Why shouldn't he face the consequences of what he did? We had to.'

For a while Wesley was unsure how to respond to her bitter tirade. He had some sympathy with what she'd said. Jamie Hursthead had been given a new beginning while Ben Restorick had no life of any sort ... and no future. The only words that came to his lips were, 'I'm sorry.' He glanced in Gerry's direction and saw him nodding in agreement.

'We don't know anything about this man's death,' said Brian Restorick firmly. 'And we're not sure we'd tell you if we did. Have you spoken to Jason State's family?'

'Not yet.'

Restorick stood up. He hadn't said it – he didn't have to. Kieran State was in a far better position to exact vengeance than this mild-mannered semi-retired architect and his wife. State knew people to whom violence was merely a tool of the trade.

'We had no idea what had become of Hursthead,' Restorick continued. 'He changed his identity so how could we? We don't have the contacts to find out that sort of thing. We don't move in that world.'

Wesley recognised this as a veiled attempt to divert their attention towards State. Restorick could well be right. How would they know that Zac Wilkinson was Jamie Hursthead, the twelve-year-old boy who'd killed their only son?

Gerry sat silently while Wesley asked more routine questions. Where had they been at the time of Hursthead's death? Had they had any contact with him since his release? Did they know he had a career as a freelance journalist and a writer of biographies? Did they know he was in Tradmouth?

The Restoricks' denials were confident but Wesley sensed

their growing impatience. He wanted to end the interview as much as they did.

When the interview was over he thanked them for their time and Brian Restorick showed them out. They had just entered the thickly carpeted hallway when Wesley noticed a colourful flyer on the hall table next to the telephone. He picked it up and handed it to Restorick.

'Mr Restorick, where did you get this?' he asked.

Restorick took it from him and stared at it. 'I don't remember. Perhaps one of us picked it up in the library.'

'That's him,' said Wesley. 'That's Jamie Hursthead.'

Restorick passed it back quickly as though it was contaminated.

THE TRUTH ABOUT WYNN STANILAND, it said. COME AND HEAR BIOGRAPHER ZAC WILKINSON TALKING ABOUT HIS EXPLOSIVE FORTHCOMING BIOGRAPHY OF THE GREAT AUTHOR AT NESTON LIBRARY.

Below was a moody photograph of Hursthead. But had the Restoricks recognised it as the same boy they'd seen day after day in court all those years ago?

If Wesley had been in their situation he'd have remembered every detail, every feature, every blemish, every mannerism, of the person who wrecked his life.

While isolation provides privacy, it also makes you vulnerable.

Wynn Staniland and Perdita had both heard the intercom: someone at the gate pressing it repeatedly, three slow buzzes each time. It had been going on for a couple of minutes and they knew whoever it was wasn't going away.

'Maybe we should answer it,' Perdita whispered in his ear. She was clinging to his arm like a frightened child.

'No,' Staniland snapped as he extricated himself from her grasping hands. He made his way over to the window slowly and stared out, his face ashen. Then the buzzing started up again.

'He's not going to go away,' she whispered. 'I think it's time to face our demons.'

He turned and took her hand. 'Whatever you think best.'

21

Wesley and Gerry barely exchanged a word during the homeward journey but each knew the other was thinking of the Restoricks. It was impossible to do otherwise.

As they neared Tradmouth Wesley broke the silence. 'What do you think? Could the Restoricks have gone to one of Hursthead's talks and recognised him?'

'If they did it would have come as a hell of a shock. You go to a library talk by an author and, lo and behold, standing up there in front of you is the person who murdered your only child. It'd feel like a kick in the teeth.'

'Don't forget Jamie Hursthead was only twelve when it happened. He was a child himself so surely he deserved some sort of second chance.'

'You're sounding like a bleeding heart liberal, Wes. You'd feel differently if it was your child he'd killed.'

Wesley knew Gerry was right. If anyone harmed one of his children he was sure he'd react exactly like the Restoricks. But whether he'd exact his revenge by killing – an eye for an eye – he couldn't be sure. He hoped he wouldn't yield to that particular temptation.

'It's only our job to catch them,' Gerry said. 'Luckily it's up to someone else to decide what happens to them next.'

'Any sign of Callum Joy?'

'All patrols are on the lookout but no sightings so far. Mind you, the mugshot we've got is a few years old. He might have changed his appearance since then.'

'He's probably lying low. Or he's miles away.' Wesley hesitated. 'How's it going with Alison?'

'I took her to the Carved Cherub last night.'

'Pam wants to go there for our anniversary. I told her we'd have to check the bank account first.'

'It wasn't that dear.' Wesley detected a note of defensiveness in Gerry's reply.

'Joyce go with you?'

'She'd already eaten by the time I got in from work.'

'Bet you were popular. What does Joyce think of the situation?'

Gerry didn't answer.

'You've still not told Sam and Rosie, have you?'

'I'm waiting for the right moment.'

'Don't leave it too long. When's Alison planning to go back to Liverpool?'

'I told her she can stay as long as she likes.'

The fondness in Gerry's words made Wesley uneasy.

When they arrived at the office a phone was ringing. Wesley didn't take much notice but a few seconds later DC Paul Johnson hurried over to him.

'Someone's been using Zac Wilkinson's debit card to withdraw money,' Paul said. 'The bank's emailing me the CCTV footage for the relevant time.'

This was the best news Wesley had had all day. The chances of it being the killer who stole the dead man's bank card were remarkably high so, with any luck, they'd soon have a picture of him ... or her.

He followed Paul to his computer where both men waited, breath held, for the email to come through.

'Well, well,' Wesley said as the image appeared on the screen. 'A familiar face. It's Callum Joy. His prints are all over the victim's cottage.'

There was a smile of satisfaction on Paul's long face. 'He must have helped himself to his old cellmate's bank card while he was there ... which suggests he knows he's dead and won't miss it.'

An hour later an up-to-date image of Callum Joy taken from the CCTV had been given to every officer and PCSO in the district. Surely it wouldn't take long to bring him in.

Karl Banville demanded another meeting at Newfield Manor. Neil found it irritating that he demanded rather than asked.

This time Neil arrived half an hour early so he could look round without Banville dogging his footsteps at every turn. He needed to make sure the structure was safe before he allowed any work to start inside it. He'd also have to assess what equipment would be required to satisfy the usual health and safety regulations, of which there were a lot these days.

He entered the ruined building through an empty side doorway, walking slowly, alert for hidden hazards. Once inside the shell of the manor he was relieved to find that things weren't as bad as he'd first feared. The walls looked solid enough, as did the floor.

He stood for a while, listening. He could hear the crows in the trees that crowded in on the house like a gang of bullies. Their cries sounded as if the birds were sharing some private joke about somebody's misfortune.

Then he heard a car approaching so he picked his way across the long-abandoned rooms and made for the front door. By some miracle the door itself still hung in place, covered with lichen and half rotted away. It must have been impressive once – but not any more.

He'd been expecting Karl Banville but instead he saw that the approaching car was a small red sporty Toyota. The car skidded to a standstill and a young man climbed out. Neil recognised him at once, even though last time he'd seen him he'd been dressed in a cloak and top hat.

'Hi,' the newcomer said, raising a hand in greeting. 'What are you doing here?' The question was a genuine enquiry rather than a challenge.

'I could ask you the same thing. Haven't I seen you before? The ghost tour?'

'Spot on. Joe Public can't get enough of ghosts and ghoulies.' He gave Neil a cheeky grin. 'Talking of ghoulies, you don't happen to know where Banville is, do you? I was hoping for a word.'

'I got the impression you two don't get along too well.'

'We have our differences. This is private property but I'm doing no harm. What damage can I do bringing a few punters here for a cheap thrill? I'm Archie Jones by the way.' He thrust out his hand and Neil shook it. It seemed like the right thing to do.

'Neil Watson. County Archaeological Unit.'

'Cool. He's not letting you dig here, is he?'

'Why?'

'He's very protective of this place, that's all. You know about the ghost?'

'What about it?'

'Her name's Mary Field. She was the heiress to the place in the eighteen eighties and she married someone her parents didn't approve of. Murdered and dumped in a pond by one of Banville's ancestors.'

'William Banville. I know all about it. Where's the pond where she died?'

Jones pointed to his right. 'Over there just beyond those trees. I can show you if you like.'

Neil hesitated. He wanted to see where Mary Field had died in such a bizarre manner. On the other hand, he was expecting Banville to join him any moment.

'Isn't there some doubt about William Banville's guilt?' Neil said nothing about Banville's desire to prove his relative's innocence. It seemed wrong to be gossiping about the man who had offered to finance the proposed excavation.

'I've done a lot of research into the case,' Jones said with a smug grin. 'Banville killed Mary all right.'

'Is that what you tell your punters?'

'Those are the facts.'

At that moment Karl Banville's car appeared round the corner of the drive and when he screeched to a halt Neil could sense the driver's anger even before he emerged from the vehicle.

'Get off my property,' he shouted to Jones. 'And don't come back.'

'Nice to see you too, Karl. Can we talk?'

Jones's question was calm and reasonable but Banville's reaction wasn't. He'd rushed forward and punched the young man in the face before Neil realised what was happening.

Neil saw blood streaming from Jones's nose and Banville stood frozen as the injured teenager staggered back to his car. Neil moved to follow him, to make sure he was all right, but he felt a restraining hand on his shoulder.

'Leave him. With any luck he won't be back,' Banville growled with satisfaction. Neil watched his gloating face. He had just witnessed a violent loss of control that seemed out of all proportion to the problem.

As he watched Jones drive off, he felt a glimmer of fear.

When Barbara Smith signed up to become a police and community support officer based at Tradmouth Police Station she'd dreamed of excitement. She'd always been a fan of cop shows and detective series – in fact anything featuring a murder. But the reality of the job so far hadn't lived up to her expectations. Her working life consisted of dealing with minor trouble: a bit of shoplifting from the local Boots; the occasional bout of minor vandalism; a smattering of drunk and disorderly at weekends; and attempting to dampen the high spirits of the Hooray Henrys, the braying youngsters who arrived with the yachting set in the summer months and treated the town and its pubs as their private playground.

Anything more interesting was instantly seized by Uniform and CID. Proper coppers. If Barbara had been younger she'd have sought to join their ranks but, as it was, she'd only embarked on her crime-fighting career in her forties after bringing up her family so she felt she'd missed that particular bus.

Today, however, Barbara had been given a job to do and she was taking it seriously. She had a photograph of the suspect and referred to it each time she passed a man of around the right age and build. Her beat partner, Ian, was keener on finding illegally parked cars than he was on proper detective work. But Barbara kept the picture of Callum Joy to hand like a talisman because it was connected to a real crime: a murder.

The Memorial Gardens were part of what Barbara liked to call her beat – one of the places where she could provide a reassuring presence to tourists and locals alike – and she walked towards the bandstand with Ian by her side. He was chewing gum, which hardly gave a good impression to her public, but she'd given up telling him. Men never listen.

She scanned the benches scattered around the little park, most bearing dedications to deceased loved ones who'd loved this place. Her own dad's bench was over near the public toilets, not the place she would have chosen but it had been the only one available at the time.

When she neared her dad's bench, as she thought of it, she saw that it was occupied by a thin young man. He was well dressed and yet something about him didn't look right. He was staring at the seagulls patrolling the path in the hope of pickings from someone's alfresco lunch and Barbara's heart beat faster as she took the photograph sur-reptitiously from her pocket.

'What is it?' Ian asked. He sounded bored and she knew he was longing to head for the market where he could nab some naughty motorists.

She grabbed his arm and led him behind a tall, bushy shrub, somewhere she could watch without being seen.

'It's him. The man in that photo we were given.'

'He'll be long gone,' said Ian the defeatist.

'I'm calling it in.'

'If you want to make an idiot of yourself,' Ian said with a sniff, eyeing a couple consuming fish and chips on a nearby bench. A smirk appeared on his lips when he saw a trio of seagulls descending like vultures on the hapless pair.

Barbara ignored him and made the call.

22

'We've got Callum Joy.'

Wesley raised his eyebrows. 'That was quick.'

'Efficiency's our middle name.' Gerry grinned with satisfaction. 'A PCSO spotted him in the Memorial Gardens sitting on a bench and called it in.'

'Very observant of him.'

'Her. Callum's down in the interview room. Are you coming?'

Wesley had expected defiance from their suspect but instead as he walked into the interview room he saw fear, even relief, on the man's face. It had a cherubic look about it; an innocent face which must have stood him in good stead in the course of his criminal career.

'How did you find me?' was Callum's first question. He sounded genuinely curious.

'Your prints were all over Jamie Hursthead's cottage. And when you used Jamie's debit card to get cash out of the ATM you were caught on camera.'

'Did Jamie report his cards missing?' There was caution in his voice, as though he was making a guess.

'How could he do that?'

'Haven't you arrested him? There were cops crawling all over his place so I thought he'd been up to his old tricks again.'

'What do you mean?' said Gerry.

Callum snorted. 'Look, I knew he'd done well for himself and he'd written books and that but I knew him when he was Jamie Hursthead ... the murderer. Don't tell me you didn't know,' he added as if he was delighted to get one over on the police.

'We knew,' said Wesley. 'What were you doing at his cottage?'

'Hasn't he told you?'

'That might be difficult. He died a few days ago.'

Callum was either an accomplished actor or his shock was genuine.

'How? Where?' he said after he'd had a few seconds to take in Wesley's news. 'When I saw the police at his place I thought he must have done something.'

'I asked you what you were doing at his cottage.'

'I needed somewhere to stay, didn't I?'

'Why's that?'

No answer.

'You might as well tell us,' said Gerry, leaning forward. 'We're very understanding, aren't we, Inspector Peterson?'

Callum thought about it for a few seconds. Then he too leaned forward, an eager light in his eyes. 'I was in this hostel in Exeter – for the homeless – and this bloke offered me work and somewhere to live. He seemed dead genuine and I thought I'd fallen on my feet.'

'What happened?'

'He drove a couple of us to this farm in the back of a Transit. Then once we got there he changed. He locked us up in this old barn place with some other blokes . . . Eastern Europeans. During the day we worked on a farm or they took us in the van to lay drives and things; cutting down trees and that. They never paid us a penny and they said if we told anyone or tried to get away they'd catch up with us and kill us, and they said they'd find our families and hurt them. They said they knew where my sister and her kids lived. At night they chained our ankles so we couldn't escape. The other guy from the hostel managed to get away when we were cutting down some trees and . . . they told us he'd been shot.'

'How many men were locked up with you?' Wesley asked.

'Six, including the lad from the hostel.'

'What can you tell us about the people who held you?'

All of a sudden he looked scared.

'You're safe,' said Wesley. 'They can't touch you now.'

Callum looked unconvinced. 'You don't know what they're like.'

'Can you describe them?'

There was a short pause. 'They covered their faces.'

Wesley and Gerry exchanged looks. He could describe them all right but the hold they had over him was still strong. 'Why didn't you come to us as soon as you escaped?'

Callum's face reddened. 'Never trusted the filth, have I? When I made it to Tradmouth and saw Jamie's face on a poster, I thought he'd help me. We shared a cell once,' he added by way of explanation. 'And there was this Russian bloke, Ivan. He was in a bad way . . . coughing and that. I wanted to go back and bring him out. Get him help.'

166

'We could have done that.'

'He's in the country illegally. If you lot get hold of him he'll be sent back and that's the last thing he wants.'

'Where is he now?'

'I borrowed Jamie's car and went back but I must have got the wrong place. I recognised one of them farm signs but everything looked different so . . . '

'If you tell us where you think it is we'll search the area.'

Callum Joy shook his head.

'If your friend Ivan's ill he needs to be cared for.' Wesley nearly added the words 'if it's not too late' but he stopped himself in time.

Neil had witnessed Karl Banville's fury at Archie Jones's defiance and he knew it would be best to tread carefully from now on. He'd heard of family loyalty but Karl's determination to prove William Banville's innocence after all those years seemed worryingly obsessive. But he was a very rich man and the offer of a fully funded excavation had been dangled before him like a tempting, juicy carrot. Even so, he wondered if there'd be a high price to pay.

After Jones's departure Banville switched back into the role of affable history enthusiast as though the violent argument had never happened and Neil found the sudden change disconcerting.

As they walked round the site, Banville revealed that the estate's accounts for 1884 showed a payment for a summer-house erected in the walled garden shortly after Mary's death. He reckoned the timing was suspicious and Neil couldn't help agreeing with him. What sort of man thinks of garden improvements when his wife has just met a violent end? Unless he has a good reason – like concealing a corpse.

The summerhouse burned down at a later date but Neil promised to make opening a trench on the spot a priority. With luck he'd be able to start work by the end of the week.

This was what Banville wanted to hear. By the time he left, the new owner of Newfield Manor was in good spirits, driving off with a friendly wave as Neil watched his SUV disappearing down the drive.

Once Neil was alone with the crows and the wind-rustled trees, the ruined house glowered down at him, challenging him to venture further. For a few moments, Neil felt reluctant to turn his back on the place; then he told himself this was ridiculous. There were no such things as ghosts, no matter what Archie Jones might say.

If he was going to be in charge of this new excavation he needed to familiarise himself with the local landscape, but he knew his motives weren't altogether worthy. He wanted to see the pool where Mary Field had met her death, which probably made him as bad as Archie's ghouls.

Although Archie's directions had been vague it didn't take him long to find the place. The pool was fringed by tall rocks on one side and on the other willows dipped their branches sadly into the dark water. The world seemed silent there, as if nature was holding its breath, and after a few seconds he realised he could hear no birdsong.

He walked to the edge of the water and gazed into its opaque depths. He'd come across pools like this before in his professional career, liminal places where sacrifices were made in more primitive times. Broken Iron Age weapons were often found in such pools, gifts to the gods of the water. He stared down at his reflection, thinking how deep it looked. He couldn't see the bottom or any sign of wildlife in the water. This was a dead place.

As he gazed down he was certain he glimpsed a reflection of something at his shoulder – the image of a pale face with hollow, pleading eyes. But when he spun round there was nothing there.

Journal of Mary Field

22 May 1884

After telling Papa I wished to take some air before dinner, I sneaked into the garden and found John waiting. I led him into the walled garden and once we were hidden from sight I enquired about the carpet bag he was carrying.

I have never before encountered a man who possesses such an air of danger. The young men Mama and Papa paraded before me have all been as dull as my nightly drink of hot milk with their perfect manners and their mild talk of mundane matters. William Banville is Mama's particular favourite. He is of a good family but I could never consider him as a suitor for he cannot share my taste for the macabre as John does.

It was almost dark so I lit my lantern, knowing the light would not be seen from the house. And when John emptied the contents of his bag onto the stone bench, I saw grim wonders that set my heart beating; wonders I will never forget until my dying day.

The death mask was a singular object: the very features of a man hanged for the brutal murder of a shopkeeper in Exeter ten years ago. I marvelled at the hanged man's expression, asking John if he thought it proved the existence of the soul for the face had a blank look, as though all humanity had departed.

John said there is no such thing as a soul and that I am foolish to believe in such matters. He does, however, acknowledge the existence of evil which, he says, is the ruler of this earth. When he speaks like that I am afraid. Yet with that fear comes an excitement such as I have never before experienced.

23

Although Callum Joy wasn't good with letters, he remembered the name on the hanging sign: Red Water Farm. After some persuasion, he shared the information with Wesley who seemed more sympathetic than most officers he'd encountered in the course of his criminal career, pointing out the possibility of reprisals if his captors ever found him again. Wesley assured him he was quite safe but he could see the fear in Callum's eyes.

When Wesley asked Rachel what she knew about Red Water Farm she told him it used to belong to an elderly couple whose two daughters hadn't wanted to take over the farming business, an increasingly common scenario these days. They'd sold it to Jack Proudfoot, the man interviewed following the death of David Gough, but she knew little about him.

As there were bound to be guns on the premises, Gerry alerted the armed response team as a precaution and arranged for the appropriate people to be on standby to deal with any slavery victims they found. When he asked

Wesley if he thought he was overreacting, Wesley agreed that if the occupants of Red Water Farm were as dangerous as Callum claimed, it would be foolish to take risks.

Wesley eyed the phone impatiently as they waited for the call, thinking of the Russian man, Ivan, who might be close to death. Would they be too late to save him? Or was the whole thing a figment of Callum Joy's imagination?

The call was taking a long time to come through so, while they were waiting, Wesley seized the chance to have another word with Callum who'd been given a break on the insistence of the duty solicitor.

He returned to the interview room and switched on the tape machine.

'Any news yet?' Joy's voice cracked with anxiety.

'We've sent a team over to the farm and we're waiting to hear. In the meantime, I want to ask a few more questions about Jamie. When you were staying at his cottage did anything unusual happen? Did he receive any calls or . . .'

Callum considered the question for a while. 'I was on my own one night and I heard someone come in. I thought Jamie had come back but it wasn't him.'

'You sure of that?'

'Yeah.' Callum began to tear apart the empty plastic cup in front of him. Something to occupy his nervous fingers.

'Was this after you last saw Jamie?'

'The day after . . . Friday night. Someone opened the front door with a key. That's why I thought it was Jamie. Then they started creeping about and I realised it couldn't be him. I thought it must be a burglar.'

'Still think that?'

'Stuff went missing. Papers and files and that. And his laptop.'

'Do you know what was in the files?'

Callum's restless fingers stopped moving. 'Reading's not my thing, is it? But I think they had something to do with his work. He was writing a book about some famous author.'

'Wynn Staniland.'

'If you say so. The odd thing is whoever broke in took the laptop but left cash . . . and the wallet with the bank cards. There was a good TV and other stuff that'd fetch a bit. Why leave all that and take a few old papers?'

'Why indeed? Did the intruder see you?'

'Nah. I was in the bedroom and I legged it down the stairs while they were in the living room. And before you ask, I never saw who it was. I wasn't going to hang about, was I?' Callum began to fidget with the wrecked plastic cup again. 'Shouldn't you find out what's going on at that farm?' There was a hint of accusation in his question.

'It's being dealt with. If these people are armed like you said we can't just rush in. If what you've told us is true they won't get away with it,' Wesley said with determination before leaving the interview room.

He returned to the CID office and found Gerry at his desk, glaring at the phone, willing it to ring. He sat down heavily on the chair opposite.

'Any news from Red Water Farm?'

As if on cue Gerry's phone rang and after a brief conversation he ended the call and sat back in his seat. 'That was the ARU. They searched Red Water Farm and found nothing. Callum's having us on.'

'He sounds convincing to me.'

'He's taking us for a ride, Wes. Probably his idea of a joke. They searched all the outbuildings and found nothing. Proudfoot's threatening to report us for harassment.'

'He might have got wind of our interest and moved the evidence.'

'There was nothing there to back up Callum's story.' Gerry sighed. 'He's a criminal, Wes. A professional liar. And we fell for it. What did he say when you spoke to him just now?'

'There was an intruder at Jamie Hursthead's cottage on Friday night; the day after Jamie's disappearance. Callum assumed it was a burglar but whoever it was had keys to the place.'

'No keys were found on Jamie's body.'

'Which might mean Callum's intruder was Jamie Hursthead's killer.'

'Don't suppose he gave you a description?'

Wesley shook his head. 'As soon as he heard the intruder downstairs he made himself scarce.' He paused. 'According to Callum the only things taken were the papers Jamie was working on and his laptop.'

Gerry sat back and raised his eyebrows. 'I thought it was odd there was no computer in that place, him being a writer. Has Callum any idea what was in the missing papers?'

'I think he finds reading a bit of a challenge.'

Gerry rolled his eyes. 'Too many like that in the prison system. Poor sods.'

'The papers and the laptop must be linked to Jamie's work, which means Wynn Staniland's biography.'

'You think Wynn Staniland might be trying to sabotage Jamie's book?' Gerry sounded sceptical.

'I can't see it somehow. But I'm going to contact Jamie's publisher and agent. He might have sent them a draft.'

Wesley leaned back and stretched, knowing it was

175

going to be another long day. And Pam was coping alone again – unless her mother descended to cause mayhem and leave her exhausted. Although she was recovering well, he couldn't help worrying about her. And Michael's venture into the realm of crime hadn't helped matters.

As soon as he left Gerry's office he decided to contact Jamie Hursthead's agent and publisher, wondering whether they knew about their author's less than savoury past. Perhaps his notoriety would be regarded as a bonus, Wesley mused cynically, some extra background colour that would draw the public's attention to the book he was writing.

He started with the editor but it turned out she was attending a book fair abroad and wouldn't be back for several days. He had more luck with Jamie's agent, a woman called Bella Cross, who began by expressing her shock at her author's untimely death. She struck Wesley as the kind who was good at choosing the right words to fit the occasion – but then words were how she earned her living.

'I was so shocked when I heard about Zac's death. He was a lovely man and a wonderfully talented writer. I assume it was a random attack. One never thinks of that sort of thing happening in a place like Devon, does one?'

Wesley didn't feel inclined to enlighten her. 'You obviously knew him well.'

'Professionally, yes. He was a very talented biographer. And the Wynn Staniland book would have made his name. Zac was very intuitive. The biography's caused a great deal of excitement because Staniland's been one of the great mysteries of the literary world for years. I mean, why does somebody produce such brilliant, groundbreaking work and then suddenly stop?' She sounded exasperated by Staniland's lack of work ethic.

'Perhaps it was something to do with his wife's suicide. Maybe Zac's biography would have shed some light on it.'

'That's what everyone was hoping.'

'Presumably you've seen a draft?'

There was a short silence on the other end of the line before she answered. 'He'd worked on a number of celebrity biographies before and when he wrote his initial proposal and sent in a draft of the first couple of chapters the publisher jumped at it. He'll have done several drafts, of course, but he doesn't like me to see it until he's satisfied with what he's done. He was going to send it through as soon as he'd finished this next draft.'

'How close was that?'

'He said about three weeks but ... '

Wesley held his breath. He had the feeling what she was about to tell him would be important. 'Then?'

'He started stalling, saying he had more research to do. A new angle he wanted to explore.'

'Any idea what it was?'

'He never liked to go into the details of his work in progress – some authors don't – but I knew he always produced good work. I'll tell you one thing though, he told me to expect some surprises. And before you ask, I did ask him to elaborate but he said I'd have to wait and see.' She hesitated. 'Tell me, Inspector, have you found his latest draft? Or his computer? There's a chance the publisher will want someone else to take over the project.'

She suddenly seemed to realise what she'd said. 'I'm sorry to sound heartless but it's an important book, one the literary world's been anticipating for a long time.'

Wesley thought it was time he broke the bad news. 'I'm sorry, Ms Cross, we've searched the cottage he was renting

177

and there's no sign of any manuscript or his laptop. The cottage was broken into so we're assuming they were taken.'

The stunned silence on the other end of the line spoke more eloquently than words. The whole project lay in ruins.

'Did he mention anything he was planning to do while he was down here, apart from working? Anyone he intended to see?'

'He mentioned a trip to Bristol. And he'd visited the Cotswolds I believe but I'm afraid I don't know any details. He kept things very close to his chest. While he was in Devon he was speaking at a few libraries, and he was going to take part in a literary festival – a place called Dukesbridge. The publisher wants to stir up as much interest in the book as possible before publication. I hope someone's let the organisers know. I believe the festival starts very soon.'

'Can you give me the organiser's details? We'd like to talk to anyone who might have had contact with him recently.'

'The chair of the committee is a man called Raynard Bishop. Zac mentioned it last time we spoke. Said the man was becoming a bit of a nuisance. He was always calling him and fussing over minor details. He said it sometimes felt as though he had a stalker.'

Wesley's ears pricked up at the last word.

'I think it was a joke.'

Wesley made a note of the name: somebody else he needed to talk to.

Wesley thanked Bella Cross and as he was about to end the call she spoke again.

'If you do come across any of his notes will you let me know? The reason I ask is, although he didn't tell me what his new angle was, he said it was something that would make the book a bestseller. He said it was something explosive.'

24

Wesley noticed there were several missed calls from Neil on his mobile but he hadn't had time to call him back. He needed to contact Raynard Bishop.

Bella Cross had given him Bishop's email address but there was a more direct way of getting in touch. His mother-in-law, Della, had wormed her way onto the committee and it was about time she made herself useful.

It took a few moments for him to psych himself up to make the call and, when he finally got through, Della's bombastic enthusiasm throbbed through the phone line, draining him of energy.

Of course she knew Raynard. Wonderful man. He's put together such an impressive programme, she said. He has a marvellous collection of Victorian puppets, you know; the type they took round fairs. Mostly ghoulish re-enactments of famous murders, the sort of thing people couldn't get enough of back then. He's saved the day by stepping in to replace Wynn Staniland's biographer. You know, the one who's been murdered.

Her last statement sounded vaguely accusing, as though she held Wesley personally responsible for Zac Wilkinson's no-show. Wesley lost patience and interrupted. 'I need to contact Mr Bishop. Do you have his address?'

'Why?' There was an edge of caution in the question, as though she feared her friend was about to become a victim of police brutality.

'Just routine.'

'That's what the police always say when they want to persecute someone.'

'You know me, Della. Am I the persecuting type?' he said, trying his best to hide his irritation.

Unable to think up a suitable reply, she provided the details without further argument. Half an hour later Wesley and Rachel arrived at Bishop's house in Whitely.

The bearded man who answered the door wore rusty black and his expression gave nothing away when Wesley and Rachel introduced themselves.

'How can I help you?' he asked in a mellifluous voice reminiscent of a 1940s BBC announcer.

The man invited them to step into a gloomy oak-panelled parlour. Wesley sensed tension behind the apparent bonhomie; either he was worried about something or perhaps he didn't trust the police for some reason.

'Do sit down, Inspector, Sergeant. What can I get you to drink?' He wrung his hands like a humble Victorian tradesman, hoping to obtain the patronage of his social betters. There was something theatrical about Raynard Bishop; an affected manner that made Wesley wonder what was really going on in his head.

'Nothing, thank you. We'd like to ask you about Zac Wilkinson. You're aware we're treating his death as suspicious.'

'Oh dear me.' Bishop slapped his hand over his mouth and Wesley saw that he was suppressing a giggle. 'I'm so sorry,' he said, dabbing his eyes with the clean white handkerchief he'd just taken from his pocket with a flourish. 'I'm unused to being interrogated by the police. It makes one a little nervous.'

'Why would you be nervous?' Rachel said sharply.

The man opened his mouth to speak then closed it again as though he'd had second thoughts.

'We're speaking to everyone who had anything to do with Mr Wilkinson,' Wesley said calmly. 'It's just routine.'

Bishop took a deep breath. 'Of course.'

'I believe you have an interest in Victorian crime,' Wesley said.

'I'm a connoisseur of famous murders. Would you care to see my collection?'

'Thank you. I'd like that very much.' He shot Rachel a warning look. She'd get nowhere with the direct approach.

As they were led into the adjoining room, he told Bishop about his connection with Della and this seemed to put the man more at ease.

The room they entered was also panelled in oak and resembled a museum; sparsely furnished with a couple of leather sofas and surrounded by exhibits. Painted figures hung on the far wall like little criminals dangling from the gallows.

'These are my puppets,' Bishop said proudly, sweeping his hand around the room. 'That's William Palmer, the famous poisoner. And Kate Webster who was hanged in 1879 for the murder of her employer Julia Thomas. Then there's Constance Kent who cut her little half-brother's throat and hid his body in the outside privy. The puppets were made by a local man called Gunster who toured the West Country with his shows in the late nineteenth century.'

'The puppets re-enacted the murders?' Wesley could hear the distaste in Rachel's voice.

'There was a huge public appetite for the gruesome in those days. Public executions were regarded as a grand day out and attracted audiences of thousands.' He pointed to the little theatres, like the Punch and Judy booths the two officers had seen as children. 'As you can see, the scenery's been beautifully painted and new puppets were made for each fresh case that came to the public's attention, providing it had sufficient notoriety.'

Wesley pointed to the puppet of a young woman with an angelic face. Undoubtedly a victim. 'Who's she?'

'That's Mary Field. Heiress to the Newfield Manor estate near Whitely. An archaeologist visited me the other day with an American gentleman called Karl Banville who's a relative of the man everyone assumed was Mary's murderer. Karl's paying for an excavation at Newfield Manor in the hope of proving William Banville's innocence once and for all.'

'How does he plan to do that?'

'I'm not sure but he's a determined man. And very wealthy. He intends to convert the Manor into an hotel but first he feels the need to clear his ancestor's name.'

'Who's the archaeologist, do you know?'

'Dr Watson.' He smiled. 'I joked about it at the time but I'm sure he's heard it many times before.'

'He has. He's a friend of mine.'

Bishop's eyes lit up. 'It's a small world. I have a friend staying with me at the moment who deals in antiquarian books and I bought a book from him about the Mary Field case. I've lent it to Karl Banville but when he returns it I can show you if you're interested.'

Bishop didn't wait for a reply. 'The book mentions that Mary was in the habit of writing a journal which was in the possession of a family in Somerset until the Second World War. My friend Peter's trying to track it down for me.'

Interesting as this sounded, Wesley couldn't forget the purpose of his visit. 'What can you tell me about Zac Wilkinson?'

Bishop's eyes flickered towards the hanging puppets. 'We had an extensive email correspondence and he agreed to speak at the festival but then he emailed me to say he was pulling out which was disastrous because he was a big attraction. The interest in Wynn Staniland has never waned, you know, even after all this time.'

'Did Zac give a reason for pulling out?'

'He said there'd been an unexpected development in his research and he didn't feel able to speak about it just yet.'

'When did you receive his email?' Wesley asked, wondering why Della hadn't thought to mention this. Perhaps he hadn't asked the right questions.

'I can show you if you like.' Bishop led them back to the living room and started up a laptop lying on the coffee table. He brought up the email and passed the computer to Wesley.

Bishop hadn't been lying. The tone of Zac Wilkinson's email was curt and he brought up Bishop's reply which struck a peevish note at first then soon turned to pleading. After telling Wilkinson he'd let them down, something Bishop considered unprofessional, he pointed out that the festival was a new project and that its success was vastly important to the community. The email ended with a plea to Zac to reconsider his decision.

But it was the timing of Zac's – or rather Jamie's – email that caught Wesley's attention and he pointed it out to Rachel, who was looking over his shoulder.

It was written at six thirty on the day he disappeared; the day he failed to turn up at Neston Library for his talk at eight. There was a good chance that it was the last thing Jamie Hursthead wrote before his death.

Pam accused Wesley of being distant that evening and he knew she was right. His mind was on Jamie's email to Bishop and he speculated about what the unexpected development might have been. He'd called the librarian at Neston to say he'd been delayed and Wesley wanted to know whether this and Bishop's email were connected.

The next morning they were due to visit Jamie Hursthead's family in York. They had been kept informed of what was going on but had chosen not to travel down to Devon. The pull of blood usually overcomes ill feeling when there's a death in the family, Wesley thought, but obviously not in this case.

He and Gerry planned to spend the night up in Yorkshire and call in on the Lombards' Leeds home while they were in the area. They'd also arranged to speak to Frank Lombard's brother, Geoff, in the hope that he'd be able to throw some light on the dead couple's lives.

It fell to Wesley to undertake the long drive and he left home with a heavy heart, even though Pam seemed remarkably cheerful. It would be the first time he'd spent a night away from her since she'd undergone her treatment but she was quick to assure him that it wasn't a problem, saying she was planning to meet friends that afternoon. She was fine, she insisted, and Michael was old enough to make himself useful in his father's absence.

Michael had been quiet since the discovery of Jamie Hursthead's body, spending much of his time in his room with his iPhone. Wesley hoped he'd been chastened by his shocking experience and when he'd forbidden him to visit Harry for the foreseeable future, he hadn't argued. Even so, Wesley felt a small nag of unease. His son's ready acquiescence after Gerry's 'little word' had been rather too easy.

He met Gerry as arranged at the station at seven thirty for an early start and was surprised to find the boss on edge, fidgeting with the papers on his desk, unable to keep still.

When he asked if something was wrong the DCI hesitated before replying. 'Alison's still staying at mine and I'm a bit nervous about leaving her with Joyce.'

'Why, what's Joyce going to do to her?' Wesley had always thought of Joyce as an even-tempered soul, hardly the sort who'd pose a threat.

'I don't think she approves of me having a love child.'

Wesley started to laugh. He couldn't help himself. 'It's a long time since I've heard that phrase, Gerry. And if Joyce disapproves of anything it's probably the amount of time you're spending with Alison.'

Gerry looked surprised. 'You think so?'

'She sees you wining and dining this new daughter of yours who turns up out of the blue while she's left at home with a meal for one. Think about it.'

Gerry bowed his head, the picture of penitence. 'I never reckoned she'd see it like that.'

'You'll have to make it up to her when we get back.'

'Maybe they'll get to be friends while I'm away,' Gerry said, his voice full of hope.

'Maybe. Had any more thoughts about taking a DNA test?'

Gerry shook his head. 'She's mine all right, Wes. She's got the Heffernan nose . . . and my eyes. I can see a resemblance between her and my Rosie too.'

Wesley looked at his watch. 'We should get going.'

It was a long and arduous journey, broken only by a couple of stops at motorway service stations, hardly Wesley's favourite places. Fortunately they encountered no major hold-ups and he was relieved when they reached York early in the afternoon.

He'd visited the city before for its historical interest but he couldn't say he knew it well. Their hotel was situated beside the River Ouse and his room had a river view. When he stood at the window looking out on the water, the sight of the pleasure boats plying up and down reminded him a bit of home. Although he was London born and bred, he now thought of Tradmouth as home. The place had crept into his soul. He supposed York was that sort of place too, a place with a past that permeated its streets and absorbed you into its very being.

He was longing to explore, to wander round the medieval streets and visit the minster he could see towering over the rooftops, reaching upwards to the blue northern sky. But there was no time. They had to speak to Jamie Hursthead's family and he wasn't looking forward to it.

The Hurstheads lived in one of the city's more prosperous suburbs: tree-lined and boasting a mixture of large Edwardian houses and pretty nineteenth-century brick-built cottages. Jamie's family home was a large, red-brick villa with half-timbered gables and a stained glass porch, and it stood in a large, neatly manicured garden.

'Nice place,' Gerry commented. 'Mind you, he's Sir Stephen. We'll have to mind our manners.'

Wesley didn't answer. He pressed the doorbell and waited.

The woman who answered the door was middle aged with bobbed hair and an ample figure. Wesley's mother would have described her as 'homely'; the antithesis of glamour. As she stood aside to let them in it was hard to read her expression. There was none of the devastated grief he usually saw on the faces of victims' parents but there was something else, a guarded look, as though she was trying hard to hide her feelings. Perhaps she wasn't sure what those feelings should be.

She was joined in the spacious square hallway by her husband, an imposing man with silver hair and well-cut casual clothes. Sir Stephen Hursthead had been knighted for his services to industry, having founded a successful engineering company. He was a man used to being in charge but now he peered at them anxiously from behind his spectacles as he invited them into the large drawing room.

After the introductions had been made, Wesley and Gerry seated themselves in a pair of hard leather armchairs while the Hurstheads took the matching sofa opposite, sitting on the edge as though they were preparing to flee.

'We're very sorry about your son,' Wesley began. 'It must have come as a great shock to you.'

The Hurstheads exchanged a look.

'Yes and no,' Stephen Hursthead said tentatively. 'You see, we'd lost all contact with Jamie. He was given a new identity, a new life, and that meant severing all ties with his old one. No family contact. That was his choice.'

'And yours?' Wesley had seen a flicker of pain in the man's eyes.

'We were assured it was for the best. We had to allow him to make a completely fresh start, which meant he was dead to us from then on.'

'That must have been hard,' Gerry chipped in.

'It was,' Mavis Hursthead said simply. 'But he was twenty-two when he was released. A man. And we have our other children – his brother and sister.'

'How did they feel about never seeing their brother?'

Mavis took a deep breath. 'Pauline and Gregory were older than Jamie and they understood.' She gave a brave smile and stood up. 'They're both doing very well,' she said before walking up to the mantelpiece and picking up a pair of photographs.

She handed the pictures to Gerry. 'That's my daughter Pauline. She lives in Whitby. She works part time as a solicitor and she has two lovely children. This is my son Gregory. He's married with three children and he's due to take over the company when Stephen retires. So you see, Chief Inspector, our other children have made a success of their lives. Jamie was always . . .'

'The black sheep of the family?' Gerry guessed.

'A difficult child. Solitary. Volatile. We thought sending him to boarding school would do him good but obviously we were wrong.'

Wesley could see it all. The awkward child who seemed like a cuckoo in their well-feathered nest. The hope that sending him away would be the making of him; only it hadn't had the desired effect. His strangeness had made him a target for Jason State's bullying and his anger had exploded into murder. After that he'd paid the price with the loss of his freedom; the loss of his family; and the loss of his own identity.

'The policeman who came to break the news told us he'd become a writer.'

Wesley heard a note of pride in Mavis's voice, perhaps a sliver of hope that her son had done something good with his life after all.

'That's right. He wrote biographies; celebrities and footballers mostly. But at the time of his death he was working on something more serious – a biography of the author, Wynn Staniland.'

Mavis looked at her husband. 'He was always a clever, creative child but I never thought he'd be able to do anything like that after . . . '

'He was renting a flat in London and although he didn't earn a fortune from his writing, he managed to make a living,' Wesley continued. 'And with the biography of Wynn Staniland, who knows how his career might have developed.' He was about to say they should be proud of him but he stopped himself in time. They could never be proud of their son because of what he'd done when he was only twelve years old; a boy on the cusp of adolescence.

'We're glad to hear it, Inspector. But it really has nothing to do with us any more.' Stephen Hursthead's words weren't convincing. However much he protested otherwise, Jamie was his son and what happened to him mattered.

'So let me get this straight,' Gerry said. 'You haven't seen or heard from your son since he was twelve?'

Both parents shook their heads and Wesley watched their faces. Any pain they felt was well concealed. They'd probably had a lot of practice.

'You never visited him in the secure unit – or when he was transferred to an adult prison?' Wesley asked, curious, wondering how he himself would feel if he was in their position. Somehow he couldn't imagine that he'd ever abandon his own flesh and blood, no matter what the circumstances.

'Jamie was adamant that he didn't want to see us and we were advised to respect his wishes. However, we did make sure we were kept informed of his progress. He did very well in his exams – even took a degree in prison – a first in English. He was a clever boy.'

This time the pain showed through, raw and hurting. Mavis turned her head away so they couldn't see her face.

'Not seeing him must have been hard for you,' Wesley said softly.

'We came to terms with it,' Stephen answered. 'I think the hardest part was dealing with the threats.'

'What threats?'

'From the other boy's family. I can understand why they reacted like that, I suppose. They'd lost a son. But then so had we.'

'What kind of threats?'

'Horrible ones,' Mavis said, her eyes brimming with tears. 'We were going to be accused of terrible things. Something dreadful was going to happen to our other children. We received parcels containing things belonging to their dead son and a few times we were sent dead birds . . . and worse.'

'I presume you're talking about Jason State's family?' said Gerry. 'It'd be typical of that lot. But although they've got a lot of nasty contacts down in Essex and London, I doubt if their writ runs up in these parts. They were trying to scare you. Nothing ever happened, did it?'

Stephen Hursthead shook his head. 'No. We soon realised

190

the threats were empty. But it was still very upsetting. And it wasn't the States who threatened us.'

'Who was it then?'

'The Restoricks. Ben Restorick's parents.'

25

Wesley drove back to the hotel in silence, stunned by the revelation about the Restoricks. It was hard to imagine anybody less likely to issue the nasty threats the Hurstheads received than the respectable Launceston architect and his wife. But grief drives people to do strange things.

He had seen the picture of Jamie Hursthead in the Restoricks' house; the flyer advertising his appearance at Neston Library on the night he disappeared. If Brian Restorick had recognised him he would have known exactly where he'd be and when. He might have lured him over to the lonely spot on the other side of the river before Jamie had a chance to set off for Neston Library on the night of his death. Jamie had received two calls from an untraceable unregistered mobile and he'd probably thought it easier to leave the car in Tradmouth and cross the river on the passenger ferry to meet his killer; witnesses had come forward who'd seen him doing just that. The calls summoning him to that deadly meeting might have been made by the Restoricks. Perhaps the phone would be found at their home.

He called Rachel to share what he'd just learned. They needed to speak to the Restoricks again as soon as possible but as it was the end of the working day, she promised to pay them a visit the next morning.

In spite of this promising new development in the Jamie Hursthead case, they were still no nearer to unravelling the mystery of the Lombards' poisoning. Wesley hoped a visit to their house the following day and a talk to Frank's brother would prove productive. And yet he couldn't get Wynn Staniland's link with all three murders out of his head; even though, in the Lombards' case, that link was tenuous to say the least.

Their night in York proved a relaxing, if short, distraction from the case. They ate at a pub in Stonegate; an ancient establishment with a framed article on the wall outlining its ghostly credentials. On their way there they passed a group of people led by a top-hatted man in a swirling black cape; one of the many ghost tours they'd seen advertised. It seemed that ghosts were big business in the city.

After they'd eaten, Gerry insisted on sampling the local beer in three different pubs. Wesley knew he should have pointed out that they were there to work and not for a pub crawl but he couldn't be bothered. Besides, he was enjoying himself and when he called Pam she sounded cheerful. She was feeling well and Michael was behaving himself; he had even tidied his room.

Wesley slept soundly that night but whether this was because of the beer or because he felt more relaxed, he wasn't sure. For a while all seemed well with the world, especially when he woke up and looked out of the window at the sun rising over the waking city, catching the towers of the minster so that they glowed like golden pillars against the cloudless sky.

He packed up his overnight case with some regret before going down to breakfast. Being in a strange city away from the bustle of the incident room was helping him organise his thoughts and when he'd woken at six he'd lain there with his eyes closed for a while, going over the cases in his head.

Jamie Hursthead's past was the most obvious motive for his murder and yet the theft of his papers and laptop, together with his agent's claim that he'd found something explosive, suggested some connection to the biography he was writing. Wynn Staniland's life had been colourful and tragic but what was there left to discover that hadn't been in every newspaper at the time?

On the other hand Callum Joy might have been lying. He might have taken the laptop himself and flogged it in a pub, destroying the papers to muddy the waters. It looked as though he'd been lying about being imprisoned at Red Water Farm so could he really be trusted?

The full English breakfast was good and Gerry shovelled it down as though he hadn't seen food in weeks. They'd arranged with the Lombards' local police station in Leeds for an officer to meet them at the house. Wesley also wanted a word with the dead couple's neighbours.

When they left the hotel at nine Wesley gave the river a regretful backwards glance as he set off for the suburbs of Leeds.

'Did you speak to Joyce last night when we got in?' he asked, breaking the silence as they drove past the sign to Tadcaster.

'No. But I spoke to Alison. She said Joyce had gone to

bed early. I asked how they were getting on and she just said OK.' He sounded disappointed, as if he'd been expecting a more gushing reply.

Wesley had programmed the Lombards' address into the sat nav and, although he never quite trusted technology, on this occasion it did its job and they soon found themselves in a neat cul-de-sac of small semi-detached houses. Cars were parked on drives but there was nobody about, not even the promised police presence.

Wesley called the local station and was told that someone would be with them as soon as possible. He hoped they'd hurry up because they'd arranged to see Geoff Lombard at work. He was a teacher in a secondary school five miles away and he'd said he'd meet them at eleven when he had a free period.

He was relieved when a patrol car arrived, entering the cul-de-sac at a stately pace and sweeping to a halt outside the Lombards' gate. The constable who got out was rotund and middle aged, the classic jolly policeman. He was also chatty, which Wesley preferred to the alternative. You could learn a lot from a chatty person.

And, as luck would have it, the constable had conducted the initial search of the premises.

'It were a bit weird,' the man said as he opened the front door. 'We found a whole file of press cuttings about that author, Wynn Staniland, and that book the bloke who was murdered down your way was writing. Come up and have a look.'

He led them upstairs into the small front bedroom over the front door. Wesley noticed that a bookcase took up one entire wall. One side was filled with non-fiction books, biographies and manuals, and the other with popular fiction;

romance with a smattering of crime. On the bottom shelf were four Wynn Staniland novels: the complete works minus the title found in the caravan. Wesley took them out to examine them and discovered that they were first editions, all signed by the author. When he pointed this out to Gerry he remarked that they'd probably be worth something.

On a small desk opposite the shelves lay an A4 folder and when Wesley opened it he found the cuttings the constable had mentioned; all apparently written since Zac Wilkinson's coming biography was announced to a waiting world.

Another file lay beneath the folder, filled with earlier cuttings about Staniland's wife's suicide. Wesley picked it up and flicked through it.

'See,' the constable said, pointing a plump finger in the direction of the file. 'They took a great interest in this Staniland. It wouldn't surprise me if she went down to Devon to see him and her husband got jealous so he killed her then killed himself.'

'We're working on the theory they were both murdered. Poisoned,' said Wesley.

'Woman's weapon, poison. She probably killed him then did away with herself. Perhaps this writer bloke rejected her advances.'

It seemed the constable had an overactive imagination but Wesley couldn't be bothered bringing him up to date on their investigation so he kept quiet.

Wesley's search turned up nothing else about Wynn Staniland's books or his private life. He read through the file of recent reports again, noticing that a piece about Perdita Staniland which speculated about her relationship with her stepfather had been circled. It had been cut from a glossy Sunday supplement, dated a couple of months ago, and had clearly been written without Perdita's cooperation. The journalist painted a picture of a stepdaughter who'd devoted herself to her genius stepfather, protecting him from the intrusions of the outside world. There was a suggestion in the article, he thought, that the stepfather/stepdaughter relationship was a little intense, hinting at something sexual. Even though it kept on the right side of the libel laws, Wesley found the speculation distasteful. Unless this was the explosive secret Jamie Hursthead had uncovered.

'If Gina was such a fan I wonder if she tried to write to Staniland,' Wesley said. 'There's no sign of any replies.'

'He's a recluse,' said Gerry. 'Maybe he never replies to fan mail.'

Gerry had a point. If anything had been received, surely it would have taken pride of place; a physical sign that her hero had acknowledged her existence.

'Me and another lad went through the house,' the constable said. 'Didn't find owt interesting.'

'Address book?'

'We've been in touch with everyone in it but nobody told us much. They both got on with people at work but didn't seem to have any particular friends. Although she was a member of a book group.'

'One that specialised in the works of Wynn Staniland?' said Wesley.

The constable tilted his head to one side, considering the suggestion. 'That's one of the questions I asked but the woman I spoke to said she never mentioned him, let alone suggested they read any of his books. Odd that.'

Wesley looked at the books, noting that they were on the bottom shelf, hardly in a place of honour. 'I think she was more interested in Staniland's private life than his books.'

'Is it worth speaking to the neighbours?' said Gerry.

'We've already spoken to them and they all say the same thing. The Lombards were pleasant enough but they didn't let on anything about their private lives. And they didn't have visitors apart from his brother, who popped in from time to time. You're going to see him later, aren't you?'

'That's right.'

'Nice bloke. The address book's by the phone in the living room if you want a look. There's a computer but there's nowt much on it … although the browsing history does feature Wynn Staniland a lot as you'd expect. No relevant emails apart from the ones booking the caravan. They only did it a couple of weeks ago. Short notice. Went on impulse, I suppose.'

'Any sign of champagne?'

The constable shook his head. 'A few bottles of white in the kitchen but no champers. We sent you details of the calls made and received on their landline, didn't we?'

'Yes,' said Wesley. 'Thanks for that but I'm afraid it wasn't much help. Mind if we take a look around?'

'Be my guest. I'd best get back to the station. Short-staffed as usual. If I leave you the key can you lock up and drop it back at the station when you're done?'

'I was hoping he'd say that,' said Gerry once the constable left. 'Don't like anyone looking over my shoulder when I'm having a good nose round.'

'He seems observant. And he has contacted everyone in the Lombards' address book, which saves us a job.'

They started upstairs in the other bedrooms, full of all the detritus of everyday life. Wesley had always found searching the unoccupied rooms of the dead unbearably sad. It was the little things that got to him: the dressing

198

gowns hanging behind the door; the toothbrushes and half-used toiletries in the bathrooms; the books sitting on the bedside table awaiting their reader's return.

He went through the Lombards' room and as he searched through drawers and wardrobes, pushing clothes and underwear to one side in search of something relevant, he felt like an intruder. The bedroom yielded nothing and neither did the spare room so, after a brief look in the bathroom, they headed for the landing.

'What about the loft?' Wesley said.

Gerry pulled a face. 'You're younger than me, Wes. Up you go.'

Wesley opened the trapdoor and hooked the ladder down. He climbed up but all he could see up there was the usual junk that people accumulate over the years. In spite of this he made a token search and it was only when he was preparing to descend the ladder that he noticed a wooden box lying in the corner. When he opened it he found it was filled with papers and in the dim light of the single bulb dangling above his head he took some out and began to read.

Some were poems of despair and sadness, written in neat square writing – the immature hand of a teenager. The handwriting looked familiar but it took Wesley a while to realise why. The directions to Addersacre they'd found in the caravan had been written in the same hand. More mature, perhaps, but undoubtedly the same.

One poem was inexpertly typed on an old-fashioned typewriter with uneven lettering. He started to read, once more feeling like an intruder, a snooper on the most intimate thoughts of a young woman – because he was sure these were the work of Gina rather than her husband, Frank.

Just as he was about to return it to the box file with the others he noticed a name at the bottom. He kept it out to show to Gerry and his heart beat faster as he carried it down the ladder.

As soon as he reached the landing his phone rang. It was Rachel.

'The Lombards' phone records have come through at last,' she said. Wesley could hear the excitement in her voice. 'Gina made two calls to Wynn Staniland's landline, one lasting ninety seconds, the other two and a half minutes.'

'He never mentioned that.'

'There's something else. Remember the unregistered mobile that called Jamie Hursthead on the night he died? Well, the same number called Gina Lombard's mobile three times in the days before they were murdered.'

Wesley said nothing for a few moments. His brain was working fast, going over the implications. Eventually he thanked Rachel and broke the news to Gerry.

'We've got our link,' Gerry said, rubbing his hands together with glee.

'And I've just found this.' The scent of musty paper wafted between them as Wesley handed over the typed poem.

As Gerry read, his mouth fell open.

'How did they get hold of this?'

'That's what I want to know.'

He took the poem back and stared at the name on the bottom: Perdita Staniland.

Journal of John Lipton

28 May 1884

Last night I met Mary again and imparted the news of yet another gruesome murder for her delectation and entertainment.

A young woman has been found in Exeter lying in a pool of blood and brain matter after the vicious attack which ended her life. She was a woman of the night so there is nobody to mourn her and she had been violated before death. I saw Mary's eyes glow with delicious horror as she devoured every detail and she suggested that Mr Gunster might make a play of it.

I recall that when my upright father took me to worship in church as a child I was told that God loves all people alike, from the high born to the lowly, and that all deserve equal consideration. Yet now I do not believe this creed of kindness. I believe some people are born to prey upon others, the strong upon the weak.

When I told Mary this she laughed and called me a philosopher.

When I enquired about Sarah's whereabouts, she asked me why I wished to know. I said her maidservant was very like her in looks but lacked her singular beauty and she looked at me strangely. Sarah, she said, had always been her father's especial favourite and she had once envied the attention he gave to a humble village child.

I asked her if her envy ever caused her to treat Sarah cruelly. She did not reply.

26

Callum Joy had been found a place in a hostel. He was safe there and the police would be able to keep an eye on him if necessary. Officially he hadn't been ruled out as a suspect for Jamie Hursthead's murder but, with the new evidence that had just come to light, Rachel was pretty sure of his innocence – of this particular crime at least.

The hostel was a disused Victorian church, long abandoned by its congregation. Inside all the ecclesiastical fittings had been stripped out and replaced by stud walls, institutional fire doors and magnolia paint. It stood on the road to Tradmouth Castle at the top of a flight of steps with an enviable view over the river and many locals had raised objections about its new role, preferring the building to become yet another upmarket restaurant or art gallery, but so far there'd been no trouble there and Rachel hoped it would stay that way.

When she asked Rob Carter if he wanted to come with her to interview a suspect he said yes at once. He was always up for some action. But when she told him the true purpose of their visit to the hostel, he found it hard to conceal his disappointment. Rachel took no notice; Rob had problems with routine but it was time he learned to deal with it.

When they arrived at the hostel Callum Joy joined them in the spartan lounge on the ground floor. It smelled of body odour and disinfectant with a faint whiff of tobacco in the background, even though smoking was strictly forbidden on the premises. Callum looked better than he had when Rachel last saw him. His face had lost its deathly pallor and he'd put on a little weight so his tracksuit no longer hung limply off his body.

They made themselves as comfortable as possible on a pair of stained chairs and Callum sat opposite, watching them hopefully.

'Did you find Ivan? Can I see him?'

Rachel shot Rob a warning look. 'I'm sorry, Callum. Our Armed Response Unit went to Red Water Farm and all they found was an angry farmer. He's threatening to sue us for mental distress.'

'He's got you fooled. Go back and have another look.'

'Last time you were interviewed you couldn't describe the men who held you captive. You see, Callum, if you can't supply more details we can only assume you've been making it all up.'

She could almost hear Callum's brain calculating the risk, balancing the potential wrath of his captors with the possibility of them being brought to justice if the police actually believed him. She hoped that after sampling a few days of safety and freedom he was about to have a change of heart, and when he opened his mouth to speak she knew her wishes had been granted.

'It's a bastard called Nev who does the dirty work. He's

the one who offered us the so-called job in the first place. Nice as pie he was . . . until he locked us up. He was the one who gave the orders.'

Rachel looked him in the eye. 'Nev? Are you sure his name's Nev?'

'I heard the other one calling him that once.'

'Other one?'

'They looked a bit alike. Could be brothers. They talked about the boss but he never showed his face.'

'You've got a vivid imagination, Callum,' Rob chipped in. 'We've been over that place. Searched everywhere. These blokes don't exist. You're telling us fairy tales.'

Rachel gave Rob's leg a crafty kick and he winced.

'You're absolutely sure it was Red Water Farm?'

'I told you. I saw the sign by the gate when I got away.'

'I understand your reading's not too good.' She wanted to sound sympathetic. She needed to gain Callum's confidence.

Callum looked at her sheepishly. 'Yeah but I knew those words. Red and water.'

'The second man, did you hear his name?'

'Don't think so. Just Nev.'

'Can you describe them?' She heard Rob give a gasp of exasperation but she blocked it out.

'Shaved heads. Big blokes.'

'So they didn't cover their faces like you said in your statement?' said Rob, earning himself a killing look from Rachel.

She ignored him and continued. 'You say six of you were held captive in a barn. All the outbuildings on Red Water Farm were searched and there was no sign of anyone being imprisoned there.'

'There were chains and everything. Your lot didn't look hard enough.'

'Maybe not,' Rachel said quietly.

'What was all that about, Sarge?' Rob asked as they walked back to the station.

'I think we've been looking in the wrong place.'

Wesley and Gerry found Geoff Lombard's school easily enough. It was a modern building with all the character of a set of shoeboxes stuck together and they found themselves at a reception desk that wouldn't have looked out of place in a corporate headquarters.

The motherly woman behind the desk made a hushed phone call and a few minutes later a man appeared. He was shorter than average with receding dark hair and his unbuttoned white lab coat gave him a youthful look even though he was probably in his forties. Geoff Lombard was younger than his dead brother but immediately Wesley saw a resemblance between the newcomer and the man he'd last seen in Colin's mortuary.

'When are you releasing my brother's body?' Geoff asked once they'd reached the privacy of the lab where Geoff taught chemistry which, he explained, would be empty for the next hour. He perched on a stool and had the relaxed look of a man with a clear conscience.

'We'll let you know as soon as possible. Shouldn't be long,' Gerry said with some sympathy.

'I'd wanted to go down there but what with work and three kids . . . ' He shrugged apologetically.

'Don't feel bad about it,' said Wesley. 'There was nothing you could have done. You'll have been told that we're treating the deaths of your brother and his wife as murder. Have you any idea who would want them dead?'

'My brother wasn't the sort to have enemies, Inspector.

He was an ordinary, unremarkable man who valued his privacy. It must be a case of mistaken identity.'

'We're considering all possibilities,' said Wesley. 'But certain aspects of the case indicate that your brother and his wife were targeted. Before they left for Devon I believe Frank told you they were going to be rich. What was that about?'

'I asked him but he wouldn't say. I'm sure it wasn't anything illegal. Frank wasn't like that.'

'What about Gina?' Gerry asked the question that had been on Wesley's lips.

'Gina's always been a bit of an enigma. Even though her and Frank had been together for years I wouldn't say I knew her well. She didn't do families.'

'We haven't been able to trace any of her relatives.'

'According to Frank there was a mother and sister she never spoke to but I couldn't tell you where to find them.'

'What was her surname before she married?'

Frank frowned in an effort to remember. 'I think it was something like Brown or Green. Her and Frank weren't actually married but she took his name – for convenience, Frank said.'

'Was there a reason they chose not to get married?'

'Some people don't,' said Geoff, twisting his wedding ring.

'We think Gina was a fan of Wynn Staniland, the author,' said Wesley.

'Was she? She never said anything about it to me . . . nor did Frank. I would have thought a good romance was more in her line. I don't think we ever talked about books – not that I spoke to her much. When I met up with Frank he was mostly on his own. I found Gina a bit difficult to tell you the truth.'

'Did Gina and your brother like champagne?'

'Doesn't everyone?' Geoff gave a nervous smile.

'You see, it looks like they were given a bottle laced with aconite. That's how they died.'

'I see.'

'You'd have the expertise to make the poison . . . from the plant monkshood, perhaps.'

Geoff bowed his head. 'I probably have but I didn't. Why would I?'

Wesley looked round the lab. True enough, the apparatus was all there.

'When Frank told you he was going to be rich, can you remember the exact words he used?'

'It was something like "We're going down to Devon to get what's owing to us. When you see me again I might be a rich man." I wondered whether it was something to do with Gina's mother or sister. Maybe she'd been left some money.'

'Their contact details weren't in her address book or on her phone. Do you know if they had a connection with Devon?'

'No idea. She never mentioned them.'

'According to her phone records the only person she rang while she was in Devon was Wynn Staniland, the author.'

'In that case I can't help you. Wish I could.'

'If you remember anything else . . . '

'I'll be in touch.'

'By the way, where were you the weekend before last?'

'Is that when . . . ?'

'The pathologist estimates they died late on the Saturday. Where were you?'

Geoff hesitated. 'I was walking in the Peak District.'

'Alone?'

'The weather was good so I decided to take the tent. My wife was going off to her parents in Lincolnshire with the kids so I treated myself to a weekend in the company of Mother Nature.' He gave a nervous smile.

'Can anyone vouch for you?'

Geoff shook his head. 'I'm afraid not. But I didn't drive down to Devon and murder my brother if that's what you're getting at.' He sounded defensive.

'Ever heard the name Jamie Hursthead?'

Geoff caught his breath. 'He was a twelve-year-old boy who killed two of his classmates.'

'You remember the case?'

A brief flicker of panic passed across Geoff's face. 'I work with kids of that age so I guess I took an interest.'

When Wesley had first met him he'd thought he was a man with nothing to hide but suddenly he wasn't so sure.

'You will catch whoever did this,' Geoff said as he walked out with them to the reception area.

Wesley told him not to worry. Sooner or later the killer of Frank and Gina Lombard would be brought to justice.

As they walked to the car Wesley glanced back and saw that Geoff was still standing there watching them.

27

In some ways Karl Banville's enthusiasm for Neil's excavation at Newfield Manor made him easy to deal with. They both wanted to start work, the sooner the better.

Neil had already asked Annabel from the County Archives to send him any relevant material about the Manor's history. Then he'd arranged for the geophysics equipment to be transported to the new site. Karl Banville wanted them to concentrate on the location of the summerhouse, erected in the walled garden shortly after Mary Field's untimely death and burned down many years later.

'Giles Billingham'll want to know why we're not starting on the main building like he asked,' Neil pointed out.

'He's not paying for all this. I am. I say where you dig.'

Neil felt a jolt to his professional pride. 'We're still required to undertake the work Giles specified.'

Banville waved his hand impatiently, as if he was swatting away an annoying wasp. 'Fine. But you dig up the summerhouse site first.'

'And if we don't find William's body there?'

'You keep looking.' He paused. 'I hope we've seen the last of that bloody ghost hunter.'

'Archie Jones. He wasn't doing any harm.'

'That's your opinion.' There was another pause. Banville stared at the ruined building in front of him for a few moments before speaking again. 'Ever heard of Wynn Staniland?'

'Yeah. He had a few hit books then he became a recluse. Why?'

'He based one of his books on the Mary Field case. *The Viper's Kiss*. I met him in the States once. He was over there promoting his first book; this was long before he went into purdah. I told him about Mary and I reckon I gave him the idea for *The Viper's Kiss*. It's probably his finest work.'

'So you've always had an interest in the case?'

'Sure. But it's only since I sold my company that I've been able to do anything about it.'

'Have you seen Staniland recently?' Neil asked.

Karl Banville walked away without answering.

It was almost eight thirty when Wesley and Gerry arrived back in Tradmouth. After a brief visit to the incident room to check whether anything new had come in, Gerry told Wesley to get home to Pam. Following up their Yorkshire discoveries could wait until tomorrow.

As Gerry walked home a veil of mist drifted in over the river, turning the town into an alien and mysterious place. When he neared Baynard's Quay a golden glow poured from the welcoming windows of the Tradmouth Arms on the corner opposite his house. Perhaps he'd take Alison and Joyce for a drink when he got in, or something to eat. He suddenly realised he was hungry.

211

The thought of Alison brought a smile to his lips as he put his key in the lock and, once inside, he paused, listening out for her greeting. But instead the voice he heard was Joyce's.

'Hello, love.' He bent forward to kiss her cheek. 'Alison about?'

Joyce pressed her lips together in disapproval and his heart sank.

'She's upstairs doing something with her hair. Been up there hours.'

Normally she'd have asked him about his trip to Yorkshire but this time there was no curiosity, just irritation.

'How long's she planning to stay?'

'I . . . I haven't liked to ask. She's just lost her mum and I don't want her to feel I'm pushing her out.'

'I've had Sam on the phone. You can't keep this from your children for much longer.'

Before he could answer Alison appeared at the top of the stairs.

'Hello, love.'

'How was Yorkshire?'

At least someone cared, Gerry thought.

'Fine. Have you two girls eaten? We could go for a bite at the Tradmouth Arms,' he said hopefully.

'Lovely.' Alison came down and reached for her jacket. 'Bit foggy out there.'

'Sea mist. We get a lot of it round here. Coming with us, Joyce?'

Joyce muttered something about having eaten already and hurried away in the direction of the living room.

'Just you and me then, kid.'

The Tradmouth Arms was pleasantly full but they managed to find a seat near the window and soon they were tucking into burger and chips. The healthy diet Joyce encouraged him to follow could be ignored for once. Besides, it felt like a special occasion.

'I've uploaded some pictures onto my phone,' said Alison when they'd finished eating. 'This is Mum. It's the most recent picture I've got.'

She passed the tiny phone to Gerry, who hesitated before fishing his reading glasses out of his pocket, reluctant to let his new-found daughter witness this sign of ageing. He put the glasses on and peered at the image of a middle-aged woman with scraped-back bleached hair and dark rings under her sunken eyes.

Although she must have changed a great deal over the unkind decades, there was something familiar about her ravaged face. But, try as he might, he still couldn't place the name Donna McQuail.

Pam hurried into the hall as soon as she heard Wesley's key in the door and brushed his mouth with a swift kiss of greeting. He was surprised how much he'd missed her. Since her operation back in the spring he'd felt an almost superstitious dread whenever they'd been parted, as though something terrible was bound to occur if he wasn't there to watch over her. She'd told him it was ridiculous but he couldn't help himself.

He received the usual enthusiastic welcome from Amelia, with news of what she'd been up to gushing out as she took his hand and danced up and down with excitement. In contrast Michael's greeting was self-consciously noncha-lant, as though his father's return home from a trip away didn't impress him in the least. Wesley watched him climb the stairs without a backward glance and, as always, he

213

couldn't help wondering whether his job, with its inevitable demands, had driven a wedge between them. Perhaps he hadn't been there when Michael needed him, he thought with a pang of parental guilt.

As soon as the children were in their rooms he heated up the dinner Pam had left for him by the microwave and took it into the living room to eat on his knee.

'How was Yorkshire?' she asked. She was sitting on the sofa, feet up, completely relaxed.

'York's lovely, even if it is full of tourists. But I didn't see as much of it as I would have liked.' He hesitated, wondering how much he could safely reveal. 'Wynn Staniland's name keeps popping up all over this inquiry. But for heaven's sake don't mention that to your mother.'

Pam rolled her eyes. 'Credit me with some discretion. He's not a suspect, is he?'

'Not so far but he seems to be a common thread.' He began to eat. He'd probably said too much but it was on his mind, nagging away like a catchy tune you can't banish from your head. Wynn Staniland: the focus of Gina Lombard's interest; the subject of Jamie Hursthead's biography.

Half an hour later they were about to watch a film when a visitor arrived on their doorstep, grinning and confident of a warm welcome.

'Good to see you, Neil,' Wesley said as his old friend stepped into the hall. 'How's it going?'

'We've started work at Newfield Manor. I'm staying at the pub in Whitely – all at Karl Banville's expense – so I thought as I was in the area, I'd pay you a call. I rang last night but Pam said you were away.'

'I was up in Yorkshire – only got back an hour ago. How

are you getting on with Banville? You weren't happy with him last time I saw you.'

'So far so good.' He turned to Pam. 'He told me he's met Wynn Staniland. You know, the author.'

Wesley put his wine glass down on the table, suddenly alert.

'Said he met him in the States years ago. Wasn't that man who was murdered writing his biography?'

Wesley nodded. 'Yes. But we're not sure that has anything to do with his death.' He paused. 'Even so, it might be worth having a word with your Mr Banville.'

'Why?'

'Just following up connections.' He grinned. 'Detective stuff.'

Wynn Staniland's name wasn't mentioned again for a while. Instead they chatted about generalities and mutual friends until they got onto the subject of Karl Banville's demands and eccentricities. Wesley and Pam listened with amusement, reclining on the sofa like a couple of ancient Romans at a lavish feast while Neil recounted his reaction to the ghost tour with appropriate dramatic gestures. But when Neil mentioned the similarities between Mary Field's supposed murder and the suicide of Wynn Staniland's wife, as well as Banville's claim that he'd given Staniland the initial idea for his best-known book, Wesley gave him his full attention.

'I always thought his wife got the idea for her suicide from her husband's book,' Pam said. 'But it might have come from the story of Mary Field.'

She shuddered and picked up the copy of *The Viper's Kiss* that was lying on the coffee table. It took her a while to locate the passage but when she found it she cleared her throat and began to read aloud.

"'Her bare feet glide over the woodland floor until she sees the river. The little pool cut off from the main flow by a spur of bank. Viper's Point. She searches the river bank and fills her pockets with stones. They feel smooth in her hands, worn by time and the relentless to and fro of the tides, and they slip in easily until her pockets are full and heavy.

"'The water is shallow at first but, even so, the shock of the cold on her flesh makes her flinch. She tells herself she must be strong as she wades out, her skirt spreading out on the surface like a parachute. But it will not save her. Nothing will.

"'When the water reaches her waist the earth stills to a stop. Even the trees fringing the river cease their gentle waving as she lowers herself into the water. No current here. Nothing to knock her off balance. Her chest is submerged. Then her neck. Then her face.

"'She shuts her eyes tight and sits down beneath the water with her back resting against a rock, waiting for death to come. And she feels perfectly at peace.'"

'I'm not surprised he gave up writing,' said Wesley. 'He'd put that method of suicide into his wife's head so he must have been eaten up with guilt. Can you imagine?'

Pam thought for a moment. 'Maybe she was punishing him . . . copying his story like that.'

But Wesley's thoughts were veering off in another direction. What if it wasn't that simple? What if it had been Wynn Staniland himself who'd not only used the story of Mary Field for his book, but to rid himself of an unwanted wife?

28

Gerry's office was empty when Wesley arrived at work the following morning, although his jacket was hanging on his personal coat stand in the corner, suggesting he wasn't far away.

Wesley made a mental note of the things he needed to do. He wanted to investigate the Hurstheads' claim that they'd been threatened by Brian Restorick and he had to follow up the discovery of Perdita Staniland's poem in the Lombards' loft: the more he thought about it the more puzzled he became.

He'd read the poem over several times. It was about a beautiful mermaid who sat on a rock singing until her throat was hoarse but nobody heard her. Then she began to scream and still nobody listened so she slipped into the water and swam away. It was a poem of teenage uncertainty and angst; a poem that made Wesley feel depressed, even though his own adolescence had been comparatively trouble-free.

After asking one of the civilian staff to track down Gina Lombard's birth certificate and National Insurance number – something he knew might take some time – he made for his desk, intending to get some routine matters out of the way before Gerry's morning briefing.

Rachel entered the office with an eager look on her face, which he recognised of old. It meant she had news.

'I spoke to Callum Joy,' she began as she perched herself on the edge of his desk.

He saw Rob Carter watching, wearing an expression of knowing speculation. He and Rachel had been the subject of gossip before but anything that might have developed between them had withered and died years ago. And Pam's illness had been the final blow so Carter could smirk all he liked. Wesley didn't care. And he hoped that, with her wedding to farmer Nigel Haynes fast approaching, Rachel didn't either.

'What did he say?'

'Even when I told him nothing was found at Red Water Farm he stuck to his story. He even named one of the two men who held him. And he gave a description. Both stocky with shaved heads.'

'That could fit a lot of people.'

'Callum said one's called Nev and the other man could be his brother. I spoke to my mum last night. She knows most people who farm around here and she told me something interesting. Do you remember that accidental shooting? David Gough from White Pool Farm.'

'I remember.'

'Remember their son, Barry? He was stocky with a shaved head. Bit shifty.'

'We can't arrest people for being a bit shifty ... much as we'd like to at times.'

218

Rachel ignored his comment, her face serious. This was no joking matter and Wesley suddenly regretted his flippancy.

'Anyway, my mum told me the Goughs had two sons, Barry and Neville. If Callum Joy was right about the name Nev ... White Pool's next door to Red Water Farm so Callum could have spotted the sign when he made his escape and assumed that's where he was held.'

She suddenly looked unsure of herself. 'My parents said David Gough used to be a good man ... '

'Used to be?'

'They said everything changed after foot-and-mouth and he never had much contact with the rest of the farming community after that, although he still carried on when a lot gave up. For his sons, I suppose.'

'Think we should follow this up?'

'I think we have to. ARU?'

Wesley didn't answer for a few moments. Sending the Armed Response Unit into White Pool Farm, especially as Mrs Gough had recently lost her husband in tragic circumstances, did seem excessive. But if that's where Callum Joy had been held it would be foolhardy not to take precautions. 'Let's see what Gerry thinks,' he said at last, feeling he was passing the buck.

As if on cue Gerry burst in, gathering his flock around him for the morning briefing. Once the briefing was over Wesley followed Gerry into his office.

'Anything new, Wes?'

'A couple of things.'

Gerry had put his head in his hands. During the briefing he'd seemed his usual confident self but now he looked like a man full of doubts. 'Go on.'

219

Wesley went through everything methodically, getting the facts clear in his own mind as well as Gerry's.

'I've sent Trish and Rach over to see the Restoricks,' said Gerry.

'Then we should have another word with Wynn Staniland. We need to know how that poem with Perdita's name on it came to be in the Lombards' loft. What if Gina Lombard knew Perdita once? What if she went to the house and met Wynn, the charismatic father figure? Maybe she developed some sort of crush on him that never went away. Hence the phone calls to the house and those press cuttings.'

'Perdita didn't recognise Gina's photograph – or her name.'

'She might have her own reasons for lying,' said Wesley. 'Perhaps something happened between her friend and her stepfather. Older man taking advantage of vulnerable girl. Maybe Perdita wanted to forget the whole thing. Either that or Gina changed beyond recognition in the intervening years. But we won't find out unless we ask. How's Alison?'

Gerry lowered his voice and glanced in the direction of the outer office, making sure nobody could overhear.

'She showed me a picture of her mum last night, Wes.'

'And?'

'Alison told me it was taken when she was ill and she'd aged so much I didn't recognise her.'

'You knew her a long time ago. Decades. People change.'

'I thought there was something familiar about her but I still don't recognise her name.'

'There were so many.' Wesley couldn't resist a wry smile at his boss's colourful past.

'Aye, there were in those days. But I'm good with names,

always have been. I'm sure I've never heard of Donna McQuail.'

'Maybe you were drunk,' Wesley suggested tentatively.

'Alison says I went out with her mum for a few weeks. It wasn't just a one-night stand . . . apparently.'

Gerry looked so forlorn that Wesley felt sorry for him.

'Perhaps it was just a brief encounter. Perhaps Alison's mum told her you went out together to make it seem less . . . sordid.'

'That'd explain it, I suppose.' Gerry sighed. 'My old gran used to have this text above her fireplace: "Be sure your sins will find you out". Perhaps she had a point.'

'What are we going to do about White Pool Farm?'

'It'll take time to get the ARU organised.'

'You think it's necessary?'

'Don't you?'

'Can't take any chances.'

Gerry picked up his phone. He needed to set the ball rolling.

The incident room was buzzing with activity and hushed conversation when Wesley and Gerry left to visit Wynn Staniland.

Wesley knew the author would be annoyed when they turned up again, just when he thought he was rid of them, but after so many years in CID he'd developed a thick skin about that kind of thing.

'Do you think we should have tried to get a search warrant?' said Gerry as they drove.

Wesley was surprised by the question. 'All we have so far is Staniland's tenuous link to the victims and that poem in the Lombards' loft in Leeds.'

'What did you make of Geoff Lombard?'

'Hasn't got much of an alibi and he'd know how to make aconite.'

'Motive?'

'He's family. You never know what goes on in families.'

'Too right, Wes.'

'You think he's in the frame?'

Gerry didn't reply and when Wesley glanced at him he saw he'd closed his eyes, as if he was taking a nap.

'Still worried about this Alison business?'

There was no answer but Gerry was easy to read – easier, he thought irreverently, than one of Wynn Staniland's award-winning novels.

It was a lot harder to gauge Staniland's thoughts as Perdita led them into his presence. He looked distant and unconcerned, as if two senior CID officers turning up on his doorstep was something that happened every day, like a visit from the postman.

'I've already told you I can't help you,' Staniland said quietly. Wesley thought he looked tired. He'd seen that look before on the faces of people under a great deal of strain.

'We'd like to ask you about the woman who was poisoned at the caravan park. Gina Lombard.'

'I've already told you I didn't know her.'

Wesley noticed that Perdita had taken up her post by the door, tense as a violin string, listening anxiously to every word her stepfather spoke.

'We were at her house in Leeds yesterday,' Gerry said. 'She had a collection of press cuttings . . . all about you.'

'Some fans can become obsessive,' Perdita said. 'Ask anyone in the public eye.'

'But Mr Staniland's chosen not to be in the public eye,' Wesley said reasonably.

'You're quite right.' Staniland gave a weary sigh. 'But I really don't see what I can do about it.'

'Has Gina Lombard ever visited this house?'

'I've already told you she hasn't.' He looked away.

'We found at poem at her house in Leeds. It's about a mermaid.'

'Well it can't be mine,' said Staniland. 'I've never written poetry in my life.'

'According to Gina's phone records she made two calls to this house the day before her death.'

Staniland raised his eyebrows and looked at Perdita. 'Did you take any calls, my dear?'

Perdita stepped forward. 'There were a couple from a woman. She wanted to speak to you but when I asked who was calling she wouldn't say so I put the phone down. I didn't know it was her. How could I?'

'The second call lasted two and a half minutes. What did she say exactly?'

Perdita frowned. 'I was explaining to her that unless she gave her name and her reason for calling there was no way I was going to bother Father.' She looked exasperated. 'Look, we get these calls from time to time. Usually journalists. I didn't think anything of it.'

Wesley took the poem, now protected in a plastic folder, out of the bag he was carrying. 'To return to the poem. Your name's on it, Ms Staniland. Did you write it?'

Perdita's hand was shaking a little as he handed her the folder. She took the poem out and studied it with a frown.

'Yes. I wrote this when I was in my teens,' she said after a while. 'Father was a writer so I thought I'd give it a try. But I've no idea how this woman got hold of it.'

223

'I've read it,' said Wesley. 'It's good. Have you continued writing?'

She shook her head. 'It wasn't for me. Besides, everyone would compare me with Father, wouldn't they?'

Wesley guessed she was right. 'The question is, how did it come to be in Gina Lombard's possession?'

Perdita shook her head, walked over to the sofa and sat down.

'That's what I'd like to know,' Staniland said, reaching over to touch his stepdaughter's hand. 'She must have stolen it but I can't imagine how.'

'Father's right. It must have been stolen.'

'When did you last see it?'

'I can't remember. It was one of those teenage things you put away and forget about.'

'How could she have stolen it if she's never been to this house?'

Stepfather and stepdaughter exchanged a look and Wesley knew there was about to be a revelation.

'Look, I think I might have seen her before,' said Staniland. 'It was a stupid lie but it seemed easier than going into details. She was a fan and she came to this house once.'

'When?'

'Many years ago. Before … before my wife died. When I was still writing.'

'At the height of your fame?'

'When things were going well for me, yes. I used to receive a lot of letters, of course, but people rarely had the audacity to intrude on my privacy and turn up in person.'

'But Gina did?'

'I never knew her name. She called here one morning saying she was a journalist and my housekeeper, Jane, let

224

her in. I was working upstairs and Jane told her I wasn't to be disturbed but the young woman insisted on waiting, saying she had an appointment. Jane was busy so she gave her a cup of tea and left her alone in here. My wife was an artist and she would have been in her studio so she didn't see her. When I came down for lunch as usual Jane told me there was a journalist waiting in the drawing room and I found her here.'

'I take it there was no appointment?' said Wesley.

'Of course not. It was a ruse. Jane was taken in by the lie but I didn't blame her.'

'What happened?'

'The girl gushed for a while, saying she was my number one fan and wanting to talk about the books. All I remember about her is that she seemed very young. Immature.' Staniland smiled. 'I never found it easy talking about my books, Inspector. The fact is that as soon as one was written I'd moved on to the next and put the previous one completely out of my mind. Like many people, this girl found this hard to understand and thought I was being deliberately obtuse. I managed to bring the encounter to an end and I never saw or thought of her again until you turned up here with her photograph. That's all I can tell you, I'm afraid.'

'She must have taken my poem when she was left alone here,' Perdita chipped in. 'I have a vague recollection of looking for it and not being able to find it. But it's such a long time ago.'

'We'd like to speak to Jane, your housekeeper. How can we get in touch with her?'

'Through a medium,' Perdita said flippantly. 'She died years ago.'

'My wife's reading *The Viper's Kiss* at the moment,' said

Wesley. 'She's enjoying it very much,' he added, thinking a little white lie wouldn't go amiss. 'Did you take the idea for the plot from the story of Mary Field?'

For a few seconds Staniland looked confused. 'Mary Field? Yes, I suppose I did.'

'Your wife took her own life in a similar way.' He felt Gerry give him a small nudge of warning.

'I find the subject painful, Inspector. It's something I'd rather not talk about.'

'I believe you know a man called Karl Banville? You met him in the States a long time ago.'

'I can't say I remember but I met so many people in those days. Why do you ask?'

'Mr Banville's just bought Mary Field's old home in Whitely; the place where she died.' He watched Staniland's face for a reaction but saw nothing. 'He claims that it was him who told you the story of Mary Field.'

'It's a well-known story. You'll find it in most of the Tales of Devon Ghosts and Murder books stocked by the tourist shops.' Wesley heard a sneer in his voice.

'A friend of mine's conducting an archaeological investigation at Newfield Manor. Mr Banville's funding it.'

Staniland turned his head away as if to emphasise his lack of interest in Karl Banville.

'You haven't been in touch with him?'

'Of course not. I don't remember him and, besides, I rarely leave this house.'

'You must go out occasionally. Who does your shopping?' Wesley asked, curious.

'Perdita has a car and ventures out once in a while for necessities. I never go with her because the outside world frightens me these days. I prefer my own company.'

He looked at Wesley intently, as though he was trying to read his thoughts. 'When I said I'd never seen that woman in the photograph before ... I hope I won't be done for wasting police time.'

'Probably not but you should have told the truth the first time.'

'Can I keep this?' Perdita interrupted, pointing to the poem.

'You'll get it back in due course,' said Wesley, returning it to his bag. 'There is just one more thing we'd like to ask.'

'What's that?' Staniland seemed relaxed now, as though he was expecting Wesley's question to be routine.

'Zac Wilkinson, your biographer, told his agent that he'd discovered something explosive while he was researching your biography. Do you know what he meant?'

Staniland didn't blink. 'At a guess, I'd say he intended to drop a hint about another book.'

'Are you writing one?'

'Not at the moment. But it's not something I can rule out completely. That's all I'm prepared to say for the moment.'

'Fair enough,' said Gerry.

'And he'd describe that as explosive?' Wesley wasn't giving up.

'I imagine it would cause a stir in the literary world, yes.'

All of a sudden Wesley heard a distant buzz which he recognised as some sort of timer going off, probably in the kitchen; a domestic intrusion that seemed out of place. Perdita looked at her stepfather before hurrying out. Staniland stood up, walked stiffly over to the French windows and turned his back on them to gaze out at the garden. It was overgrown but Wesley guessed there were no gardeners these days. Staniland and his stepdaughter lived in their own world, sealed off from the outside.

Next to Wesley on a side table was a framed photograph of stepfather and stepdaughter side by side. Wesley picked it up to examine it and noticed a join down the centre of the picture, as if somebody else had been edited out and the two ends married together. Staniland's back was still turned so he gave the picture a small shake. When Gerry saw what he was doing he repositioned himself to shield him from sight if Staniland decided to turn around.

The photo slipped a little to reveal the edge of another person; someone who'd once had pride of place in the centre but whose presence had for some reason been erased.

Journal of Mary Field

4 June 1884

John says he loves me and my heart sings with joy. His people are humble and he makes no secret of this. His father is a blacksmith from a village not far from Bristol in the County of Somerset and I know my family would forbid our alliance. When I tell him I do not care about their approval he points out that I am not yet of age and they could make me a prisoner in their house if they so wish. I assure him that we can rely on Sarah's help and promise to put my mind to the problem. In the meantime I will play the dutiful daughter to perfection.

He calls me his lamb and I scold him for using such an endearment. I am no meek creature of scant wit. I wish to be his equal in all we share.

William Banville called upon me today and when Mama greeted him she simpered like a lovesick serving maid. I told her I had no wish to see him but she insisted we all take tea in the drawing room. I sat on the edge of my chair wearing my best tea gown of grey silk, making awkward conversation while Mama beamed with approval. I do not like the rapacious way Banville looks at me, as though he wishes to devour my very soul. I am afraid he will discover my plans and betray me out of spite. Love so easily turns to malice when it is thwarted and I must thwart all William's hopes.

John will meet me tonight and we will elope. Sarah helped me pack my valise and she is sworn to secrecy. She says my father will not suspect her because of the fondness he bore her as a child and she promises to play the innocent when my absence is discovered. We are to go to Somerset, to the village where John grew up. There the vicar will marry us and we will be one. How I long to be his, body and soul.

On Father's death, I will be mistress of Newfield and John will be master.

29

'You say the summerhouse burned down in the early nineteen thirties?' said Neil. 'Sorry to tell you this, Karl, but burned material can mess up geophysics results.'

'That won't stop you digging there?' Neil detected a note of anxiety in Banville's question.

'I'd rather begin at the house. But I know you're keen to find out what's under the summerhouse so that's where we'll start.'

Banville didn't bother to hide his relief and by ten thirty Neil had opened his first trench on the site which produced a lot of burned debris: shards of blue and white pottery, a trio of clay pipes and a small gold ring. A wedding ring, perhaps. This latter find made Banville very excited.

'Mary Field wasn't wearing her wedding ring when they found her. They said William Banville took it off her dead finger in a fit of jealous rage because she'd chosen to marry John Lipton instead of him.'

'You think he threw it away here?' said Neil. The neatness of the find made him sceptical.

'No, don't you see? If he'd killed her he would have thrown it in the pond when he put her there. He'd have wanted to get rid of it as soon as possible. Psychology.'

He sounded triumphant, as if he'd solved the case already and exonerated his ancestor of all suspicion. But Neil could see holes in his argument.

After Banville left for a meeting with some developers about his proposed hotel, the digging continued. Neil had a brief to look for a human burial but this wasn't something he'd shared with his colleagues. He thought it best to leave them in ignorance of Karl Banville's obsession.

He was walking to his car to fetch an extra measuring tape when he heard another car approaching up the drive and saw Archie Jones's red Toyota emerging from the bushes. After the reception he'd had from Banville last time, he was surprised to see him back.

'Hi,' Jones said as he climbed out of the car. He looked confident but Neil was soon to learn why. 'I waited till I saw Banville leave. I don't think he likes me.' The boy grinned. 'Found any bodies yet?'

'Not yet.'

Neil found Jones irritating; too cocky for his own good. Perhaps, Neil thought, he'd been like that himself at eighteen when he knew everything.

Archie asked how the dig was going and Neil thought it would do no harm to give him a quick tour of the trench, although when he allowed him to peep into the finds tray, he saw disappointment on the boy's face. No doubt he'd expected something more exciting: long-lost Viking silver, perhaps, or rich medieval jewels accidentally dropped by a fleeing king. Fat chance.

'I discovered something interesting about Karl Banville the other day,' Jones said as they were strolling back to the car.

'What's that?'

'Bet he hasn't told you he's a local lad.'

'I thought he was born in the USA and he's only here because he'd been researching his family tree and found out about William Banville. That's what he told me anyway.'

'Well, he was telling you porkies. He was born in Plymouth. Only went over to the States when he was in his twenties. Why would he lie about something like that?'

'Perhaps he thinks being American gives him a touch of glamour,' said Neil with a hint of sarcasm. He was getting fed up with Archie Jones.

'If you let me know when he definitely won't be around, I can arrange to bring my ghost hunters here. What the eye doesn't see and all that.' He gave Neil a wink. It was a while since anybody had done that and Neil found the experience disconcerting.

'I've got better things to do than act as your lookout. Banville's your problem, not mine.'

Archie Jones gave a theatrical shrug and drove off.

When Wesley returned to the incident room he asked to see all the statements taken following the discovery of Jamie Hursthead's body. He needed to find out who Jamie had interviewed in the course of his research into the life and work of Wynn Staniland.

Wesley sat at his desk going through each statement and after half an hour he found what he was looking for.

Several weeks before his murder Jamie Hursthead had interviewed a woman who lived on the edge of the fishing port of Bloxham, not so very far from Addersacre, a woman whose late husband had once worked as Wynn Staniland's gardener.

Her name was Ethel Rinton and Wesley wanted to speak to her. But first he had to deal with the imminent raid on the Goughs' farm; something his visit to Wynn Staniland and his daughter had driven from his mind.

When he heard Rachel say his name he looked up from his computer screen.

'I went to see the Restoricks with Trish as you asked and they admitted sending those things to the Hurstheads. Mr Restorick said they were going through a bad patch at the time and they regret it now. But he insists they had nothing to do with Jamie's murder.'

'Believe him?'

She considered the question for a moment. 'I think so but I wouldn't cross them off our suspect list by any means.' She paused. 'I've also had a good chat with Jack Proudfoot at Red Water Farm,' she said. 'He was reluctant to talk at first but when I played the Farmer's Daughter card he opened up. According to Proudfoot the Goughs were quite cooperative when he first took on the tenancy at Red Water. But around the time David Gough handed over the running of the farm to his sons, they broke off all contact. A couple of Proudfoot's sheep strayed onto the Goughs' land and the sons threatened Proudfoot with a shotgun and told him to get off their land, although they did return the sheep eventually – brought them over in a trailer and dumped them outside Proudfoot's farmhouse. They made it quite clear that visitors weren't welcome.'

'Why didn't he tell us this when we searched his farm?'

'He thought he was suspected of shooting David Gough so he didn't want to admit he had a bad relationship with the family. The officers who spoke to him didn't mention this suspected slavery business so he didn't put two and two together.'

'But now he has?'

She looked at her watch. 'He reckons the Gough boys are bad news.' She hesitated, looking sheepish. 'I asked Nigel about them and it turns out he's been hearing stories.'

'What kind of stories?'

'He's heard whispers that they've been diversifying. Organising casual labour; tree-felling; laying driveways and all that.'

'Using slave labour.'

'Possibly. But it's all just rumours. The ARU are waiting for the go-ahead.'

'Then we'd better give it. I'll tell the boss.'

He broke the news to Gerry, torn between following up his new lead on the Jamie Hursthead case and seeing the raid on Gough's farm through. Then he thought of Callum Joy and his concern for his Russian friend, Ivan, and he knew the interview with Ethel Rinton would have to wait.

30

The image of those men shielding their faces from the light in that windowless barn and the stench from the galvanised bucket in the corner would stay with Wesley for the rest of his life. As soon as the padlock was smashed and the doors flung open, the men cowered back, as if they feared a beating. But it was the sight of the chains that horrified him most of all.

The men were thin but not emaciated. The Gough brothers knew that, to get the maximum amount of work out of them, they had to be kept nourished. And their clothes were dirty but not ragged. They'd been used to lay drives and fell trees so they had to be seen in public. He could only imagine what kind of threats had been used to keep them from giving the game away. The men had lived in fear: fear for their lives, for their families' lives, even fear of the police.

In the event the ARU were stood down because Nev and Barry Gough came quietly. It was their recently widowed mother who gave the most trouble. At first she claimed she had no idea what had been going on. Her boys had taken over the running of the farm from their father, she said, and they'd had their own ideas about diversifying. She'd thought the men who slept in the barn were just casual labourers. She began crying hysterically but Wesley suspected the loss of control was an act put on for his benefit.

'You OK?' Rachel said. She was standing by his side, watching as the ambulances disappeared down the farm track, taking the men to Tradmouth Hospital to be checked out.

'I will be when those bastards are behind bars. We'll need to take statements from the men and re-interview Callum Joy.'

'The premises are being searched,' she said as an officer emerged from the back door of the farmhouse carrying a shotgun swathed in plastic. 'We'll have no trouble getting a conviction.'

'Let's hope not. But if they get a good solicitor . . . '

'Don't be such a pessimist,' she said, touching his arm.

Wesley sighed. 'There's nothing more we can do here and I need to get over to Bloxham and talk to Wynn Staniland's gardener's widow.'

'Bit of a tenuous connection.'

'Jamie Hursthead interviewed her for his biography and I'm wondering whether she told him anything important.'

'Why do you think Staniland has anything to do with his death? What about the Restoricks or that villain in the Home Counties – Kieran State?'

'Kieran State's in Spain.'

'The likes of him have minions to do their dirty work.'

He knew Rachel had a point. Brian Restorick and Kieran State were still very much in the frame. But Wynn

Staniland intrigued him; and he was the one connection between Jamie Hursthead and the Lombards.

'About the Lombards,' she said as though she'd read his thoughts. 'The Goughs own the caravan park where they died. If they found out what Nev and Barry were up to, who's to say they weren't killed to shut them up? The Gough brothers could come and go on that caravan site without comment and they knew exactly where the Lombards were staying. It'd be a simple matter to put that champagne bottle on their caravan steps.'

Wesley didn't reply for a few moments. Even though he couldn't see poisoned champagne as the Gough brothers' weapon of choice, Rachel could be right. A major crime had been uncovered a stone's throw from where the Lombards died so a connection was possible. Perhaps the Lombards saw something and had to be silenced.

'I still need to speak to Mrs Rinton. Coming with me?'

'OK,' she said without enthusiasm, as though she suspected him of wasting valuable time.

Gerry had stayed behind in the office to coordinate things so Wesley called to tell him that the Gough brothers were being brought in. Gerry said it sounded like a good result.

Wesley had hoped to avoid the rush hour but he found himself stuck in the queue for the car ferry while the frustratingly slow vessel chugged to and fro, letting only a few vehicles on at a time. He was tempted to tell Rachel to put on the blue light but he curbed his impatience and enjoyed the scenery until they were on the Queenswear side of the river following the sat nav directions to Jasmine View Cottage just outside Bloxham, just a mile from Addersacre.

Although the name of the house conjured images of chocolate-box prettiness, the reality was disappointing. A small, 1960s brick-built bungalow that had seen better days, surrounded by a patch of scrubby grass. The few straggly shrubs in the front garden suggested that Mrs Rinton had left all the gardening to her late husband.

Mrs Rinton herself was a well-built woman with a tight grey perm and a mean mouth that rarely smiled.

'Are you from the police?' she said in a surprisingly strong voice when she answered the door, looking them up and down as if she suspected they were imposters intent on fleecing her of her life savings.

'Yes, Mrs Rinton,' said Wesley, holding out his ID. 'I hope you don't mind answering some questions for us.'

She stared at him as though he was a specimen under a microscope. 'I wasn't expecting anyone coloured,' she said accusingly once he was over the threshold.

Wesley saw Rachel flinch at the woman's casual racism.

'Nothing wrong with your eyesight, is there?'

'Nothing wrong with my hearing either. You don't have to shout. Who's this girl?' she said turning her gaze on Rachel. 'Looks as if she could do with a good meal.'

Rachel couldn't think of an appropriate reply and once they were seated in the cluttered living room which smelled faintly of cabbage, it was Wesley who did the talking.

'I believe you had another visitor a while ago. A young man called Zac Wilkinson. He was a writer.'

'Posh lad. Wouldn't have trusted him further than I can spit.'

'What makes you say that?' Wesley asked.

'When you get to my age you can tell. And I didn't like the way he spoke about my Eric . . . like he was just something in a story. All he wanted was scandal but I didn't give him any.'

239

'Do you know any?' Wesley asked.

'I might do. But I didn't tell him.'

'Will you tell us?' said Wesley.

'Why should I? Police were no help to me when I needed them. My husband was murdered but they kept on saying it was an accident. Doctors, coroner, all the same. Wouldn't listen.'

'Can you tell us what happened to your husband, Mrs Rinton?'

She sniffed and gave Wesley a sideways look. 'They said he mistook a poisonous plant for parsley and ate some but I told them my Stan never ate parsley in his life. Then they tried to make out he'd scratched himself on some roses and the poison got into his bloodstream. The coroner said it was accidental death and he warned about the dangers of dealing with poisonous plants. It made the local paper at the time. Big spread.'

'But you think he was murdered?'

'The coroner said it was an accident so that was that. They treated me as if I was stupid . . . just like his lordship.'

'His lordship?'

'Staniland. Treated the likes of us like we was something he'd trodden in.'

'If your husband was poisoned, Mrs Rinton, who do you think was responsible?'

She tapped the side of her nose. 'I've got my suspicions.'

'What are they?' Wesley asked quietly. He watched Ethel as she weighed up the benefits of sharing her thoughts.

Eventually she spoke. 'That Jane Whitsun called herself a housekeeper but she was a common little whore. Eric found her and Staniland together you know. He liked Mrs Staniland – she was a gentle soul – so he told Staniland he was going to tell her. Said she should know what that husband of hers was like.'

'Did he tell her?'

'No. She was away in London at the time – something to do with her paintings; she was an artist, you know. By the time she got back he'd thought better of it but Jane and Staniland wouldn't have wanted to take the risk, would they? Not when Rosemary had the house and all the money. Do you know when Mrs Staniland died he destroyed all her paintings – burned them.'

Wesley saw Rachel raise her eyebrows. This certainly shed some light on Staniland's relationship with his late wife.

'We've spoken to Mr Staniland and nothing was mentioned about an affair with the housekeeper. Although that might have been because his daughter was there.'

'Perdita? Eric always said she was a rose bush short of a herbaceous border. She isn't his, you know. She was Mrs Staniland's by "a previous relationship" as they say. Eric reckoned Staniland only married Rosemary for her money. Mind you, I've heard it all went to Perdita when she died.'

'All the more reason for him to keep in with Perdita, then,' Rachel observed. 'She still lives with him.'

Ethel looked at her as if she'd only just noticed her sitting there. 'So I've heard, not that I've seen her since my Eric died and I moved out here.'

'Did you tell Zac Wilkinson all this?' Wesley asked.

'I've already said: I didn't like him. Don't you listen?' she snapped. 'I didn't think much of Wynn Staniland but I don't think people's dirty linen should be washed in public.'

'You can trust us to be discreet,' said Wesley. He didn't bother to add: 'Unless your evidence is needed in court.'

241

'I told him about the man though.'

Wesley shifted forward a couple of inches.

'What man?'

'The one who used to live at Addersacre with Staniland. Hung around like a bad smell, he did.'

'Tell us about him.'

'Eric reckoned something was going on between him and Staniland.'

'Something ... sexual?' Wesley ventured, earning himself a purse-lipped look of disapproval.

'Nothing like that, I'm sure: Staniland was one for the ladies. Mind you, you never know these days, do you? Eric said Staniland never looked comfortable when this man was around. Said he used to hear them arguing.'

'What about?'

'Don't ask me.'

'Do you know this man's name?' Wesley took his notebook from his pocket in anticipation.

'Eric called him Mr La-di-da. Reckoned he had something to do with Staniland's books but I don't know.'

'Can you describe him?'

'Only saw him a couple of times and then not to speak to. He was around Staniland's age. Tall. Thin. Had a beard. And he talked posh – not that he ever talked to the likes of Eric and me,' she added. Wesley could hear years of pent-up resentment in her voice.

'Tell us what happened when Mrs Staniland died.'

'Why don't you read about it yourself? It was in all the papers.'

'We'd like to hear your version.'

'She went out for a walk one day and didn't come back. Then they found her in the sea pool, sitting bolt upright with the water just over her head. They say she'd drugged herself before she ... you know.'

'I've heard something similar happened in the nineteenth century. A local murder case.'

Ethel Rinton shook her head but her permed white curls didn't shift a centimetre.

'The man you told us about – was he at Addersacre when it happened?'

'Probably. He was a permanent fixture until he buggered off around the time Jane Whitsun did away with herself. That was three dead: my Eric, then Mrs Staniland, then Jane Whitsun. Addersacre's an unlucky house. Wouldn't catch me living there.'

'Did Jane Whitsun have any relatives?'

'There's a younger sister.'

'Do you know her name?'

She stared out of the window, as though she was making a great effort to remember.

Then her eyes lit up in recognition. 'It's Julie but I don't know her married name. She works in the library in Neston. Nice woman. Not like her sister at all but there was a big age gap between them.'

'Did you tell Zac Wilkinson about her?'

'Why should I?' she said with a note of malevolence.

Wesley stood up to leave. 'You've been a great help. Thank you.' He'd reached the front door when he turned to face her. There was one final question he needed to ask. 'By the way, what was the poison that killed your husband?'

'Monkshood. They say he should never have touched it without taking precautions.'

Wesley's mind had started working overtime. Monkshood – aconite – was the poison that had killed the Lombards.

31

Ivan had been kept in hospital while the other men from White Pool Farm were found emergency accommodation. Although their future was uncertain, at least they were safe now the Gough brothers were in custody. Gerry reckoned it was a good result.

As soon as Wesley returned from his interview with Ethel Rinton – an interview that had raised more questions than answers – he was accosted by one of the detective constables who'd been drafted in to help with the murder investigations. The young man seemed nervous but Wesley gave him an encouraging smile and asked what he could do for him.

'You know that caravan park where that couple were found?'

'What about it?'

'One of the men we found at White Pool Farm is a Russian called Ilya. He speaks quite good English and he said the Goughs sent them to build a fence in a field with lots of little metal houses; I think he meant caravans. There was new fencing behind the Lombards' caravan and I wondered if it might be worth asking him if he noticed anything. Shall I bring him in?'

'Yes. But take it easy, won't you? After what he's been through ...'

The DC nodded. He understood.

Half an hour later Wesley was face to face with Ilya over a cup of tea. He'd chosen the room set apart for dealing with vulnerable witnesses and victims of crime. In a bid to appear unintimidating it was furnished in pale wood with a pair of squashy sofas and patterned wallpaper on one wall. A kettle and tea bags were provided as well as a tiny fridge for milk. And even the cups were china, a rare treat for Wesley who was used to the bilge which passed for tea from the machine in the corridor.

Ilya was a small, gaunt man with a shaved head and watchful eyes. He had a tired, haggard look about him and Wesley suspected he was younger than he appeared. He stared at Wesley with suspicion and Wesley wasn't sure whether this was because he wasn't used to meeting someone with dark skin or because he had a deep-rooted fear of the police.

'How are you?' Wesley used the sympathetic professional tone of a doctor, or a social worker. That was the impression he needed to give if this man was to trust him.

'Not good,' Ilya replied in heavily accented English as he fidgeted nervously with the hem of his tracksuit top. 'How is Ivan? He very sick.'

'He's in hospital. They're looking after him. He'll be OK.'

Ilya shook his head as though he couldn't bring himself to believe it.

'We've arrested the men who held you captive. They'll go to prison.'

Ilya nodded. 'They are very ... cruel man.'

Wesley continued the questioning, relieved that Ilya understood most of what he was saying. He only stumbled over the English words a few times, sometimes misunderstanding, sometimes needing explanation, and eventually Wesley felt able to steer the conversation towards the Cliff View Caravan Park.

'This man and woman were staying in a caravan by the fence. Did you see them?' He produced photographs of Gina and Frank Lombard and Ilya studied them for what seemed to Wesley like a long time.

'I see these peoples. They shout. Angry.'

'Did you hear what they said?'

Wesley held his breath waiting for the answer.

'I want to better my English so I listen. She say she frightened then he say she has to go or she let him down. He say she should get what is hers. He say they get money.'

'Are you sure that's what they said?'

'They speak loud. I understand. Then Nev comes and says I do not work.'

'Did Nev hear what the people in the caravan were saying?'

Ilya bowed his head. 'I think so.'

'Did you see Nev speak to the people in the caravan?'

Ilya thought for a moment. 'Caravan man say to him we make too much noise and Nev say sorry. All nice. When back at farm he beat me with chain.'

He twisted round and raised his sweatshirt to reveal the scars on his back, half healed but still red and sore. Wesley gave an involuntary gasp.

'What about woman?' said Ilya.

'What woman?'

'Woman in charge. Old woman.'

'Do you mean Mrs Gough?'

'Old woman worst of lot. Others not see but I see one day. She give orders.'

Wesley stared at the man before him, thinking how appearances so often deceive.

Joan Gough had been brought in half an hour before and given a cup of tea in the interview room. No kid glove treatment this time. The chair was uncomfortable and the tea came from the machine.

The other captives from White Pool Farm had been interviewed through interpreters and a few had mentioned unprompted that they'd heard a female voice outside the barn issuing harsh orders to the two men who'd tormented them. Although they hadn't actually seen her and couldn't understand all she said, they assumed she was in charge. Gerry sent someone over to have another word with Callum Joy but he pleaded ignorance. Perhaps she'd been careful when she knew he was around because he spoke English.

In view of this new development, Wesley couldn't help wondering if Mrs Gough had something to do with her husband's death. Maybe his shooting hadn't been an accident after all. He told the interviewing officers to question her about it and about the man Joy claimed had disappeared. There was always a chance they could secure a murder conviction.

Callum Joy had mentioned a man who'd gone missing so a further search of the farm had been ordered. This time they were looking for graves, although Rachel had pointed out that there were other ways to dispose of a body on a farm – ways that left no trace – so perhaps they'd never know the truth.

Rachel walked into the office, a preoccupied look on her face as though she was wrestling with some intractable problem which was threatening to defeat her. Wesley caught her attention as she passed his desk.

'Everything OK?'

'I've just interviewed Joan Gough. It was surreal. She asked after my parents as though nothing had happened. Then she started asking when she could go home and when we were going to release her boys because she needed them on the farm.'

'What did you say?'

'I was worried about the livestock so I called Jack Proudfoot and he's agreed to see to the milking and check on the animals until we can reach a more permanent solution. When I told Joan what I'd arranged and said she was lucky to have a good neighbour she lost it – said I had no right to interfere. I don't think she realises the seriousness of the situation.'

'Do you think we have enough on her to get a conviction?'

'None of the men actually saw her so if she gets a clever lawyer our evidence might not stand up in court. I can see her playing the poor widow card and saying it was something the boys thought up on their own.' She sighed. 'I rang my parents to tell them and my mum told me the Goughs changed after the foot-and-mouth outbreak.'

'That's a long time ago.'

'It's something the farmers who were affected will never forget. I called Nigel too. He used to know the Gough boys years ago when they all went to Young Farmers meetings in happier times. He said they'd always been under their mother's thumb.'

'We need to get Nev and Barry to talk.'

'To shop their own mother?' Rachel sounded sceptical.

'We can always try.'

Wesley brought Neville Gough up to the interview room, playing the sympathetic official who understood the pressure he was under. But Nev denied knowing anything about the Lombards and when Wesley told him about Ilya's claim that he'd overheard the couple's argument, Nev said he couldn't remember. Wesley decided to let it go for now and give him time to consider the matter. Gerry, who had always lacked his patience, told him he should have pushed harder.

It was almost nine by the time he reached home and Michael thundered down the stairs to greet him in the hall.

Wesley was hungry but he could tell his son wanted to talk so eating would have to wait. Pam emerged from the living room and gave him a wan smile. She looked pale again, as if she'd been doing too much. She shot back into the room before he could ask her how she was.

'How's it going?' Wesley asked.

Michael shrugged. 'Nathaniel's asked me to stay over at his on Saturday night. Is that OK?'

'As long as it's OK with his mum.'

'She says it's no problem.' Michael hovered in the hall for a moment then vanished upstairs again, no doubt to contact his friends from the isolation of his room. Wesley couldn't understand what they could find to say to each other and he suddenly felt old. Then he remembered someone saying that it was everybody's ultimate fate to turn into their parents.

He joined Pam after putting the dinner she'd left for him into the microwave.

'It's OK if he stays at Nathaniel's on Saturday night, isn't it?' he asked. 'I've just said he can go.'

'It's Nathaniel's. There's nothing to worry about.'

'But after last time . . . '

'I sometimes think we're over-protective.'

'My parents were and it never did Maritia and me any harm.'

'Della let me do as I liked and my dad was too soft to say anything.' She smiled. 'I turned out OK, didn't I?'

He took her in his arms, more cautiously than he would have done before her treatment. Nowadays he tended to treat her more like a delicate doll than a human being.

'I won't break,' she whispered in his ear.

'I know but . . . '

She stopped the words with a kiss and they held each other for a while.

'Sorry I'm so late,' he said, breaking the silence.

'I didn't expect you back early. The local news said two men were arrested for keeping slaves on a farm in Stoke Beeching. Were you involved in . . . ?'

'Yes. That's one case we've wrapped up. Only three murders to go.'

Before Pam could say anything the phone started to ring and she answered. As soon as Wesley realised it was Della on the other end of the line, he hurried to the kitchen to fetch his food.

He'd just taken his plate out of the microwave when Pam appeared at the door. 'Della's on her way round. And I warn you, she's not in a good mood . . . especially with the police.'

'What are we supposed to have done now?'

'Who knows?'

They only enjoyed half an hour of peace before he found out. Della entered the house like a whirlwind, her scarves bright around her neck, tearing off her black velvet coat and throwing it onto the banisters. Her arrival brought the children out of their rooms but as soon as they realised who it was they disappeared again.

Wesley stood up as Della entered the living room, not out of politeness but preparing for flight if necessary.

'Your lot are bloody incompetent,' she said, looking him in the eye.

'Sit down, Della. Cup of tea? Glass of wine?' In his mind he added hemlock to the list.

'Red wine,' she ordered. 'A large one.'

Before he could fetch it she began her tirade. 'We pay our taxes for proper policing and we might as well have the Keystone Cops. They didn't even send anyone out.'

'That'll be the funding cuts,' said Wesley with studied patience. 'If something's routine and not life-threatening . . .'

'That's not good enough.'

'I agree with you but—'

'So what are you going to do about it?'

'I can't do anything until you tell me what's happened.'

This seemed to calm her a little. He saw that Pam had picked up her book; still Wynn Staniland's *The Viper's Kiss* – she was ploughing through it slowly. He couldn't get away from the case even at home. She began to read, ignoring her mother's complaints. She'd always had the knack of switching off when her mother became too irritating.

'Our office was broken into this lunchtime while we were all out.'

'Your office?'

251

'The Literary Festival office at the Dukesbridge Arts Centre. A laptop was stolen along with a purse from Yolanda's handbag. And a radio. At least they didn't make a mess.'

'How did they get in?'

To his surprise, Della blushed. 'Yolanda forgot to lock the door. A lot of people use the Arts Centre – disadvantaged teenagers and the like. Not that I'm accusing anyone,' she said swiftly.

'And because the door was unlocked, you're not insured?'

'The constable I spoke to on the phone wasn't at all sympathetic. He said someone would come over tomorrow and not to touch anything in the meantime. We can't afford to lose the computer. We're running the festival on a shoe-string as it is.'

'I suppose you want me to chase it up for you?'

The fire of righteous anger suddenly vanished from Della's eyes, replaced by meek gratitude. 'If you would, Wesley, that'd be wonderful.'

A glass of wine later Della left, duly appeased.

32

'You mean to say Kieran State's been in the country all this time? I thought he was sunning himself in the Costa del Crime.' Gerry didn't sound pleased about the news that had greeted him first thing the following morning.

'That's what his wife told the local police. Turns out she was lying, sir.'

Gerry stood staring at the unsuspecting young constable who'd brought him the news as if she was personally responsible for Mrs State's deception.

'His local police say he's chosen to make a voluntary statement, sir.'

'That's good of him. We'll lay on a limo to bring him over and get the champers on ice.'

The constable bowed her head and suppressed a nervous giggle. She'd never been quite sure how to take the DCI's sense of humour.

'I want him brought over asap. If people lie to us they've usually got something to hide.'

The clock on the office wall told Gerry it was seven thirty, time for his morning briefing, but first of all he wanted to speak to Wesley, who was deep in conversation with Rachel. They looked like a pair of conspirators and when he caught Wesley's eye he saw him whisper something to Rachel that made her smile.

When Wesley joined him Gerry noticed there was a secretive half-smile on his lips.

'Something you want to share with me, Wes?'

'I was just telling Rachel we had a visit from my mother-in-law last night. There's been a break-in at the Dukesbridge Literary Festival office and she seems to think I can pull some strings. I had to explain about the budget cuts in words of one syllable.'

'Anything taken?'

'A computer. A purse. A radio. Hardly the crime of the century. I've had a word with Dukesbridge nick and they're sending someone to take fingerprints this morning.'

'Good.' Now he'd got the trivialities out of the way it was time for the important news. 'I've just heard that Kieran State's wife was telling porkies. He wasn't sunning himself in the Costa del Sol at the time of Jamie Hursthead's murder after all. She said she lied because she couldn't face having her son's death raked up again.'

'I take it you don't believe her.'

'I wouldn't believe Kieran State if he told me the grass was green. He's a villain, Wes. Record as long as the Amazon.'

'Is there any proof he was here killing Hursthead?'

'Not yet. But I've asked traffic to check whether any cars registered to him appear on their fancy number plate recognition system. I've also asked them to do the same with

254

all vehicles belonging to the Restoricks. They knew exactly where the victim would be at the relevant time. And they were the ones who threatened the Hursthead family.'

Wesley thought about the Restoricks; they didn't seem the killing sort but anyone was capable of murder given the right provocation. 'Even if they're in the frame for Hursthead's murder there's no suggestion of any connection with the Lombards.'

'You're right, Wes. Perhaps we've been barking up the wrong tree all along with this Wynn Staniland business.' Gerry sounded despondent.

An array of possibilities danced through Wesley's head, each as elusive as the last. After half a minute of thoughtful silence he spoke. 'I want to follow something up.'

'What?'

'Staniland's housekeeper killed herself shortly after his wife's suicide. I want to speak to her sister.'

'You're chasing shadows, Wes.' Gerry sounded exasperated. 'Two families out there have lost sons thanks to Jamie Hursthead and maybe the Lombards killed themselves after all. Perhaps the grand money-making scheme Frank mentioned to his brother didn't work out.'

But Wesley wasn't giving up. 'The Stanilands' gardener died of aconite poisoning – same as the Lombards. The inquest found he'd been handling poisonous plants without taking precautions but . . . '

'It's probably a coincidence. Anyway, why would Staniland want Jamie Hursthead dead? He'd agreed to cooperate with the biography. As for the Lombards, it looks like Gina was a fan and authors don't go round killing their fans.'

Wesley shook his head. 'Humour me, Gerry. I'll go and

see the housekeeper's sister and if it gets us nowhere we'll concentrate on State and the Restoricks.'

Gerry gave him an indulgent smile, like a fond uncle giving permission for a play session with a new train set.

Wesley made a call and established that Julie – married name Shepherd – who worked at Neston Library was the very person who'd reported Jamie Hursthead missing when he'd failed to turn up for his talk. It seemed like an omen.

He went to the library alone, preferring an informal chat to an official visit. After parking in the municipal car park he walked down the sloping high street past its colourful new age shops to the new library, which stood in a small alleyway. As he entered the building he passed a group of mothers with toddlers who were proudly clutching picture books in their tiny hands. He'd arrived on Mother and Toddler morning and he had the uncomfortable feeling that he was intruding.

He asked for Julie at the counter and was pointed in the direction of a woman with shoulder-length fair hair and a kindly face. It was hard to guess her age but, if she was Jane Whitsun's sister, he thought she must look younger than her years. He waited until she'd finished dealing tactfully with a small boy who was reluctant to return his cardboard book in the shape of a tractor and she suggested they talk in the staffroom.

After the customary cup of tea was offered and accepted, Wesley explained the purpose of his visit.

'I thought it'd be about poor Zac Wilkinson,' she said, surprised. 'I arranged the event, you see, and I still keep thinking about it.' Her hand fluttered as if to still her pounding heart. 'I met him, you know. He came here and

256

I helped him with his research. When I told him my sister used to be Wynn Staniland's housekeeper, he was very keen to talk about her.'

'Your number was on his phone but we assumed it was connected to his talk.'

'That as well, of course. But we did meet. We had a coffee in town. I liked him.'

Wesley sipped his tea. It was too strong but he didn't care. He had a feeling he was about to discover something important.

'What did you tell him?'

'Not much. My sister was twelve years older than me and I was only sixteen when she died. We didn't talk much about her job. All I know is that she and Wynn Staniland were close.'

'Do you mean they were lovers?'

'I don't know for sure but it wouldn't surprise me. Jane was very attractive and around Staniland's age. I understand his marriage wasn't particularly happy. It can't have been because his wife killed herself, didn't she?'

'Do you know anything about that?'

'Only that she copied the method he described in one of his books, *The Viper's Kiss*. I imagine she did it like that to get back at him.'

'I've heard he took that plot from a real-life incident – a nineteenth-century murder in Whitely.'

'I've heard that too. We have a very good local history section if you want to look it up,' she added hopefully. 'But if you're thinking there was anything suspicious about Rosemary Staniland's death, I'm sure you're wrong. It was investigated at the time and the verdict was suicide.'

Wesley said nothing. The more he found out about Wynn

Staniland, the more certain he was that the man was at the centre of everything, like a spider sitting in its web, waiting for prey.

'Staniland stopped writing after that. Any chance it was Rosemary who actually wrote the books?'

Julie smiled. 'I suppose it's a possibility but she'd have no reason not to publish under her own name, would she? Anyway, she was an artist and I think that's where her interest and talent lay.'

'I've spoken to the widow of Staniland's gardener. His name was Eric Rinton and he died from accidental poisoning.'

A knowing smile appeared on Julie's face. 'I used to work over at Bloxham Library and Ethel was one of our regulars.' She paused. 'She isn't the easiest of women to get along with.' Wesley had the feeling that, for Julie, this was damning criticism indeed.

'She told me her husband was murdered.' He wondered whether to mention that her main suspect was Julie's late sister but decided against it.

Julie rolled her eyes. 'Ethel's always had a taste for crime novels – the more lurid the better,' she said as though this explained everything.

'She said something about a man who used to stay at Addersacre. She described him as tall and bearded, with a posh voice. She thought he might have had something to do with his publisher.'

'I remember Jane saying that a friend of Wynn's from his Oxford days moved in for a while. I had the impression she didn't like him much.'

'Why was that?'

'I was the kid sister. She didn't confide in me.'

'Did she mention his name?'

'She might have done at the time but I really can't remember. Sorry.'

'You're sure he was at Oxford with Wynn?'

She suddenly looked unsure of herself. 'I think so. But it's a long time ago.'

'I'm sorry to ask you this but how did your sister commit suicide?'

'She poisoned herself.'

'Aconite?'

She raised her eyebrows. 'If you already knew why are you asking?'

'I didn't know. It was a guess. Did she leave a note?'

'She said Rosemary Staniland killed herself because of Wynn's affair with her. She felt she'd caused her death and she couldn't live with the guilt.'

'Was that in character?'

Julie said nothing for a few moments. 'As I said, she was a lot older than me and it was only after she died that I realised how little I knew about her. The honest answer is I don't know.'

'Ethel Rinton said her husband had caught Jane and Staniland together and threatened to tell Rosemary. She thinks Jane killed him to ensure his silence.'

'That's nonsense.' Julie didn't sound too sure of herself.

'Was the note she left handwritten?'

'It was typed. She acted as Wynn's secretary as well as his housekeeper.'

'She typed his books?'

'I presume so but she never talked about it.'

'Did you ever think your sister's death might not have been a straightforward suicide?'

Wesley saw a look of uncertainty in her eyes. 'The police did a thorough investigation at the time.'

'There were three deaths within three months of each other. The gardener, Rosemary, then your sister. Did it ever cross your mind that this might not be a coincidence?'

A shadow passed across Julie's face. He knew he'd reawakened painful memories but it couldn't be avoided.

'A few months after it happened I heard a rumour that Jane killed Rosemary; drugged her, helped her down to the pool and let her drown and then she killed herself in a fit of remorse. But I refused to believe it,' she said quietly. 'I'm sorry, Inspector, but if you dig too deep there's a chance you might stir up something terrible. I've got children and if it does turn out their aunt was a murderer . . .' She didn't have to finish the sentence.

'Did you tell Zac everything you've told me?'

'I told him what I knew about Staniland, which wasn't much, but I didn't want to talk about my sister's death. I didn't want that raked up in his book.'

He could hear children's voices drifting in from behind the closed door, reminding him of the world outside.

'Do you intend to look into Jane's death – reopen the case?' Her words held a hint of dread.

Wesley stood up. 'If your sister's death wasn't suicide, I want to get justice for her.'

'And if you find out the rumours were true and she killed Rosemary Staniland?'

Wesley didn't answer Julie's question and as he returned to the car he feared he'd said too much, assumed too much. But ideas were swirling around his head. A summer day; a gardener who'd seen something he shouldn't. An inconvenient wife. An even more inconvenient housekeeper who knew secrets she couldn't be trusted to keep.

And Wynn Staniland's friend – Mr La-di-da. Did he have anything to do with what happened back then ... or more recently? Wynn Staniland had a lot of questions to answer.

The geophysics in the rest of the walled garden wasn't conclusive. The ground had been disturbed too much over the years, Neil explained to Karl Banville, doing his best to keep his professional cool. Yes, there were anomalies but they could be long-buried garden features. As for the murdered body of William Banville, he told the man's descendant not to get his hopes up.

To his surprise Banville produced a photograph – fragile and sepia – of a young man in tweeds with dark hair and a luxuriant moustache, awkwardly posed beside an aspidistra. 'It was found among some family papers. Turn it over.'

Neil saw the name William Banville and the date May 1882 written on the reverse in faded copperplate.

Banville pointed to the man's left hand. 'If you find him he'll be easy to identify. He lost half his middle finger in a childhood accident.'

Neil said nothing and returned to work, hoping the man wasn't in for a big disappointment. But even if they didn't find what Banville was looking for, excavating the old garden was an interesting exercise. The original layout could even be reconstructed as part of the renovation of the manor; perhaps he'd suggest it to Banville.

Work was continuing in the trench they'd opened on the site of the summerhouse. They were taking things slowly because there were a lot of charred artefacts amongst the debris to be recorded and photographed and as Neil watched he wondered how Banville would react if William Banville wasn't found. How would he take it if William's innocence couldn't be proved? What if he had killed Mary Field and fled, just as everyone thought at the time?

He began digging in the summerhouse trench, scraping the earth away carefully, and he'd been working for an hour when he heard a voice calling his name. One of his PhD students, a dark-haired young woman called Emily, was standing in trench two a few yards away, trowel in hand, staring at the ground.

'Neil, you know that geophysics anomaly? It's a statue. A nymph with one leg; the other's broken off. Looks nineteenth-century.'

'Great. Carry on,' said Neil. That explained the body-sized anomaly, the one that had looked the most promising.

He was wondering how to break the bad news to Banville when a speck of white appeared in the soil he'd been trowelling. He continued and as the thing was gradually revealed he held his breath. Had someone buried a much-loved pet in this part of the garden? Or ... ?

He called Emily over to help and slowly the bones emerged from the ground.

Only it definitely wasn't William Banville. Instead it was the fully articulated skeleton of a woman.

Journal of John Lipton

6 June 1884

We are married; joined till death us do part. And now all Mary possesses is mine.

When I took her to my father's cottage after the wedding I saw a look of distaste pass across her face. She had thought me a gentleman, an assumption I went to great pains to encourage, but now she knows the truth. I am the son of a humble blacksmith who has desires above his station and I have married with an heiress.

Our mutual interest in death and murder is no longer of such importance and, as I took possession of her body on our wedding night, she lay still as a corpse beneath me as though all the passion she professed during our meetings in the walled garden has vanished at the discovery of my origins.

I think often of Sarah and that kiss we shared together. I do not think that she would be so cold.

I instructed Mary not to send word of our marriage to her father because there will be time enough to break the news when we see him face to face. To my relief she acquiesced and now I must consider when it will be best to return to Newfield Manor.

We stay at the inn for there is little room in my father's house. Besides, I cannot bear his pious carping. He says he is pleased I have found a wife and tells me a good marriage is a blessing and that my wild days are over. My father is a fool.

33

If Wesley had had access to Jamie Hursthead's research notes, he might have been able to learn the identity of the mysterious Mr La-di-da without disturbing Wynn Staniland again. But everything connected to the biography he'd been writing had been stolen from his cottage which, Wesley thought, was probably significant in itself.

He was pondering the problem when Gerry returned to the CID office with news that Kieran State was being brought in for questioning. Did Wesley want to do the honours when he arrived?

Wesley said he'd leave it to Gerry: let him grab the glory if State turned out to be their man. Gerry looked at him questioningly and said he wouldn't take no for an answer. Wesley was going to be in at the kill whether he liked it or not.

Once they'd finished going through their strategy, Wesley scanned his notes. He was sure he was missing something, although he couldn't think what it was. After a while he pushed the notes aside and stared out of the window, remembering his conversation with Julie Shepherd and wondering exactly where her sister, Jane Whitsun, had fitted into the Staniland household.

He needed to speak to Wynn Staniland again, even though another visit might be construed as harassment. If the man Ethel Rinton called Mr La-di-da was an old friend of Staniland's from his Oxford days, all it would take to identify him was a direct question – unless Staniland had something to hide.

His thoughts were interrupted by a call from Dukesbridge Police Station.

'Just thought you'd like to know, sir,' said the enthusiastic officer on the other end of the line. Wesley envisaged him as young and untainted by the weary cynicism that overtakes so many in their chosen profession after a decade or so dealing with the worst of human nature. 'That break-in at the Arts Centre. We've found a set of prints that don't match the ones we took for elimination purposes. Obviously recent.'

'What about them?' said Wesley, sensing he was about to hear something important.

'This is going to sound a bit daft but ... Well, the truth is, sir, they appear to belong to a dead man.'

The body Neil had found definitely wasn't William Banville's. The bones were those of a slightly built woman and, in his professional opinion, she'd been in the earth a long time.

He liked to use Wesley as his first police contact whenever human remains were found. With his archaeology degree, his friend knew the subtleties of death, ancient and modern, and how to tell which was which from the context of the discovery. But today his luck was out. Wesley was unavailable so he left a message: human remains had been found at Newfield Manor and he was contacting a forensic anthropologist who would, hopefully, confirm that the burial was of no interest to the police.

After the arrangements had been made he took out his phone. There was something he needed to check; a postscript to the Mary Field case that appeared in some accounts of her murder but not others.

Around the time of Mary's death, her maid Sarah left her employ and vanished from all records. It was rumoured that she'd been seen in the company of William Banville and there was speculation that they were in league. There were even those who said that Sarah helped to lure the hapless Mary to her terrible fate before fleeing to another part of the country. Or maybe fleeing abroad with William Banville.

If the bones they'd just found turned out to be Sarah's, then it solved the mystery of the fate, although Neil had no idea how he was going to prove it was her. All he knew was that he had to tell Karl Banville the skeleton wasn't the one he was hoping to find.

He made the call and when he broke the news there was a long silence on the other end of the line before Banville ordered him to carry on digging. The discovery of the woman made no difference. William Banville was innocent and Neil was going to prove it.

The constable from Dukesbridge was quite adamant. The computer never lied.

Wesley asked for the details of the fingerprints' owner to be emailed through and once he had the information up on the screen, he printed it out and made his way to Gerry's office.

'Something wrong?' Rachel asked as he passed her desk.

He could see Gerry was busy on the phone; it would do no harm to get Rachel's opinion while he waited for him to finish. 'Do you remember that break-in at Dukesbridge Arts Centre – the Literary Festival office?'

'What about it?'

'They sent someone round the next day to dust for prints. Some belonged to a couple of young tearaways who've got form for this sort of thing. Hopefully Dukesbridge are picking them up as we speak.'

'You'd think they'd have learned to wear gloves by now,' said Rachel, rolling her eyes.

But Wesley wasn't interested in the pair of incompetent young opportunists. 'They also found another set of prints; a suspect in a 1968 murder inquiry who disappeared without a trace.'

'Like Lord Lucan?'

Wesley smiled. 'Not dissimilar. His name was Robert Valdun and he was at Oxford studying English. He was a brilliant student, by all accounts, but he had problems: drugs and drink. Went seriously off the rails.'

'Just shows you, even people who get into Oxford can be spectacularly stupid.' Rachel's verdict was swift and merciless. 'Who was he supposed to have murdered?'

Wesley studied the printout in his hands. 'Valdun dropped out of his course at the beginning of his final year but he stayed on in Oxford, moved into a bedsit and took a job as an assistant in a library in the suburbs. He became infatuated with a bar maid called Suzie Grant who worked at a pub near his old college. According to her colleagues

Valdun sat in the bar most nights watching her and waiting for her shift to finish.'

'On his own?'

'Mostly. But sometimes he was with another man.'

'Who?'

'Another student, the bar staff said. Although he wasn't there on the night Suzie died so the police never spoke to him.'

'Sounds like he was stalking her.' Wesley could hear the disapproval in Rachel's voice.

'Not exactly. Suzie gave him some encouragement and he often walked her home. On the night she died he hung around until she'd finished her shift and they left the pub together. She was found strangled in her flat the following day.'

'I take it he was questioned?'

'Yes and he admitted they'd gone back to her place and had sex. After that, according to his statement, she said she had to be up early in the morning so he went home and took some acid – he was experimenting with drugs a lot in those days. I guess it was the height of the swinging sixties. Way before our time.' He smiled. 'Anyway, he claimed he was completely out of it and he couldn't remember what happened for the rest of the night. He swore she'd been alive when he left her and he was certain he didn't go back – although the officers who interviewed him asked him how he could be so sure if he couldn't remember anything about the evening.'

'Good point,' said Rachel.

'The forensic evidence stacked up against him so the local police went to his bedsit to arrest him only to find he'd gone and, in spite of extensive enquiries, nobody knew where. Then some days later his clothes were found on a beach in Norfolk. A one-way train ticket was found in his pocket and another note saying he couldn't go on any more and that this was the best way for everyone.'

'Was his body ever found?'

'No. But we're talking about the North Sea. Bodies can go in and never turn up for years . . . if at all.'

'What about his family?'

'Both parents died in a car accident when he was a teenager at boarding school and he was an only child. There was nobody to miss him. Sad.'

'Not if he was guilty of killing that woman,' Rachel said righteously. 'And you say his fingerprints have been found at the Arts Centre in Dukesbridge?'

'By some miracle the prints are still on file but they're still trying to find a photograph of him so we can ask the people who work there if they recognise him. It might be worth contacting Thames Valley to see if there are any retired officers who remember the case.'

Wesley consulted the printout again. 'Suzie Grant was twenty-three and she too was a university dropout. She'd been disowned by her parents for throwing in her course so she took the pub job to earn a living. Reading between the lines I think she had problems.'

'Doesn't mean she deserved to be murdered.'

Wesley felt hurt by the implication that he was unsympathetic, even guilty of snobbery. 'I never said that.' His eyes met hers. 'You're touchy today.'

She looked away.

'Everything OK?' He could see she looked tired, as though she hadn't slept.

'It's this Gough thing. Nigel and my parents won't stop talking about it.'

Wesley understood. The Goughs' misdeeds had sent ripples through the whole farming community. Someone they knew had done a terrible thing, driven to evil by a bitter cocktail of greed and circumstances.

He saw that Gerry had finished his call. 'I'd better tell the boss about Robert Valdun.'

Rachel raised her eyebrows. 'Do you think it's relevant to our case?'

'I've absolutely no idea,' Wesley said before heading for Gerry's office.

Millicombe Antiquarian Books smelled musty; the odour of old damp books together with something more unpleasant. But Raynard Bishop was used to the smell, even finding it comforting.

It was here he'd found an old leather-bound book containing the first reference to the puppet shows that were to become his obsession. One illustration featured a monstrous representation of the infamous murder of the Ratcliffe Highway victims and the interest this ignited had encouraged him to delve deeper into the subject, hungry for every morsel of information. Eventually this had led him to the treasure in the Goughs' barn – Gunster's show almost in its entirety – and now his collection had grown to the extent that he was now able to put on his own shows for a modern-day audience to rival those of his predecessor. But he still retained the true collector's greed for the novel and surprising.

Raynard stood in the gloom and watched the well-heeled holidaymakers drift past the window in their white jeans and pastel waterproofs. Hardly any of them ever ventured inside. They brought their reading matter from home or bought it from the clean, well-lit bookshop down the road.

He felt something approaching pride as he watched Peter Walsingham trawl the dusty volumes on the shelves for some rare treasure that would take his fancy. They'd met through their mutual interest in books and he felt they were kindred spirits.

'You haven't got to rush back to Scotland, have you?' Raynard asked as they left the shop. A lot hung on the answer.

'Not if you don't want me to.' Peter had no trace of a Scottish accent, even though he'd lived there so long.

Raynard felt a rush of relief and touched his companion's hand lightly. For so many years he'd longed for someone to share his life; to take away the loneliness he tried so hard to banish with shows and committees. And since Peter had come to stay he'd dared to hope even though, so far, Peter had shown no signs of reciprocating his interest.

'Why don't you help me with the puppet shows? I'm getting a lot of bookings nowadays.'

Peter smiled. 'Why not? I'm thinking of sticking around. I like it round here.'

Raynard felt a sudden glow of happiness. He'd met Peter online when he'd been searching for material on notable Victorian murders and marionette shows. Peter had found his treasured book about the Mary Field case and now he was trying to track down the ultimate prize – Mary's own private journal; the book many contemporary accounts said existed but which had become lost over the intervening years. Mary Field had brought them together so Raynard had a lot to thank her for.

Peter was older than he was but still attractive, and his interests and passions perfectly aligned with Raynard's. It was a long time since he'd felt like this about another human being; not since his university days when he'd abandoned his studies because of another person, a mistake that had ultimately led to disaster.

'I read about those farmers,' Peter said as they climbed into Raynard's car, a twenty-year-old VW which still served him well. 'The ones who kept those men as slaves. Isn't that where you found the Gunster puppets?'

'That's right. The man who sold them said he was descended from Gunster himself.' Raynard thought for a moment. 'The theatre and marionettes had been lying neglected there for over a hundred years and he wanted rid of them because he was clearing out a barn. Weren't those men found in a barn? Perhaps ... '

'Don't think about it,' said Peter.

Their eyes met and Peter took something from his pocket, a small brown book, unremarkable in appearance. 'I spotted this on the net; a dealer in Somerset was selling it,' he said. 'I've been saving it. I think it's what you've been looking for.'

He held the book up tantalisingly, as if he was about to snatch it away. Then he handed the tiny, tattered volume to Raynard.

When he opened it he saw the neat handwriting, the ink faded with age, and his hands began to shake. From the name in the front Raynard knew that this was the treasure he'd been waiting for all his life.

34

Although Gerry found Wesley's news about Robert Valdun's fingerprints intriguing, he couldn't see what it had to do with the case that had been bugging him for the past couple of weeks.

Even so, he knew Wesley was anxious to contact Thames Valley Police, so he told him to go ahead but not to let himself get sidetracked. Wesley pointed out that Wynn Staniland must have studied English at Oxford around the same time as Robert Valdun and this tenuous link seemed to excite him, especially as the identity of Staniland's mysterious Oxford friend remained so elusive.

Gerry, however, pointed out that a lot of people passed through Oxford. Until they established a definite connection between Valdun and Staniland, they couldn't afford to hare off after false leads. Besides, they had more urgent things to worry about than a dead man's fingerprints at the scene of a burglary. The Gough brothers were blaming their dead father for everything, claiming they'd been dragged into the operation against their will. As for their mother, they insisted she knew nothing.

While he was preparing to tackle the overtime budget that was squatting on his desk like a monstrous toad, he received a call from his daughter, Rosie. It didn't take Gerry long to realise something had upset her.

'What is it, love?'

'I was in Tradmouth so I call at the house and when I open the door there's this woman there. She says her name's Alison and . . . she says she's your daughter. What's going on, Dad?'

There was an edge of hysteria in Rosie's voice and Gerry was suddenly lost for words.

'I can explain, love. Look, can we talk tonight. I—'

As soon as Rosie slammed the phone down it rang again. This time he heard Alison's voice.

'I'm going home to Liverpool,' she said, stifling a sob.

Gerry experienced an unexpected tug of loss; a dread that the daughter he'd only just found was going to leave him and possibly never return. 'Have you got to go now, love? Can't it wait? I've just had Rosie on and she said she'd seen you. She's had a bit of a shock, that's all. It's my fault. I should have told her earlier.'

'Sorry, Gerry. I've got to get back to work soon anyway. Don't want to lose me job.'

She hadn't called him Dad yet and he wasn't sure how he felt about that.

'Rosie went ballistic,' she said with another sob. 'She told me to get out. Called me a liar. It's best all round if I go. I should give you some space to sort things out.'

He was tempted to tell her to take no notice. But Rosie was a hard woman to ignore.

'You'll come back?'

Another silence. Then 'I hope so, I really do.'

The line went dead. Gerry was left feeling angry with Rosie, and angry with himself for not handling things better. He heard someone saying his name and saw Wesley standing in the doorway. When he asked if everything was OK Gerry answered automatically. Yes. Fine. He needed time to think before he confided in anybody.

'Kieran State's arrived,' said Wesley. 'He's waiting in the interview room.'

Gerry scratched his head. 'OK. Let's go and have a word.'

'I never killed Jamie Hursthead and you can't prove otherwise.'

Kieran State's eyes shifted from one officer to the other, as though he was trying to work out who was the most likely to believe what he was saying.

'But you'd discovered his new identity.'

State grunted. 'He didn't make much effort to stay under the radar, did he? Writing books and giving bloody talks. No shame about what he did to my boy.'

Wesley saw Gerry nod as though he thought the man had a point.

'But I never touched him and that's God's honest truth. I've got witnesses.'

'Who?'

'My wife. A couple of my associates who came round for a drink on the night you say he was murdered. I wasn't here and you can't prove I was.'

'Did Brian Restorick tell you where Jamie was?' Wesley asked.

No answer.

'We can go through your phone records ... and Restorick's,' said Wesley. 'We can easily find out.'

State looked at his solicitor. He'd brought him with him specially, like a king with his personal physician in attendance. The solicitor – a sharp-featured man in an immaculate suit – gave a slight nod as if to say Wesley was right and there was no point holding back.

'OK. Brian called me to say Hursthead was here in Devon using another name and he was going to give a talk at some library. Said his picture was plastered all over posters. You can understand why he was angry.'

'What did you do with this information?'

Another glance at the solicitor. 'Nothing.'

'Did you come here and look for him? Or send one of your associates?' said Gerry.

'How could I? Brian never knew where he lived.'

Wesley leaned forward. 'But he knew where Hursthead was going to be that evening. He could have told you.'

'I've already said. This is the first time I've ever been here. And before you ask, I didn't send anyone here to do my dirty work neither.'

'What about Brian?'

'Brian's not the type to get his hands dirty. But I called him when I heard Hursthead's body had been found. Asked him if he'd done it.'

'What did he say?'

'Said he knew nothing about it and I believed him. Look, I'm telling you the truth.'

Wesley guessed that this wasn't all that had passed between State and Restorick, but when he pressed State he stuck to his story.

'What do you think?' he asked Gerry after the interview was over.

'My gut feeling says he's telling the truth, more or less,' said Gerry. There was something absent-minded about his reply.

·'If his alibis check out we've no reason to hold him. We'll have to let him go.'

Gerry nodded.

'What about Restorick?'

'We bring him in.' Gerry sighed. 'I don't like doing this, Wes. Restorick and State both lost their kids.'

Wesley was about to say something about people not taking the law into their own hands but the words wouldn't come. Like any parent, he knew he might feel the need for vengeance should he ever be unlucky enough to find himself in the same situation.

Once back in the office, he gave the order. Kieran State was to be released on bail pending further enquiries and Brian Restorick was to be brought in for questioning.

Michael's sister was at a friend's so he was the sole focus of his mother's attention. She'd always fussed but she'd been worse since she'd been off work with more time on her hands to think and worry. She hadn't been the same since her operation; the operation they tried to hide from him because they thought he was just a kid who wouldn't understand. But he did. His mum had had cancer just like the mum of one of the girls at school, only her mum died last year. He avoided the girl because every time he saw her he was reminded of that terrible fact.

He followed Pam into the kitchen and watched as she began to unpack the dishwasher.

'I'll do that for you, Mum,' he said, leaping forward to help.

But rather than giving him effusive thanks, she looked at him suspiciously. 'You OK?'

He resisted the temptation to snap back a brilliantly sarcastic reply. 'Why shouldn't I be?'

Pam put her arms around him and kissed the top of his head. He was as tall as she was now and she had to stand on tiptoe. He stood there longing to escape her embrace; angry with her for fussing; angry with her for being ill; angry that there was a chance he might lose her.

He felt his phone vibrate in his pocket. Another message and he could guess what it would say: it was time to sort out the arrangements.

'You remember I asked if I could stay at Nathaniel's tomorrow night?'

He saw his mum's smile freeze.

'Harry won't be there, will he? Only after last time . . . '

'That'll never happen again. Promise. It'll just be me and Nathaniel.'

Pam held him close. 'Love you.'

'Love you too,' he replied automatically.

As soon as he made his escape he rushed up the stairs and shut his bedroom door so that he could message Harry to say he'd be there. He was up for it, especially if Archie was going to pay them. He was going to be a ghost.

When Wesley looked at his watch he saw it was four thirty which meant, as far as a major murder inquiry goes, the day was still young. Thames Valley hadn't yet got back to him with a photograph of Robert Valdun and he felt he couldn't make any progress until he had one. He wanted to show it to Ethel Rinton; and then possibly to Wynn Staniland. All sorts of ideas were forming in his head, each more fantastical than the last. But until he had that photograph, he couldn't move forward.

It was five o'clock by the time Oxford sent through a picture of a dark-haired young man with a thin, earnest face and the sunken eyes of a habitual drug user. It was an intelligent face, he thought, and not obviously the face of a killer, even though he knew only too well that murderers come in all sorts of guises.

He stared at the image, running through all the people he'd met in connection with the case in his mind, but nothing clicked. He was as sure as he could be he'd never seen the man in the photograph before; and he was equally sure that he'd be able to recognise him if their paths did cross in the future because he'd always been good with faces.

Brian Restorick had been out when the officers called to bring him in for questioning and he wasn't expected back for another couple of hours. His wife said he was playing golf, which seemed somehow inappropriate to Wesley in the circumstances.

While he was waiting for Restorick to turn up, he thought he'd seize the opportunity to show Robert Valdun's photograph to Ethel Rinton. He told Gerry where he was going but the DCI was busy bringing the chief super up to date with developments so he drove to her cottage alone.

As he brought the car to a halt outside he saw a yellowing net curtain twitch at the window and when Ethel answered the door she didn't seem pleased to see him.

'I suppose you'd better come in,' she muttered resentfully and led him into the living room where an unappetising smell of cooking hung in the air. The reek of cabbage again.

Mingled with shepherd's pie, at a guess. The dirty crockery was still on the little table in the corner; a single plate veiled in a film of congealed brown with a knife and fork laid on it as neatly as it would be in any upmarket restaurant.

'Sorry to disturb your dinner.'

'You're lucky. I've just finished.' She began to busy herself clearing the dishes away, carrying them into the kitchen.

'I'd like to ask you a few more questions if that's all right,' he said.

'I've told you everything I know.'

Wesley ignored the hostility in her voice. 'Do you recognise this man?' He passed her the photograph. 'Is this the man who used to stay with Wynn Staniland? The one your late husband called Mr La-di-da?'

She held the picture at a distance and studied it, a frown deepening the furrows on her time-worn face. After a few moments she gave her verdict. 'It could be him. Mind you, he had a beard back then and I only saw him at a distance.' She squinted at the picture again. 'There is a resemblance.'

Wesley felt a thrill of triumph; the triumph of a man who's gambled on an outsider who's just come romping home to win against the odds.

'His name's Robert Valdun. Did you ever hear that name mentioned?'

'I didn't move in their circles so I was never introduced,' she said bitterly.

'Can you tell me anything you remember about him, however small?'

'I told you everything last time you came. If I was you, I'd ask Staniland.'

When he stood up to leave she looked worried. Maybe, in spite of her cold welcome, she didn't want him to go.

'Are you sure there's nothing else you want to tell me?'

'Quite sure. Now if you've finished, I've got things to do.'

'Take care.' Wesley touched her arm and she flinched at the gesture of sympathy as if he'd stubbed out a lighted cigarette on her flesh.

'Are you going to speak to Staniland?' she asked.

Wesley nodded.

'Then maybe it should be you who needs to take care,' she muttered, slamming the door behind him.

35

Karl Banville sensed Raynard Bishop's excitement throbbing down the phone line as he announced that he'd made an important discovery. Karl, used to Bishop's tendency to overdramatise, made the appropriate noises and told him to bring his new find round, assuming it was something to do with his precious puppets.

His disappointment at the discovery of the young woman's skeleton in the walled garden still stung. But the work would carry on until he found what he was looking for. He was a rich man, and could afford to fund the excavation for as long as it took.

As he left the confines of the house to head for the walled garden he turned to look back and glimpsed something in one of the first-floor windows. He'd seen it before; that impression of a human shape, shifting and misty, there for a second then gone. If anybody had told him a few years ago that he'd start believing in ghosts, he'd have said they were crazy, but since he'd begun to delve into his family tree – his very roots – many things had changed.

When he heard a car engine approaching up the drive he stood alert like an animal scenting a potential predator, hoping it wasn't Archie Jones who habitually ignored such legal niceties as trespass. However, when the car appeared he recognised it as Raynard Bishop's and fixed a smile of welcome to his face as Bishop sprang from the driver's seat waving a small, dirty-looking book.

'My friend Peter bought it online from a dealer who was doing a house clearance in Somerset.'

Bishop thrust the book towards him and Banville caught a whiff of old paper.

'It's Mary's journal,' Bishop gloated. 'I knew it existed somewhere.'

'Does it prove William's innocence?' If it didn't, Banville couldn't share Bishop's enthusiasm.

'Read it for yourself but take good care of it and let me have it back as soon as possible.'

Banville took the book and opened it carefully at the first page, his hand shaking with nerves.

It was approaching seven o'clock when Wesley called the office to see whether Brian Restorick had been brought in for questioning. A subdued Gerry answered in the negative. After Restorick had played his round of golf he'd told his companions he was going home but he'd never turned up. Mrs Restorick was worried and all patrols were on the lookout.

When Wesley said he wanted to speak to Wynn Staniland again Gerry sounded a note of caution. 'We'll have to take care he doesn't complain of harassment.'

'We've no choice, Gerry. Ethel Rinton seemed pretty sure the Oxford suspect, Robert Valdun, used to stay at Addersacre around the time Staniland's wife died.'

'Was this before or after the murder of Suzie Grant?'

'Suzie died in 1968 and Rosemary killed herself in 1983.'

'So Valdun disappears when he realises the Oxford police are about to charge him and he leaves his clothes on the beach so everyone assumes he's topped himself. Then a few years later he turns up at Addersacre. If this Ethel Rinton's right, Staniland was hiding a man on the run.'

'Valdun's prints were found at the Arts Festival offices which means he's still around. We need to see what Staniland knows about it.'

Gerry paused. 'Every stone we turn over we find Wynn Staniland underneath.'

Wesley made a number of calls to Oxford; some to the police there and some to the university. If possible he wanted to speak to Staniland's old tutor. The author was now seventy so he hadn't held out much hope but, to his surprise, he managed to get a name – a Professor Pargeter, long retired and, if he was still alive, well into his nineties. Now it was a question of tracking him down.

They decided to postpone their visit to Wynn Staniland until the following morning. They'd turn up first thing, Wesley said, and hopefully catch him off guard.

Gerry left work first that evening, saying he had important things to see to. Since Alison's arrival on the scene he'd felt the need to be more secretive, even though it went against his nature. He hadn't told Wesley that Rosie had found out about his secret daughter's existence. It was something he needed to sort out himself.

By the time he reached Baynard's Quay the sun was beginning to go down and the drinkers, a cross section of holidaymakers and yachting types in spotless white jeans, were spilling out of the Tradmouth Arms onto the waterside benches. It was a warm evening and he couldn't blame them for making the most of it.

He opened the front door, hoping Alison had changed her mind and decided to stay a few more days. But he was greeted by the kind of heavy silence found only in a house that has known centuries of souls, in this case seafaring ones. He closed the door behind him and called Alison's name. There was no reply.

Gerry arrived at work early the next morning, marching in without a word of greeting and shutting himself in his office. When Wesley offered to take over the morning briefing Gerry said yes: there were things he needed to do. Wesley knew something was wrong but, for the time being, Gerry didn't seem prepared to share and he was unwilling to intrude on his privacy.

'Restorick's still not turned up,' Gerry said when Wesley was about to leave his office. 'His wife's reported him missing.'

'Think he's avoiding us?'

Gerry turned his Biro over and over in his fingers. 'All patrols are on the lookout for him. Think he's our man, Wes?'

'Not sure but we need to find him.'

'Somehow I can't see him killing the Lombards, can you?'

Gerry was right. There was a chance the Lombards' deaths had nothing to do with Jamie Hursthead. But the

Staniland connection to all three deaths nagged away at the back of his mind.

As soon as the briefing was over Wesley drove to Wynn Staniland's house with Rachel. In the bright morning sunlight Addersacre looked even more shabby and neglected than he remembered and the rambling rose around the doorway blossomed with desiccated brown blooms. Even in the height of summer, with the rest of Devon lush and green, the place had a dead feel about it.

Staniland greeted them with resignation and led them into the drawing room. He moved slowly, as though he'd suddenly aged, and Wesley could sense little of the charisma that had been so evident at their last meeting, almost as though the man could no longer be bothered to make the effort.

There was no sign of Perdita and when Wesley asked where she was the answer was vague. She was in the garden or she might have gone for a swim. She liked swimming.

Wesley was glad of the chance to talk to Staniland alone without the protective presence of his stepdaughter and he wasted no time. He produced the photograph of Robert Valdun and, as Staniland studied it, he caught Rachel's eye. Today she'd scraped her hair back in a neat bun which made her look severe and formidable. Perhaps this was the impression she wanted to give.

'Where did you get this?'

Wesley ignored Staniland's question and asked one of his own. 'Do you recognise him?'

'Should I?'

'I understand he was a friend of yours.'

'What gave you that idea?'

'Was he or wasn't he?'

'He looks familiar, although it's not a good picture – a mugshot, isn't that what you call it?'

'So who is he?'

Staniland waited several moments before replying, as though he was weighing up how much to reveal. 'OK. I used to know him a lifetime ago. His name was Robert and he was up at Oxford with me but he dropped out in his third year as I remember. Problems with drugs. Some people can't handle the pressure. Sad.'

'The story goes that he killed a woman and went on the run. His clothes were found on a beach. Everyone assumed he was dead.'

Staniland's expression gave nothing away.

'It now looks as though his suicide was faked.' He paused to let his words sink in. 'We have reason to believe he was staying here at this house a few years later. Did you help him get away?'

'That's ridiculous,' Staniland muttered.

'He was seen here at about the time your wife died and we have evidence that he's still around. Have you seen him recently?'

Staniland handed the picture back and shook his head. 'I hardly knew the man at Oxford and I doubt if I'd know him if I saw him again now. People change. *Anno Domini* and all that.'

'But he came here when your wife was alive?'

A flicker of alarm passed across Staniland's face. 'You've been misinformed, Inspector. I'm sorry you've had *another* wasted journey.'

The door opened and Perdita stepped into the room. Her hair was hanging in damp strands, suggesting Staniland had been right about the swimming. She looked at her stepfather enquiringly.

'The officers are just going, my dear.'

Wesley felt the urge to stand his ground but he knew it would be a futile gesture. They would learn no more until they could confront Staniland with solid proof.

'He's lying,' Rachel said as they walked back to the car. 'He's not even good at it.'

'Unless Mrs Rinton's mistaken.'

'Do you think she is?'

Wesley shook his head but he couldn't be absolutely sure. While Ethel Rinton had appeared to recognise the photograph all right, he wouldn't have put it past her to indulge in a spot of mischief-making.

Now all he had to do was to find out whether it was Staniland or Ethel who was telling the truth.

36

The female skeleton found in the grounds of Newfield Manor had been removed for further examination. But, while Neil and his colleagues were keen to know how the unknown woman came to be there, Karl Banville dismissed the mystery as an irrelevance. His only question was how soon the diggers could carry on seeking their real goal: the body of William Banville.

Because Karl Banville was footing the bill Neil was in no position to object, so he left Emily to extend the trench where the skeleton had been found.

Banville stood watching in silence and Neil saw him take something from his pocket and stare at it intently. He was close enough to see it was the photograph of William Banville.

'Keep digging,' Banville said, returning the photograph to his pocket. 'I'm going to the village to get lunch.'

Banville's constant scrutiny was getting on Neil's nerves and when he walked away Neil felt relieved. He'd just lifted some flagstones to reveal compacted earth alive with wriggling worms when he heard a shout from the newly extended summerhouse trench.

'I think there's another one.'

He abandoned work and rushed over to where Emily was working. She was standing perfectly still, pointing at the creamy white orb of a skull peeping from the soil. Neil could see the brow above the eye sockets, thick and prominent.

The skeleton wasn't buried as deeply as the first and this time it was definitely male. Neil made the obligatory calls to the police and the coroner before calling the forensic anthropologist back. She joked that he was keeping her busy while the coroner's officer said wearily that he hoped there weren't any more. Wesley, on the other hand, sounded interested and promised to come over to have a look as soon as he was free.

While Neil was waiting for them all to arrive, he watched as painstaking work continued to release the bones from the earth. Emily was working on the hands with a delicate leaf trowel and when she stopped what she was doing and spoke, he gave her his full attention.

'I think the middle finger on the left hand's missing. I can't see it in the soil . . .'

'You sure?' In Neil's experience the small bones of a skeleton's fingers and toes can often go astray.

'What's that you said?'

Neil swung round. Karl Banville had returned and he was standing at the edge of the trench with a wrapped sandwich in his hand. Emily repeated what she'd told Neil and Banville's eyes lit up with excitement.

'We've found him,' he announced loudly. He took something from his pocket then passed it to Emily. She took it gingerly in her soil-stained hands, holding the thing by the edges. It was the old sepia photograph Neil had seen before.

'If it is him,' Neil said as Emily handed the picture back, 'it means he didn't run away. He died here and someone buried him here in the walled garden a few feet away from the woman. A double grave later covered by a substantial summerhouse. You've got your proof at last, Karl.'

A look of sheer triumph appeared on Banville's face, the sort of look Neil had only seen before on gold medal winners standing on the podium at the Olympics.

'Jenny. It's Pam. Michael's forgotten his bag. Shall I pop it round?'

There was silence at the other end of the line.

'You there, Jenny?'

'Yes, Pam. Sorry. I thought you said something about Michael's bag.'

'That's right. He is staying the night with Nathaniel, isn't he? Or shall I pick him up?'

Another silence. Then: 'Pam, I think you've made a mistake. Michael's not here. Hang on, I'll go and ask Nathaniel if he knows anything.'

Pam felt a paralysing panic rising inside her. Michael wasn't where he said he'd be. Her son was missing and every dreadful scenario ran through her head. Headlines about missing children flashed up; visions of fatal accidents and predatory paedophiles. She felt helpless, like screaming.

She heard Jenny's voice again, full of sympathy like a doctor breaking bad news; like the doctor who'd told her about her cancer.

'I'm sorry, Pam, Nathaniel doesn't know where he is.

Look, is there anything I can do? Have you contacted his other friends? I can make a few calls if you like.'

Pam felt tears stinging her eyes as she took a deep, calming breath. 'Thanks, Jenny. If you could.'

'I'll ring you as soon as I hear anything,' Jenny said.

Pam shut her eyes. She had to think. There was one number she could try. Michael had been told he couldn't go to Harry Jones's but now she hoped – prayed – that he was there.

Journal of Mary Lipton

16 June 1884

I am a married woman and yet I have no joy of it. When John took me to his father's house I was quite unprepared for what I would see. I had thought him a gentleman and he had lied when he told me his father was a physician in Taunton. When I challenged him he laughed and said his father, as a blacksmith, is adept at treating horses so he lied but a little.

John agreed that we should return to Whitely and that I should throw myself on my father's mercy. He said we must do all in our power to prevent him from altering his will. I am his flesh and blood after all.

Father received me in his study on my arrival. I was prepared for his anger but nothing prepared me for his cold indifference and the news that he has summoned Mr Bearstowe, his solicitor, to attend him tomorrow. I know what this heralds: I am to be disinherited; thrown out without a penny as punishment for my hasty marriage.

John is awaiting me in my chamber with Sarah, who is unpacking my valise while John lies on my bed, the bed I have slept in since childhood, watching her. He stands and I see him glance at Sarah as though they are conspirators. How my distress causes me to imagine all sorts of evil.

'Because of you my inheritance is lost,' I say, close to tears, and he tells me I am wrong.

I do not understand how he can remain so calm.

37

They had their costumes – a pair of white sheets pinched from Harry's airing cupboard – which they stuffed into rucksacks before climbing into Archie's car. Archie had promised them a percentage of his profits. Even so, as they drove down the narrow lanes towards Whitely, Michael was starting to have misgivings, especially when he caught sight of the ruined house squatting in its overgrown garden like an ogre's palace. It had no roof and the windows looked like pits of darkness where something evil might be hiding.

Archie told them it was easy to get inside through the ground-floor windows or, failing that, through a door round the back that was falling off its hinges. Their job was to crouch behind the front bay window when they heard Archie's minibus arrive and then flit across the empty windows. They had orders to keep it subtle: no ghostly whooping or waving of sheets. It had to be believable; nothing more than a tantalising glimpse.

Archie was going off to pick up the punters in Tradmouth

and he'd be back in half an hour. In the meantime, they were on their own.

'You're not scared are you?' Harry said with relish.

'Course not.'

He climbed through the window and Michael scrambled in after him. It was gloomy inside the house and, although the upper floors had vanished long ago, the ruined partition walls still stood, separating the rooms and turning the place into a shadowy maze. After a few moments Harry tore off to explore, leaving Michael alone, frozen to the spot, listening. Then he heard Harry calling and when he followed the sound he found him in a room at the far end of the house where the skeleton of a large bay window overlooked a garden long returned to nature.

'How long till Archie comes back?' Michael asked. Although it was a warm night he was shivering with cold.

'He won't be long. They found a body here, you know.'

'Yeah, I know. My Uncle Neil found it. He's an archaeologist,' he said, hoping this might impress.

'Want to see if it's still there?'

'They'll have moved it. Let's go out to the front.'

'Why? Feeling spooked?'

'Course not. But we can't see Archie arriving from here.' Michael made a great effort to sound nonchalant. When he'd agreed to the venture, when he'd lied about staying at Nathaniel's, Harry's plan had sounded like fun; now though it felt like a mistake. He fingered the mobile phone in his pocket, tempted to call his dad. But he'd get into trouble for lying and besides, such a loss of face was out of the question.

He'd started to make for the front door when he heard Harry whisper, 'What's that?'

'It's just an engine. Must be your brother.'

'Too early.' For the first time Harry sounded uneasy.
'Builders?'

Harry bobbed down behind the window and Michael
did the same. A car door slammed somewhere in the distance and there were voices. Men's voices, getting closer.

'Come and see the house,' he heard one of them say and
when he caught Harry's eye Michael saw that his companion's bravado had vanished and he looked as terrified as
he was.

'Run,' Harry hissed. But as they neared the door three
large figures blocked their exit.

'You're trespassing.' The man's accent was American and
he sounded angry.

Harry dodged forward past the men but Michael was too
slow. He was stuck there in that maze of crumbling walls
and in his panic he couldn't remember the way out.

Michael edged away until his back came into contact
with a mossy wall, cold as dead flesh. Then, in the gloom,
he saw a doorway, a dark rectangle in the wall. He darted
towards it, hoping it would lead to a way out, but as soon as
he crossed over the shadowy threshold he knew he'd made
a mistake.

The floor plunged away and when he tumbled into the
void he felt a sharp pain.

Wesley had felt uncomfortable about Michael's friendship with Harry ever since the boys had pocketed Jamie
Hursthead's valuables but he'd assumed, perhaps optimisti-
cally, that a telling-off from Gerry had done the trick. Now
he bitterly regretted not keeping a closer eye on his son. On
the other hand, Michael had deceived them about where

he was spending the night and Wesley knew only too well that the forbidden could be enticing.

When he received the call from his sobbing son, he didn't hesitate. He drove too fast down the narrow lanes to Whitely, his mind fuddled with anxiety. Michael was in trouble. He was hurt. He called Pam to say their son had been in touch and that he was safe. He'd call her again when he knew more.

He knew the way to Newfield Manor because he'd looked in when Neil found his skeletons. In the gathering twilight the place looked more threatening than before.

He put his foot down and the car bounced its way down the drive. As he hit the brake he saw three men standing beside a Range Rover but there was no sign of Michael and his heart lurched with panic. He slammed the car door behind him and rushed over.

To his relief he saw Michael sitting in the back seat of the Range Rover, looking small and frightened, and he felt a sudden rush of the parental protective instinct that had kicked in the moment his children were born.

Ignoring the men who were hovering there as if they had no idea what to do, he leaned into the car to give the boy a reassuring hug. Michael only stopped short of flinging himself against Wesley's body when he realised he was too old for that sort of thing.

Wesley recognised two of the men as Karl Banville and Raynard Bishop from the Dukesbridge Literary Festival. The third man had sloped off into the shadows of the ruined manor as though he was embarrassed by the potentially awkward scene and didn't want to get involved.

Banville, Neil's erstwhile benefactor, spoke first. 'I think he's twisted his ankle,' he said. 'He was trespassing with another boy and—'

Wesley turned to Michael. He was his priority now. 'You all right?'

Michael sniffed and nodded.

'Can you walk?'

As if to demonstrate, Michael slid off the seat and limped a few steps.

'Nothing broken,' Raynard Bishop said with forced bonhomie.

'He said they were playing ghosts,' said Banville. 'Archie Jones put them up to it. They were trespassing on private property.'

'But you won't be pressing charges, Mr Banville,' Wesley said, making a great effort to maintain a cool professionalism. He left Michael's side and ushered Banville out of earshot.

'No harm's been done and I think they've learned their lesson, don't you?' He looked at Michael, head bowed and contrite, tears staining his face, and could have added that at least one of them had. 'Besides, my son's been hurt. This place is in a dangerous state and there's nothing to stop children wandering in here. Health and Safety would have a field day.'

He held his breath and watched Banville's expression change from determination to indecision.

'Boys will be boys and all that,' said Raynard Bishop who had edged towards them to listen to the exchange. 'We've met before, Inspector. You'll remember you came to question me about Zac Wilkinson's murder.'

'Of course,' Wesley said. 'Well, if you don't mind, Mr Banville, I'm going to take my son to A & E to get that leg checked out.'

Banville bowed his head. 'Of course.'

Wesley hadn't paid much attention to the third man who was hovering half out of sight in the doorway of the ruined building. But as he began to make for the car, supporting Michael, the stranger stepped forward and, although the light had almost faded, Wesley could see him properly for the first time.

Wesley settled Michael in the passenger seat and told him not to move before retracing his steps.

'We haven't been introduced,' said Wesley, studying the stranger's face in the dim light.

'This is Peter Walsingham. He's staying with me,' said Bishop, as though he was introducing a friend at a normal social occasion.

Walsingham offered his hand to Wesley, who took it. The man's palms were damp.

With a glance towards Michael, Wesley took his notebook from his pocket, playing the efficient copper. 'If you gentlemen could write down your names and addresses, just in case there are any repercussions and we need to speak to you again.'

Once the three men had obliged, Wesley thanked them before joining his son in the car and slipping the notebook carefully into an evidence bag he had in his pocket.

'How's the leg?' he asked when they were halfway down the drive.

'It hurts. We were only messing about.' The boy was on the verge of tears.

Wesley was angry; angry about the lies and about the worry Pam had had to endure. She'd sounded shaken when he'd spoken to her. This was something she could do without.

Harry had made his escape, leaving Michael hurt, badly

for all he knew. Wesley intended to make sure someone in uniform visited the Jones household to have a word.

Before Wesley could say anything, a minibus loomed ahead of them, travelling towards the house.

'It's Archie with his ghost tour people,' Michael said.

Wesley stopped the car and when he flashed his headlights the minibus came to a screeching halt.

He wound the window down. 'I wouldn't go up there if I were you.'

Without a word Archie Jones turned the minibus round and Wesley saw a row of curious faces staring out at him. If they'd hoped for a glimpse of spectral activity at Newfield Manor, they were in for a disappointment.

Wesley drove in silence, aware of his son brooding in the passenger seat. When they were halfway to Tradmouth he spoke again, his voice shaking. 'I'm upset because you lied to us. Your mum was worried sick and you could have been badly hurt.'

'I never thought . . . ' Michael had started to sob and Wesley was sure his message had got through this time. 'I'll send someone round to have a word with Harry in the morning.'

But Harry Jones wasn't the only problem on his mind. If his suspicions were correct, the killer of Suzie Grant had just returned from the dead to be near his old friend, Wynn Staniland.

38

Now that Alison had returned to work in the exclusive clothes shop in Liverpool One, Devon seemed a long way away. Yet as she served the customers, she couldn't tear her thoughts away from that cobbled quayside in Tradmouth where her real father lived. She'd travelled to the South-West without a plan but the decision about her future had been made for her by her father's daughter – her new-found half-sister. Rosie Heffernan had treated her like an interloper, which was understandable. Though it still hurt.

Just before closing time an encounter with an awkward customer, the wife of a premiership footballer who treated her like a junior housemaid, put her in a bad mood, as did the late arrival of her bus home. So when she reached her terraced house in Aigburth she wasn't in any mood to continue sorting through her late mother's things; the things piled high on the chair awaiting her attention.

But she knew the sooner she did it, the sooner the pile would disappear so, after eating the M&S meal for one she'd bought for herself that lunchtime, she switched on the TV to provide the illusion of company, and began work.

The first shoebox she opened contained photographs and she started to sift through them, glad that her mother had had the foresight to write comments on the back. Discovering the old photographs resurrected memories, good and bad, and she sat cross-legged on the floor, surrounded by images of her childhood. Relatives she hadn't seen for years and embarrassing fashions. Near the bottom of the box she found pictures of her mother that must have been taken in the years before Alison was born. Her mother looked so young in them . . . and glamorous; a carefree girl dressed up to the nines. In one she was with a young man and Alison turned the picture over to read what was written on the back.

Me with Gerry.

As Alison studied the picture closely she felt light-headed and her heart began to thump in her chest. She needed to speak to the man she'd started to think of as her father again.

The next morning she rang her boss at the shop to say she wasn't feeling well and set off back to Devon.

Neil had agreed that his team would work at weekends and since the developments in the walled garden it would have taken a lot to keep him away. As soon as he arrived at Newfield Manor on Sunday morning Karl Banville took him to one side.

'We had some trouble here last night. Kids trespassing. One of them hurt himself. It was a good job I was showing

Raynard Bishop and his friend over the Manor. If nobody had been here the kid could have been trapped. His father's that policeman friend of yours.'

'Is Michael all right?' Neil sounded worried.

'The kid's fine. Twisted ankle and injured pride. I said I wouldn't press charges.'

'Very good of you,' Neil said with a hint of irony, resolving to call Wesley later to get his version of events.

'I invited Raynard and his friend over because he's made an important discovery.'

He went on to tell Neil that Bishop's friend, the second-hand book dealer, had located a journal apparently written by Mary Field. Mary's name didn't actually appear but the journal told the familiar story of her terrible fate. William Banville's clumsy courtship; the clandestine romance with John Lipton and the secret wedding, followed by the untimely deaths of Mary's wealthy parents. The trouble was, the last entry had been made a couple of weeks before the writer's death so it threw no light on what had actually happened.

'Have you got it with you?' Neil asked, curious to see it for himself.

Banville delved into his pocket and took out a small, leather-bound book. 'Raynard's lent it to me with strict instructions to take good care of it.' He wrinkled his nose. 'It's quite disparaging about William. Mary Field must have been a bitch.'

Neil took the book from Banville's outstretched hand.

'I'll read it during my lunch break. Is there anything in it that helps us identify our female skeleton?'

Banville shook his head. 'But I'm sure whoever killed William also buried the woman, aren't you?'

'Well, we know the skeleton can't be Mary. She's buried in the parish church.'

To Neil's relief Banville left the team to it for the rest of the morning and when lunchtime arrived Neil made for the pop-up gazebo which served as a site hut to enjoy the sandwich he'd bought at the supermarket on his way to Whitely. Once he'd settled down to fill his stomach he began reading Mary Field's journal.

Banville was right. The story was there although, frustratingly, there were no entries for the period leading up to Mary's death. However, it was the deaths of her parents that caught his interest first. Both had apparently died of some sort of food poisoning and Mary and her new husband regarded their deaths as part of the great scheme of things and asked no questions. Neil reflected that they lived in an age where death was a constant companion so perhaps it had been easier back then to accept tragedy philosophically. On the other hand, perhaps they weren't keen to encourage the authorities to examine things too closely and in Neil's opinion the writer's account seemed remarkably callous.

Soon after Mary's clandestine wedding and her parents' deaths, she and her new husband had summoned the family solicitor to make wills. She left her darling John everything she possessed and John did likewise, although everything he possessed had originally belonged to his wife. There was a vague mention of further provisions although Mary didn't go into detail, but it planted a seed in Neil's mind. He recognised the name of the solicitor in Tradmouth and, as luck would have it, the firm still existed and his colleague Emily's father was one of the present-day partners. Which meant it might be possible to do some detective work.

He made his way to the interior of the house where a

trench had just been opened and spoke to Emily, who was hard at work with a spade, clearing the ground in order to find the original floor.

'Emily, can I have a word?' he said. And when he explained his plans her face lit up with the excitement of the chase.

Wesley left Michael in bed, his leg bandaged and his confidence bruised. Playing the stern paterfamilias didn't come easily to Wesley so he hadn't given him a hard time when they'd returned from A & E, and Pam had just been relieved that her son was safe.

When he reached the station first thing the following morning there were things he wanted to follow up. The officer he'd spoken to in Oxford had provided contact details for Professor Pargeter, who was in his nineties and still enjoying a peaceful retirement in the Cotswolds. Jamie Hursthead's agent, Bella Cross, had mentioned that her client had travelled to the Cotswolds in the course of his research, and Wesley wondered whether Pargeter had been the reason for his visit.

When he called the professor he was relieved to discover that the man's mind and memory were as sharp as ever. And after Pargeter confirmed that he had indeed spoken to the man who'd introduced himself as Zac Wilkinson, an interesting conversation followed that helped to clarify things in Wesley's mind ... and raised several new possibilities.

Wesley also sent his notebook off to be examined for fingerprints, saying he needed the results back as soon as possible. By eleven o'clock he had his answer.

He'd already established that Raynard Bishop's friend,

Peter Walsingham, was a book dealer based in Scotland who did a good deal of his business online. His second-hand and rare book business seemed modestly successful and must have provided him with a living that, although not lavish, was probably comfortable. However, when he delved further into the man's background, he found that there was no record of a Peter Walsingham of the appropriate age in any official records before 1992. At first Wesley wondered whether he'd been living abroad but when the fingerprint results came back he knew there was a more sinister explanation.

Wesley had to share what he'd learned – or rather what he hadn't learned – with Gerry. But first Gerry had news of his own to impart.

'Brian Restorick's been picked up. He was with a . . . lady. Turns out they've been carrying on for years.'

Wesley slumped down in his chair. 'Has it been checked out?'

Gerry nodded. 'His wife was in the dark. And after what happened to their son . . . '

'He couldn't leave her.'

'He says it was his wife who threatened the Hurstheads. It looks as though he couldn't take the strain any longer, what with everything being dug up again. He says he went to stay with his girlfriend for a few days because he just couldn't face going home.'

'You have to feel sorry for him.'

'He didn't do it, Wes. I'm pretty sure of that.'

'What about the wife? They gave each other an alibi for the time of Hursthead's murder.'

'She doesn't drive. Besides, I've had someone checking whether Restorick's car was out and about that night and it wasn't caught on any of our cameras. Nor was any car registered to Kieran State or his known associates. I reckon they're both in the clear. It's back to square one,' he said with a despondent sigh.

Wesley's news couldn't wait any longer. He hoped it would cheer Gerry up.

'I've found Robert Valdun,' said Wesley. The DCI listened intently as he recounted everything he'd learned.

'So he's staying with Raynard Bishop and using the name Peter Walsingham? Are you sure?'

'His prints match the ones Thames Valley sent over. There's no doubt about it.'

'You've actually seen him?'

Wesley hesitated, reluctant to talk about Michael's latest trouble. Revealing to Gerry that his stern telling-off of a few days ago had had no effect on the boy might seem like a criticism. 'Yes, I met him last night. His face seemed familiar but I couldn't be certain. A lot of time's passed since that picture was taken.'

'If we can pull him in for the Oxford murder I'm sure Thames Valley will be delighted. When's he being picked up?'

'It's not that straightforward, Gerry. I think he might be connected with our recent murders as well. Ethel Rinton told us he used to stay with Wynn Staniland so if Hursthead found out Staniland sheltered a murderer . . . '

'What about the Lombards?'

'Not sure yet. But I don't think Staniland's told us the whole truth about his dealings with Gina.'

'If she knew about Staniland harbouring Valdun she might have been blackmailing him. Perhaps that's where Frank's riches were going to come from.'

'But why wait all this time?' Wesley sighed. 'We'd better go and have yet another word with Mr Staniland.'

The officers sent to Bishop's address found nobody at home. Then on Wesley's suggestion they spoke to Karl Banville at the swish riverside apartment in Tradmouth he was using for the duration of his visit but he swore he'd had no communication with Peter Walsingham since the previous night.

Wesley knew one person who might be able to help. He called Della, only to discover that Bishop had been expected at the Festival offices that morning but he hadn't turned up. Once he'd managed to get his mother-in-law off the phone, he began to wonder whether his unexpected encounter with the man who was calling himself Peter Walsingham the previous night had caused Bishop to panic. Or, if Walsingham thought his true identity was about to be revealed, maybe there was a chance that Bishop was in danger.

To Wesley the obvious place to look was Addersacre, the home of Robert Valdun's old friend from his Oxford days. Wesley knew Staniland would be heartily sick of their intrusion into his well-guarded privacy by now but he had no choice.

Gerry insisted on going with him, saying that Wesley might be awed by these literary types but he didn't intend to pussyfoot around. Wesley allowed himself a secret smile at the boss's assumptions. It wasn't that Staniland overawed him, it was just that the man was an enigma he hadn't quite managed to work out yet and dealing with him required tact.

When they arrived at Addersacre Perdita greeted them with 'Not you again,' as if they were persistent cold callers who wouldn't give up.

'Afraid so,' said Wesley. 'We need to ask a few more questions.'

Perdita mumbled something about a solicitor.

'That's your choice, Ms Staniland,' said Wesley. 'Is your stepfather at home?'

She hesitated, as if she was tempted to deny it, then disappeared upstairs, leaving them waiting in the hallway.

'Do you reckon they've got Valdun hidden somewhere?' Gerry asked gleefully. 'Shoved him in a priest hole maybe?'

Before Wesley could reply Wynn Staniland appeared at the top of the stairs.

'You're wasting your time,' he said as if he was humouring a pair of backward children. 'I've told you everything I know.'

He descended the staircase stiffly, Perdita hovering behind him protectively. Wesley suspected he was putting on the old man act for their benefit.

They followed Staniland into the drawing room where they sat facing him. In spite of the warmth of the August day, his devoted stepdaughter draped a tartan rug over his knees. Wesley suspected this was another piece of theatre, designed to make them feel guilty about harassing a vulnerable pensioner. Yet Staniland looked anything but vulnerable as he watched them, taking in every detail of his adversaries as though he was storing the information for future battles. Wesley sensed his sharp intelligence. He'd seen him use charm and now he was using weakness; and Wesley couldn't help wondering about the real Wynn Staniland behind the masks he chose to wear.

'We're looking for Robert Valdun,' Wesley began. 'Did you know he was staying in the area?'

A look of frustration appeared on Perdita's face as her

father shook his head. 'We've already told you, Father knew him slightly at Oxford but that was back in the nineteen sixties. He hasn't seen him for years.'

Staniland looked perfectly calm but Wesley saw his knuckles turn white as he tightened his grip on the arms of his chair.

'Do you know where Robert Valdun is?'

Staniland shook his head vigorously and Perdita placed a comforting hand on his shoulder. 'You seem to know more about him than I do.'

'Do you have a secret, Mr Staniland? Did Zac Wilkinson discover something in the course of his research? Something you were desperate to keep quiet? Something connected with Robert Valdun?'

There was a split second of silence before Perdita spoke. 'This is beginning to feel like harassment.'

'Tell us everything you know about Robert Valdun and maybe we'll leave you in peace,' said Wesley. 'I think you sheltered him when he was on the run after faking his suicide following the Oxford murder.'

'Robert killed himself and you can't prove otherwise.'

'He's staying a few miles away from here . . . in a village called Whitely? I saw him last night.'

Staniland turned his head and stared out of the window. 'You're mistaken, Inspector.'

'Has Valdun been in contact?'

'No.'

Wesley heard a soft creak which seemed to come from the ceiling above their heads. It might have been one of the inevitable sounds of an old house. Or it might have been a footstep.

'Is he here now?'

'Of course not.'

'We can get a search warrant.' Gerry made it sound like a threat.

Perdita Staniland stood up, blocking Wesley's view of her father.

'Come back when you've got one. But you won't find anything.'

She was calling their bluff. Wesley made a move to leave and Gerry followed. 'If Valdun gets in touch, you will let us know,' Wesley said to Perdita when they reached the front door.

'Of course.' Perdita sounded relieved that she was getting rid of them at last.

'We should have stayed,' Gerry said once the front door had closed behind them.

'Did you see it?'

'What?'

'The jacket hanging on the stand in the hall. It had a pin on the lapel. Dukesbridge Literary Festival.'

'So?'

'Staniland refused to have anything to do with the festival.'

'Are we going to get that warrant?'

'If we leave now he'll be gone by the time we get back,' Wesley said before retracing his steps to the front door.

'What are you doing?'

Wesley didn't answer. Ignoring the front door he walked round the house. When he reached the drawing-room window he stopped and signalled to Gerry to keep back, then leaned forward, trying to see without being seen. After a few moments he turned to Gerry with a thumbs-up signal.

They circled the house until they reached the back door.

Wesley tried the handle and the door swung open silently as though the hinges had been recently oiled.

It was his lucky day.

Ethel Rinton hoped she hadn't told the police too much. It would be a shame to spoil things now she knew the truth. Knowledge can be used to your advantage.

In her lonely, silent hours she often thought about her husband's death, reliving it over and over again. People didn't realise that poison was a terrible way to die. Someone had to pay for what happened to Eric and now at last she had the chance to take her revenge; to come out on top for once in her life.

When Zac Wilkinson turned up to talk to her, she'd shared her suspicions with him, even though she hadn't been absolutely certain back then. With hindsight she knew it had been stupid to say so much but he'd been the first person who'd taken her seriously in years. He'd provided a sympathetic ear and the facts, as she knew them, had tumbled out before she could stop herself. Now Wilkinson was dead, murdered, and she couldn't help wondering if this was because he'd followed up what she'd told him. Maybe he'd dug too deep and awoken the sleeping serpent.

When Eric was alive he'd kept newspaper cuttings about his employer, Wynn Staniland. Staniland been lauded as a genius. He'd won prizes and awards and this had made him and his private life public property. Eric had been proud to tell everyone that he worked for someone famous and he'd revered Staniland as some sort of hero. Ethel had always suspected the Stanilands sneered at her husband in private.

Being the gardener's wife, she'd had little to do with the family back then, although that didn't mean she hadn't used Eric as a source of salacious gossip. She'd taken an interest in the goings-on at Addersacre and Jane Whitsun, the housekeeper who'd also called herself Mr Staniland's secretary, had been the focus of particular curiosity. She knew Staniland had been carrying on with her behind his poor wife's back but in those days his behaviour had been excused by his fame. Ethel had talked to a woman who'd tried to read one of his books once and she said it was incomprehensible rubbish; give her a good Mills and Boon any day.

After Eric's death there had been no more pieces about Staniland snipped out of the newspaper and Ethel had stuffed the box of cuttings out of sight in the back of a drawer in the spare bedroom. However, she still liked to keep reports of local crimes – preferably murders – gloating over the details in her long, lonely hours and trying to piece the mysteries together. She'd often thought she'd have made a good policewoman but when she was young that hadn't been an option.

She kept her crime reports in a cardboard folder by the TV and she opened it now because there was something she wanted to check; something about the couple who'd been found dead in that caravan.

She located the cutting she was looking for and stared at the photograph of the couple in summer clothes, taken in happier times. 'Can you help us trace this couple's movements?' the caption said. But it wasn't their movements that interested Ethel. She'd always thought something was badly wrong at Addersacre and now she knew what it was.

39

Staniland and his stepdaughter had lied. Robert Valdun had been there under their roof. He'd disappeared upstairs as soon as Wesley and Gerry arrived, sneaking down again as soon as they'd left. Wesley had seen him through the window, talking to the Stanilands in their drawing room, smirking at the idiocy of the local force. If Wesley hadn't heard that soft footstep in the room above, he would have missed out on the satisfaction of bringing him in for questioning.

As it was they called a patrol car to transport him back to the interview suite at Tradmouth Police Station and the man who'd been introduced to Wesley as Peter Walsingham the previous night wore a puzzled look on his face as he climbed into the back, as though he wasn't quite sure why he was being taken in for questioning. But the act didn't fool Wesley for a moment.

Before they returned to the station Wesley wanted to hear what Staniland had to say for himself. Perdita had left her stepfather alone to face the questioning and when he asked where she was he was told she'd gone to her room with a headache.

Staniland sat down and stared into space, as though he was trying to think up an explanation that would exonerate him from blame. Wynn was an accomplished weaver of tales so Wesley expected it to be a good one.

'You told us you hadn't seen Robert Valdun and yet he was here in your house.' He let the question hang in the air and inclined his head politely.

'He asked me not to tell anyone he was here. After what happened, he's wary of the police.'

Wesley saw Gerry's mouth fall open in astonishment.

'If he murdered someone that's hardly surprising. Why have you been shielding him, Mr Staniland? What hold does he have over you?'

The author looked away and Wesley knew he'd hit a nerve. He repeated the question.

'He's an old friend, that's all.'

'He's a murderer,' said Gerry.

'He assured me that girl's death was an accident.'

'Her name was Suzie Grant,' said Wesley, irritated. He sat forward so his face was closer to Staniland's. 'Did Zac Wilkinson find out about your relationship with Valdun? His cottage was burgled and his notes and laptop were taken. He discovered the truth about your friend, didn't he? He found out he was here when your wife died – and that he's still alive. He found out you've been shielding a murderer all these years.'

When there was no reply, Wesley carried on, his mind turning over the possibilities.

'I've been wondering why your books stopped after your

317

wife's death. I don't think it was grief. You'd been conduct-ing an affair with your housekeeper.'

Staniland said nothing.

'Robert Valdun left this house soon after Rosemary died, didn't he? Just when you needed a friend he abandoned you. Why was that?'

Staniland looked at Wesley. 'Rosemary's death generated a lot of interest and Robert was afraid he'd be discovered so he thought it best to leave. I didn't hear from him for many years and it was a shock when he contacted me again a few weeks ago. He'd been living up in Scotland and he was down here visiting someone – something to do with his second-hand book business.' He swallowed. 'Only I think he really came back here because he'd heard about the biography.'

'He wanted to make sure his secret didn't come out.'

Staniland nodded slowly.

'I've spoken to Professor Pargeter. You remember your old tutor? He must have been a young man when you knew him but he's in his nineties now. However, there's nothing wrong with his memory.'

Staniland appeared to be surprised by the sudden change of subject. Then his face clouded with worry, as though he could guess what was coming.

'Professor Pargeter was very surprised at your success. According to him, you didn't have much talent.' Wesley let the words sink in for a moment. 'Let me tell you what I think happened. You'd been out of university a few years when you met Rosemary, a wealthy older woman. You came to live at Addersacre, her old family home, and you were an aspiring writer, except things weren't going well. Then your old friend, Robert, turns up. He'd disappeared years before

318

to avoid being arrested for murder and everyone assumed he was dead. Only I think you helped him escape.'

Staniland said nothing.

'Professor Pargeter was very keen to tell me that Robert Valdun displayed a prodigious talent in his student days – stunningly fresh and original was how he described it. He told Zac Wilkinson all this, by the way.'

He fixed his eyes on Staniland, who was staring ahead, as though in a trance.

'Robert was on the run, living abroad since murdering Suzie Grant, but when he turned up you didn't betray him to the police. On the contrary, you allowed him to move in with you and stay for as long as he wanted so he became part of the ménage here. Why was that?' Staniland stared out of the window, expressionless.

'Whatever hold he had over you, it must have been something major.' Wesley saw Gerry raise his eyebrows. 'I think Robert Valdun wrote your books. I think he turned up with the manuscripts but he couldn't do anything with them because he was a wanted man. Instead he agreed to publish them under your name and give you a share of the profits. You'd get the glory while he amassed a comfortable income. Then it all came to an end when Rosemary died.'

There was no mistaking the look of devastation on Wynn Staniland's face. His secret was out at last.

'Did Rosemary find out what was going on? Did Robert kill her? Or did you?'

Staniland sat perfectly still for a few seconds before answering in a whisper. 'She killed herself. Read the inquest report.'

'But I'm right about the books. Did Valdun write them?'

'Yes,' he said as though he found it painful to utter the word. 'And he's written five more in the intervening years.'

'Does he want you to publish them under your name again?'

Staniland nodded.

'How do you feel about that?'

'I've become used to a life of privacy on my own terms so I told him I didn't want to. That's what we were talking about when you turned up.'

'Was this Zac Wilkinson's explosive discovery?'

'Zac didn't know about it. How could he? I was hardly likely to tell him the truth, was I?'

'Perhaps he found out somehow. Or perhaps he put two and two together after speaking to Professor Pargeter. Where did Valdun go when he left here after Rosemary died?'

'When he first disappeared – after he'd faked his death – he went to Canada and he decided to go back there. He'd managed to acquire a false passport using the name of a dead baby – that sort of thing was easier in those days.'

'He became Peter Walsingham?'

'That's right.'

There was a long period of silence and Wesley waited, hoping Staniland wouldn't be able to resist filling it with the truth. Eventually his patience was rewarded.

'When Robert first came back from Canada he had three novels and asked me to publish them under my name. One of them was *The Viper's Kiss*; my greatest hit. That's how it started and he wrote the other two while he was living here. When Rosemary died I gave him a large sum of money to disappear again because her death attracted such a lot of attention, especially as she'd copied the suicide method from *The Viper's Kiss*. I think she did that to get at me . . . or Robert. I'm not sure which.'

'She knew about your deception?'

'Not at first but she found out. Of course, the writing fizzled out after Robert left. I tried but I couldn't manage it on my own.'

'I don't understand why you agreed to cooperate with Zac's biography.'

'He was going to write it anyway so I thought if I had some sort of control . . . '

'But it didn't work out like that, did it? Zac was thorough and there was a real risk he'd uncover your secret. That's why you killed him.'

'I didn't.'

'Or did your stepdaughter do it to protect you?'

'She knows nothing about this. Besides, it makes no difference to her whether I wrote the damned books or not. She's a wealthy woman in her own right.'

'But you're close. You must be or she wouldn't be here.'

'We get along,' he said quickly. 'And Perdita's . . . fragile. I'm not sure how she'd survive in the outside world. It can be a cruel place.'

Wesley knew Staniland was right. Perdita had no reason to hide her stepfather's secret and she certainly had no reason to do Valdun any favours.

'That leaves you, Mr Staniland. If you were exposed as a fraud, you'd be ruined.'

'Not financially. My late wife left me well provided for.' He gave a bitter smile. 'I admit I enjoyed my years of fame; all the parties; the women; the glory. But in the end the strain of living a lie took its toll and anonymity came as a relief.'

321

'But you'll lose your anonymity if this becomes a scandal,' said Gerry. 'The newspapers will think all their birthdays have come at once.'

'Things might be hard for a time but it'll soon blow over. I'll go away for a while.'

'If that's the case why didn't you come clean earlier?'

'And betray Robert? He's an old friend. And I don't betray my friends.'

'What about the Lombards? What did they know about your little deception?'

'I've already told you, I know nothing about them. The woman was obviously a fan of my work – Robert's work – but that's all I can tell you. Now if that's all, I'd be grateful if you'd leave.'

'We'd like you to come down to the station with us,' said Gerry.

'If I refuse?'

'Then you're under arrest in connection of the murder of Zac Wilkinson, alias Jamie Hursthead.'

Ethel Rinton reckoned someone needed to be taught a lesson. It was high time she had some compensation for all the years of struggle and humiliation while certain people breezed through life, cheating and flouting every rule she'd been brought up to live by.

She took her tattered old address book out of the drawer and found the number. Then she picked up the phone and put it down again. This needed some thought.

Journal of Mary Lipton

17 June 1884

Father died in great agony last night and Mother is gravely ill. John said it was the crab they ate at supper. John and I dined privately and we ate no crab because neither of us share my parents' taste for it.

Cook is distraught, saying the crab was the freshest she'd seen and it had been bought at the seafront in Tradmouth that very morning. I have instructed her to leave at once and Sarah says she knows of a reliable woman to replace her.

The doctor agrees with John that the crab was the cause of Father's demise, especially as his heart was weak.

Sarah sits with my mother, who appears to be close to death. The doctor says he will return in a few hours.

When Mr Bearstowe arrived at the house I told him the news and sent him away. There will be no need of his services now.

40

Neil had always known it was good to have friends in high places – or even in solicitors' offices. When he'd asked Emily she'd reacted like a bloodhound on the scent and made the call to her father without hesitation.

Neil feared the nineteenth-century archives of Bearstowe, James and Greaves would have been thrown out years ago in a fit of modernisation but, fortuitously, they were still in the basement where they'd always been. It was good to know tradition still counted for something in the modern world of the law.

Neil was conscious of his dishevelled state as he walked into the office behind Emily but the unflappable receptionist appeared to regard the arrival of two soil-stained archaeologists as a routine matter and directed them to Emily's father's office.

Soon they were in the basement with Emily's father, Keith, a rotund man in a slightly shabby grey suit who'd been infected with his daughter's enthusiasm. For half an hour they heaved boxes around in an attempt to locate the Lipton papers, sending clouds of dust into the dimly lit air. Then, once they found what they were looking for, they returned with the box to Keith's office.

They clustered round the box, Keith ignoring the drying soil flaking off the archaeologists' clothing onto the pristine carpet. Neil allowed him to do the honours and when he lifted the lid a fresh layer of dust landed on his desk. The papers inside were yellowed with age and when Keith spread them out he began to study them.

'There's a will here. Standard stuff. And there's this.' Neil saw Keith scratch his head. '"Only to be opened in the event of my death".'

Keith slid a paper knife through the seal on the envelope and flattened the contents on his blotter.

'What does it say?' Emily asked, voicing the question Neil was longing to ask.

'I think it's a confession.'

'To Mary Field's murder?'

Keith handed the sheet of yellowed paper to Neil. 'See for yourself.'

Rachel and Trish Walton questioned Wynn Staniland at some length in the interview room but he revealed nothing more. As Wesley and Gerry watched behind the two-way mirror Staniland admitted to harbouring Robert Valdun all those years ago but denied knowing anything about the deaths of the Lombards and Zac Wilkinson.

Afterwards Wesley and Gerry decided to conduct the interview with Robert Valdun themselves but, with the encouragement of his solicitor, each question was answered with a 'no comment'.

Then he appeared to relax a little, as though he was confident he had the upper hand.

'You've been staying with Raynard Bishop. Tell us about your relationship with him,' said Wesley.

'You want to know if we're lovers?' Valdun said with an amused half-smile. 'It sometimes pays to let people believe what they want to believe. But I assure you Ray knows nothing about my past.'

Wesley tailored his next question to appeal to the man's vanity.

'You wrote books that won awards. You must be blessed with a considerable talent. It must have been hard to see Wynn taking all the credit.'

'I received my cut.'

'He sent you the royalties?'

'He kept a little for his trouble but he paid the lion's share into my account. That was the agreement and it's allowed me to indulge my passion for rare books and build up a nice little business. Until recently Wynn and I have had no personal contact. I only got in touch again when I heard about the biography. I thought it was time I came back from the dead.'

'And let Wynn know you want to publish five more books.'

'I see he's already told you.'

'Why did you leave Devon in 1983?'

'Because Rosemary and Jane died and the police were sniffing around. I thought it wise to make myself scarce but I'd been planning it for some time anyway.'

'Were you having an affair with Rosemary?'

Valdun looked shocked. 'Whatever gave you that idea? Rosemary was hardly my type. She was too ... needy.

Between you and me, Wynn married her for her money. She was a wealthy woman.'

'He inherited everything?'

'He has the house for his lifetime but, as far as I'm aware, Perdita got everything else.'

'She's never married or been in a relationship.'

'She's what they describe as unstable. It can't be easy for Wynn but they seem close.'

'Am I right in thinking Perdita's Rosemary's daughter by her previous marriage?'

'A previous relationship. Nobody knows who her father was. Wynn's the only father she's known.'

'What can you tell me about Rosemary's death?'

For a while Valdun didn't reply. Then a distant look appeared in his eyes. 'It was very like Mary Field's.' The man's thin lips twitched upwards in a smile. 'I used to stay with an aunt round here when I was a child and the case has fascinated me ever since I learned about it – the woman sitting down to die beneath the water; so calm; so deliberate. Sitting on a rock like a mermaid: half fish, half woman.'

'Wasn't Mary Field murdered?'

'I didn't let a little detail like that get in the way of my imagination, Inspector.'

'The Field case features in one of your books, *The Viper's Kiss*. Rosemary used the same method when she killed herself.'

'As I said, it's always fascinated me.' The faint smile remained on his lips, as though he was nursing a secret. Playing games.

'Did you kill Suzie Grant in Oxford?'

'To tell you the truth I really can't remember.' He bowed his head. 'I had problems at the time.'

'Drink? Drugs?'

'I used anything I could lay my hands on. Anything that would bring about oblivion. I was a mess back then. The only thing I had was my writing . . . and I lost that to Wynn. I sometimes wonder . . .'

'What?'

'Nothing.' He shook his head sadly then turned to his solicitor. 'Any chance of bail?'

Wesley stopped the tape and left the room, Gerry following behind.

The past had been intruding into Julie Shepherd's thoughts ever since she'd spoken to the police. During all those years filled with work and family, she'd pushed her sister Jane to the back of her mind because she couldn't bear to think of the sadness of her lonely end in that room at Addersacre, racked with guilt about another woman's death and gasping in pain as the world turned black. Their mother had spoken of it in hospital just before she'd passed away, saying she wished Jane had never clapped eyes on Wynn Staniland.

After that Julie had done her best to get on with her life, reminded of the tragedy only when she saw one of Staniland's novels on the shelves at work. She hadn't been looking forward to Zac Wilkinson's talk and she'd been secretly relieved when it hadn't gone ahead. This made her feel guilty – as though it was she who'd wished him dead.

It was her day off, the first day she'd spent alone since the police had come calling, and she'd planned to use the time to do some sorting out. She went to the old cupboard in the garage where the box containing her dead sister's things was stored, stuffed to the back and forgotten. She'd brought it home with the rest of her mother's things when she'd cleared out her childhood home, shoving it away because she feared it would contain memories too agonising to bear.

She hadn't looked at the box in years but now she carried it into the living room, knelt on the floor and opened the lid, closing her eyes for a moment, unwilling to look at those reminders of Jane's existence. Then she forced herself to take out each item and lay it carefully on the coffee table.

When she unfolded an unpromising sheet of paper she discovered that it was a note from Wynn Staniland and her hand shook as she began to read. He appeared to be apologising for something but she couldn't quite understand what it was. Then she read another note – then another – and gradually everything became clearer. He was saying he was sorry, apologising to Jane, his lover, rather than his wife and Julie wondered why. What hold had Jane had over him? And who was the girl he mentioned? His other love?

There was a diary too, a cheap desk version with a separate page for each day. Now curiosity made her turn each page and it became obvious that Jane had only made entries in it when she felt particularly aggrieved. As she read on she began to realise how little she'd known about her elder sister and what had happened at Addersacre that summer. Jane mentioned people she'd never even heard of, one person in particular. How could she have been so unaware for so many years?

Once she'd finished reading she sat stunned, wondering what to do. This was something the police should be told. It might mean nothing. But on the other hand, it might be just what they were looking for.

Ethel Rinton had the upper hand and it was a heady and unfamiliar feeling.

'We need to talk,' she said sweetly. It was a phrase she'd heard in TV soap operas but one she'd never had the opportunity to use before. 'I've found something you wouldn't want the police to get hold of and I've got a proposition.' She was careful to keep her voice even, reasonable, as if she was discussing some everyday matter. 'I'm sure we can come to some arrangement. It would suit me if you came to my house at three.'

She went on to name her terms. Then the line went dead.

41

'Wynn Staniland was released a couple of hours ago. We had no reason to hold him.'

Wesley could see the disappointment on Gerry's face, like a child whose favourite toy has been taken away.

'Harbouring a fugitive? Deception?'

'That's up to the CPS.'

In spite of passing his inspector's exams Wesley wasn't too clear about the legal rights and wrongs of using a ghost writer and passing the work off as your own: he expected lots of people, particularly celebrities, had done it. 'He's got a good solicitor, Gerry,' he said as though this explained everything.

Before he could say anything else the phone rang. It was a call from the front desk saying there was somebody who wanted to see DCI Heffernan and Inspector Peterson. Curious, Gerry went down and Wesley said he'd follow once he'd made a phone call.

When he reached the foyer, Gerry was greeted with the sight of Callum Joy sitting on the plastic bench. He looked smarter than when Gerry had last seen him, and his face was rounder, more cherubic.

As soon as he saw Gerry he stood up and shifted from foot to foot nervously.

'How are you doing, Callum?'

'Well, thank you, Mr Heffernan.' There was an awkward moment of silence before he carried on. 'I've got myself a job – a proper job with an agricultural suppliers. It's in the warehouse, but it's got prospects.'

Gerry beamed, genuinely delighted, and gave his hand a hearty shake. 'Pleased to hear it, Callum. Well done. Don't take this the wrong way, lad, but I hope we don't see you here again – professionally, that is.'

'You won't, Mr Heffernan.' He studied his trainers for a few seconds. Gerry noticed that they looked new. 'There's something else . . .'

At that moment Wesley appeared through the door beside the front desk and Callum swung round.

'Callum's come to tell us about his new job,' said Gerry at his most avuncular.

Callum repeated the news of his good fortune for Wesley's benefit and was rewarded with noises of approval and wishes of good luck.

'What was it you wanted to tell me?' Gerry asked.

Callum blushed and opened the rucksack he was carrying. He took out an iPad, together with its charger, and handed it to Wesley. 'I found this in Jamie's car and when I heard he'd been murdered . . . I thought I'd better hand it in. I won't get into trouble for . . . ?'

'You've brought it in, haven't you?' said Wesley.

After more handshakes, Wesley and Gerry saw Callum off the premises and made their way back upstairs.

'Very honest of him,' said Gerry. 'I'm surprised he didn't flog it.'

'He probably intended to then he realised it was important – and hot. We need to see exactly what's on it.'

'I'll leave that to you, Wes. Let me know what you find, won't you? I've got paperwork.'

Back in the CID office it didn't take Wesley long to locate the notes Jamie had made in the course of his research. But it wasn't until he'd trawled through a lot of material that the word 'Bristol' and a photograph caught his eye: something he hadn't expected to see. And beneath the photograph was a cryptic sentence which made his heart beat faster. He was pondering his new discovery when Rob Carter looked in.

'There's been a call for you from a Julie Shepherd. Could you call her back. She says it's urgent.'

It took Wesley a second or two to recall that Julie was Jane Whitsun's sister. When he'd spoken to her at the library he was sure she'd told him all she knew about the Staniland household and he wondered what could be so urgent.

When he went to tell Gerry about Julie's call, the DCI picked up a budget report that was squatting on his desk.

'The chief super wants this yesterday so you deal with it, Wes,' said Gerry. Then he threw the report to one side and it landed on the floor. 'On the other hand . . .'

Wesley called Julie to say they'd be round in ten minutes. The paperwork could wait.

Julie Shepherd lived in Tradmouth at the top of the town, not far from Wesley's house. There was a smart Mini parked outside her modern detached bungalow and they were shown into an immaculate lounge, a homage to every interior design magazine Wesley had ever flicked through in the dentist's waiting room. The only thing out of place was an embroidery frame standing next to an armchair occupied by a sleek tortoiseshell cat. The cat was stretched out, completely relaxed, but the woman in front of him was fidgeting, restless with worry.

'Why did you want to see us?' Gerry asked.

'I've been looking through Jane's things and I found a note from Wynn Staniland apologising for an affair he was having. I don't know whether it's important but I thought you should know.'

'Who was he having the affair with?'

'I'm not sure but Jane's diary mentions a friend of Perdita's who used to stay at Addersacre. It's obvious Jane thought she was using Perdita to worm her way into the household. She also says Perdita and Wynn didn't get on.'

'Have you seen Perdita recently?'

'I don't think I've ever seen her. I never went to Addersacre when Jane was there and I've heard Perdita avoids Tradmouth and Bloxham; anywhere she might be recognised and set tongues wagging. I suppose she values her privacy. Just like Wynn.'

'What was Perdita's friend called?'

'Jane just refers to her in her diary as the Little Bitch.'

Wesley looked at Gerry. Was it possible that Gina Lombard had been the Little Bitch? Was that why she'd kept Perdita's poem; as a souvenir of her time in Wynn's unconventional household?

'I wanted to speak to someone who was around at the time so I got Ethel Rinton's number from my colleague at the library. When I tried to call her she said she had someone with her and couldn't talk. But she sounded strange . . . nervous.'

'Did she say who was with her?'

'No. But when I said I wanted to talk about Wynn Staniland she slammed the phone down.' Julie suddenly looked embarrassed. 'Sorry. I'm probably wasting your time.'

'No. You've done the right thing.'

Before Wesley could say any more his phone rang. It was Rachel and she sounded excited.

'We've traced Gina Lombard's National Insurance number. We couldn't find a birth certificate for her but we've got hold of another you might be interested in.'

Wesley listened carefully as she gave the details. When the call was finished he asked for a word with Gerry in private and steered him into the hall, aware that Julie, in the lounge, would probably be straining to hear.

Once he'd heard what Wesley had to say Gerry headed towards the front door. They needed to ask Wynn Staniland more questions. On his release from questioning he'd taken a taxi to Addersacre so he should have arrived there a couple of hours ago.

After thanking Julie they set off. And when they arrived at Addersacre Wesley had the feeling something was badly wrong.

42

Wynn Staniland flung open the door to admit them then, without a word, he turned his back and made for the drawing room. Wesley could sense his anger and irritation as they followed.

'What do you want now?' Staniland snapped as he sat down heavily. 'I've only just got back from your police station.'

To Wesley's relief there was no sign of the attentive stepdaughter.

'Have you seen Ethel Rinton today?'

'Who?' The question came out as an indignant squeak.

'The widow of your former gardener. She had a visitor. Was it you?'

'Why on earth would I want to visit her?'

Wesley watched him intently, wishing he could read his expression.

'I'd like to know what happened to Perdita's friend – the one Jane Whitsun called the "Little Bitch".'

'I don't know what you're talking about.' Staniland stood up and walked to the window, staring out at the overgrown garden.

An idea had been forming in Wesley's head since he'd seen the picture on Jamie's iPad and if he was right all his previous assumptions would be turned upside down.

'You never got on with Perdita, did you?' he said. 'After her mother's death she left here. Got away from you.'

'Rosemary's death hit her hard and she left for a week or so to sort herself out, that's all. Then she came back. We comforted each other.'

'Sexually?'

Gerry's question surprised Wesley but he would have asked it himself in time.

'She's my daughter.' Staniland still had his back to Wesley so that he couldn't see his face.

'Stepdaughter. No blood relation.'

'That makes no difference.'

Staniland turned. 'You should watch what you say.'

'I'm wondering where her friend comes into all this. You remember her friend who used to stay here?'

'Vaguely.'

'What was her name, by the way?'

'I don't remember.'

'Try.'

Staniland took a few moments to answer. 'Theresa. Terry.'

'We need to speak to her.'

'I don't know where she is and neither does Perdita. They lost touch years ago.'

Wesley took Jamie's iPad from his bag and found the photograph labelled 'Bristol'. A thin teenage girl wearing

337

a striped summer dress with a full skirt; a school uniform. Her hair was mousy and her hands were clasped in front of her. The girl standing next to her was dressed identically but she looked more confident. She was around the same height and build as her companion and the same physical type but her hair was darker and fell around her shoulders.

'Who is this?' Wesley asked, pointing to the mousy girl.

Staniland took the iPad from him, glanced at it and passed it back. 'That's Terry.'

Wesley studied it again and passed it to Gerry, who took it with a puzzled frown.

'And that's Perdita?'

'Yes.'

'The girl you say is Terry has a birthmark near her elbow.'

'So?'

'The woman we found dead in the caravan had a similar birthmark. I was at the postmortem.'

'You're saying that was Terry?'

Wesley shook his head. 'I think the dead woman was Perdita. We couldn't find out anything about Gina Lombard's past because it was made up. A work of fiction.' He paused before making his next revelation. 'One of my colleagues found Perdita's birth certificate: her full name is Perdita Regina.'

'My late wife had a taste for fancy names,' Staniland said bitterly.

'I think Perdita started using her middle name when she left here and she shortened it to Gina. She met Frank Lombard, shed her past and became Gina Lombard. When she ran away from here after her mother's death I don't think she realised she was due to inherit her fortune. If she'd known I'm sure she would have been back sooner claiming what was hers.'

Wesley recalled the press cutting found in the Lombards' house in Leeds, the circled article about the reclusive author living with his daughter, Perdita, who'd inherited Rosemary's considerable wealth. Rosemary Staniland had been a modest woman with a bohemian disregard for money. The young Perdita had probably assumed the family's wealth came from Wynn's books.

'Perdita lives here with me. You've met her.'

'That's not Perdita. The real Perdita read an article in a magazine, probably written to stir up interest in Zac Wilkinson's coming biography. Just imagine how she felt when she realised Terry, her former friend, had taken her place.'

Staniland smiled as though he pitied Wesley's naiveté. 'This is ridiculous.'

'Only you didn't regard Terry as a surrogate daughter, did you, Mr Staniland? She became your lover and you conspired together to make sure you kept a firm hold on Perdita's inheritance when she left after her mother's death, not intending to come back. Where's Terry now?'

'How should I know?'

'Liar.' Gerry moved forward and put his face close to Staniland's.

Wesley touched the boss's arm; a warning gesture. 'Your whole life's been a lie, Mr Staniland,' he said quietly. 'First your writing and now your so-called daughter. Why should we believe a word you say?'

'Because it's true. I don't know where Terry is.'

'Your stepdaughter has a car?' Wesley hadn't noticed one during his visits but there were outbuildings round the back and how else would a household that didn't welcome visitors obtain the necessities of life?

'Yes. But . . . '

'Is it still here?'

Wynn hesitated before leading them outside to a detached garage at the back of the house, his every step laboured as though he was trying to make a point. When they reached the garage the door was open and it was empty.

Wesley took Gerry by the arm and led him out of earshot. 'We need to get someone over to Ethel Rinton's cottage. Fast.'

Journal of John Lipton

1 July 1884

I had expected my wife to be more distressed at the death of her parents but I ought to have known better. She is a cold, strange woman; the eagerness with which she embraces the topic of violent murder should have told me that. She thinks I share her love of the macabre but she is mistaken. I merely used it to bait my trap and now she and her fortune are mine.

She reads the newspaper each day in the hope of finding some new gruesome death to take her fancy. Last night she asked me to invite Mr Gunster to the house to present another performance and she sulked when I explained that this would not be suitable for a house that is meant to be in mourning.

Now Mary has come into her inheritance, I fear for her sanity, as does Sarah. William Banville called to express his condolences. Mary received him but I could not tell what he made of my wife's behaviour as he spoke only to her and said nothing to me.

Sarah and I have become closer of late and she confides in me. Today she revealed that she has a secret, one so momentous she fears it will shock me.

Sarah told me that she too is Sir Cuthbert's daughter for her mother, a poor village woman who once worked at Newfield as a laundry maid, whispered the truth on her deathbed. Sarah is Mary's half-sister but her base birth condemns her to the life of a servant. I did not tell her that I have suspected the nature of this secret for some time because of the resemblance between maid and mistress.

I never visit Mary's bed now as I take my solace in Sarah's arms. I have exchanged mistress for maid. Sister for sister. Does this make me a wicked man?

43

Wesley and Gerry arrived at Ethel Rinton's cottage to find no sign of life, although Wesley had the feeling he was being watched from behind the opaque net curtains.

He hammered on the door while Gerry circled the building in search of an open window. But they were all tightly shut in spite of the August heat, which meant that drastic action was needed.

Wesley stood by the back door, looking for something to break the glass. Then he spotted the shed. Edith had been married to a gardener so the tools of his trade might still be there.

He was in luck. The flimsy padlock intended to secure the shed door was dangling loose so he pushed the door open and saw spades, trowels and garden forks hanging in order of size from a neat row of hooks. Wesley grabbed a spade and ran to the back door. The tinkle of breaking glass filled the silence and he reached in to unlock the door. He stepped inside, ignoring the glass crunching beneath his feet, and made for the small front parlour.

Ethel was slumped on the floor beside the settee. Wesley could hear her rasping breath and as he shifted her into the recovery position she gave a faint moan. Gerry was already calling the ambulance, punching out nine nine nine with his chubby fingers.

'Poison?' he asked when he ended the call.

'Looks like it.' Wesley put on his crime scene gloves and picked up the solitary bone china teacup. There was a matching pot on the table, still warm. Wesley reckoned Ethel wouldn't have gone to the trouble of using the best china if she'd been alone.

'Only one cup,' Gerry observed.

'Look in the kitchen. I'll bet our killer's washed it up to cover her tracks.'

'Where has she gone?' Gerry said.

Wesley shook his head. If Terry had been Ethel's companion, she was in her car so she could be headed anywhere. He alerted Traffic but if she stuck to the network of country lanes there'd be no cameras to pinpoint her movements. He picked up the empty cup again and when he swirled the dregs around he saw a powdery deposit that definitely wasn't tea.

Then an idea suddenly came to him. 'I know where she'll be.'

'Who? Perdita?'

'Terry. The real Perdita died in that caravan with Frank Lombard. She'd been enjoying the quiet life up north until her husband got greedy. This whole case has been about identity, Gerry. Jamie becoming Zac; Valdun becoming Walsingham. We need to get back to Addersacre. Call for backup to meet us there.'

The ambulance and a patrol car arrived while Gerry

344

was making the phone call; he'd known Wesley too long to suspect him of overdramatising.

Wesley didn't know what Ethel's chances were but they didn't look good. They left her with the patrol officers and the paramedics and headed back to Addersacre. Once Staniland had answered the intercom, saying Perdita had returned home but had gone straight out for a swim, the gates opened painfully slowly. Wesley drove fast through the overgrown grounds towards the sea and pulled up beside a black Toyota parked next to the path leading down to the shore: the car that belonged to the woman they'd known as Perdita.

He leaped out and took the path towards the pool where Rosemary Staniland died.

'You think she's down there?' said Gerry breathlessly, trying to keep up.

Wesley didn't answer.

The path sloped downwards to the English Channel and Wesley could see the sea pool at the bottom of the cliff, like a bowl carved from the rocks. The water in the pool was flat calm, unlike the restless sea around it. As he drew closer he saw brown hair spread out on the glistening surface like the fronds of a delicate plant. A woman was swimming, executing an elegant breast stroke. She wore an emerald green one-piece costume and looked at one with the water. Wesley watched her for a while until she reached the edge of the pool and stopped swimming, flicking back her wet hair. When she became aware of his presence she stood up.

'We need a word,' he shouted over the rush of the waves.

Her reply was swallowed by the breeze so Wesley moved closer. 'Get out of the water, Terry. Now.'

She flinched at the use of her real name and slipped back beneath the water.

'Come and get me,' she shouted defiantly as she surfaced, pushing herself off to perform a smooth back crawl.

'Ethel Rinton's still alive. She's told us everything.' It was worth a lie to get at the truth. But there was no tape or attendant solicitor so if she chose to answer it would be her word against his.

The movement in the water suddenly stopped. Then she flipped over and swam with effortless grace to the other side of the pool; the side nearest the cliffs surrounded by rocks. If she reached the rocks and climbed up then she could make it round the headland to the next bay.

She began to haul herself out but the rocks were coated in seaweed, as slippery as sheet ice. She tried a second time, then a third but each time she slithered back into the pool. On her fourth attempt she found a foothold. Then without warning she plunged backwards, hitting her head and vanishing beneath the surface of the water, motionless.

'Well, I'm not going in,' said Gerry behind him. 'I can't swim.'

Wesley had no choice. Slowed by the sodden weight of his clothes, he waded in, his steps frustratingly slow like in a nightmare, and when the water deepened he swam in a clumsy crawl towards the unconscious woman.

Working on instinct and adrenalin, he struggled to pull Terry to the side of the pool. The faint sound of police sirens drifted over on the breeze, getting nearer, as he hauled her limp body from the water while Gerry helped him land her on the sand like a massive fish.

Wesley was surprised at how quickly his training kicked in and when he turned her over into the recovery position she spluttered and emptied the contents of her stomach and lungs. She was alive.

She came round quickly and once the paramedics had taken her away, a uniformed constable keeping her company in the ambulance, watching her like an anxious relative, Wesley sat on the rocks with his head in his hands, sopping wet. He felt Gerry's hand on his shoulder. 'She'll live, Wes. You could get a commendation for this.'

Wesley looked up. 'What about Ethel?'

'No news yet. They're taking Terry to Tradmouth Hospital. Fancy conducting the interview once she's fit?'

'Try and stop me.'

44

'Sorry, Neil, this is a bad time. We've just made an arrest. Can it wait?' said Wesley.

'Promise this won't take a moment.'

Wesley craned his neck to see the wall clock. Terry had been taken to hospital for a check-up but he'd been assured she'd soon be released and brought to the station for questioning. Gerry reckoned they already had enough to charge her and he was planning a celebration that evening. Wesley hoped nothing would stop it going ahead.

He'd gone home to change his wet clothes in a patrol car driven by a young constable who'd appeared to find his predicament amusing. Now he was waiting for Gerry to return from the chief super's office. As soon as Terry arrived Gerry wanted to observe the interview; he wanted to be in at the end.

'This arrest?' Neil continued. 'Is it something to do with the puppet man – Reynard Bishop? He's a mate of Karl Banville and I heard you were questioning him.'

'It's not Bishop.' Wesley hesitated, wondering how much to tell him. 'Although an associate of his is in custody for something else.'

'What? Who?'

Wesley didn't answer. He didn't have time for long explanations. 'What did you want to tell me?'

'It's our skeletons. Would you believe the killer left a confession with his solicitor? Not to be opened until after his death.'

If only all murderers were so obliging, Wesley thought to himself. He looked at his watch. Terry hadn't yet arrived so it would do no harm to hear what Neil had to say. Besides, he was interested. 'Go on.'

He listened as Neil outlined his discovery but Gerry walked in before he could ask any questions.

'Sorry, mate, got to go. See you tonight maybe. We usually have a little celebration in the Tradmouth Arms when a case is wrapped up. Come if you like.'

'Might well do. Cheers.'

Wesley wondered whether to call Pam to ask if she could get a babysitter and join the festivities. It was time she got out and enjoyed herself, even if it was only with his police colleagues.

But Gerry interrupted his thoughts. He'd just received a call from the officer guarding Terry at Tradmouth Hospital to say she was on her way. While they'd been waiting Rachel had made enquiries and discovered that one of the numbers they'd found on the iPad Callum Joy had returned to them belonged to a Miss Holt, a retired teacher who'd worked at a boarding school near Bristol.

Miss Holt remembered Theresa Sildon well and told Rachel that she'd been brought up by her grandparents near Bristol and became close to Perdita Staniland when she was sent to board at the school. Miss Holt had received a visit from Zac Wilkinson and she'd told him everything she knew.

The trip to Bristol Jamie Hursthead mentioned to his agent had been puzzling Wesley; a small, annoying piece of the jigsaw that had appeared not to fit. But now he knew he'd gone there in search of the truth about Terry. Presumably he'd found it and that was why he'd had to die.

Perdita, according to Miss Holt, had been the sensitive sort, someone who was easily led, and Terry had taken advantage and wormed her way into an intense relationship with the girl. The pair had become inseparable, she said, and Terry had stayed with Perdita at Addersacre in the school holidays.

Terry had no criminal record but she'd been a difficult, rebellious and sexually precocious teenager and her grandparents had been only too pleased to pass the responsibility over to the school and were, no doubt, relieved when Perdita's unconventional family had taken her under their wing.

That was all Miss Holt was able to tell them but when Rachel dug further she found that Theresa Sildon vanished from all records after the age of seventeen and nobody had bothered to report her missing.

When the call came through to say Terry had arrived, Wesley and Rachel made for the interview room where the suspect was waiting for them. Rachel, looking businesslike in her neat black suit, had a file beneath her arm. She was a good interviewer and he suspected Terry was about to meet her match.

Wesley walked into the room first as Gerry slipped next

door to observe the interview through the two-way mirror. Terry had a solicitor with her, a sharp-featured young woman who would, no doubt, be keen to do things by the book and play on her client's recent bout of concussion if necessary, even though the FME had said she was fit to face questioning.

Wesley let Rachel begin as soon as they'd recited their names for the tape.

'We know all about you, Terry. I've been talking to one of your old teachers,' she began while Wesley sat silently, his eyes fixed on the prisoner. The green swimming costume had been swapped for a grey tracksuit and her hair had dried to a halo of curls. She looked almost angelic, apart from the dressing on her forehead where she'd gashed her head on the rocks.

Terry pressed her lips together and looked away. 'You know nothing about me.'

'I know you and Perdita were friends.' When this got no reaction, Rachel gave a swift résumé of everything they had so far but Terry stayed silent.

It was Wesley's turn to speak. 'The real Perdita saw an article in a magazine saying that Wynn Staniland lived in seclusion with his stepdaughter, Perdita, who'd inherited her mother's fortune. We found the cutting in her house in Leeds. She came down here to see what was going on. She never realised she was in line for an inheritance all those years ago, did she?'

Terry gave her solicitor a sideways look, as if to check she was paying attention. 'She hadn't a clue. All she wanted to do was get away from Wynn.'

'And you encouraged her?'

'Why not? That's what she wanted. She left and swore

351

she was never coming back. She was going to get a new life and start again. She hated Wynn and blamed him for her mum's suicide.' Terry rolled her eyes. 'She was ridiculously naive. She'd led a sheltered life.'

'And you stole that life. You were supposed to be her friend.'

Terry gave him a cold smile. 'It was all Wynn's idea. Perdita had gone – she just wanted to get away. When her mother was alive she did all she could to break up her marriage to Wynn. And when we were at school together I had to listen to her going on about him, pouring out all that poison. Then she took me home with her one holiday and when I actually met him I knew she'd been lying. He was wonderful. I'd never met anyone like him before.'

'You fell for him?'

She pursed her lips. 'Wynn and I became close but not like that.'

'Jane Whitsun thought you were lovers. Was it you she referred to in her diary as the "Little Bitch"?'

'Jane Whitsun was a jealous cow.'

'Tell us what happened when Perdita left.'

'She took off one day saying she was never coming back and Wynn said that if I pretended to be her I could claim the money left to her in her mother's will.' She sighed. 'There weren't going to be any more books because Robert had buggered off abroad but we had Rosemary's money so Wynn and I lived happily for years. The world didn't intrude and nobody ever questioned that I was Perdita. She'd been away at school most of the time and she hated living at Addersacre so she never made any friends locally; it wasn't hard to become her.' She gave Wesley a bitter smile. 'I lost my own identity but that was a small price to pay. It

352

wasn't much of an identity anyway and my grandparents were glad to get rid of me. They bred cats, you know, and they thought more of their animals than they did of me. I just got in the way.'

Wesley could sense the pain behind her words and for a brief moment he almost felt sorry for her. Then he remembered the people she'd killed.

'Why did you try to poison Ethel Rinton?'

'She called me to say she'd seen a picture of the woman in the caravan – the one the police circulated. She said she knew I was an imposter because she'd recognised Perdita's birthmark from an old press cutting her husband kept and she wanted money to keep quiet.'

'So you poisoned her?'

'She's still alive?' She looked disappointed.

Wesley didn't answer. 'Let's get back to your deception. You stayed on at Addersacre after Perdita walked out. I'm guessing it was the first time you'd had anything approaching a stable home,'

She gave him a look that told him he was spot on. At last she'd found a home and that was why she'd endured those years of seclusion with a recluse.

'You must have been afraid Perdita would come back one day and ruin everything.'

She bowed her head. 'If it happened I knew wc'd have to deal with it.'

'We? Does Wynn know you killed Perdita and her partner?'

She shook her head. 'He knows nothing about it.'

'Perdita made two phone calls to Addersacre. Was it you who spoke to her?'

'Yes.'

'Lucky,' said Rachel but Terry ignored her.

'Wynn never answers the phone. He leaves that to me in case . . .'

'I'm guessing she wanted to see Wynn and you couldn't let that happen, could you, Terry?' said Wesley. 'You went to the caravan park and left a bottle of poisoned champagne. Where did you get it? It's a rare vintage.'

'Is it? There are a lot of bottles in the cellar left over from Wynn's party days.'

'Did you take it and inject it with poison?'

'No comment.'

'Your room at Addersacre's been searched and they found an unregistered mobile phone. Perdita received a call from that number and so did the man you knew as Zac Wilkinson shortly before his death.' He noticed the solicitor was no longer looking so confident. 'How did you know you'd got the right caravan when you left the champagne? Or didn't you care? If some innocent person had been killed . . .'

'Of course I cared,' she said, almost indignant.

Wesley glanced at Rachel and saw a look of triumph on her face.

'Perdita told me where she was staying. As far as she was concerned I was still Terry, her old friend who'd got it together with her wicked stepfather. I said I wanted to talk to her and told her I'd come to the caravan park because Wynn wasn't well and the shock might kill him. She believed me.'

'You used aconite. Monkshood. Where did you get it?'

'As well as breeding cats my grandmother was a great one for herbalism. I used to hang around and watch her even though she didn't like it so I learned all about poisons. There's a lot of monkshood in the garden at Addersacre.'

'Did you use it on Eric Rinton, the gardener? Did you silence him when he found out about your relationship with Wynn?'

'That was an accident. Monkshood's dangerous stuff. You have to treat it with respect and he obviously didn't.'

'But you killed Jane Whitsun. She died around the time you decided to take Perdita's place. She had to go if your deception was going to work. You made her death look like suicide.'

Wesley saw the ghost of a smile on her pale lips. 'No comment.'

He took a deep breath. 'Zac Wilkinson discovered your secret so you had to get rid of him too. Did you arrange to meet him in the woods to speak in private? Did you say you were going to tell him something that would make his biography a best seller? You didn't use poison that time. Perhaps there was no way of persuading him to take it and you certainly didn't want to speak to him at the house because you didn't want a body on your hands. He told his agent he'd discovered something explosive. Was that your deception? Or was it Wynn's? He didn't even write the books that made him so famous so what could be more explosive than that?'

'No comment.' She smiled as though she was pleased with her answer.

'When Zac was off his guard, you hit him. You killed him.'

'Prove it.'

Wesley had reached the limits of his patience. He ended the interview and left the room.

Journal of John Lipton

18 July 1884

Sarah assumed a remarkable strength of character while Mary grew feebler in mind and kept to her room. Then Sarah made a suggestion so outrageous that I thought she spoke in jest. However, when I found Mary dead in her bed the next morning I knew Sarah's words had been no idle musings. She had suggested poisoning Mary so that she could take her place and enjoy the fruits of her rightful inheritance. When I asked her if Sir Cuthbert and his wife had been poisoned in the same manner she refused to answer.

She insisted that I dismiss the servants before Mary's death was discovered, telling them the house was to be shut up, and this I did.

I buried Mary in the walled garden and, even though I'd had no love for my wife, I felt some sadness laying her to rest in the place of our strange courtship.

Now Sarah has appointed new servants from out of the district and she queens it over her new household. She is now Mary Lipton and I am the keeper of her secret.

45

Terry was refusing to confess, answering each question with a stubborn 'no comment'. But Wesley and Gerry were sure they had enough evidence to satisfy the CPS so she was charged with the murders of Perdita Regina Lombard, Frank Lombard and Jamie Hursthead, alias Zac Wilkinson, and remanded in custody. Wesley was pretty sure she'd killed Jane Whitsun as well but unless Terry confessed there was no way of proving it.

The attempted murder of Ethel Rinton had clinched their case: Terry's fingerprints had been found in her cottage. She'd made a fundamental mistake.

Ethel was still in a critical condition and it looked likely that Terry would soon be facing another murder charge. Gerry wondered whether Ethel's prognosis was the reason Wesley made an excuse to leave the team's drinks celebration at the Tradmouth Arms early the previous evening, saying Pam wasn't feeling well and he had to get home. He'd seemed quiet, as though something was on his mind, and when Gerry asked him whether something was wrong, Wesley gave nothing away.

Gerry was about to leave the station and step out into the warmth of the evening sun when the automatic door swished open. He stopped and a spontaneous smile appeared on his lips.

'Alison, love. I wasn't expecting you back so soon.' He wasn't a cheek-kisser but he made an exception in her case and, in his enthusiasm, failed to notice the guarded expression on her face.

There were no words of greeting. She came straight to the point. 'Gerry, I've got something to tell you. I would have told you over the phone but . . . '

He took her elbow gently and led her outside the police station, out of earshot of the woman on the front desk. The warmth of the air hit him and he steered Alison through the strolling tourists in the Memorial Gardens until he found a free bench that wasn't covered in seagull droppings.

'What is it, love?' he said as they sat down. 'Something happened up in Liverpool? Is it work? You can stay with me as long as you like, you know that.'

'Shut up, Gerry, and listen.'

Her sudden assertiveness silenced him. She took something out of her shoulder bag: a photograph, the muted colours faded with time.

'It's my mum and that's you, isn't it?'

Gerry stared at the picture for a few seconds before he answered. 'You're right, that's me and . . . Her name was Selina. Selina Parry.'

Alison shook her head. 'That's my mum. That's Donna McQuail.'

Gerry swallowed hard. 'She told me her name was Selina. I went round to her flat one day but she'd gone.'

'I spoke to her sister – my aunty. She said Mum pulled that stunt a few times, thinking up names to make herself sound more glamorous and—'

'She told me she worked on the perfume counter at George Henry Lee's.'

Alison shook her head. 'Nothing so posh. She worked in Sayers cake factory. She left Liverpool when she found she was expecting me . . . went to an aunt in Wales.'

Gerry felt tears pricking his eyes. 'Oh, love. I'm sorry. I had no idea she was . . .'

'It's not your fault, Dad. It's just how she was. She liked to pretend – to imagine she had a more exciting life than she did.'

Gerry wanted to take his daughter in his arms and give her a hug but a couple of uniformed constables had just emerged from the station and were staring in his direction.

Gerry's heart ached so much that he could barely speak. 'I'll make it up to you, love,' he said softly when he'd composed himself.

At that moment he hated Donna McQuail, the woman who'd lived a fantasy that had deprived him of a daughter.

'I'll have to get back to Liverpool soon,' Alison said, seeing the tears forming in his eyes. 'Fancy a drink tonight?'

Gerry blinked the tears away and forced out a smile. 'That'd be great, love. Mind if I bring Joyce along?'

46

A week had passed and Terry Sildon was on remand awaiting trial for murder. She still hadn't made a full confession but, as far as Wesley and Gerry were concerned, her guilt was certain.

Robert Valdun too had been locked up, charged with the murder of Suzie Grant back in 1968, and Thames Valley said they'd be only too happy to take him off their hands once Tradmouth CID had finished questioning him about their case. While Gerry reckoned they could safely hand him over and let Thames Valley deal with him, something made Wesley advise delay.

That evening he left work at a reasonable time because Pam had tickets for a performance at the Literary Festival her mother had been so busy organising. He'd been tempted to make an excuse but his conscience got the better of him once he'd discovered she'd arranged for a neighbour to babysit. Michael had objected to the term, pointing out that he was no baby, but he'd been subdued since that night at

Newfield Manor so he didn't argue. There'd been no more mention of Harry so, with luck, he was off the scene for good.

When he arrived home Pam greeted him in the hall and handed him a letter topped by the hospital logo that had become so familiar over the last months.

'My appointment's come through – the results of the latest tests.'

Wesley took her hand. 'I'll come with you.'

'You don't have to.'

'I want to.'

She changed the subject, saying her mother had booked a table for them at a Dukesbridge pub so they could eat before the performance.

To Wesley's relief Della didn't join them for their meal. Instead they ate in peace before walking hand in hand to the library by the harbour where the show was to be held. He had no idea what they were going to see and he didn't particularly care. He was glad of anything to take his mind off work, especially since Ethel Rinton's death a couple of days before – another murder to add to Terry Sildon's list of crimes.

A glass of wine was handed to him as soon as he entered the building and as he sipped he began to relax. Then he spotted Neil in the doorway with a young woman.

'You never called me,' Neil said accusingly when he made his way over, the young woman following.

'Sorry. I've been busy.' He glanced at Pam, who was studying Neil's companion with barely disguised curiosity. 'What is it you wanted to tell me?'

Neil looked at his watch. 'You'll see later. This is Emily, by the way. She's been helping me with some research.'

Pam raised her eyebrows. 'How's Lucy?' she asked pointedly, her eyes fixed on Emily. Wesley could sense her disapproval; she'd always liked Lucy and felt some loyalty towards her.

'Still in Orkney. I spoke to her yesterday.' He gave a slight shake of the head as if he'd read Pam's thoughts and was eager to reassure her that his relationship with Emily was purely archaeological.

The blinds in the library had been drawn and the shelves pushed to one side to create a large seating area. One end of the space was partitioned off by a curtain and Wesley and Pam watched as Neil and Emily disappeared behind it without explanation.

Once they were seated the lights went out, leaving the audience in semi-darkness. Then the curtain swung aside to reveal a puppet theatre with elaborately painted scenery. His heart skipped a beat. It was the one he'd seen before in Raynard Bishop's parlour.

He held his breath and felt Pam's hand on his as Bishop appeared to make the introductions.

'You look as if you've seen a ghost,' she whispered.

He didn't answer and settled down to watch as the puppets re-enacted the murder of Mary Field. Mary's parents were depicted as decrepit and greedy, John Lipton as a romantic hero who swept the wilful Mary off her feet and William Banville as a moustached villain, eaten up with murderous jealousy. Mary's maidservant, Sarah, only had a supporting role as confidante to the unfortunate victim. One of the voices behind the puppets was definitely Neil's. He wasn't much of an actor but he played the part of John Lipton with gusto. Mary's puppet was voiced by Emily and the voice of William Banville was decidedly transatlantic. Karl Banville had made no attempt to disguise his accent.

Once the performance was over the puppet masters emerged to acknowledge the polite applause which halted when Raynard Bishop stepped to the front and raised his hand.

'You've just witnessed a re-enactment of the murder of Mary Field, a notorious local case,' he began before going on to explain in some detail how the puppet theatre and puppets had been a popular form of entertainment in the nineteenth century. His enthusiasm seemed undimmed by the shock of discovering that his recent house guest was wanted for murder. Wesley recognised an obsessive when he saw one.

Some in the audience started to fidget at this unexpected history lesson, until Bishop announced that Dr Watson had something important to say. He moved aside to let Neil take his place, watched by Karl Banville who was wearing a smug grin on his face.

Neil looked around. 'My recent excavation at Newfield Manor has uncovered evidence to prove that the performance you've just seen was a lie,' he began, causing an embarrassed murmuring in the audience. 'Rather than disappearing abroad, William Banville was murdered by the same person who killed Mary. New evidence has recently come to light in the form of a confession left with the real killer's solicitor with instructions that it wasn't to be read until after his death.'

He held the sheet of paper in his hand in front of him like a herald's proclamation.

'"I, John Lipton, do hereby confess that I concealed the murder of my wife, Mary, whom I married solely for her inheritance. Mary's maidservant, Sarah, envied her mistress because her mother had told her that she too was Sir Cuthbert's daughter, born of an illicit liaison. Sarah had a great hatred for the half-sister who had no inkling of their kinship and she desired her death above all things, thinking in her muddled way that she would have a claim on her wealth, an idea I encouraged.

"'Sarah administered a large dose of laudanum to her mistress one night, causing her death as she intended. She insisted that we bury Mary in secret in the walled garden which is a private place and not overlooked, saying she, as her half-sister, would take her place. The servants were dismissed and new ones hired and she planned that we should live as man and wife. I readily agreed until it transpired that Sarah was not the pliant creature I had first thought. Soon she made excessive demands of me and desired to go to London, where nobody knew Mary, and live in society enjoying her newly acquired wealth to the full.

"'The humble maidservant was much altered and after several weeks the situation became intolerable. I feared she would fritter away Mary's inheritance and my dreams of prosperity would come to nothing so I went on business to Bristol, giving the servants the night off, and paid Mr Gunster's son, Enoch, the sum of one hundred pounds to commit the deed in my absence. When I returned the next morning Gunster informed me Sarah was dead. Gunster's son had strangled her before placing her in the pool near the woods. I had assumed her death would be taken for a simple drowning but when I heard that marks of violence had been found upon her neck I feared the truth would emerge so I lured William Banville to the walled garden, saying I wished to speak with him. There I killed him with a spade and buried his body near to Mary's, resolving to claim that he was responsible for the death of my wife and had fled the country to avoid justice.

"'I live with the knowledge of these terrible deeds weighing heavily on my conscience so I wish to set these matters down in order that the truth will be known after my death and William Banville will be cleared of all blame.'"

Neil lowered the confession and a long silence followed before he spoke again. Wesley could see people looking at each other; some whispering behind their hands; all waiting for Neil to continue.

'Gunster and his son purchased a farm near Stoke Beeching with the proceeds of their crime and the puppets you have just seen lay undiscovered in a barn there for years. I can't help wondering why they chose to re-enact the crime they committed in their show. Maybe it was to reinforce the idea of William Banville's guilt but I guess we'll never know. If anyone has any questions . . . '

When the evening was over, Wesley stood up, oblivious to Pam's suggestion that they meet Neil for a drink. Raynard Bishop's puppet show had given him a lot to think about.

47

The next day Wesley knocked on Wynn Staniland's front door. There had been no security at the gates today and they'd opened with a hefty push.

When Wesley and Gerry reached the house they found it silent, as if nothing lived or breathed inside. Wesley stood beside Gerry, looking up at the windows for signs of activity. There was something he needed to ask. It wouldn't change anything – not really – but he wanted to know whether his suspicions were correct.

'He's not in. Or he's not answering.'

'What do we do now?' Gerry shifted from foot to foot, restless.

'We find him.'

Wesley walked away from the door and Gerry followed, trotting to keep up with Wesley's fast pace.

'Surely he won't be down here,' Gerry said as they descended the steep path leading to the sea.

Wesley said nothing. He had to check out the scene of

Rosemary's death. If Staniland wanted to put an end to everything, this was where he'd do it.

When they reached the sand they quickened their pace and soon the sea pool came into sight. As they drew nearer Wesley saw something in the water, floating just below the surface. His instincts had been right. He stopped and Gerry almost cannoned into him.

'Is it . . . ?'

Without replying Wesley ran over to the pool where Rosemary Staniland had drowned and looked down on what he'd first taken to be the body of Wynn Staniland, floating face down beneath the summer sky. But now he realised that it was only clothes. There was no body. But behind them was the hungry sea.

'Where's Michael?'

Pam paused, as if she was about to impart bad news. 'He's gone to Nathaniel's.'

'That's good . . . isn't it?'

'He insisted on going alone and I hadn't the strength to argue. I might ring Nat's mum and see if he's arrived safely.'

'I think he's learned his lesson. We've got to trust him.'

But she wasn't listening. 'I said one of us will pick him up later.'

Wesley nodded in agreement, although he thought she was being unnecessarily cautious. She looked tired and her hospital appointment was imminent so he knew he'd be the one to go.

She looked at him and frowned. 'Are you all right?'

It had been a tough day but he hadn't thought it showed. He took a deep breath.

'We went to interview Wynn Staniland . . .'

'And?'

'We found his clothes by the sea pool at Addersacre. The place where his wife died.'

Pam looked stunned by the news.

'Just his clothes?'

Wesley nodded.

'Was it suicide or ... ?' She hesitated. 'You don't think he's faked his own death, do you?'

Wesley didn't know. There was still so much he didn't understand.

Until the next day, when Wynn Staniland's body was washed up in Tradmouth harbour on the high tide.

48

Terry Sildon obtained permission from the authorities to attend Wynn Staniland's funeral. It was a quiet affair and sparsely attended. A cremation conducted by a duty clergyman who'd never known the man in life and seemed embarrassed by what he'd learned of his death. The scandal caused by his deception had ensured the literary community stayed well away.

Wesley watched Terry as she sat, straight-backed, listening intently to the impersonal service, handcuffed to a prison officer who looked as if he'd rather be somewhere else. When the service was over the tiny congregation walked out into the sunshine and Terry approached Wesley, her escort in tow.

'Inspector Peterson. Fancy seeing you here.'

Wesley saw that her eyes were red. She'd been crying. Somehow he hadn't expected genuine emotion.

'Can I have a word with you?' Wesley said.

Gerry, who was sticking close by his side, gave him a

questioning look as they walked back into the institutional little chapel and sat down in the back pew.

'You didn't tell us the whole truth, did you, Terry?' Wesley said quietly. 'You and Wynn weren't lovers. You're his daughter. That's why you stayed with him at Addersacre all these years. He was your father. Family.'

Her head was bowed so he couldn't see her face and her response took a long time to come.

'You've got it right, Inspector. Well done. He got my mother pregnant when they were both eighteen. A brief encounter, according to my grandmother.'

'Where is your mother?'

'Still alive as far as I know but I haven't seen or heard of her for years. And I don't want to. She handed me over to her parents when I was little. They didn't want me so I thought I might have more luck with my father and when Perdita turned up at school ... It was as if it was meant. You thought Wynn and I were lovers but you couldn't have been more wrong. I just wanted the money. And my father.'

'You killed Jane Whitsun?'

Terry said nothing for a few moments then 'There's no harm in telling you now, I don't suppose. My father was infatuated with her. He hardly noticed me when she was around.'

Her words suddenly made everything clear. 'Did you kill Rosemary?'

She smiled. 'It was easy to put the pills in her drink then take her for a little walk when she was half conscious. I was doing Father a favour. He didn't love her. He was better off without her.'

'You killed Perdita when she came back and threatened to ruin the life you'd built for yourself. And Zac Wilkinson when there was a danger he'd find out the truth about what you'd done.'

'We thought we could control what Zac wrote but he started poking around in all sorts of places he shouldn't. I couldn't let him carry on.'

'What was your relationship with Robert Valdun?'

She looked uncomfortable. 'Robert was just there. Wynn needed him. He protected him.'

'Why?'

'Because of the books, I suppose.'

'I think there was more to it than that. I've been through the details of the Suzie Grant case and Valdun admits he and Wynn were together earlier that evening. Valdun went back to Suzie's but later he met up with Wynn again and he spent the rest of the night high on drugs. Valdun was so far gone he couldn't remember what happened and he took Wynn's word for it that he'd been the one who'd killed Suzie. Valdun told us Wynn fancied Suzie and I think Wynn went to her flat while Robert was insensible to try his luck with her. When she fought him off he killed her. Strangled her.'

Wesley saw it all. Wynn's encounter with the girl he'd fancied; the girl who'd willingly slept with his friend, Robert; who'd preferred a drug-addled loser to himself. He imagined Wynn's loss of control when Suzie rejected his clumsy advances. Then he seized the opportunity to manipulate his damaged but supremely talented friend into believing he'd caused her death, making him beholden to him for life.

In that chaotic moment he'd become the ultimate puppet master and he suspected that only Terry knew the truth. But, unless she decided to talk, it would be hard to prove.

'You know what really happened, don't you, Terry? Wynn couldn't keep something like that quiet forever so he confessed to you.'

One look at Terry's face told him he was right.

'And now Robert Valdun's serving time for a murder he didn't commit. Why don't you do the right thing, Terry? Wynn's dead. You've got nothing to lose.'

'When Robert was at Addersacre he treated me like some stupid little girl. Why should I do him any favours?'

At the prison officer's signal she began to walk away, turning her head to look back at Wesley.

Gerry put a hand on his shoulder. 'Don't worry, Wes. I don't think we got it wrong about Valdun.'

But he knew Gerry was wrong this time and he wanted to prove it.

That night he arrived home and found Pam smiling. She looked better than she had in ages, he thought. More colour in her cheeks and much less tired. She'd been for her appointment at the hospital to receive the results of her latest tests that day and the news was good. The best. She'd been given the all clear. And, with everything that had been happening, he'd forgotten. He hadn't even been there with her.

Terry sat in the prison library, her cheap ballpoint poised over the notebook.

She and Wynn had shared everything. Every secret. He'd known she was a killer and she'd known about his own inner darkness. That sin he'd committed all those decades ago.

Now Wynn had gone, the policeman's words kept running through her head. 'Wynn's dead. You've got nothing to lose.'

She'd liked the inspector. He was different, not just because of the colour of his skin. It was as if he'd looked inside her soul and understood

Perhaps he was right. She had nothing to lose by doing one good deed in the wicked world she'd created for herself.

She began to write.

Sometimes it's good to be a ghost. Somebody who doesn't exist.

But Robert Valdun did exist back then. He walked. He talked. He breathed. Even though nobody paid him any attention.

He recalled that hot night in 1980. Wynn's latest book launch at some swish London hotel. When he closed his eyes he could see the people sipping their cheap white wine, looking straight through him. Wynn had thought it amusing to invite him, and there was no danger he'd be recognised – not with that beard.

If only they'd known he was the creator; all those non-entities who thought they were as wise as gods with their pretentious prattle, wearing their smug smiles as they voiced meaningless opinions.

He remembered watching from the edge of the room while they fawned over the chosen one. He recalled how he nudged the elbow of a scrawny young woman dressed entirely in black like a Victorian widow in her first days of mourning. He could still see the wine spilling from her glass, leaving a dark patch on her dress, as he murmured an insincere apology. She'd looked away as though he was beneath her attention. If only she'd known that his writing was the reason they were all there.

Wynn had too much to drink that night. But why

shouldn't he? He was celebrating his achievement. Robert's achievement. Robert had raised his half-empty glass to him and saw him turn pale.

That was decades ago. Now things had changed. As Robert sat in the prison library where he spent so much of his time, he thought of the letter he'd received from the publisher the previous day. The new novels he'd written during his years in Scotland pretending to be someone he wasn't had been accepted. And, thanks to the efforts of Raynard Bishop, his antiquarian book business would be waiting for him when he was released.

He only wished he'd been able to attend Wynn's funeral. Wynn who'd been so good to him. Wynn who shielded him from the police after he did that terrible thing. He'd been so drunk and stoned that the night of Suzie Grant's death had always been a blank. He'd had to rely on Wynn to fill him in on the facts but he'd known he could trust him.

He thought of the future as he queued up in the canteen, talking to nobody and keeping his head down because he had nothing in common with his fellow inmates.

A few hours later he was summoned to the governor's office and told that new evidence had come to light. A woman called Theresa Sildon had made a statement and his case was going to be reviewed.

He walked out of the office with a smile on his face.

Sometimes it's good to be a ghost. But it's a lot better to be alive.

AUTHOR'S NOTE

In 1827 Thomas de Quincy published an essay entitled *On Murder Considered as One of the Fine Arts*, which introduced the idea that crime, particularly murder, could be treated as a form of entertainment. Thus began the craze for plays, books, memorabilia and even murder tourism that persists to this day. Life undoubtedly became more comfortable for many in the nineteenth century as the wild perils of the previous century were banished by safer streets, better lighting and an organised police force. Perhaps this is what made the vicarious enjoyment of 'horrible murder' so fashionable.

Today we tend to think of our Victorian forebears as a buttoned-up, puritanical bunch but often the ideal of family life (as upheld by Queen Victoria and her family) was little more than a facade and hypocrisy was rife. You only have to look at the entertainments the Victorians enjoyed to discover a dark side to their upright piety. Notorious murder cases held a grim fascination and, until they ended in 1868, public executions attracted particularly good audiences.

Special trains were often laid on for hangings which were scheduled for noon on market days to ensure a large crowd.

The author, Thomas Hardy, was just sixteen in 1856 when he watched Elizabeth Martha Brown hang at Dorchester jail for killing her husband. Perhaps the experience inspired the finale of one of his most famous novels, *Tess of the D'Urbervilles*.

Murder was popular entertainment, as I suppose it is today, and a notorious and gruesome case would hold a particular fascination for aficionados. Some of the cases I mention in this book – for example the Ratcliffe Highway Murders – became the subject of broadsides and pamphlets published to satisfy the public craving for ever more grisly detail. Melodramas were performed in theatres throughout the land and touring marionette troupes staged productions at fairs and village greens. These troupes were run by families who carved, dressed and operated the marionettes. The audience's appetite for the re-enactment of well-known murders was insatiable. Maria Marten or Murder in the Red Barn was particularly popular.

The fictitious murder of Mary Field in this book was inspired by a real-life case. In 1884 a young woman called Laura Dimes lived in a large house called Oldstone near the village of Blackawton in South Devon. One morning Laura went for a ride and was later found dead in bizarre circumstances, sitting upright in a pond in nearby woods. The water came over her head and, strangely, she was still wearing her riding top hat. There was no sign of violence on her body (nor any sign of drowning) and the inquest passed a verdict of accidental death.

The matter would have rested there until it was discovered that Laura had secretly married a rather shady young man three weeks before her death. Her new husband was apprehended and put on trial but was acquitted through lack of evidence. Ten years after the trial Oldstone burned down and nobody has ever attempted to rebuild it. To this day the unfortunate Laura is said to haunt the spot which is now, as historian Professor W. G. Hoskins describes it, 'a dark and melancholy ruin among the chestnuts, the nettles and the elder'.